MINDGAMES

Deborah Nicholson

Further Titles by Deborah Nicholson

Novels:

House Report
A Kate Carpenter Mystery

Evening the Score
A Kate Carpenter Mystery

Sins of the Mother
A Kate Carpenter Mystery

Flirting With Disaster
A Kate Carpenter Mystery

Liar, Liar
A Kate Carpenter Mystery

Ghost of a Chance (2012)
A Kate Carpenter Mystery

A Very Bad Day
A bloody sexy short story

The Pain Diaries: A Love Story
Adapted from the play

Stop Lying (2012)
A personal journey through weight loss and change

Plays:
The Pain Diaries, a love story

First World Publication and Electronic Edition released 2011.
Copyright © 2010 by Deborah Nicholson
All rights reserved.
The moral right of the author has been asserted.
ISBN 978-1-4636818-2-1
Except where actual historical events and characters are being described for the storyline of this novel, all situations in this publication are fictitious and any resemblance to living persons is purely coincidental.

EBook Design by 52 Novels

Cover Design Clayton Hansen Design, Calgary, Alberta.
Photographs © Deborah Nicholson

Edition July 2011

I work with some really great people. They spend their days helping people overcome severe pain and, since I came along, helping me find creative ways to kills people (on paper, of course). They seem to have a lot of ideas on how to do that, for which I am grateful..

This book is dedicated to my less than evil anesthesiologist colleagues: Drs. Martin Scanlon, Chris Spanswick, Geoff Hawboldt, Darryl Guglielmin and to an adorably evil pharmacist (just kidding), Don McIntosh. Also, without the guidance of Dr. Sharon Habermann, my psychology would have been completely fictional.

Without your help, this would have just been a great idea, not a book!

I donate my time and money to various charitable organizations. I believe that those of us that are blessed should pay it forward, whatever your favourite cause. One of the ways I do that is to donate 10% of the profits of all my novels to various charities.

For this novel, my donation will go to Calgary Health Trust to help fund a Pain Residency program. These doctors do good all day but they're outnumbered and we need to train more people to help treat patients in pain.

1965

It was the smell that got most people. That aseptic sharp sterile smell, burning your nostrils, overlaid with the sickly sweet, slightly metallic scent of fresh warm blood. It closed their throats, sent them running for the nearest bucket or sometimes their eyes just rolled to the back of their heads and they folded up upon themselves into a neat little pile on the floor. One more thing for the nurses to clean up.

But this was his first time in an operating room and he was trying very hard to control his nerves. Fainting, gagging or retching would destroy the image that he had spent so much time creating. He was working very hard to be the perfect student and was determined to be the smartest, the fastest, the first to the question, the first with the answer, the first to complete a task. And now he had to be the last one standing. The one who could make it through the first time in an operating room without doing anything that would lessen him in the eyes of his esteemed professors. He breathed deeply under his mask, slowly and regularly. His freshly scrubbed hands were clasped in front of him, one nail digging into the palm of his other hand. The worst part was that he didn't really know what to expect. If he had a script or could have known what the plan was, it would be easier. But this was a mystery to be unraveled in front of this year's batch of green students. A test to determine their worth. So he continued to breathe deeply, concentrating on naming the bones of the human body in his head, starting with the metatarsals and working his way up. He was up to the patella when the patient was wheeled in.

She was a middle-aged woman, slightly overweight, and very happy thanks to an expert dosing of preoperative medications by the anesthesiologist. Her pupils were dilated, there was a smile on her face, and she softly hummed some unnamed tune as they transferred her from the gurney to the operating table. He lost his concentration on naming the bones of the human skeleton somewhere around the seventh thoracic vertebra, and was mesmerized by the woman on the table. The nurses had removed her gown and draped her demurely under a sheet for the time being. The anesthetist entered the room and took his place at the head of the table. He checked her intravenous line and checked her vital signs.

'How are you doing Norma,' he asked.

'When the moon hits your eye like a big pizza pie…'

'I guess you're doing fine,' he laughed and then turned to the students. 'Norma is a forty-two year old female, G-three P-three and is joining us today for a cholecystectomy. Norma is a textbook case of gallbladder disease: fair, fat and forty.'

One of the students giggled and then quickly stopped when he realized he was the only one doing so.

'Now, I would say Norma has had a favourable reaction to her preoperative medications and is ready for her perioperative sedation. I will be administering standard doses of standard medications for sleep and a muscle relaxant. Does anyone care to tell me what those might be?'

The silence from the students was deafening.

'As I suspected. Perhaps before you come into an operating room again you might read a book on anesthesia. Remember gentlemen, it's a little hard for the glamorous surgeon to operate on a patient that is awake and squealing. Anesthesia is a very important part of surgery. Pay some attention to it.'

The doctor picked up a needle and injected it into the patient's IV line.

'You're going to feel very sleepy, Norma,' he told the patient. 'And when you wake up in a few hours, you'll feel much better. No more pain when you're eating those fried chicken dinners with your family on Sunday afternoons.'

The anesthetist watched the patient close her eyes and waited a moment.

'Norma,' he said. 'Can you hear me Norma?'

He pressed his thumb into her breastbone, trying to induce a pain response, but she didn't move. He injected another fluid into her IV and then quickly intubated her. He listened to her chest to ensure that his tube was placed properly, and then ensured that the monitors were running properly. When he was satisfied, he turned back to the students and smiled.

'In my specialty, we say there are three levels of anesthesia. Asleep, awake and dead. I would say this patient is successfully in the sleep phase of her surgery. I hope the surgeon is able to do a competent job and we do not have to downgrade her condition.'

The nurses were busy prepping the patient for surgery, cleaning her skin with an iodine solution and draping her abdomen. Some were busy counting instrument packets. The students watched the activity with building excitement, knowing that soon the surgeon would arrive and they would get to see that first cut, get their first peek inside a human body.

But not Beckman. He was intrigued by the anesthesiologist and he watched closely while the doctor scribbled some information onto a form. Here was a man who held this woman's life in his hands, and was confident enough about it that he sat back and started working on a crossword puzzle while everything unfolded around him.

After the surgery, he approached the anesthetist and spoke with him. It was never too early to start cultivating mentors.

Chapter 1

There was total silence in the room. No glasses clinked, no cigarettes were lit, no coins jingled and no one even dared to breathe. All eyes focused on the television, afraid to miss anything, as the tied championship game came down to the wire. And then a stick was drawn back, a puck shot out and, almost in slow motion, it flew across the ice, towards the goalie, who tried to judge the path of the oncoming projectile and position himself between it and the crease. Almost magically, the puck spun and whether by design or by divine intervention, and it snaked around the awaiting goaltender and into the net behind him.

'Hurray, Stanley Cup champions!' she cheered, raising her glass in the air, too inebriated to aim for her companions glasses.

'Cheers,' the other two answered in unison and then they all broke down in drunken giggles. These men had two traditions, one was watching the Stanley Cup together every year, for the past three years now, and the second tradition was to drink copious amounts of alcohol while carrying out the first tradition.

'Who won again?' Ian asked.

'Who was playing?' Ben answered.

'You're not asking me, are you?' Sara laughed. 'I don't even like football.'

'Hockey,' Ian corrected her loudly, wondering why they had let his sister into this men's only event. 'This is a Stanley Cup party, therefore we were watching hockey.'

'Well, my thesis outline has been approved, so frankly that's what I've been celebrating,' she informed him. 'That fact that there is a game on just happened to be a happy coincidence.'

'Oh, my God, you may actually get your Master's done without having to get an extension,' Ian laughed at her. 'Cheers to that.'

They all held their glasses up in the air again. The group had started the evening with beer and switched to scotch at some point. The line of empty bottles on the table illustrated the course the evening had taken. She set her glass down on the coffee table and stood up unsteadily.

'Oh, I think I may have to stay here tonight,' she informed the men, grabbing the back of the chair to steady herself. 'I don't think I should drive home 'cuz I don't think I can even walk to the car right now.'

'Your room is always ready for you, sis,' Ian said.

'Thank you.' She stood up trying to decide the best way to exit the living room.

'Where you going?' Ben asked.

'To the bathroom,' she giggled as she tried to step over him and crashed into him instead, landing on his lap. 'Oops.'

'Can I help you?' he asked, smiling as her face came within inches of his, smelling her perfume and finding himself suddenly attracted to this charming drunken girl.

'You know,' she began, her lips almost brushing against his. 'You're kind of cute, Ben. Too bad I'm seeing somebody already.'

'Yes it is,' he sighed, helping her up and standing up himself to steady her.

'Whoa, I feel really, really dizzy,' she said. 'What kind of scotch have I been drinking?'

11

And then she toppled over, but Ben caught her smartly in his arms. He picked her up and turned to Ian.

'I'm just going to put her to bed,' he said. But Ian's eyes were closed and he was snoring softly.

Ben's gait suddenly became very steady as he carried Sara to the bedroom and laid her down on the bed. He went back into the living room for his briefcase and returned, setting it on the dresser and opening it up. He pulled out a hypodermic needle and a vial marked Haldol, not an unusual cargo for a psychiatrist. There was no reason to sedate a drunken young woman, already passed out on the bed, but that was not his intent. The label on the vial was to fool anyone who was looking too closely, and not designed to divulge its real contents. He filled the syringe, tapped out the air and brought it over to the bed where she lay. He slid her jeans off her hip, pinched some skin between his fingers and injected the drug. He slid her jeans back up and returned the hypodermic to his briefcase, and locked it securely. He came back to the bed and pulled the comforter up over the girl, then he sat on the edge of the bed, picking up her wrist and measuring her pulse. When he was satisfied, he tucked her hand back under the blanket and made himself comfortable, studying her face, her breathing and waiting another five minutes.

'All right, Sara, lets see how you do with this. Now, I just want you to relax. You might be experiencing some strange feelings, but don't fight it, just let it happen. Just let your mind wander and go wherever it wants to go. All right, now I want you to repeat after me. *I wonder what happened.* Can you say that for me?'

He waited, very patiently, looking for a reaction.

'*I wonder what happened*, just try saying it. *I wonder what happened. I wonder what happened.*'

'I won...' she tried to command her lips to work.

'Good girl. Now try once more. *I wonder what happened.*'

'I wonder wha' happ...'

'Good girl,' he took her wrist and felt her pulse again.

'Good girl. You just went somewhere didn't you?'

He watched her eyelids flutter, as if she were in some sort of frantic REM state.

'It'll be over in a minute, don't panic just let it happen,' he whispered, his voice like silk. 'I knew you would be a good candidate.'

In another minute her eyelids stopped fluttering and she appeared to be sleeping peacefully.

'That's very good for the first time, my dear. You just have a good night's sleep now and we'll try this again in another couple of weeks. We'll give these drugs a chance to work on your brain and see what happens.'

He tucked her in, making sure she was comfortable, before returning his briefcase to the front door, where he had dropped it when he first arrived. Ben went back into the kitchen and got three beers out of the fridge, pouring two down the sink and taking a swig out of the other one. He brought all the bottles, both full and empty, to the living room and set them on the coffee table in front of his chair. This would make it appear that he had drunk as much as everyone else, if anyone was counting empties in the morning. He didn't worry about the scotch glasses, the ones that he had added the sedatives to, ensuring that his friends would pass out peaceably and on schedule, as he would clean those up himself in the morning. With the three of them, all pitching in to clean up the mess, there would be nothing suspicious about that. He grabbed the remote and turned the volume down on the TV. He was pretty sure Ian wouldn't wake up with what he had slipped in his last drink, but it was always better to be safe than sorry. Ben made himself comfortable in the over sized armchair, putting his feet up on the ottoman and tucked the cushion up under his head. Then he channel surfed, sipped his beer and waited for sleep to overtake him.

Chapter 2

Ben jumped when he heard the sound of glass crashing, but then he quickly remembered where he was and what he was supposed to be doing and tried to slow his reaction time

'Ow, keep it down out there,' he moaned, holding his head, pretending to nurse a hangover.

'Sorry,' Sara apologized, coming into the living room and leaning over the couch. 'I knocked over a bottle trying to get to the coffee pot. We're not very tidy drunks.'

She didn't look too good, Ben thought. Her face was quite pale and her eyes sunken and black ringed. He'd seen this reaction before and it usually cleared up within twenty four hours, but he wanted to keep an eye on her just in case. It usually only happened to the ones that were quite susceptible to the drugs, which was another good sign. He wanted to reach over and feel her forehead, see if it was warm, check her blood pressure, ask her about her dreams. But he fought the urge to be a doctor and just tried to search her eyes for clues.

She noticed him studying her and hurried back into the kitchen to hide her self-consciousness and suddenly warm, blushing cheeks.

'You don't look so hot either,' she called from the kitchen, searching for the makings for some morning coffee, which she desperately needed right now. 'Do you have any idea where my idiot brother keeps the coffee filters?'

'Sorry,' he called into the kitchen. 'I wasn't staring at you, just lost in space. I'll trade you coffee filters for aspirin.'

'Check the medicine cabinet in his bathroom,' she told him. 'That's where he used to keep them.'

'Should I wake him up?' Ben said. 'He's not being a particularly good host, is he?'

'You can wake him up if you want to but you better run real fast after you do. He's a bit of a grumpy bear when he's got a hangover.'

'Understood,' Ben said, reaching over and checking Ian's pulse just to be sure everything was okay, considering he was still sleeping so soundly. Ian groaned and rolled over, pulling an afghan off the back of the couch over his head.

'Besides, I gave up on the coffee filter thing, I used a paper towel. I need coffee and I need coffee now'

'You used paper towel as the filter?' Ben said, giving up on Ian and standing in the kitchen door.

'Uh yeah. Man, you went to college. You're supposed to learn how to make ketchup soup and use paper towels for coffee filters and that kind of stuff. How come you don't know these things?'

'Sara, my name is Bennett Johnston Aaron Douglas. My father invented the coated paper clip. I spent every summer in the Hamptons. I have never been without a coffee filter in my life. As a matter of fact, I didn't even know you needed filters until I was eighteen years old because somebody else always made the coffee for me.'

'You're a snob, Ben.'

'Yes I am. But I was raised that way, it's not like I had a choice.'

'Well, you haven't lived yet, Ben, but you're about to,' she said, pouring him a cup of coffee and handing it to him.

Ben took the cup but sniffed gingerly at it, not daring to take a drink.

Sara opened the fridge and pulled out some cream, taking it and her cup to the kitchen table.

'Are you going to get those aspirin?' she asked.

'Sure,' he said, setting his cup on the table beside hers.

'Because I'd really like some too.'

Ben made his way down the hall to the bathroom, opening up the medicine cabinet and finding the aspirin. He grabbed the bottle and brought it back into the kitchen, pulling out a chair and joining Sara at the table.

'Well?' she asked.

'Success,' he smiled, holding the bottle up.

'Gimme!' she said greedily.

Ben unscrewed the cap from the bottle and tapped a couple of aspirin into her outstretched hand.

'Keep going,' she asked, not moving her hand.

He tapped one more pill into her hand before she took the bottle and swallowed five of the tablets.

'Like your liver much?' he asked.

'You don't have the headache that I have right now,' she said. 'My liver is just going to have to toughen up.'

'You have a bad headache?' he asked, concern clouding his eyes. He automatically reached out and took her wrist, feeling her pulse.

'Yes doctor, I have a headache,' she laughed, pulling her hand away from his grasp. 'I drank enough alcohol last night to fall an elephant. Do you think it's some sort of a red flag symptom that I might have a headache?'

'Sorry, just habit I guess,' he laughed, screwing the top back on the aspirin bottle.

'Ben, you're a shrink, not a doc.'

'I went to medical school just like the rest of them,' he insisted.

'You not going to take any of those aspirin?' she asked.

'Oh, yeah,' he laughed outwardly, but inside was already berating himself for almost blowing his cover. 'I guess I better if I want my head to clear up today, huh?'

'That and drink your coffee,' she said.

'Paper towels are okay for filters?' he asked.

'I'm alive and I've been doing it for years.'

He popped the aspirin and then took a swig of coffee. 'Okay, you win. I don't think I can taste a difference.'

'Top up?' she asked, bringing the pot over and filling her cup.

'Sure,' he said. 'What are we going to do about your brother?'

'Let him sleep,' she said. 'It's Sunday, he has nothing better to do.'

'You think he's okay on the couch?'

'Ben, in the real world, a lot of us have spent many a night sleeping on our sofas. I know that must be a shock to your feather bed, goose down duvet lifestyle, but it's the truth.'

'I've slept on my sofa,' he protested.

'Yeah, well I'm sure your sofa cost three times what my bed did, so I don't see that as such a hardship for you.'

'You're the snob,' Ben told her.

'Me? A snob? Because you're rich and I'm not?'

'You didn't exactly grow up on the streets,' he said.

'I wonder…'

He watched as her eyes grew distant and for a moment, he knew she wasn't in the room with him. But then she was back. He sipped his coffee and tried to cover up his smile. So far, all the signs were pointing to the fact that Sara might be his most successful candidate.

'I better get going,' Sara said, feeling slightly out of sorts. 'I have to call Paul and let him know I'll be home in time for lunch.'

'Why didn't he come over last night?' Ben asked.

'Paul and Ian don't get along very well,' Sara explained. 'Ian doesn't think Paul is good enough for me and Paul thinks Ian is an over protective big brother. They just can't seem to meet in the middle.'

'That's too bad.'

'It is too bad,' she sighed. 'Since mom and dad are gone, those two are all that I have.'

Her sentence was punctuated by the ring of her cell phone. She looked down at her call display, forced a smile on her face and answered it.

'Hello? Hi Paul. Yes I'm still here…'

Ben stood up and moved back into the living room, trying to give Sara some privacy.

'I know I said I'd try to come home…' she said, her voice rising in frustration.

Ben sat in the arm chair he had slept in, sipping his coffee.

'Is that Paul on the phone?' Ian's voice came out from under the blanket.

'I think so,' Ben said.

'Why doesn't that girl have the sense she was born with and dump that bastard.'

'Ian, you know that everyone has to learn these things for themselves.'

'I'm coming home right now…' they heard Sara say from the kitchen. 'If you would just lower your voice…'

'There's coffee on,' Ben was uncomfortable being a part of this and needed a good excuse to leave before the brother sister fight broke out, which he predicted would be about ten seconds after Sara hung up the phone.

'Fuck,' Ian said, throwing the blankets off and storming into the kitchen. 'Sara, hang up.'

Or sooner, Ben thought to himself, gathering up his coat.

'Ian, shush. No, Paul, not you. Look, I'm hanging up and getting in my car right now.'

'So hang up,' Ian said.

'Goodbye,' she said, hanging up and snapping the phone shut angrily.

'It's about time,' Ian said, fussing with a coffee cup. 'Where'd you put the cream?'

'Nice compassion there, Ian. What year psychology did you learn that in?'

'The cream?'

'Crap, you talk to me like Paul does.'

'Sara, I'm sorry. You know how I feel about him.'

'Ian, I wish you would just lay off this for now. Please,' she begged. 'The cream's on the table.'

Ian turned and poured cream into his coffee cup. When he turned back, Sara had her coat on and her bag over her shoulder.

'Oh, come on, don't go,' he said. 'Not when you're mad at me.'

'I'm not mad, Ian. But I have to go.'

'Come on, you know that after a big drunk we always go out for some greasy bacon and eggs at Denny's.'

'Paul's waiting for me,' she said, wrapping him in a hug. 'Things are just different now. Paul is in my life and I have to treat him like he counts, okay?'

'Yes things are definitely different now.'

'Ian, please don't make me leave mad with this hanging between us,' she said. 'You know we agreed to never do that after mom and dad's accident.'

'Sara, I swear I love you unconditionally. I just don't love the choices you make.'

'Ah, you'll make such a good dad some day,' Sara teased, as she kissed him quickly on the cheek. 'I'll see you Monday.'

'Love you,' he called after her. He flopped down on the couch and looked at Ben.

'So, feel like breakfast at Denny's?' he asked.

'What's Denny's?' Ben asked.

'Oh, stick with me dude, there is so much I have to teach you.'

Chapter 3

Fuck, I hate these mornings, she thought, pulling the brush through her sleep tangled hair, trying to get it under control, and pulled into a pony tail while she listened to him stomping around downstairs. She had her shirt on but not buttoned and her jeans lay on the bed waiting for her.

'Come on Sara, we're going to be late,' Paul yelled from the front door.

Why did they have to do this every single morning. They could have such good times, when he chose to not be an angry bastard. So why did he keep choosing to be an angry bastard? And why did she keep putting up with it?

'That's easy, she answered herself in the mirror. 'Because if I leave, I have to deal with all those *I told you so's* from all my friends. And then I have to deal with the fact that I'm actually talking to myself.'

'Sara,' he bellowed, 'I'm leaving in two minutes with or without you.'

'Chill out,' she mumbled.

'What?' he called up.

'Coming,' she tried again, forcing the sweetness into her voice. It was forced, it wasn't as easy to be agreeable and pleasant as it used to be. These rushed mornings always ruined her entire day. She felt like she was playing catch up all day long and always ended up forgetting something important in order to get out the door and appease him.

'I'm leaving in two minutes with or without you,' he called up again, and she heard the kitchen door slam and the roar of the engine as he started the SUV.

Sara finally tamed her hair, pulled on her jeans and boots and buttoned her shirt then raced down to the kitchen. He could have told her the night before that he had to leave early today, but that wasn't his style. He liked to watch her race after him. And apparently, she did it well, because this was becoming their normal morning routine. She was beginning to think that he was just trying to see how far he could push her. She was beginning to wonder how far she could be pushed.

Sara grabbed her laptop and her backpack and hurried out the door. She hoped she still had a granola bar in her backpack, because breakfast was something else she lost out on, on these mornings. She struggled with her key in the lock, fumbling from the pressure she felt, and when her key finally turned she realized she'd forgotten her coffee go-cup in the kitchen. He already had the car in reverse and was now honking for her to get in. She decided she would rather go without her morning coffee than have him yell at her one more time for making him late.

'Come on,' he yelled out the open window.

Sara raced around to the passenger side and got in the car, getting her seatbelt buckled just as he slammed down the accelerator and screeched out of the driveway.

'Take it easy, big guy,' she tried to calm him. 'We won't get there any faster if you get us in an accident.'

'Well if you could manage to get up on time...' he began, but she noticed his foot lightened up on the accelerator a little. 'You've got your shirt buttoned up wrong.'

Sara looked down and saw her mistake. She dropped her stuff onto the floor and fixed her shirt. Then she pulled her Blackberry out of her backpack and pulled up her schedule for the day. She was just switching over to check tomorrow's schedule when something caught her eye out the window. Paul noticed it too.

'I wondered what happened there?' Paul asked.

I wonder too, Sarah thought, as she craned her neck trying to get a better view.

Their car slowed almost to a stop as Sara stared at the fence along the side of the freeway. A big gash rendered it in two and she could almost picture the car that must have lost control and ran off the road, causing the tear. She could almost hear the screeching of tires, the horn honking and then that scream. Suddenly, she felt dizzy and sick to her stomach. It felt like there was a knife going through her head, following by the howling of a gale force wind. She was having a stroke, or maybe an aneurism, she was sure of it. She turned forward to tell Paul that she needed to get to a hospital when she noticed a car in their lane, coming straight at them and the scream that had only been in her mind a moment ago was suddenly ringing through the interior of the car. Paul slammed on the brakes and veered to the right, trying to get out of the path of the oncoming car, and suddenly they were heading into the same spot in the fence. Sara braced herself on the dashboard and screamed again.

Paul slammed on the brakes and pulled onto the shoulder, as the car skidded to a halt.

'What the hell is wrong with you?' he asked, turning to stare at her.

Sara stared back at him and then out the window at the fence, and then down the road. Where was the car that had been seconds away from hitting them? Why weren't they halfway through the fence? The smell of burning rubber was hot in her nostrils as Paul slammed the brakes, trying to stop before they hit the gulley but now Sara stared down the freeway and saw a normal, peaceful traffic pattern, just like every other morning. She was totally confused. A second ago they had been headed off the road toward the fence. She turned slowly back to Paul.

'There was a car,' she tried to explain.

'What do you mean?' he asked.

'There was a car in this lane. Coming straight at us.'

'Sara, are you doing drugs or something? There was no car. You just started screaming and grabbed the dashboard. You almost scared me to death.'

'Paul, I swear to you there was a car coming at us. You were trying to avoid it and we were heading straight for the same spot in the fence….' She turned and looked. She heard that scream again, but it wasn't her voice she heard this time. And then she began to recognize the sounds, the cars and then she saw a reflection of a face in the windshield, but it was her reflection, it was another girl just before that poor girl plunged through the windshield to her death.

'If you don't tell me what you're talking about….' He began to threaten her.

'Oh, God,' she sobbed, pictures filling her mind. 'It wasn't us.'

'Shit, Sara, now we're really late and you aren't making things any better.'

'It was Michelle,' Sara whispered.

'What was Michelle?'

'It was Michelle. It was her car. Jim was driving. Oh my God, there was a car coming straight at them. They veered to miss him and drove through the fence. She died, Paul. Michelle died.'

'Are you just doing this because I rushed you this morning? Is this how you're trying to get even with me?' He asked, as he slammed the car back into gear and pulled out into traffic.

'Michelle went through the windshield. I saw it. She had undone her seatbelt to get something out of the backseat when it happened. She went through the windshield and she died.'

Paul honked at a car that cut him off, but appeared to be ignoring Sara.

'Paul, I'm serious,' she insisted, her heart racing. 'Take me to Ian's office.'

'Sara, I'm dropping you off at school and then I'm going to work. I don't have time for your crazy shit.'

'Paul, take me to Ian's office now or let me out of the car,' she commanded.

He was shocked by the tone of her voice and scowled at her, but pulled into the turning lane and headed to her brother's office.

'Fine,' was the best response he could manage.

Ian was Sara's older brother and a successful clinical psychologist. Sara had worked with him on a couple of research projects during her high school years and fell in love with the work. She had tried medical school, thinking that psychiatry would be even more interesting, but after a year of dissection and blood letting she discovered that she was not as interested in the inside of the human body as she was in the inside of the human mind, and she switched to psychology. She was just finishing her Masters and planning on joining her brother in practice while she completed her doctorate over the next few years. He was going to do the clinical work, and she would mostly do the research, but they could cover for each other as required. She had it all planned out.

Michelle and Sara had been best friends ever since the day they first met in kindergarten. They had stuck together like glue until they graduated from high school. That was when Sara started University and Michelle started looking for a job. They may have had a lot of things in common, but scholarship was not one of them. Sara had talked Ian into letting Michelle take over as secretary in his practise and was surprised at how well it had worked out. Michelle had run Ian's office for him ever since. They had worked together now for almost six years and the two families just grew closer and closer as the years went on. Sara had always joked about them all retiring together and spending their retirement years on a porch in their rocking chairs, psychoanalyzing everyone in the neighbourhood.

Paul pulled the vehicle into the parking lot of the medical building where Ian's office was located and Sara jumped out before it had even fully stopped, racing into the building. Paul had pulled away, screeching tires and shooting gravel. He did not come in with her, did not even check to make sure she was okay. Just what she had expected.

She punched the elevator button, but when it was too slow coming, she raced up the three flights of stairs and to her brother's office. Sara stood outside the door for a minute, gathering her thoughts and her courage. Ian Hunter M.Sc., Ph.D., Psychologist, the sign read. She was proud every time she saw that and would be even more proud when her name was up there beside his. Sara got her breathing under control, put her hand on the door handle and turned it, not realizing that her life was about to change forever.

In the reception area, Ian sat on the edge of Michelle's desk. He was talking to two police officers. Sara knew in an instant she had been right about everything. Ian looked up and met her eyes. She saw the sadness in them and felt herself finally lose control. She ran across the room and let Ian wrap her in his arms.

A few hours later Ian had managed to cancel all the day's patients. The police had left a couple of hours ago, and by the time Ian had seen them out and locked the office doors, Sara had found a bottle of scotch, a present from a grateful patient, and poured a couple of glasses. He had joined her on the couch without protest. For a long time, they just sat there and sipped their drinks. Then, slowly, they started to talk about Michelle and shared stories from years past. Finally, Ian brought up what had been bothering him since his sister first appeared in his office that morning.

'Sara?' he asked. 'Why did you come here this morning?'

'Huh?' she asked, her senses slowed from the alcohol that had stopped burning her throat and was now warming her brain.

'You had classes this morning. Why did you come here

instead?'

'I don't know, I must have mixed up my days.'

'You never mix up your days.'

'Well, I don't know, I guess I didn't have enough coffee this morning or something.'

'Sara, you got here and you knew. When you first opened the office door, you knew already. I saw it in your eyes. You knew what had happened before you saw the police in my office.'

'I don't know what you mean.'

'How did you know?' he asked.

She hesitated for a long time. But Ian was a psychologist. He was used to uncomfortable silences and he had no problem waiting them out, while the person he was interviewing struggled through the process of finding an answer.

'How did I know about Michelle?' Sara asked.

'Yes Sara,' he sighed. 'How did you know about Michelle?'

Again she hesitated, but this time only for a moment. Then she took a deep breath and decided she had to tell him. He was her brother and a very intuitive psychologist and she had never been able to hide anything from him.

'Paul was driving me to school and we passed where it happened.'

'But the police said it happened really early this morning. When Jim and Michelle were coming back from the airport. The accident should have been all cleaned up by the time you guys drove past.'

'There was a hole in the fence,' Sara said, as if that explained everything.

'I don't get it.'

'Ian, you'll think I'm crazy.'

'I already think you're crazy,' he smiled at her.

'Okay, we were driving past the place where the accident happened and I saw the hole in the fence where their car had veered off the road and gone through it. And then suddenly, I saw everything. I saw the accident.'

'What do you mean?'

'I mean I had a vision or something. I saw a car coming at them. I saw them swerve and go off the road. And I saw Michelle go through the windshield.' Sara took another big swig of her scotch.

'Don't be ridiculous,' he told her. 'You must have just seen the hole in the fence and your imagination got the better of you. Your brain saw the hole in the fence and created a story to go with it.'

'It wasn't like that,' Sara told him. 'I know things, Ian, I know things that I couldn't have known unless I'd been there.'

'Like what?' he asked, and she heard the disbelief creeping through in the tone of his voice.

'I know she had her seatbelt off. She was reaching around to get something out of the back seat. Jim was making a smart ass comment like always. And then I heard her scream and I saw the whole thing. She saw her face, you know? She saw her face reflected in the windshield just before she went through it. She was so scared.'

'Sara, you know the mind is a weird thing. It compensates for times when it knows you can't deal with something. It makes up stories and fills in blank spaces. You know there is a much more plausible explanation than suddenly having visions.'

'It's true though, Ian, I don't care if you believe me or don't believe me. Paul didn't either. But it's like I know what happened. It's like I was in the car with them.'

'Well, it was a big shock to all of us. I mean we've known Michelle since you guys were just little kids. So I say we just shouldn't worry about you having visions or whatever, as long as you're okay now.'

'All right,' Sara agreed, knowing there was no way to convince him.

'And another thing,' Ian said. 'I don't think you should go home tonight.'

'Oh, Ian, don't do this now,' Sara begged him.

'He dumped you off here and drove off,' Ian said. 'He

hasn't even called once today to see how you are. Sara, you deserve better than that.'

'But what am I supposed to do?' she asked.

'Come home with me. Back to the family house where you belong. You know your bedroom is still waiting for you.'

'Moving back to mom and dad's house at twenty five years old? Isn't that kind of pathetic?' she asked.

'It's not mom and dad's house anymore. It's ours, they left it to us.'

'It's yours Ian, remember, I sold you my half so I could pay for university.'

'You know what I mean,' he chided her.

'I know what you mean, Ian,' she scolded him. 'Just like you know what I mean.'

'What I mean is you have to take a hard look at the relationship you're in. Sara, you deserve to be treated better than Paul treats you.'

'I can't just throw away five years of my life,' she protested. 'Paul and I have history. We've built a life together.'

'Some life.'

'Ian.'

'Sara, don't you remember mom and dad's marriage? They were happy. You had a good marriage modeled for you. Why are you stuck in this bad relationship?'

'Ian…'

'Why can't you just leave? Why keep trying to turn something that is broken and not working into a relationship?'

'He's all I have.'

'No, he isn't,' Ian sighed, suddenly realizing where this had all come from. 'Sara, I know you had a hard time when mom and dad died. You were in your last year of high school and that's hard enough on its own. But then you had to deal with the loss and me moving in to look after you and everything that went along with that. But you were never alone and you will never been alone. You will always have me.'

'Ian, I know how you feel about Paul, but now is not the

time,' Sara begged, blinking back the tears that were forming in her eyes.

'Okay, okay, but remember the offer is always open.' He wrapped his arm around her shoulder and pulled her close to him. 'You always have a home to come back to.'

Later, Ian dropped Sara off at her place. It was dark and empty and Ian offered to come in with her, so she wouldn't be alone. But Sara put on her brave face and insisted she would be fine and Paul would be home any minute, even though she knew that wasn't what would happen.

Sara let herself into the empty, dark house and tried to wake it up and bring it to life. She turned on lights and started dinner, watered plants and put a CD on the stereo. She had almost succeeded in lifting her mood and making the house seem less empty when Paul finally got home, four hours later. He didn't offer an explanation for being late and she didn't ask. There was no point. His stories were always good, always plausible, she just didn't know if she believed them or not. The temperature in the house seemed to drop ten degrees as he ate his over-cooked dinner and she avoided any sort of confrontation, hiding behind a text book in abnormal psychology. He never asked her about her day either. Didn't ask about Michelle or if Sara was all right or why she had suddenly started having visions. He just ate his dinner, drank his beer and then disappeared into the den. She heard him turn on the computer as she grabbed his plate off the table and scraped the leftovers into the garbage can. She loaded the dishes in the dishwasher and turned it on, then sat down at the table with her text book. She heard his fingers clicking over the keyboard, as he chatted with all the people on the internet that he seemed to find infinitely more interesting than she was.

Another typical evening in my life, she sighed inwardly, flipping the page of her book. She wondered why she stayed, why she fought with Ian every time he suggested she move back home. She wondered why she felt she deserved to be unhappy and when she would finally find the chapter in one of her psychology books that explained her behavior.

Chapter 4

It had been a long week for Sara. She kept thinking how nice it would be if she could just call Michelle, her best friend, and talk to her. She needed to talk about Paul, about how her boyfriend was never around now that she really needed him to be there for her. Instead of being there for her, Paul had been working late and going out with his friends. She needed to decide what she was going to do, how she was going to get out of this mess, and Michelle had been the only one she could talk to about him. Michelle was the only one who never judged her or argued with her, she just listened, knowing eventually Sara would answer her own questions.

Sara also needed to talk to her friend about her thesis advisor and how the professor was making her crazy, questioning every comma she typed. And she really needed to talk about death and dying, about loss and mourning. But it was her best friend that she was mourning. It was Michelle who was gone, Michelle who would never be able to listen to her again. And Sara would never be able to listen to Michelle, give her advice or share her problems.

It had been two long days since the accident and the vision. Two days of tiptoeing around Paul because she couldn't handle a fight or even some minor name calling right now. Sara had gone to class, but found her mind wandering and simply couldn't concentrate.. She talked to her professors, had found a substitute teacher for the class she was supposed to teach and went home and tried to keep busy. She made dinner and tidied up the house, but not with any amount of caring. It was just keeping busy, something to make the time pass. She dusted and rearranged her CDs. She ironed clothes and bleached grout around the bathroom tiles. The only time she felt better was when she was with Ian, he had known Michelle almost as well as she had and they could share their sorrow. Ian had met her for coffee every day, giving them both a chance to talk. Paul never had much to say about any of it, offering a simple I'm sorry one morning. But Sara knew he was getting fed up with her moping and wished she would just get over it.

Ian seemed to be doing much better than Sara. He had found a temp for the office and had managed to get someone to cover for him for a couple of days. He had his patients to focus on, something to take his thoughts away from himself. Sara wished she could do the same.

It was Friday, a week later, when they finally got to say goodbye to their friend. The day had dawned cool and gray, perfect for a funeral. Sara had got up that morning, feeling a strange sense of peace, knowing that today would provide some closure and she could begin to move forward again. Paul was supposed to pick her up, so they could go to the church together. But he had called from the office, explaining that he was tied up on with some sort of a big project, and told her he would just meet her at the church instead. Sara had called Ian to see if he could give her a ride and he had agreed, of course. He had also very kindly avoided saying anything negative about Paul. And suddenly, she realized the time, and that he would be here in ten minutes and she didn't know where the morning had gone. She stood in the bathroom, staring at herself in the mirror. She had on a black jacket and skirt, with a white button down blouse underneath. She wore her mother's pearls. Michelle had always loved them and actually wore them on her wedding day. Something borrowed and something old, Michelle had laughed, two things knocked off the list at once. She had taken care of the rest of the list with her new blue garter. Sara ran her fingers over the smooth pearls and smiled at the memory. She wore her shoulder length hair down and straight, tucked behind her ears to keep it out of her face. She held two lipsticks in her hand, trying to decide what would be less celebratory, brick red or peach glow. She had been staring at them for five minutes, stalled by indecision, when there was a knock on the door. She took both the lipsticks downstairs and opened the door, letting her brother in.

'Ian, I don't know which lipstick to wear,' she said, frantically holding them out to him.

'Sara, it doesn't matter,' he smiled sadly at her. 'But I like this one.'

She looked down at the peach and turned back to the bathroom. After touching up her lips, she slid into her pumps, grabbed her purse and went back to the kitchen. Ian sat quietly at the table, not rushing her. He knew this was going to be hard on both of them and he had allowed himself plenty of time.

'You ready for this?' he asked.

'I didn't know I had a choice,' she said.

'Well, yeah, about that...' he laughed. 'Come on, it's not going to get any easier the more we think about it.'

'I guess you're right.'

Sara followed him out to the car, got in and buckled herself up. She had been obsessive about seatbelts in the last few days, double checking the latch and pulling it tightly around her.

They got to the church with plenty of time to spare. Ian went inside, to talk to Michelle's family. Sara stood outside, waiting for Paul. She didn't want to go in there alone and have to explain to everyone why Paul wasn't there. She pulled her jacket tightly around her and checked her watch for the fourth time. Sara had been waiting for at least twenty minutes when Ian came out to check on her.

'Sara?' he asked. 'I think they're getting ready to start in there.'

'He's not here yet.' She explained. 'Just another minute or two.'

'I wonder what could have happened to him?' Ian asked sarcastically.

Yeah, I wonder too, Sarah thought, but didn't give Ian the satisfaction of saying it out loud.

The sky suddenly swirled over her head, clouds moving as if they were being run at fast-forward through a movie projector. For a moment her vision blurred and she thought she was going to faint. Then, everything cleared, but she wasn't at the church any longer, she was at Paul's office. And he was there too, sitting on the armchair that was in the corner, across from his ornate cherry-wood desk, his secretary sitting on top of him. Her blouse was unbuttoned and swept back on her shoulders, revealing firm breasts, erect nipples just inches from Paul's face. Her skirt was pulled up around her waist. She was straddling Paul, moving slowly up and down. His hands were on her naked waist, pulling her forward until he could reach a breast and take a nipple in his mouth. He caressed it, flicking his tongue over it, as Sara had felt him do it to her hundreds of times. She could hear the throaty giggle arise from deep within the secretary's throat. The woman began moving faster, sweat forming on her brow, leaning closer to kiss Paul. He moved his mouth from her breast to her lips, his hands moving up to caress her nipples. The woman moaned, a low moan, emanating from deep within her, building in intensity as her movements became more frantic…

'No,' Sara screamed, slamming her fist against the wall of the building, hoping the pain would take away the images that filled her mind.

'What?' Ian asked, grabbing her by the shoulders, to keep her from hitting anything else.

Sara worked hard to get her breathing under control, and concentrated on not collapsing as the world swam back into focus around her. She fought the urge to scream out loud, blinking her eyes rapidly to try and clear the last wisp of the vision that seemed to be burned into her brain.

'Sara, what is it?' Ian asked, concern beginning to cloud his face.

'Nothing,' Sara said, shaking her head, trying to shake the vision away. 'Nothing. I guess I'm just a little more emotional than I thought.'

'Sara, this isn't like you. There's something you're not telling me.' Ian insisted.

'Ian, I'm fine,' she promised. 'Come on, let's go. You said the service was about to start, right?'

'Right.'

'Okay, let's go.' She took pulled his hand off her shoulder and took it in hers, leading him inside the building.

'And Ian?'

'Yeah?'

'I'd like to come home with you tonight. Maybe stay for a while?' she asked. 'Do you still have my bed made up for me?'

'I told you that you would always have a place to come to,' he said, finally relaxing, the concerned look leaving his face. 'We can pick some of your stuff up after the reception and then get you settled in.'

'Thanks,' she smiled weakly, and then they entered the church.

'Come on, Ben's holding a spot for us,' Ian said, as he led her down the aisle.

Sara smiled when she saw Ben, and he slid over a bit, making room for her and Ian in the pew beside him. He looked at the dark circles forming under her eyes and took her hand in his.

'You okay?' he asked.

'Not really.'

'You don't look good Sara,' Ben insisted.

'A bit of a headache,' she said. 'I think it's all the stress. I'll be fine.'

But she felt his hand going to her wrist and feeling for her pulse. She smiled, happy to be surrounded by two men who actually cared for her.

It had been a long, hard afternoon. Michelle's parents were in more pain than Sara had ever thought possible. They had held each other and laughed and cried for most of the afternoon. When she and Ian had finally been able to pull themselves away, she was emotionally drained. Ian had led her out to his car, with Ben close behind.

'So what's up now?' Ben asked, holding the car door open for her.

'I'm going to take Sara to her place and she's going to pack up a few things and stay with me for a few days,' Ian said.

A thousand questions passed through Ben's mind but he decided now was not the time to address them.

'Why don't I come over later,' Ben suggested. 'I could bring a bottle of wine and some pizza?'

'No,' Sara said.

'Really, it's no trouble.'

'No, I meant I prefer Chinese,' she laughed. 'Mu-shu pork?'

'Mu-shu pork it is. And those dumplings I like. Around six o'clock okay with you?'

'Six is great,' Ian said, climbing into the car.

Ben closed the door on the passenger side and waved as they pulled out of the parking lot.

They arrived at Sara's house and it was dark, as always. She convinced Ian to wait in the car and let herself in to the house. She hardly had the energy to turn the lock, let alone to fill a suitcase but she had even less energy to deal with Paul tonight. So she tossed in jeans and t-shirts and her makeup bag. Sara stopped at the kitchen table and put her laptop and research notes into her backpack and closed it up. She grabbed a piece of paper to write a note for Paul, explaining where she was, when she saw lights turning into the driveway. Paul was home.

'Fuck,' she said out loud, crumpling up her note and throwing it in the garbage.

Paul threw the door open and slammed it behind him.

'What's your brother doing sitting in his car in the driveway?'

'He's waiting for me,' Sara admitted.

'More funeral stuff?' Paul asked. 'I thought that was this afternoon.'

'Yeah, it was. And thanks for being there for me.'

'Sara, I called you and told you I had a deadline at work I had to deal with,' he said, his voice slowing as if he was talking to a small child. 'If you had a problem with that, why didn't you say something then?'

'I didn't say anything because I actually believed you. Because I hadn't seen you fucking your secretary. That was what I had a problem with.'

'What are you talking about?' he asked.

'You sat in that ugly armchair that I have always hated and you fucked her. You even left the blinds open, because it excited her to think that somebody might be watching you two.'

'You're crazy.'

'No, I have been crazy to put up with your shit and the lousy way you treat me,' she said, surprised at the venomous sound of her voice. 'I think now I'm finally getting sane. And I'm leaving you.'

'You are not,' he said, grabbing her arm.

'Paul, it's over,' she said. 'There is nothing you can do. Now take your hand off me.'

He didn't move for several long seconds and then slowly his hand dropped from her arm.

'You can't prove anything.'

'I don't have to,' she said. 'We both know it's true.'

'You bitch,' he screamed at her, as she picked up her suitcase and her backpack. 'If you walk out of that door, don't you ever think about coming back. Not even for the rest of your things!'

Sara looked at him, suddenly not able to remember why she had spent the last five years of her life with him, living like this, and she let herself out the door. Ian had his hand on the doorknob and she almost ran into him as she pushed the door open.

'I asked you to wait in the car,' she said.

'I heard some yelling. I was worried about you.'

'I'm okay,' she assured him. 'Come on, let's get out of here.'

At Ian's house, she dumped her bag on the floor of her old bedroom and fell on the bed. When Sara had moved out, Ian had replaced the twin beds of her teenaged years with a nice queen size bed. He said it was to make it a proper guest room. But he had always hoped she would see the light and he wanted a safe and comfortable place for her to come home to.

'Do you want a beer?' Ian called up from downstairs.

'Sure.'

'You don't mind if Ben comes over tonight do you?' Ian asked. 'He's admitted a couple of my patients to the hospital and I'd like to find out what he thinks.'

'No, Ben's cool,' Sara yelled down the stairs. 'And I can just stay up here while you guys talk about your patients.'

'No you can't,' Ian yelled. 'You can come and join us for Chinese food. You're officially my research assistant. The patient confidentiality form covers you too.'

'What if I want to stay up here,' she called down to him.

'It not healthy, Sara. You come down here and have dinner with us.'

'You're not my mother,' Sara yelled, regretting instantly what she had just said.

And there was no answer from Ian. She pulled herself off the bed and headed downstairs. It was never a good move to alienate everyone in your life in the same day.

By the time Ben and the Chinese food arrived, Ian and Sara had made up over a beer and everyone was smiling again. Sara laid out some plates and opened a beer for Ben. He dropped his stuff at the front door and joined them at the table. Ben and Ian had met in their first year of university. They lost touch when Ben headed off to medical school and Ian went into psychology but they met up a few years later, after finishing their residencies in different ends of the country, but occasionally worked together. Ian referred to Ben when he had patients who needed psychiatric care or hospitalization and Ben referred all his patients that needed community counseling to Ian. They were very close, consulting each other about patients, doing research and spending every Sunday together during hockey season. Ben had always liked Sara, coaching her through her research and exams, as she made her way through university. Ian sat back and watched them the two of them throughout the years, wondering what would have happened if Paul hadn't been in the picture.

Ben hung his suit jacket over the back of the chair, sat down, grabbed his beer and held it up in the air.

'Cheers to surviving the day,' he smiled at Sara.

She picked up her beer and clinked it against his and then Ian's. 'I will toast to that.'

Ian joined in, 'Me too.'

'Help yourself,' Sara said, opening one of the take out dishes and passing it around. 'Looks like there's lots here.'

'Well, I have a big problem deciding what to get at a Chinese restaurant. I want it all.' he laughed.

'Physician heal thyself,' Sara teased him.

'So, do we want to talk about today?' he asked. 'Or am I in charge of picking a totally innocuous subject absolutely unrelated to anything serious?'

The phone rang and they all sat silently, listening to it ring two more times before the answering machine picked up.

'It's Paul,' the voice rang out over the speaker. 'Sara, I'm sorry you were upset today but I think you're acting like a child and you need to come home right now…Sara, I know you're there, pick up the phone….Sara…..pick up the fucking ph…'

The answering machine cut him off and they all sat in silence for another moment.

'I vote for innocuous,' Sara finally said.

'All right. Well, how's Paul?' Ben asked, trying to sound naive.

Sara froze for a moment as the phone rang again. Ian jumped in quickly and turned the ringer off on the phone and the volume down on the answering machine.

'Did you see that one patient I called you about this morning?' Ian asked, sitting back down at the table and digging into the chow-mein.

Ben read the look on Sara's face. 'I'm here if you ever need to talk about it,' he told her, and then turned to Ian. 'I did see him today. He's on Dr. Adams' unit but I consulted.'

'So did he manage to eat today?' Ian continued, trying to avoid the original subject.

'I think so,' Ben said, turning back to study Sara's face again. When he was satisfied she was going to be okay he turned his full attention back to Ian. 'Yes, he ate today. And kept it down. I think he's finally adjusting to the new meds. I had an interesting chat with him too. I left a long dictation for you. It should be in the chart by tomorrow.'

'Thanks,' Ian said. 'Anything else I need to know about before tomorrow?'

'No, same old stuff. Nothing urgent, no big breakthroughs. Sorry, I tried to cure them all for you, but three days just isn't enough time, even for someone as good as me.' Ben laughed.

'I left Paul today,' Sara said, softly.

Ben and Ian both turned to her.

'Sorry,' she laughed. 'I haven't lost my mind. I just had to say that out loud.'

'Do you like the way it sounds?' Ian asked.

'Yeah, I think I do,' Sara said, a smile slowly breaking across her face.

'Here's to dumping Paul,' Ben said, bringing his beer up to toast again. But this time he looked at Sara a little differently then he had before, a twinkle in his eye. 'And what are you doing next Friday night?'

She laughed. 'I'll probably need a little time to get over him. How about Saturday night instead?'

It was late. Sara had gone to bed hours ago, leaving the two men to talk sports or patients or whatever it was they talked about when she wasn't around. But she just tossed and turned. She couldn't get her brain to turn off. There was a soft knock at her door and it opened a crack.

'Sara?'

'Ben?' she asked, sitting up and pulling the blankets modestly up around her. 'Is everything okay?'

'Fine, he said, letting himself in and sitting on the side of the bed. 'It was you I was worried about.'

'Me? Why?'

'Because you've been tossing and turning up here for hours.'

'You can hear me down there?'

'I heard you go to the bathroom three or four times. Sara, I can give you something to help you sleep tonight if you'd like.'

'I'm not a big fan of sleep meds,' she admitted.

'Just tonight,' he said. 'I'm not even offering to write a prescription. Just something I have in my medical bag.'

She looked at him and nodded her head. He pulled a pill bottle out of his pocket and shook two into her hand.

'You'll feel better in the morning,' he assured her, as she swallowed the pills and took a sip of water. 'Now get under those covers and just relax.'

She did as she was ordered, and he tucked the covers around her. Sara could already feel the medication taking effect, as her body relaxed and her thoughts grew thick and muddy.

'Sleep well, Sara,' he said, leaning over and kissing her lightly on her forehead.

Ben let himself quietly out of her bedroom and went back downstairs and into the living room.

'She's asleep,' Ben confirmed. 'Now what did you want to talk to me about?'

Ian reached over and got his beer, taking a long drink while he worked out what to say.

'There's something I need to know,' Ian said. 'And I need the truth.'

'What?' Ben asked.

'Did you inject Sara?'

'What are you talking about?' Ben asked.

'You know exactly what I'm talking about,' Ian said. 'You've wanted to do her for months and I forbade it. You remember that, right?'

'Of course I do'

'But you injected her anyway?'

'Ian…'

'She's having visions, Ben. She had a vision about Michelle's death. She saw every detail of the accident. I didn't put it together then, I thought she was just out of her mind with grief. But then today, she knew that Paul was cheating on her. She knew it without anyone telling her or without any hard proof. I'm convinced she had a vision before we went into the church. You injected her.'

'Yes,' Ben admitted, his head held in shame, sorry that Ian had found out this way. 'But Ian, I was right. She's an amazing test subject.'

'She's not a test subject, Ben, she's my sister.'

'But she's already having perfectly clear visions. And there aren't any signs of distress.'

'How many times?' Ian asked.

'What?'

'How many times have you injected her?'

'Once.'

'Do they know?'

'No, they don't. I didn't have approval from them to do her either. I thought I'd tell them when it proved to be successful. As it has, Ian. Think about it, we will have a test subject who will not only thrive but will be able to tell us what she's seen, and do it coherently. No more scared little kids.'

'Ben, you've got to get a hold of yourself. This is Sara, this is my sister and I love her. And I am never going to let anything happen to her. Do you understand me?'

'Ian, after all this time, we finally have a subject that can…'

42

'Ben,' he shouted at him. 'Stop it! Just stop it! Now here's the deal. You will not inject her again, ever. We know that it sometimes reverses itself after one injection…'

'Yes, if the patient doesn't die within 48 hours of the first injection, the condition will reverse itself unless the next injection is given within fourteen days. Ian, we know all this already, we know how it doesn't work. Don't you want to know how it does work?'

'You will never inject Sara again under any circumstances. And if you do, I will go to the press and tell them everything. Do we understand each other?'

'Yes.'

'Ben, I thought you liked Sara, why would you do this to her?'

'I love Sara, Ian. That's why. Because I love her and together, the three of us, we could make miracles happen.'

'You need to stay away from her, Ben. And you need to get out of my house.'

'I'll go home,' Ben said, getting up and putting his jacket on. 'But I can't stay away from her. And you and I have work to do together. This isn't one of those jobs you can just quit.'

1970

He walked down the hallway like he owned the place. It was the only way to get the respect he deserved. When he first walked into this hospital he was surprised to realize that most of the nurses actually knew more than he did. There he was, fresh from years of medical school, his newly minted degree hanging on the wall, everyone calling him doctor and these women could out-perform him on almost any task. Not that he was given many glamorous jobs. As a first year resident he had spent most of his time with vomiting street people, evacuating constipated bowels and starting IV lines on veins that had been abused for years.

The nurses knew that these new doctors were a menace to society, as well, and they treated them that way. He was just another wet behind the ears resident, sent to make their lives more difficult. They would have to watch his every move, make sure he was doing more good than harm, and clean up all his messes after him. And they resented the additional burden on their time. Every August this happened; a new crop of these useless first year residents appeared. And it didn't matter how cute or charming Beckman was, they weren't about to fall for his looks when they knew he made three times the salary they did and yet they would have to spend the next year covering for him. And that's how they treated him.

About three quarters of the way through his first year, he realized that he didn't have to take it and he stood up for himself. He started speaking to the nurses like the more seasoned doctors did, ordering them around. Nurses were there to serve the doctors and he made sure they were fetching and carrying for him, too. He demanded the respect that his years of education had earned him. And he made sure that if he couldn't start an IV or some other minor procedure, that it never went further than the exam room. He didn't care if they liked him or not, it wasn't the nurses who were going to advance his career.

But to ensure that they wouldn't sabotage his career, Beckman picked out one of the prettier senior nurses and he started dating her. A dinner in a nice restaurant, a passionate kiss with the promise of much more to follow, and she took care of the other nurses, who then left him alone. That got him through the final months of his first year. And after spending that first year rotating through the various departments, he moved to the surgical floor and began working with the anesthesiologists. The nurses here had a little more respect for him, but unfortunately, the doctors had less. He spent two more painful years working his way up the ladder, doing all the scut work and menial tasks that the senior residents didn't want to do.

But, in the end, it had all been worth it. Because today, for the first time, he sat at the head of the table, waiting for his patient to be brought in. An anesthetist would be around, would check his meds and supervise his intubations, but this was his case and his patient. And then the door opened and the gurney came through, his patient on board. He watched as the nurses got the patient settled on the operating table and covered him up with a warm blanket.

'Hello, Mr. Sanders, I'm Dr. Beckman. We met briefly yesterday.'

'I remember, Doctor,' the man answered, looking very

nervous.

'How are you feeling?'

'Like I'd rather be somewhere else, to be honest,' he tried a laugh.

'Well, we'll have you asleep in just a minute, and then when you wake up, this will all be over.'

He applied the electrocardiogram leads to the patient and checked his equipment. All the monitors seemed to be fine and the IV line was patent. He turned to his chart and waited for the attending to appear, so he could proceed. And shortly, he arrived.

'Beckman,' he said sharply. 'What have we got?'

'Mr. Sanders is a 52 year old male, slightly obese but in good health otherwise. He uses tobacco at a pack a day, alcohol at three beers a night and works as a bricklayer. He has developed a right inguinal hernia and presents for a herniorraphy. There is nothing in his history or family history to contraindicate a general anesthetic and he has had a successful surgery on the contralateral side four years ago.'

The senior doctor took the chart, reviewed the plan and signed off.

'I'll be in the lounge. Just page me if you need me.'

Beckman smiled, glad to be alone, and picked up the syringe he had prepared.

'All right, Mr. Sanders, you might feel a slight burning and then you're going to feel very, very sleepy. Can you count backwards from one hundred for me please?'

'One hundred, ninety nine, ninety …six…eighty ….two….'

It was a textbook perfect induction. Beckman filled in his chart report and waited for the surgeon to come in, pleased that everything was ready and waiting for him.

'Morning Dr. Morton,' one of the nurses called, and Beckman looked up to see the surgeon being gowned and gloved.

'Good morning all,' he boomed, his voice more that like of a Broadway actor than a surgeon in an operating theatre.

'Morning,' they all greeted, almost in unison.

The surgeon took his place at the operating table.

'Who are you?' he asked briskly.

'Andrew Beckman,' he answered quickly.

'Resident?' he asked.

'Yes sir.'

'What year?'

'Fourth, sir.'

'Well, try not to kill my patient please.'

'Sir,' Beckman muttered, not sure what an appropriate answer would be.

The nurses all giggled and the surgeon held out his hand for a scalpel.

'All right, apparently this gentleman has not been able to have sex with his wife for over a year. Let's get him fixed up before she divorces him.'

'Yes doctor,' the nurse said, handing him a scalpel and a suction device to the surgical resident.

'But from the size of his penis, I'm not sure if she's really missing anything at all. Too bad there's nothing we can do to help him with that while we're here.'

They all laughed with the surgeon, although some of them looked uncomfortable. Beckman had never understood surgeons who felt the need to joke about the patients, He was always very aware that the patient was still in the room with them. But he was still just a fourth year resident and not ready to confront a surgeon about his attitude. He quietly turned back to his chart and scribbled more notes.

Beckman was tired; he hadn't realized how stressful running his own cases was going to be. But they were all alive and well and awaiting him in the recovery room. He pulled his lab coat on over his scrubs and went to do a final check on his three cases. The appendectomy had a little nausea, so he wrote orders for Gravol in her chart. The bunionectomy seemed to be doing fine and was awake and joking with the nurses. The herniorraphy was drifting in and out of sleep. Beckman pulled the chart and went and listened to his heart and lungs, just to make sure everything was okay. The patient's eyes fluttered open when he put the cold stethoscope to his chest.

'Hello Mr. Sanders,' Beckman smiled down at his patient. 'It's all over and you're still in the recovery room.'

'I know,' he croaked through a dry and irritated throat.

'We'll have you back in your room in no time and I'm sure Dr. Morton will be around to see you.'

'I want a new surgeon,' the man said.

'Mr. Sanders, you'll feel better in a few hours. You still have a lot of drugs in your system…'

'I don't want that asshole touching me,' he said, more firmly.

'Mr. Sanders, please just close your eyes and rest for a minute. You'll feel much better in the morning.'

'He made fun of me.'

'What?'

'During the operation. I trusted him to fix my hernia and he made fun of my sex life.'

'What are you talking about?' Beckman asked, not believing what he was hearing.

Sanders grabbed Beckman's shoulder and pulled himself up.

'If that asshole comes into my room, I'll knock him into next week. You tell them that. And I want a new doctor looking after me.'

'Nurse,' Beckman called. 'Get me 10 mg of midazolam.

'I mean it,' Sanders said, his eyes fluttering, looking as if he was going to faint.

The nurse appeared and injected the sedative into the patient's IV line, and he fell back on the bed, eyes closed, sleeping peacefully.

'What was that about?' she asked.

'I don't know,' Beckman lied. 'Probably just an adverse

reaction to one of the medications. Do vitals every fifteen minutes for the next hour and make sure he's settled down and then we can discharge him back to his floor.'

'Yes doctor.'

Beckman stared down at the sleeping patient for another couple of minutes, wishing he could get inside his brain and find out what was going on. How did he know what Morton had said during the surgery, when he was supposed to have been totally unconscious and every instrument and monitor had confirmed that he was? Beckman pulled a notebook from his pocket and wrote today's date and time, and then recorded all of the patient's comments. He went back to the nursing desk and pulled the chart, so he could record all the pre-op and perioperative medications too. This had turned into a very interesting case.

The next day, Beckman was in an empty operating room, preparing for his second day of surgery. He wanted to double check the monitors that he had placed on Mr. Sanders yesterday to ensure they were calibrated and not malfunctioning. The attending walked by and noticed Beckman working away.

'You trying to make points, Beckman?'

'Sir?'

'You're here two hours early before your first scheduled surgery? Trying to make the rest of us look bad?'

'No sir. I just wanted to double check everything.'

'Did something happen or are you just one of those doctors who doesn't trust these new fangled machines?' he laughed.

'Sir, something interesting happened in my herniorraphy procedure yesterday.'

'And what is that?'

'The patient reports he remembered something that the surgeon said during the procedure.'

'Oh, is that your first one?'

'Sir?'

'Look, Beckman, you're going to be working under me for another year, have you got a first name?'

'Andrew, sir.'

'And I'm Mark,' he said, sliding a stool over and taking a seat. 'Andy, you will see and hear some strange things in the recovery room. Patients have some amazing stories.'

'But they're just stories?'

'I think so. My theory is that the patient probably read up on the surgery and between that and the drugs we administer, they create some sort of false memory.'

'Mark, this was much more than that.'

'Well, there was a senior anesthetist here who believed that the patients who reported these events were physiologically resistant to the sleep medications but not the muscle relaxants. So basically he said that we were paralyzing them but not anesthetizing them and they were conscious for the entire procedure but had no way of telling us.'

'And the monitors wouldn't be able to pick that up. If I noticed a little tachycardia or hypertension, I would have assumed it was a reaction to the medications and treated him for it.'

'That's right. When in fact it would mean the patient was feeling everything, every cut and every stitch, and was reacting in terror and pain. As you can imagine that is a very unpopular theory around here. That particular doctor has actually lost his privileges and is now practicing in a very small hospital somewhere in the mid-west, I believe.'

'Oh.'

'Andy, you seem like a good man. You're a smart student and you treat the patients well. I just wanted you to know this because I think it would be a shame to derail your career before it was even started. Do you understand what I'm saying?'

'That things like this aren't really talked about.'

'See, I knew you were a smart man. Now, you finish up here and get yourself a cup of coffee. You need to spend some time in the doctor's lounge and get to know everyone here if you want some good references.'

'I know. You can never start too soon,' Beckman said.

'Yes, you're a very smart doctor,' he patted him on the back as he got up off the stool. 'Let's get together for a beer after you're done today and discuss how your cases went.'

'Yes sir,' Beckman said.

'It's Mark!'

Chapter 5

Sara sat at the kitchen table, several books spread out on the table in front of her, with her transcribed research notes piled underneath them. Organized chaos was how she referred to it. Ian just called it chaos. She had been living with Ian for almost a week now and was quite enjoying the peace and quiet. Paul had called several times, but Ian was screening her calls and for now she was happy not to have to deal with the situation. Psychologically unsound, perhaps, but she felt happier than she had in years. And at this moment her life would be complete if she never had to talk to Paul again.

Ian was out tonight, on a date, which was something he hadn't done in a long time. It seemed they were breaking out of the shells they had surrounded themselves with since their parents had died. Sara smiled and she searched through her notes for a reference she knew she had recorded somewhere, when her phone rang. She was totally focused on her paper and picked it up before she realized what she had done. Don't let it be Paul, she prayed silently.

'Hello?' she asked timidly.

'Sara?' It was Paul.

'What do you want?' she asked, her temerity switching easily to anger.

'I want to know how you're doing. I also want to know why you're not here right now and why you're living at your brother's house. And while we're at it, maybe you can share with me when you're planning on coming home?'

'I am home.'

'Sara, this is unacceptable. I came home a week ago and you're pulling out of the driveway with suitcases in hand and saying you'll be staying at your brother's place. Don't you think you at least owe me some sort of explanation?'

'Only if you owe me an explanation for why you were fucking your secretary while I was alone at my best friend's funeral.'

'I don't know what you're talking about. I told you I had an emergency at work that I had to deal with.'

'Well, from what I saw, she was pretty pleased with the way you dealt with her. See, that's the problem with you. You're so great in bed that it takes a long time to realize what a real bastard you are when you're out of bed.'

'There is no way you could have seen us,' Paul said. 'How do you know?'

'You just told me,' Sara spat at him and then hung the phone up.

A part of her hoped it would ring again, and he would be begging for her forgiveness, but all that followed was silence. She wasn't sure how long she waited, staring at the phone, but she jumped when there was a knock at the door behind her. Sara got up and opened the door.

'Ben?' she asked, surprised to see him standing there. 'I'm sorry but Ian's not home tonight.'

'I'm not here for Ian,' he laughed.

'I don't understand.'

'Why aren't you ready?' he asked, looking down at her sweat pants and t-shirt.

'Ready? For what?'

'I believe we have a date tonight,' he explained. 'It's Saturday night.'

When she looked confused, he continued his explanation.

'Remember, I had suggested Friday night but you thought Saturday might give you more time to get over Paul?' Ben smiled at her, laughter in his eyes.

'You were serious?' she asked.

'Well, sort of. Actually, I just thought it might do you good to get out of the house for a little while. Maybe a movie and then a drink?'

'I really should be working on my thesis,' she explained, pointing to the mess of books that sat on the kitchen table. 'I seem to be a little behind.'

'You've got six months before it's due and at least another six months of extensions after that if you need them.'

'Are you trying to corrupt me?' she asked. 'Advising me on extensions already?'

'Well, I've been accused of worse.'

'Ben, it's really nice of you to think of me…'

'Come on, lets get out and get some fresh air. It'll help clear your head.'

'Ben, you know I really can't date you right now,' she said, watching his face for a reaction. 'I mean, I just moved out a week ago. I haven't even picked up the rest of my stuff yet.'

'Yeah, I'll get over it. Look, Sara, we're friends. Come to a movie with your friend. I swear I'll help you with your thesis tomorrow, if I can.'

'You're willing to do thesis research with me tomorrow if I see a movie with you tonight?' she asked.

'Sure.'

'Wow, you must be pretty desperate,' she laughed at him. 'How long since you've been on a date?'

'I'm a single, handsome, rich and very eligible doctor,' Ben told her. 'I'm not that desperate. And I believe you're the one that is supposed to be irresistibly attracted to me.'

'Yeah, well I'm going to be a doctor too,' she said. 'I don't need to marry one.'

'I was just thinking more along the lines of a movie, but we could talk about that marriage thing later, maybe.'

She laughed at him. 'Come on in and have a seat while I change.'

'You look fine,' he told her, sitting at the table and pulling her laptop in front of him. 'Can I read this?'

'Sure you can. And I don't look fine. But I will in five minutes. Besides, you should at least get your money's worth.'

'Oh, I'm paying?'

'You said you were the rich doctor, too late to back out now,' she said. 'I'll be right back.'

Ben had the rich doctor car to go with the rich doctor façade and Sara decided she liked this world and was looking forward to the day she could afford the fully loaded Lexus, with the heated leather seats. He parked, came around to open the door for her and she reluctantly let him help her out.

'Too bad there's not a drive-in theatre left in town. I could happily stay in that car all night.'

'Yeah, I bet you tell all the guys that.'

'What are we going to see?' Sara asked, as they made their way across the parking lot.

'What do you want to see?'

'I'm an out of touch student. I don't know what's playing, who's starring in anything or what's good or bad,' she said, staring up at the movie posters for the theatre complex. 'You pick and I promise I won't complain if I don't like it.'

'You sure?' he asked.

'I trust you.'

'You shouldn't,' he laughed. He paid the cashier while Sara got a place in the concession line up.

'What would you like?' he asked, looking up at the menu.

'This part is my treat,' Sara told him. 'You got the movie, I can get the treats.'

'Nope, let me. Remember, rich doctor and poor student.'

'Ben, that's not really fair to you.'

'Maybe I like being taken advantage of!'

'Okay, but then you have to let me make a nice dinner for you and Ian sometime this week.'

'You cook?' he asked.

'Now don't get all excited. I just do the basic stuff, like spaghetti or chili. Nothing fancy at all. But it's edible.'

'Well, I look forward to that,' he laughed, his hand brushing over her back as he guided her through the line up. 'Food like my mom used to make.'

'That's where I learned it from, my mom,' she said, feeling a shiver run through her at his touch. 'So, shall we share a large popcorn?'

'Extra butter?'

'Absolutely.'

'And what would you like to drink?' he asked.

He carried the pop and popcorn while she loaded up with napkins and then led the way into the theatre.

'Where do you like to sit?' he asked her, as they stood at the back of the theatre, perusing the seating.

'I like the middle,' she said. 'There's some room down there.'

'Lead the way.'

They settled in their seats and she grabbed a handful of popcorn and started munching.

'So what's this about?' she asked.

'It's a ghost story.'

'Are you serious?'

'Absolutely.'

'I should warn you, I'm a jumper when I get scared. I could be sitting in your lap through most of this movie.'

'I certainly hope so,' he smiled at her, eyes twinkling.

She stared into those twinkling eyes, not being able to pull away, feeling a tingle running through her entire body. She hadn't felt like this in a long time.

'Ben, have you ever done something that is just so wrong that every fibre of your being is screaming at you to stop and yet you can't?' she asked, staring back at him, her pulse racing.

'Yes I have, actually. Why do you ask?'

'Because I just have a horrible feeling that that's how this evening is going to be ending.'

He leaned closer to her and kissed her, his lips just softly brushing over hers with a promise of more to come.

'Good,' he smiled. 'Just let me know if there's anything I can do to help things along.'

He set the popcorn in her lap and draped his arm around her shoulders. She leaned over and snuggled up to him.

'Only because it's a scary movie,' she told him, her smile giving her away.

As they walked out of the theatre she reached over and took his hand in hers. He accepted it without comment.

'So, that wasn't so bad,' she said.

'Yeah, it'll just be our little secret that you screamed like a girl fifteen or twenty times.'

'I am a girl.'

'Okay, I admit I have noticed that,' he laughed. 'It's almost midnight. I better get you home.'

He opened the car door and she slipped into the seat. He closed the door and came around to the driver's side, getting in and turning the heat on for her.

'Yeah, I suppose I should get to bed,' she said. 'My thesis awaits tomorrow.'

'That seat should warm up soon.'

'Thanks,' she smiled shyly at him. 'Remember what I said earlier? About making a big mistake tonight?'

'Yeah.'

'Well, I was still thinking I might like to do that. Have you got any beer at your place?'

'No, but I have a nice Merlot that I was saving for a special occasion,' he slipped the gearshift into drive and turned into the street. 'But Sara, I don't know about this. I mean, I'm a psychiatrist and I just can't help feeling that I'm taking advantage of you when you're in a vulnerable state. And your brother and I work together. Maybe I should just take you home?'

'Did you ever think I might just be using you?' she asked. 'I might not even want to see you tomorrow.'

'Wow, my dream date,' he laughed, and turned the car toward his house.

He pulled into his driveway, turned the car off and came around to the passenger side. He took her hand and led her up the front steps. He didn't let go when he opened the door and led her into the dark hallway. He reached over to turn on the light and she grabbed his hand and stopped him. She unbuttoned his coat and slid it over his shoulders, letting it drop to the floor. He leaned over and kissed her, sliding his hands under her coat and slipping it off her shoulders. He wrapped his arms around her and pulled her tightly to him, letting his kisses wander down her neck. His hands found the buttons on her blouse and started to unbutton them, but then he pulled himself away.

'Ben?' she asked.

'I don't want to do this here,' he told her, and picked her up and carried her down the hall to the bedroom.

'This is much better,' she agreed.

He laid her gently on the bed and then lay down beside her, staring at her face. She rolled over and kissed him, gently and unsure at first, and then more aggressively as she began to feel more secure in her decision. He began unbuttoning and unzipping every fastener he could find, while she frantically tried to do the same. Their hands got tangled up while she was trying to pull his sweater over his head and he laughed, pulling the offending garment off himself. He finally got her bra off and moved his tongue down her neck toward the firm nipples that were calling out to him. He heard a soft moan escape the back of her throat when he finally took it in his mouth. And then the phone rang.

'Oh God,' she whispered breathlessly in his ear. 'Don't

answer it.'

'I have to,' he said.

She rolled over, letting him get up. He sat up, doing up his pants and reached for the phone on the night stand.

'Hello?'

Sara noticed his face harden as he listened to the voice on the other end.

'Now?' he asked. 'This is not a good time. Who the hell decided to do that?'

Ben got up and paced the room.

'Fuck,' he cursed into the receiver. 'I can't believe you've done this.'

Sara sat up, sensing what was coming.

'Of course I'll be there, the patient needs me, but heads are going to roll in the morning. You tell him he better be packing his bags right now.'

Ben slammed the phone down and turned to see Sara with her bra on already, buttoning up her blouse.

'It's a patient,' he told her.

'I know. You don't have to explain or apologize; I understand the whole patient thing.'

He walked around the bed and kissed her one last time.

'You're great, you know?'

'Oh yeah, people tell me that all day long.'

'Sara, one of the greatest regrets in my life is going to be that I didn't get to finish what I started here tonight.'

She smiled at him as she tucked her blouse into her pants.

'I told you this was one of those great mistakes, so it's probably for the best.' She smiled up at him as she sat on the bed and pulled on her shoes. 'Can I just call a cab?'

'I'll drive you home,' he said. 'It's on my way.'

'To the hospital?' she asked.

'It's a private patient in a private clinic,' he reassured her. 'I have time to get you home.'

'Thanks.'

She followed him down the hall where he picked her coat

up off the floor, shook it out and helped her on with it.

'Maybe I can give you a call tomorrow and we can do something?'

'Maybe,' she agreed. 'Give me a call and we'll see how stupid I feel about all this after I've slept on it for the night.'

'You don't need to feel stupid about this. Sara, do you know how long I've been hoping you might give me a chance some day? That maybe you'd be back on the market?'

'What, I'm a piece of meat now?' she asked.

'Well, it was better than saying how long I've been waiting for you to come to your senses and leave that jerk, don't you think?'

'I see your point,' she laughed. 'Call me tomorrow, we'll talk.'

They drove home in relative silence. He pulled into Sara's driveway and she leaned over and kissed him on the cheek before getting out of the car. She stood in the driveway while he backed out and drove away. She stood there long after he was gone, wondering what she was thinking to have even thought about doing this with Ben tonight. Ben, her brother's best friend.

'I wonder what would have happened if that phone hadn't rang?' she thought out loud.

The sky opened up and clouds swirled through her head, filling her brain with thunder and lightening. Gale force winds forced her over onto the cold pavement. Her heart was beating so fast she was worried her chest might explode when suddenly everything cleared and she was lying on Ben's bed. She was naked and sleeping, and he was watching her. He stood in the shadows, staring at her, a loving smile on his face. But then he raised his hand and there was something in it. He started coming towards her, holding something over her then bringing it down. Sara couldn't see what it was, but she was scared. She tried to focus her eyes, get a clearer picture when the wind starting blowing outside, rattling the shutters.

'No,' she screamed.

'Sara,' he said. 'Sara, it's okay.'

'No, get away from me,' she screamed, pushing at the body that was looming over her.

'Sara,' he said harshly and then her face was stinging. She opened her eyes, and saw Ian standing over her, his hand cocked to slap her face again.

'Stop!' she cried.

'Sara, are you awake?' he asked.

'Don't hit me,' she said. 'I'm awake.'

He reached down and pulled her up off the ground. 'Let's get you inside.'

'What happened?' she asked. 'What am I doing out here?'

'I think you just fainted, Sara. You'll be okay. Let's get you into bed. It's all the stress.'

Sara let Ian lead her into the house. She dropped her coat at the front door, pushed Ian away and went to her bedroom. She was freezing so she ran a hot bath and climbed in. As she lay in the bathtub, she was curious as to why Ian hadn't wanted to rush her to the hospital or a doctor or something. Why was he so convinced it was stress. He usually worried endlessly about everything. But she was exhausted. She dried herself off, fell into bed and was asleep before she could worry about anything else.

Downstairs, Ian listened to Sara get into the bath and then picked up the phone and dialed Ben's cell phone number.

'Hello?' Ben said after two rings.

'Where the fuck are you?' Ian asked.

'I'm on my way to the clinic,' Ben said. 'That idiot old man injected two kids this afternoon and now their blood pressure is out of control.'

'I just found Sara unconscious on the driveway,' Ian said. 'I think she was having a vision.'

Ben smiled but didn't share his joy with Ian.

'We went and saw a movie and I just dropped her off a few minutes ago,' he told Ian. 'She was fine then.'

'Where were you?' he demanded.

'We just went to a movie and then had a drink. God, Ian, you need to chill out.'

'I told you to leave her alone,' Ian said.

'You told me not to inject her again,' Ben said. 'And I haven't. Even though she is proving to be the most successful subject we've ever had. God, Ian, do you know what we are losing here?'

'We're saving my sister,' Ian said. 'Which is what we should be doing for some of these kids we are losing.'

'What, are you getting a conscience all of a sudden?'

'Ben, how many kids have to die?'

'I'm not going to have this conversation with you right now,' Ben said. 'I'm almost at the clinic. Look, we'll talk this week, okay?'

'You leave Sara alone,' Ian threatened him.

'I haven't done a thing to her,' Ben reassured him. 'Look, I have to go. She's okay, isn't she?'

'She's fine now, just a little disoriented.'

'Okay, I'll check her out this week and we'll talk. These visions should stop soon,' Ben said.

'They better,' Ian said, before slamming the phone back down in its cradle.

Chapter 6

Sara was in the lecture hall. She had just finished up with her class of first year Psych students and was wondering why people chose teaching as a profession. She hated everything about it except for the fact that it allowed her to continue with her Master's program. She wondered if the students hated her. Either way, Psych 101 was not an overly inspiring course at the best of times but at least her students were all getting good marks, so she must be doing something right. She wrote a few notes, gathered up her books and started stuffing things into her backpack. There was a knock at the door and she answered without turning.

'Sorry, I don't have office hours today. You can book with me through the Psych office.'

'Ms. Sara Hunter?' a female voice called.

'Yes?' she turned, and saw a man and a woman crossing the room towards her.

The woman reached into her pocket and pulled out a small wallet, flipping it open and showing a police detective's badge.

'I'm Detective Roberts, this is Detective Grassi.'

'Is my brother okay?' she asked, worried.

'Your brother is fine as far as I know,' Detective Roberts said. 'We just wanted to ask you about Paul Whyte.'

'The stuff I took from the house was all mine,' Sara sighed. She knew Paul would keep trying to cause problems in her life but never suspected he would call the police on her.

'I'm sorry?' the woman said, not understanding Sara's answer.

'Ms. Hunter, we're here because Mr. Whyte has been reported as missing,' Detective Grassi explained.

'Excuse me?' Sara asked.

'His office has reported that he hasn't been in for three days,' Detective Roberts took over the conversation. 'According to the people we spoke to, you are his girlfriend…'

'Was his girlfriend,' Sara corrected them.

'Was?' Roberts asked. 'How long has this been the case?'

'Since I found out he was fucking his secretary,' Sara said, bitterness creeping out, and the immediately regretted her words. 'A couple of weeks, I guess.'

'Have you seen him since?'

'No. He's been phoning me, dropping by, but my brother has been intercepting his visits.'

'I wonder if you could tell me where you've been for the past several days,' she said.

'Are you accusing me of doing something to him?' Sara asked.

'No, we're just trying to piece together where he might have gone and what might have happened.'

'Look, anyone you talk to will tell you that we had a very acrimonious relationship. I finally had the good sense to leave him and I literally have not seen him or talked to him since that day. My brother and I went to the house to get some of my stuff when Paul was at work. That's all I know.'

'Can you tell us where he liked to hang out? Did he have a favourite bar or club he went to?'

'I don't know,' Sara said. 'He didn't really share that kind of stuff with me. I just waited at home for him and never questioned what he did. You could check his computer. I know he liked to chat on those internet sites.'

'And he had a relationship with his secretary?' Roberts asked.

'Yes.'

'How do you know this?' she asked. 'Were you having him followed?'

'I saw them. Through his office window.'

'I'm sorry.'

'Not half as sorry as I was,' Sara said. 'Look, there's really nothing I can help you with.'

Detective Roberts pulled a business card out of her pocket and handed it over to Sara. 'Maybe you could call me if you think of anything else?'

'I'll do that,' Sara said, putting the card in her backpack and zipping it closed. 'Thank you.'

She slung the pack over her shoulder and left the lecture hall, walking quickly down the corridor, afraid the police might be following her. She didn't know why she was scared of them, except there was some sort of faint, almost forgotten memory ticking at the corner of her conscious mind. Something about what had happened to Paul. And she didn't know how she knew it, but she knew the police couldn't find out about it or she would be in more trouble than she could get out of.

'Well?' Roberts asked her partner.

'Well, it sounds like she was one of those stupid young girls who got mixed up with an idiot. It's nice to see she managed to get out of it before we ended up interviewing her in the emergency room.'

'You always do that,' Roberts said, putting her notebook back in her pocket.

'Do what?'

'Fall for the girl. God, how did you ever make detective?'

'I didn't fall for the girl. I just happened to believe what she was saying.'

'Same difference.'

'Look, Roberts, I think the one we need to psychoanalyze

here is you. How come you never believe the girl? Overbearing mother? Repressing your lesbian side?'

'I could have you cited for sexual harassment,' she warned him.

'Yeah, you started it,' he said. 'Saying I fell for the girl.'

'Well, I still think she knows something she's not telling us.'

'See, Roberts, if you had just said that in the first place we could have avoided this whole sexual harassment conversation,' Detective Grassi said. 'I think she knows something she's not telling us too.'

'Matt Grassi, there are some times I think you might be the most brilliant detective on the force.'

'Don't get all carried away here. What made you suspect her?' he asked.

'The fact that she said she saw her boyfriend and the secretary going at it in his office.'

'Yeah?'

'His office is on the twenty-fifth floor.'

'Good deduction.'

'What made you suspicious?' she asked him.

'The fact that she didn't fall for my smile.'

'Spare me,' Roberts said, leading him out of the lecture hall.

'No, really, they all fall for my smile,' he laughed, turning to smile at one of the coeds that passed by and was rewarded with a warm smile in return. 'See?'

Sara pounded on the door, hoping someone was there, wishing she had phoned first, but then the door opened and Ben's face poked around the corner.

'You're home!'

'I usually work from home a couple of days a week,' he said. 'Nice surprise to see you here though.'

'I'm sorry; I should have called you first.'

'Sara, what's wrong?' Ben asked, reaching out, grabbing her arm and pulling her inside the house.

'Look, I tried to get a hold of Ian first, but apparently he's in some sort of a workshop or something and he's not supposed to be back at the office until six.'

'Sara, take a deep breath,' Ben told her, pulling her jacket off and leading her into the kitchen. He sat her down on a chair and plugged the kettle in, making a pot of tea. He set a steaming cup in front of her and sat down at the table. 'Now, tell me what happened. Why are you so upset?'

'The police came to see me after my class today.'

'What?' he asked, keeping his face neutral despite the fact that he could feel his blood pressure spiking.

'Paul's missing. I think they think I did it,' she spat out almost manically.

And then his blood pressure returned to normal. It was perfectly reasonable that the police would talk to Sara. But their interest would be short lived after the initial questions. Nothing would point to Sara and if they were too interested in her, Ben could make them go away.

'Sara, calm down,' Ben said, acting concerned. 'What do you mean Paul's missing?'

'I don't know. They said his office called and he hasn't been in for three days.'

'Well, he's probably off somewhere wishing he treated you better.'

'Doubtful,' Sara said.

'Or off with his secretary then,' Ben said softly.

'Much more likely.'

'Look, Sara, it's perfectly normal for them to question people who knew Paul. They always do that when someone disappears. And if they get anything useful from you, they follow it up. If not, they move on to the next person. Eventually they'll either find him or his file will go into one of those black hole filing cabinets where no one ever figures out what happened and no one really cares.'

'But I just left him, surely they'll think that I had motive to hurt him.'

'Maybe you had motive to cut off his balls or something, but not to kill him and make him disappear. Look, sweetie, they'll talk to me and they'll talk to Ian and they'll talk to all the other people that might have something to do with Paul and we'll all tell them what an asshole he was and how glad we are you finally left him, and then they'll move on. A man like that has probably made a few enemies over the years.'

'I suppose you're right.'

'I am right,' he insisted, pouring more tea into her empty cup.

'God, Ben, I'm sorry to have bugged you. But you always make me feel like everything is going to be okay. You must get sick of me and my problems though.'

'Sara, this is what friends do for each other,' Ben said, taking her hand. 'We help each other through the rough times.'

'Yeah, well so far it's all my rough times and none of yours.'

'It's just your turn,' he said. 'Some day it will be my turn and you'll have to endlessly listen to my problems.'

'Oh, God, I'm sorry…'

'No, I'm just joking,' he said. 'I will listen to you as long as you need me. I'm honoured that you feel safe enough to come to me.'

'Now don't get all psychiatric on me,' she laughed.

He brushed his hand across her cheek and she felt her face flush at his touch.

'I love you, Sara.'

She just stared at him, unable to respond.

'Please don't feel bad,' he said. 'I don't expect you to answer me. And I don't mean to scare you. As a matter of fact I didn't even mean to let that slip out at all.'

'Ben, you know I just can't match that level of commitment right now.'

'I totally know that,' he said. 'Please tell me that I haven't ruined our friendship.'

'No, you haven't ruined our friendship,' Sara said. 'I hope I haven't either.'

'No, you could never ruin the way I feel about you,' he promised her.

'Look, I better get going,' Sara said, pushing her chair away from the table.

'No, don't leave,' he begged. 'Let's get a bite to eat or something.'

'I don't know if that's a good idea,' she said. 'I'm kind of tired and I think I should just go home.'

'Please. Look I'll call Ian's answering service and leave a message for him to meet us somewhere. Safety in numbers and all. Then you know I won't say or do anything else stupid for the rest of the evening.'

'Okay, Sara gave in. 'Where do you want to go?'

It was late and there weren't many lights burning in the squad room. Detective Grassi sat at his desk, but his partner was nowhere to be found. He had come back after dinner. He wanted to check out some things about Sara Hunter, psychology student. He had only been half joking with Roberts about Sara not responding to his charms, but there was something deeper about her that was bothering him. There was a look in her eyes, just for a moment, like she had been caught, when they first identified themselves. He wanted to find out what she thought she had been caught at. And he was finding some interesting things. Her parents had died in a mysterious fire in a hotel while they were visiting the coast of Maine. Fourteen people had died but the cause of the fire had never been found. Sara had responded by finishing high school and moving in with Paul upon graduation. Two months later her brother had deposited enough money in her bank account to get her right through her PhD and further if she wanted.

The brother was also an interesting case. He had quit his job at the University despite that fact that he was a fully tenured professor by then. He had moved home to be with Sara through her last year of high school and expanded his clinical practice. He had also become involved in some sort of private research project, but because it was privately funded, the detective was hitting endless brick walls in trying to get more information on that subject. But Detective Matthew Grassi was nothing if not persistent, and he was pretty sure that his smile might work on Dr. Christina Stevenson, another doctor that was listed as a researcher on the project. He didn't think Dr. Stevenson would be a pushover but people gave away a lot without realizing that they were giving away anything. He had spent years working on his smile, just to gain that extra power over the females he was interviewing.

He turned off his desk lamp, and decided to call it a night. He would get up early and see Dr. Stevenson on his way in, without Detective Roberts at his side, bringing him down. The hospital had said her first surgery was at nine in the morning, and she would be in her office at seven thirty. So he would be there waiting for her and just see if she had anything to hide.

1973

He hung his suit jacket in the locker and pulled on his lab coat. He ran his hands down the sides of the coat, smoothing it out, checking for wrinkles. It was his first day and he wanted to look good. His wife had spent the evening before laying out his clothes for him, ironing them, checking his tie for errant stains. He had watched proudly as she fussed, pleased with the choice he had made in her. They would make a great team, him out there changing the world and her waiting for him, making sure he had a nice peaceful home to come back to. She had been angry when he wanted her to give up her nursing career at first, but once their son had come along, she seemed to be busy enough and it seemed that she no longer resented his wishes.

He clipped his nice, new shiny hospital ID badge onto his pocket and then left the changing room. He approached the desk, where the charge nurse stood, sorting through charts.

'Good morning, Dr. Beckman,' she smiled in greeting.

'Morning Judith. Looks like you've scheduled a busy day for my first full day in the operating room.'

'We like to test out you new guys,' she laughed. 'Actually, it's just the busy season right now. You'd think we were running ads on two for one chole's or something.'

'Oh, well, better busy than sitting around with nothing to do.'

'That's right. So is there anything you need help finding?'

'I seem to be able to find my way around pretty well after the orientation. The only thing I don't know is where to find is a good cup of coffee.'

The nurse laughed. 'Well, you'll find a good cup of coffee at the restaurant just down the street. But if you'll settle for hot and brown, there's a pot brewing in the nurse's lounge. Anyone can help themselves. It's a dime a cup. Not worth it but that's what we charge anyway.'

'Thanks, Judith. I'll see you later.'

Beckman managed a cup of coffee and a few words with some of the other doctors, who were already on the floor, before he was due in his first procedure. He had met the patient the day before, when he did the pre-op screening exam. She was a pleasant forty-year-old female who presented with no history of note and had had a previous uneventful general anesthesia during a cesarean section. She presented for a simple hysterectomy, to get rid of a uterus that was now more trouble than it was worth. The surgeon of record was a competent man who took pride in his work and had not caused any problems in his fifteen years on staff at the hospital. It was the type of surgery where the anesthetist could sit back and relax with a good book if he wanted to, because there would really be nothing else to do. The patient was wheeled into the operating room, joking nervously with the nurses.

'Hello, Barbara, are you ready for today?' Beckman asked, smiling down at her, as he checked the IV lines.

'I guess,' she smiled back. 'Any chance you can arrange for a tummy tuck while I'm here?'

'I'll see what your doctor has to say,' he laughed. He pulled a syringe from the tray he had prepared and filled it. 'Now Barbara, you're going to feel sleepy. Can you count backwards from a hundred for me?'

He plunged the needle into the IV line and watched his

patient's face as the liquid entered her vein.

'One hundred, ninety nine, ninety eight, ninety…'

And she was out. He held the oxygen mask on her face for a moment and then set it aside. He pulled out the equipment he had prepared and expertly intubated the patient. He hooked her up to the oxygen, checked his equipment, checked her vital signs and then sat back on his stool, waiting for the surgeon to make his entrance.

'She's out,' he informed the waiting team.

They pulled off her blanket and gown, disinfected her abdomen, and expertly draped her in preparation for surgery. Two nurses were counting instruments on a tray when the doors opened and the surgeon arrived. He held out his arms and was wrapped in a sterile robe, gloves pulled expertly onto his outstretched hands, and then he made his way over to the table.

'Morning everyone,' he smiled. 'Andy, how's she doing?'

'She's ready for you, Jim,' Beckman said, still feeling slightly uncomfortable at using first names with senior staff. 'She went under without complication.'

'Ladies?' he asked, turning to the nurses.

'Everything here is ready doctor,' one of them answered. 'Instrument counts complete.'

'Alright, scalpel please,' he said, holding out his hand.

And that was almost the last normal moment of what was supposed to be this quiet and peaceful surgery. There was a tumor, hidden away in a little fold, attached to her ovary.

'Forceps,' the surgeon called, hoping to pull the tumor out of the way and see what kind of a mess this procedure was going to turn into.

But suddenly there was blood everywhere. The forceps had made a tiny hole in one of the arteries feeding the tumor. A simple hysterectomy was suddenly converted to an emergency procedure, with people racing in and out of the operating room. Blood was brought up from the blood bank, a resident who had been holding a retractor was replaced by another surgeon who was frantically trying to suction the blood out of the field so the tumor could be found again and the bleeding stopped. Beckman pumped blood into the poor woman, trying to keep the volume up in her veins. Another IV line was set up, fluids were hung. And then her heart stopped and monitors screeched, medications were called for and administered and after twenty frantic minutes that felt more like twenty years, the bleeding artery was clamped off and the tumor removed. The patient's heart was beating again, and the surgeon closed up the gaping wound in her abdomen.

Beckman left a resident in charge while the surgeons stitched up her wound, and went out to find the woman's family. Her husband sat in the waiting room, calmly smoking a cigarette and reading a dime store novel. He looked up and smiled as Beckman approached him.

'You all finished in there, Doctor?' he asked.

'They're just closing her up,' Beckman said, sitting down beside the man. 'We had a little bit of trouble and I just wanted to let you know what happened.'

'What kind of trouble?'

'The operation started out just fine, but once they got inside her, they found a tumor. Unfortunately, it bled quite a bit while they were removing it. We have her stabilized now though.'

'A tumor?'

'Yes, I'm afraid it was a tumor.'

'What kind of tumor?'

'Well, they'll send it to the lab and the doctor there will test it and let us know. But I have to be honest; it's probably not good news.'

The man made a choking sound, like his throat had suddenly closed and he couldn't catch his breath. Beckman put his hand on the man's shoulder and squeezed, trying to offer some reassurance. And then he stood up.

'I'm going to go and get her settled in recovery. The surgeon will be out to see you later.'

The man nodded, but he couldn't speak. Beckman made his way back down the hallway and into the operating room again. The nurses were just signing off on the instrument counts and the surgeons were pulling off their gloves. Beckman took over from the resident, and leaned over the still sleeping woman, surprised by how much compassion he was feeling for her. He began to slowly pull her out of her drug-induced sleep, sad that she was being awoken only to suffer what would undoubtedly be a slow and drawn out death from the cancer they had just discovered.

Her eyes opened and he leaned over, so she could see him.

'Okay Barbara, we're just going to take this tube out now. Can you cough for me?'

She coughed and she was extubated. He placed an oxygen mask over her face and held it firmly in place. She rolled her head, trying to get away from the mask and he lifted it up for a minute.

'It's okay, Barbara,' he said. 'It's just a little oxygen.'

'I don't want to die,' she said.

'What?'

'The tumor. It was cancer. I saw it. You told my husband about it. Oh, God, poor Frank. Why did you leave him sitting alone out there after you told him that?'

'Barbara?'

'Why did you work so hard to save me just so I could die from cancer?' she asked, tears streaming down her face.

'It's okay,' he said, putting the mask over her face. 'Just breathe deeply. You're having a bad dream from the drugs.'

She breathed the oxygen in, and soon her breathing slowed and she went back to sleep. He let the nurses take over her care and turned to write his orders on the chart.

Dr. Beckman made sure his patient was settled in the recovery room and stable, then, wrote up his post-op orders and went back to the locker room. He pulled his notebook out of the locker and opened it up to a blank page. He carefully recorded the day's date and the name of the patient. Then he recorded all the medications she had received, all her medical history and exactly what she had said. He tucked the notebook safely back into his locker, locked it and, went to the doctors lounge. He pulled out his Dictaphone and dictated a note on this patient while the surgery was still fresh in his mind. He wanted to make sure the record was complete in case the husband decided to sue later; complete except for the patient's rambling memories of events that she should have known nothing about.

Dr. Andrew Beckman was a proud man. He had been working as an anesthesiologist for almost a year and was proud to be working at this prestigious hospital. He was involved in several research projects and had many notebooks filled with his own private research regarding patients' memories of their operations. He was surprised at how many of them had such interesting things to say if you just asked them Now he had been called into the Medical Directors office, it could only be good news. Maybe the research grant he had applied for had come through, or maybe he was about to get his first promotion. Either way, he sat there sipping coffee and trying to keep his face neutral as the director flipped through some files on his desk.

'Thanks for coming up to see me Andy,' he started.

'It's my pleasure Dr. Fanning.'

'Andy, I'll just cut to the chase here. You've been with us for almost a year now, and you've done a real good job in the OR.'

'Why thank you sir.'

'Which is why I'm so distressed about this complaint we've had.'

'Complaint, sir?'

'Several of the nurses in the recovery room have said you've been questioning patients after their procedures. Asking them if they remembered anything about their surgery.'

'Sir, I think the nurses might have been taking my questions out of context…'

'Well, that might be so, but we've had two patients complain as well. They said you were asking them to tell you what they remembered. And they were both quite confused as to why they should be expected to remember an event they were supposed to be unconscious for.'

'Well, sir, you know that some patients report…'

'Andy, I'm actually not here to ask you to explain this to me. I know exactly what you're trying to do. You're not the first gas pusher to have patients talk to them about this. We all know it happens. That is we all know except the patients. Good Lord, man, could you imagine what would happen if the patients thought they stayed awake through their surgery? It would create mass panic. People would be dying of appendicitis before they would come in to have them removed.'

'Dr. Fanning, I think you may be exaggerating slightly.'

'Perhaps. But the bottom line is, Dr. Beckman, that at this hospital we do not sanction the belief that some patients might be awake during their surgery nor do we sanction any type of research being done without approval of the board of directors and the Ethics Committee.'

Beckman took a deep breath, trying to hold his growing anger and frustration in check.

'You're right, Dr. Fanning, I am sorry and it won't happen again.'

'Well, you're right about that. It won't happen again because you won't be working at this hospital. Your privileges are revoked as of now. I have recruited other doctors to cover your procedures.'

'You're firing me?' Beckman asked, disbelief in his voice.

'We're going to let you resign,' Fanning said. 'And trust me Beckman, this is a very generous offer. If we fire you when you haven't completed your first year, you'll be lucky to get a job in Mexico.'

'But it's not fair.'

'There are certain lines, Andy, and unfortunately you have crossed one of them. Now, would you like to sign the letter of resignation or should I contact our legal department?'

Beckman picked up the letter that the director had slid across his desk and read it. It was innocuous, moving on to other opportunities, thank you for everything you've done, nothing that condemned either party to any wrong doing. Beckman pulled a pen out of his lab coat and signed the letter.

'You'll regret this one day,' Beckman said, standing up to leave.

'I'm an old man at the end of my career,' Fanning said. 'I doubt I'll regret anything when I'm retired on the beaches of Florida. However, I suggest you should think about your career, Andy. You have a lot of years to go before you get to the point of not worrying about what you're doing.'

It was probably good advice, but Beckman didn't stay long enough to listen, slamming the door behind him as he hurried to clean out his locker and leave this place.

Chapter 7

Matt Grassi sat in the reception area, smiling at the receptionist, making sure she didn't forget he was there. He had a to-go latte in his hand, with an extra shot of espresso, as he wasn't exactly known as a morning person. Matt had pulled on a blue sweater and his well-worn leather jacket, an outfit that many women had commented on in the past, and he knew he looked good in them. He wasn't above using his wiles to get information. For example, he had put on his Levi's that were fresh out of the washing machine, still a nice tight fit and not stretched or sagging yet. Women had been doing it for years, he thought, why shouldn't he use it too. They had already proved it worked.

Detective Grassi checked his watch again, it was almost eight o'clock. He had waited long enough. He was just about to get up and be a little firmer with his request, maybe flash the badge as well as the teeth, when the receptionist waved to him, signaling that he could go into the office now. He picked up his coffee cup and walked down the hall to the door marked Christina Stevenson, PhD, MD, Department of Anesthesiology. He knocked lightly and waited outside the door.

'Come in.'

He pushed the door open and stopped dead in his tracks, his smile freezing on his face. Christina Stevenson was a lovely looking woman. She was already dressed in her scrubs, ready for surgery, and the robin's blue colour set off the stunningly beautiful eyes that shone out from underneath a shockingly grey thatch of hair. She smiled in greeting and her eyes were suddenly encased by fine lines shooting out in every direction.

'Detective Grassi?' she asked, holding out her hand to him. There was a slight wobble under her arm, loose skin just like his mother had. She was about the age of his mother, he estimated.

'Yes, thank you for seeing me, Dr. Stevenson,' he smiled. How had he remembered to look up everything about her except the year she graduated from medical school?

'No problem. I've only got about ten minutes and then I'm off to see some patients. I hope that's enough time.'

'I've only got a couple of quick questions,' he said.

'Please have a seat, Detective,' she motioned to a well-worn chair across from her desk. 'I'd offer you coffee but it appears you have that taken care of already.'

'Yes, I'm fine,' he said. He set his coffee on the edge of her desk then pulled out his notebook. Since he wasn't secure about charming someone his mother's age, he decided he would play bumbling young man, try and play on her motherly instincts. 'Sorry, I had this ready last night.'

'Maybe you should start drinking a little less caffeine,' the doctor suggested. 'It can do strange things to people.'

'Oh, here we go,' he laughed nervously. 'I should probably eat better and exercise more too, right?'

'Not bad advice.'

'Doctor, we're investigating the disappearance of a man named Paul Whyte.'

'I don't believe I know anyone by that name. Is he a patient?'

'No, he's not a patient. I found your name when I stumbled across a research project in my investigation. I believe you are involved in that project too. Something listed under Beckman

Pharmaceuticals Sleep Study.'

'Yes, I'm one of the doctors attached to that study. But I'm afraid, due to confidentiality issues, that's all I can say. Is Mr. Whyte a patient in the study?'

'No, but he is an acquaintance of two other doctors involved in it. Dr. Ian Hunter and Dr. Benjamin Douglas.'

'I'm afraid I haven't met either of them yet,' she told him. 'I'm certainly not being much help to you, am I?'

'Well, that's the way my days go,' he said. 'I chase leads and most of them turn out to be nothing. But you have to check everything out just in case.'

'Sort of like diagnosing a patient.'

'I guess it is a little bit. Thanks for your time, Dr. Stevenson. Could I leave my card with you just in case anything comes to mind later?'

'Certainly,' she said, taking his card and studying it.

'Thanks again,' he said, letting himself out of the office.

When the door closed behind him, she reached for her telephone and dialed the number she had memorized.

'Hello, extension three five nine please.' She waited until the connection was made. 'Yes, it's Dr. Stevenson, ID number seven three four slash alpha seventy two. There have been some inquiries about the project.'

'Yes, I'll be at the hospital all day. Thank you.' And she hung the phone up.

Matt Grassi pulled his head away from her door, and started down the hallway. He tossed his empty coffee cup into the nearest garbage can and hurried out to his car. Yes, people told you all sorts of things, whether they meant to or not. He might not know how much yet, but he did know this wasn't a dead end.

At the other end of the day, Sara sat in another waiting room, hoping her brother was going to be finished soon. He had promised to review her thesis tonight, at least what she had done of it, before she did another edit and rewrote the opening chapter for the fifteenth time. But Ian was running late with his last patient. Finally, the door opened and a boy came out. The social worker who had been seated across from Sara got up to take him back to the group home he was living in. Sara locked the door behind them and made her way into Ian's private office. She tossed her diskette onto his desk and lay down on the couch.

'Hello to you, too.' she greeted him, adjusting the pillow under her head.

'Sorry, I'm just trying to get a few notes down while it's still fresh,' he explained. 'You would understand if you ever dealt with real patient's instead of just books.'

'I like research,' she protested. 'So what's his story? What's wrong with him?'

'You know I can't tell you about my social service patients. They can't sign a consent form regarding your study and the Department of Children's Services doesn't want them involved in research,' he lectured. 'But I do wonder what happened to him too. I know there was some sort of big trauma but I just can't get through to him yet. He's a really tough cookie and I just don't know how I'm going to…'

Sara felt the room start to spin and her brother's voice faded off into the distance, nothing more than an annoying buzzing as she tried to pull herself out of the fugue she felt overtaking her. She grabbed hold of the side of the couch, afraid she was going to slide off as the spinning became faster and faster and the wind started to blow. No matter how she tried to direct her mind, it pulled her deeper and deeper. And then when it stopped, she wasn't in her brother's office any longer. She didn't know where she was, she looked around frantically but she didn't recognize anything about this place. It looked like a bedroom, a dingy, dirty bedroom that needed a lot of cleaning and a little sunlight. The windows were boarded over and there were no pictures on the walls to give any sort of indication of who might call this room their own. The only light source came from a small bedside table lamp. She knew there was someone on the bed; she could smell the fear coming from him before she actually saw the little boy tied to the bed. He was naked and he was covered with cigarette burns. She watched as his father reached down and burned him again, putting his cigarette out on the boy's chest. She felt that he wanted to scream, but his mouth and nose were held shut with duct tape. And suddenly she could feel him, feel what he was feeling. The fear was overwhelming. She felt her heart racing in her chest, the jagged pain of her lungs trying to keep up with her racing heart but they could not keep up. The father only left a little hole in the tape for him to breathe through, by his left nostril, so he could get just enough air to keep him from passing out. The father loved to watch the panic in his eyes as he struggled for breath, as his little ribs shook and strained as he tried to fill his lungs. And then somehow the duct tape came loose and she could scream. Finally she could scream. And all the terror and panic and hate came from the bottom of his soul and made its way out of his tiny bruised mouth.

'Noooo!!!' they seemed to scream together.

'Sara?' Ian looked up from his work at his desk, not even aware of what she'd just been through.

'Nooo!!' she screamed again, hoping she was loud enough to bring help to that helpless little boy trapped in that bedroom.

'Sara,' Ian ran to the couch and started shaking her. 'Sara, wake up, what's wrong?'

Sara's vision blurred again and suddenly all she could see was Ian's face over hers.

'What's going on?' she gasped, trying to get more air into her aching lungs.

'You tell me,' his hand went to her wrist and felt her pulse. 'Holy, crap, Sara, you're going to blow a gasket. You're going to start hyperventilating. Come on, long deep breath in through your nose.'

Some how Sara managed to follow his instructions, as he went back to his desk and grabbed his stethoscope and blood pressure cuff. He wrapped it around Sara's arm, despite her protests that she was fine.

'What is wrong with you?' he said as he got the reading. 'Your blood pressure is through the roof.'

'I know what happened,' she whispered, tears starting to fill her eyes.

'What are you talking about?'

'I know what happened,' she said, getting louder. 'I know what happened to Bobby Johnson and I know who did it to him.'

'Bobby Johnson?' Ian asked. 'How the hell do you know the kid's name?'

'I know everything,' she said, pushing herself up into a sitting position. 'I had a vision Ian. I was there in that poor little kid's bedroom and I know what happened to him.'

'Don't be ridiculous,' he said.

'I swear to God,' she said. 'I had a vision. And it's not the first one I've had.'

'Tell me what you think happened, then,' Ian said, sitting beside her on the couch.

'It always happens in this dark and dirty bedroom,' she began, and she told him everything she had seen.

Ian had sent Sara home in a cab while he went to the group home to see his patient. Sara sat in the living room, waiting for Ian to come home. She saw the car pull into the driveway but she didn't move. She heard the front door open and he came in, closing it after him. Then he stepped into the living room. He reached over to turn a light on.

'Don't,' she stopped him.

'Okay.'

'Well?' she asked.

'You were right,' he admitted, sitting across from her.

'You confronted him?' she asked.

'No I didn't confront him. I talked to him. I mentioned one thing. I just asked him to tell me about the bedroom in his house. And suddenly every little detail came spilling out. I checked him into the hospital for the night; I wanted to make sure he was being looked after properly. That's why I'm so late.

You were right about absolutely everything. Sara, how did you know?' he asked the question, but he already knew the answer. He knew that Ben had ignored his warning and injected his sister again. But he couldn't tell her yet. He didn't know how to tell her that she was going to die.

'I don't know Ian, I really don't know,' she leaned forward and held her head in her hands. 'Am I going crazy? I mean first it was Michelle and the car accident and now she's gone. Then it was Paul and his secretary and now he's totally disappeared off the face of the earth. And now this little boy. I could sort of understand the first two, because I knew them. But I've never seen Bobby before in my life. And I don't ever want to see the kind of things I saw happening to him again. It felt like it was happening to me.'

'I don't know what's going on either,' Ian lied to her. 'I think I might be crazy for thinking this is real. But Sara we're going to get to the bottom of this. We're going to find out what's going on with you and fix it. I promise.'

There was a noise from the kitchen and Ian looked up to see Ben standing at the entrance with two cups of tea in his hands.

'Ben?' Ian asked. 'What are you doing here?'

'I called him. I couldn't stand to sit here alone and wait for you. Ian, I was so scared I didn't know what to else to do.' She leaned closer to Ian and whispered to him. 'I didn't tell him what was going on yet. I thought he'd probably drug me and check me into the psych ward.'

Ian stared at Ben for a long time. Finally, Ben made the first move and brought the tea in, setting a cup in front of Sara. He sat at the opposite end of the couch, sensing that might ease Ian's mind right now if he kept his distance from Sara. He wasn't sure if Ian knew about the second injection. If so, this might be a dangerous place for him right now.

'Is there something going on between you two?' Sara asked, feeling the tension rising.

'We just need to talk about a patient,' Ben said. 'Someone

we can't seem to agree on.'

'Well, I need to go to bed anyway,' Sara said, getting up. She gave Ben a quick kiss on the forehead and did the same for her brother. 'I'm totally exhausted. You guys go a few rounds or whatever it is you need to do.'

They stared across the room at each other for a long time. Long past the time they heard her door shut, long past the time the light coming from under her door was extinguished. Long enough to assure she was asleep and they had total privacy.

'Don't tell me you did this to her?' Ian finally asked, trying to keep his voice low.

'Ian, we talked about this.'

'Yeah, we talked about this and I told you that I thought it was a fucking crazy idea and that I would kill you with my bare hands if you touched her again.'

'I didn't think you meant it,' Ben laughed. 'Ian, quit thinking like a brother and start thinking like a doctor. We finally have a perfect test subject.'

'This isn't funny!' Ian hissed at him.

'Ian, you've acted like this every time we've brought in a new test subject. I've always understood that you don't have the guts to do the clinical work the way I do. And that's fine, we complement each other. You collate the data and do all the preadmission interviews. I do the clinical work. Now we discussed the results and we both agreed that we needed to try an older subject because the children just weren't working out.'

'And I told you I was finished with this. I would not be responsible for another life being destroyed. And then you take my sister. You are killing my sister.'

'You can't just walk away from this Ian. You can't just quit and go find another research grant somewhere else. This is serious. The people that are paying us don't let people just quit. And you know that Sara fit all the parameters we set out for our next subject. And you know how I feel about her. I'm not going to let anything happen to her.'

'You're not going to let anything happen to her?' Ian kicked at the coffee table in frustration, knocking everything off the top of it.

'You're going to wake her up,' Ben warned him.

'She should be awake. She has the right to know what you've done to her.'

'But Ian, it's working. Look at the visions she's having.'

'How many injections have you given her?' Ian demanded.

'Two.'

'Then she's going to die,' he sobbed. 'They all die.'

'They only die if we stop now. Some live.'

'We are going to stop now,' Ian said.

'Stop? Now you're the one who's out of his fucking mind.

'There's no way I'm letting you carry on. In the morning, I'm checking her into the hospital and I'm going to tell the doctors everything and hope they can save her.'

'Ian, I've had more success with her in the last few weeks than I have with all the other subjects over the last year. She's our breakthrough, don't you see?'

'She's my sister, you bastard.'

'Ian, you've got to get over the emotional baggage about this. I want you to come to the clinic tomorrow and review my data on her. It'll blow your mind.'

'I won't be a part of this.'

'Ian, you already are a part of this. Do you have any idea what will happen to you if you try and quit?' Ben asked him.

'Nothing will happen. I'll go to the press and that will be that.'

'Ian, don't do it. It won't work.'

'Get out of my house,' Ian said. 'And I don't want you coming back here ever again.'

'Sara may have something to say about that,' Ben said.

'Not after I tell her what you've been doing to her.'

'You're making the biggest mistake of your life.'

'No, you are,' he said, opening the door and waiting for Ben to leave. 'You should probably start running now, because come morning I'm going to start talking and I don't plan on stopping for a long time.'

Ben grabbed his jacket and made his way through the door.

'Is there nothing I can say to change your mind?' he asked. 'You used to think this was such important work we were doing.'

'It was important work. But it's gotten totally out of hand. I can't live with myself any longer Ben; I don't know how you can.'

'I can because we've finally had some success. Ian, if we quit now, all those people that died will mean nothing. Don't let their deaths be meaningless, we have to carry on.'

'The only life that matters to me is my sister's.'

'And she is going to be a huge success. She's going to make us famous.'

'Yes, and all it will have cost you is the life of the woman we both love.'

And then he slammed the door on his friend. Ian stood at the door, making sure Ben actually left. And then he wiped at the tears that were clouding his eyes. He turned off the lights and made his way upstairs. He stopped at Sara's door, peeking inside and watching her sleep peacefully, not having a clue as to what was happening to her. And then he closed the door quietly and went into his bedroom. He turned on his laptop and started to prepare the statement that he was going to release to the press tomorrow.

1993

Beckman sat nervously in the locker room, preparing for his next procedure. The patient was a young boy of thirteen, in for a simple appendectomy. Good candidate, as all his preoperative screens had revealed. Beckman thumbed through his notebook, double-checking his dosages and indications in a patient this age. When he was satisfied, he pulled a vial from his suit jacket and filled a syringe. Then he capped the syringe and tucked it away in his lab coat, returning the vial and notebook to his locker and securing it. He no longer used the combination lock that the hospital had provided, but had replaced it with his own. He had also labeled everything innocently enough, the vial of drug was labeled as insulin and his notebook was all done in his own personal short hand. But he was still not willing to take too many chances and risk this great opportunity for research that he had here.

When he was sure everything was secure, he got up and went into the operating room. He made sure the meds he had ordered were there and laid his own syringe amongst them. He continued with his preoperative chores, reviewing the chart and starting his anesthesia report. The patient was wheeled in and Beckman chatted with him for a moment or two, his typical reassuring pre-op speech, and then filled the patient's veins with drugs, sending him into a paralyzed sleep. Beckman hyperventilated the patient and then expertly intubated him, hooking up the required machinery and monitors. He watched the readouts for a moment, recording what was necessary, and then after a quick look around to ensure no one was watching him, he took the extra syringe and pushed the drugs into the patient's IV line. He capped the used syringe and tossed it into the sharps container, where it became one of hundreds of needles that would be disposed of at the end of the day, safely anonymous. He sat back and pulled out his crossword puzzle, waiting for the surgeon to arrive and the procedure to begin. He smiled thinking back to the day when as a medical student he first crossed the threshold of the operating room, and was amazed by the anesthetist sitting at the head of the table, doing the same thing. About an hour or so later, he put down his puzzle, as the surgeon wrapped up the procedure.

'All right boys and girls, everything looks nice and tidy. I'm going to let my resident close today and I'm going to go grab a sandwich before my next procedure. Do some nice stitching there, huh? He's a handsome young lad and I'm sure the girls will soon be after him. We want to make him look good.'

'Yes doctor.'

The resident took her time, as they all did, painstakingly making sure every stitch was neat and even, afraid to raise the ire of the surgeon with a sloppy job. Finally, the wound was dressed and Beckman started to wake his patient up. He extubated the boy and checked his monitors. Satisfied all was well, he leaned over the boy, very close to his ear.

'Do you know what happened?' he whispered to the boy.

'Surgery.'

'Do you know what happened during surgery?' Beckman prompted. 'Tell me what happened.'

'Left a gauze in,' the boy said. 'The nurse broke up with her boyfriend, he hit her. And she wasn't counting right.'

Beckman was disappointed. He didn't want to hear nonsense like that. Two nurses signed off on the instrument count and he knew it was fine. Another failure. He followed the boy to recovery, just in case he started to talk about anything else, but there was nothing. Beckman wrote up his orders and signed the anesthesia report, before heading back to the doctor's lounge for a bite of lunch himself.

It was eight days later when Beckman was woken from a sound sleep by the sound of his pager going off. He was the anesthetist on-call and he quickly dressed and hurried to the hospital. He found his resident waiting for him in the doctor's locker room.

'This better be good.'

'It is,' the resident assured him. 'Thirteen years old, one week post appendectomy. Spiking a high fever. He presented to the emergency room convulsing with a fever of 105.2. They managed to get it down a bit, but he is still tachy with shallow resps. Ultrasound shows intraperitoneal abscess and the surgeon is scrubbing now. But this kid's really unstable and I wasn't confident enough to do the anesthesia myself.'

'Okay, good call. Start prepping him and I'll be there in two minutes.'

Beckman pulled out his notebook and turned back to his notes from a week ago. The boy had said something about the sponge count. Beckman was suddenly very excited now, and ready to do everything in his power to save this boy. He closed his locker and hurried into the operating room.

The resident had been correct, the young man was very sick. Not the type of patient you looked forward to operating on, as they tended to go south very quickly, especially at this age. But Beckman medicated him very carefully and got him under while managing to keep his vital signs stable.

'That was an amazing procedure,' the resident babbled, sitting beside on the bench in the locker room. 'I've never seen anything like that.'

'The patient died.'

'Oh, I know and that's a terrible thing. But when they cut into the peritoneum, that pus must have shot three feet into the air.'

'It was a massive infection that the poor boy's body just couldn't fight.'

'And all that because of one sponge.'

'One sponge and a perforated appendix that probably already left a nice little bit of bacterium in the peritoneum.'

'It was still very cool.'

'Please try to remember that the boy died and the surgeon is telling his parents right at this very moment.'

'I know,' the resident said. 'I don't wish people harm. But I learned more from that one procedure than I've learned from my last ten.'

'Leave me alone, boy,' Beckman said harshly. 'Go share your schoolboy enthusiasm with some other schoolboy. I don't appreciate it!'

The resident opened his mouth to apologize but thought better of it when he saw the look on Beckman's face, and turned and left the room quickly. Beckman opened his locker and pulled out his notebook. He was worried. Not about that poor boy or his family, but about the fact that the body was now headed for an autopsy. And Beckman had no idea whether or not his little drug cocktail would have metabolized out of his system yet. He made a few notes, then changed and headed for home.

It was a month later when his world began to fall apart. He had that same resident, sitting by his side at the head of the table. The one he found so annoying. But he realized now he probably shouldn't have been quite so sharp with him. They sat, poised over the patient, prepared to administer the medication, when three men walked into the operating room.

'Dr. Beckman, please stop what you're doing and come with me.'

'I'm sorry; I have a patient here about to have surgery.'

'Dr. Beckman, if you do not put that syringe down, I will have security restrain you. Do you understand?'

Beckman set the needle back on the tray and turned to the

resident. He thought he noted a look of triumph in those eyes, but he couldn't be sure. He stood up and the resident slid into his place at the head of the table.

'What about this patient?' Beckman asked, as he followed the men through the doors and into the corridor.

'There will be another attending along in a minute. Dr. Beckman, I am Jerome Peters. I am chief legal counsel for this hospital. I am here to inform you that there are two police officers waiting by your locker with a subpoena to inventory the contents of your locker.'

'What are you talking about?' Beckman asked, fear creeping into the pit of his stomach.

'Dr. Beckman, several residents have reported you are using drugs on the patients that you will not identify, or that you identify improperly. They suspect you may be testing some new drugs and that you don't want anyone to know about it. Further more an autopsy on one of your patients has revealed certain drugs in his system that should not be there. You are being accused of unethical practices.'

'I have absolutely no idea what you're talking about.'

'Dr. Beckman, we believe you are experimenting on patients. Why or with what, we have no idea. The hospital has no choice but to protect itself by charging you. Your locker will be searched and you will be arrested. Do you understand Dr. Beckman?'

And then he realized that his life had changed forever. But he had to come up with a way to save his research.

Two years and hundreds of thousands of dollars later, Andrew Beckman was no longer a doctor. There had been many behind the scenes deals between his lawyers and the hospital lawyers and the medical association lawyers and in the end he had had to relinquish his medical license and pay all the legal costs, but at least he was a free man without a criminal record. And as soon as the last papers were signed and the deal done, Beckman took what little he did have left, and went into partnership with a failing pharmaceutical company. One of the pay-offs of his years of research was the development of a new local anesthetic. In another twelve months or so, it would be on the market and he would recoup all that he had lost and more. But the best part was that it gave him the chance to continue his research without any interference.

Chapter 8

There was a noise. Sara was sitting on the beach, watching the seals playing in the surf, but there was some sort of annoying noise that wouldn't stop. She finally realized it was a cell phone. And then she wondered why a seal would have a cell phone. And then it all made sense. She sat upright and grabbed the phone beside her bed that was still ringing.

'Hello?' she answered, still trying to shake the dream from her head.

'Sara?'

'Ben? Ben, what's wrong? What time is it?'

'It's just after five,' Ben said. 'I'm sorry to wake you. I've got to talk to Ian. It's about a patient.'

'I'll get him,' Sara said, laying the receiver on her pillow and trudging down the darkened hallway.

'Ian,' she said, knocking on his door. 'Ian.'

'What?'

She opened the door and stuck her head through the crack. 'Telephone. It's Ben. He said there's a patient emergency.'

'Okay,' Ian said, sounding like he was pushing through a dream as she had done moments ago.

Sara turned and headed back to the bedroom. She picked up the receiver and put it to her ear.

'I've got it now, Sara,' Ian said.

She clicked the off button and turned over and went back to sleep.

Ian stared at the phone for a long time before he put it to his ear. He was exhausted since he had been up most of the night, scouring the newspaper websites, choosing the reporters he was going to call in the morning. He didn't believe this phone call was about a patient emergency. He was pretty sure it was Ben with either one last plea or one last threat before the sun rose.

'Dr. Hunter here,' he finally said into the receiver.

'It's Ben.'

'I don't think we have anything to talk about.'

'It's not what you think, Ian. It's the Porter boy. He's been throwing PVC's. We're trying to get him stabilized but he's calling for you.'

'How do I know you're not lying?'

'Because I don't think he's going to make it through the next couple of hours and I don't want him to die alone. He wants you with him and I want to give him his last wish.'

'Okay. How do you suggest I get there?'

'Go to your office. I'll send a car. That way there's no need to explain to Sara why a limo is picking you up to see a patient.'

'Fine, I'll be there in about fifteen minutes.'

'Thanks Ian.'

'This isn't for you,' Ian told him, before hanging up the phone. He stormed out of bed, dressed, brushed his hair and his teeth and splashed cold water on his face, trying to wash away the last vestiges of sleep. Then he poked his head in Sara's room. She was sound asleep, so he decided he would call her later and let her know what was going on rather than wake her again. He let himself quietly out of the house and got into his car, and headed for the office.

There were the seals again, only this time the ocean was rough and stormy and they were all barking at her. She called out to them, not understanding what they were trying to tell her. Until finally it all made sense and she sat bolt upright. The doorbell rang again and she jumped out of bed, pulling her robe on and racing for the door. The sun was just rising, and her stomach was sinking as she raced down the stairs. There was never good news at this time of the morning. She was expecting to see a crushed Ian standing there, having lost his keys after losing a patient, distraught and needing her comfort. Instead, she saw Ben standing at the door, flanked by Detectives Grassi and Roberts. She took a step back from the door, refusing to open it. Somehow knowing when she did that everything was going to change again.

'Sara, open the door,' Ben said. 'It's okay.'

'No, it's not.'

'Sara, please, just open the door.'

She just stood there, not knowing what to do.

'I'll break the glass,' Detective Roberts said.

'No,' Ben said. 'Sara, please, for me.'

Slowly, Sara walked towards the door and flipped the lock into the open position. Then she took a couple of steps backwards, wanting to run but there was no response from her legs. She told her feet to move but they just stayed planted on the floor.

Ben opened the door and crossed the threshold, the two detectives beside him.

'Ms. Hunter,' Detective Grassi started, coming closer to her. 'I am very sorry to tell you that at 6:15 this morning we found your brother...'

'No!' she screamed, not wanting him to finish his sentence.

'We found your brother in his office. He was shot. It appears that someone thought there were drugs in his office and broke in. He must have walked in on them.'

Sara felt her legs beginning to move now. Only they were moving towards the floor, giving out from under her as she lost touch with the world around her. Two sets of strong hands reached out and grabbed her, pulling her over to the couch before she could hit the ground.

'My bag is in my car, Detective,' Ben said. 'If you wouldn't mind.'

'I'll get it,' Roberts said, racing out to the driveway.

'Doctor?' Detective Grassi asked.

'I think she's just in shock,' Ben said. 'I'll check her vital signs. We'll give her a few minutes. If she doesn't come around quickly, I may have to sedate her for a while.'

'We'd really like to talk to her.'

'I know,' Ben said. 'I'll do my best. But I'm not going to put her in any danger. If she needs to be sedated, that's what I'll do. I may even have her admitted to the hospital for a couple of days.'

Grassi sat back in the armchair and sighed. He always hated it when well meaning doctors got in the way. And psychiatrists were the worst. Grassi thought people could handle way more than any psychiatrist ever gave them credit for.

Roberts handed Ben his bag and then looked around the living room. 'Is there a phone here?'

'In the kitchen,' Ben said, pointing to the doorway.

She looked at Grassi and he nodded, then she disappeared into the kitchen.

Ben wrapped a blood pressure cuff around Sara's arm and pumped it up. Then he checked her pulse and listened to her chest. When he was satisfied he turned to Detective Grassi.

'She seems okay, I think she just fainted. But I want you to swear you're going to take it easy on her when she wakes up.'

'I promise.'

'Because I can have an ambulance here and have her admitted to the hospital before you can get the second question out of your mouth.'

'I understand, doctor,' he said, a little of his frustration showing in his voice.

Ben ignored him and leaned over Sara.

'Sara,' he called, gently but firmly. 'Can you hear me Sara?'

There was no response and he called out a little more loudly, pressing his knuckles firmly into her breastbone. This time Sara responded, her eyes opening and trying to focus.

'What?' she asked. 'What is it?'

And then she looked at Detective Grassi's face over Ben's shoulder.

'It wasn't a dream,' she said, as tears filled her eyes.

'It wasn't a dream,' Ben said.

'Ian's gone?' she asked.

'He's gone,' Detective Grassi said.

'Oh, God,' she sobbed. 'He was all I had.'

Ben wrapped her in his arms, holding her closely to him. 'You're not alone Sara. You'll never be alone.'

Detective Grassi watched Ben closely, noticing that he held on to Sara just a little more firmly than she was holding on to him.

'Where is he?' she said suddenly, pushing Ben away from her.

'Excuse me?'

'Where is he? Where's Ian?'

'He's in the hospital morgue,' Detective Grassi said.

'I need to see him.'

'I don't think that's a good idea,' Ben said. 'Why don't you wait until he's at the funeral home and he's been cleaned up a little bit.'

'No, I want to see him now.'

'I'll drive you down,' Detective Grassi said. 'Detective Roberts can stay with Dr. Douglas and take care of things here.'

'I don't think I should leave her alone,' Ben protested.

'I won't be alone. I'll be with Detective Grassi,' Sara said, making up her mind as she got up off the sofa. 'I'll just get dressed. I won't be long.'

Sara disappeared up the stairs and Ben sat on the couch, closing his bag and turning to the detective.

'This doesn't make me particularly happy,' he informed him.

'I was pretty sure it wouldn't.'

'Then why did you suggest it?'

'She was the one that wanted to see her brother. I just wanted a few minutes alone to talk with her.'

'Well, you're doing it against my medical advice,' Ben warned him.

'Let me just get one thing clear here. Are you her doctor or her boyfriend?'

'Well, I, uh,' Ben started.

'That's what I thought.'

Sara came back down the stairs dressed in jeans and a sweatshirt. She had her hair pulled back in a sloppy ponytail and her face was washed but free of makeup.

'Can we go now?' she asked, sensing the tension between the two men.

'I wish you would reconsider,' Ben said.

'I need to see him Ben. That's the end of this conversation. Are you ready, Detective Grassi?'

'Roberts,' he bellowed. 'I'm going to the hospital. You've got Dr. Douglas.'

'Okay,' she said, poking her head around the corner. 'I'm almost finished with the phone records. I'll be with you shortly, Dr. Douglas.'

Detective Grassi stood up and held the front door open for Sara. She grabbed her backpack and followed him out the door. She buckled herself into the car and sat silently while he pulled the car out of the driveway and started down the road.

'So are you going to ask me for my alibi?' she said.

'I'm assuming you were in bed alone, since we found Dr. Douglas all tucked in at his house.'

'What do you mean by that?'

'Well, you two looked a little bit cozy, I thought that maybe…'

'You thought wrong. He's an old family friend.'

'I'm sorry.'

'So now am I a suspect?'

'No. It was obviously somebody looking for drugs and your brother just got in the way.'

'What a waste,' she said. 'My brother was a psychologist. He couldn't prescribe medications. The most he had in his office was a bottle of aspirin for when he got a migraine.'

'That's interesting.'

'Have you caught the guy who did it?' she asked.

'No. We're still in the gathering evidence stage. We'll have to see where it takes us.'

'I need you to find this guy.'

'I know,' the detective said. 'Did your brother often go in to his office that early?'

'Well, sometimes. But I didn't think he was going to the office at all. Ben called early this morning and said there was a patient at the hospital he needed to see. Some sort of emergency. I thought that's where he would be headed.'

'Maybe something happened?'

'Ben might have called him on his cell and told him to meet him somewhere else. I don't know. I do some research with some of Ian's patient's but I don't know all of them. Especially the ones he consults with Ben on.'

'So you're a teacher?'

'Detective Grassi, you're very cute and you play the bumbling charmer very well, but I'm pretty sure you're not half as clueless as you pretend to be. I'm pretty sure you know exactly what I do.'

'You are a master's psychology student, you teach part time, you do some research with your brother and you spend an inordinate amount of time worrying about your thesis.'

'Yes, yes and how the hell did you know that last one?'

'It was an educated guess.'

'Well, Detective Grassi...'

'You can call me Matt.'

'So I'll feel closer to you? I'll be more likely to share my secrets with you?'

'No. Okay, yes. But it is nicer. And then I could call you Sara and we could sound like civilized adults here.'

'Okay, Matt. But I'm afraid I don't have any secrets to share with you.'

'Do you know a Dr. Christina Stevenson?' he asked.

'Nope.'

'Were you involved in the research your brother is doing with Ben Douglas?'

'Nope. I knew nothing about that at all. Ian told me he had to sign one of the strictest confidentiality agreements he had ever seen. So he couldn't even tell me who he was doing the research for.'

'Is that a usual practice?'

'Well, private industry is usually a handled a little different than public research. He didn't seem alarmed by it.'

Matt pulled the car into a red zone in the hospital and turned the engine off.

'You can't park here,' Sara said.

'I can actually park anywhere I want,' he said. 'I have police ID.'

He flipped the sun visor down, showing his police parking permit and got out of the car. Sara followed him, feeling her stomach start to churn.

'I think I'm going to be sick,' Sara said, as they got into the elevator and he pushed the button for the basement.

'Slow deep breaths,' he told her. 'You can do this. If you really want to?'

'Are you sure?'

'Slow deep breaths,' he repeated, and she followed his instructions.

She followed him down the hallway and waited while he talked to the attendant. They were kept waiting another few moments while Ian was brought into position for viewing.

'Why do you want to do this Sara?' he asked her.

'I need to see for myself,' she said. 'It doesn't seem real. When mom and dad died, I couldn't see them, and it took me years to deal with that. I just need to see Ian, to see for myself.'

'Are you ready?' Detective Grassi asked her.

She nodded, not sure she could speak. Her head was

spinning and she thought she was going to be sick. Matt put his hand lightly on her back, holding her steady, and led her into the viewing area. She walked slowly over to the stretcher where Ian waited, a hospital blanket covering his body, folded back at his shoulders so she could see his face.

'Oh, Ian,' she said, her voice catching in her throat. She felt her legs start to shake, but they didn't give way this time. She gently touched his cheek with her hand. 'He's so cold.'

'He can't feel it,' Matt said.

'Did he suffer?' she asked, the detective and then turned back to her brother. 'Were you scared, Ian? Did you know what was happening?'

'They said it was quick,' Matt told her. 'The bullet hit the femoral artery in his leg and he would have lost consciousness very quickly.'

'That's good,' she said, caressing his cheek, brushing the hair off his forehead. 'Ian, I promise you I'll find out who did this.'

And she felt a strange peace settle over her. She had a mission now, something to keep her going and keep her focused. She was going to find out who did this to her brother.

And then she leaned over and kissed his cheek. 'Goodbye big brother. I'm going to miss you.'

'Are you ready to go?' Matt asked.

'I'm ready,' she said, taking his arm. 'Do you mind?'

'Are you okay?' he asked, feeling her lean on him.

'I'm fine,' she said. 'I just feel a little shaky.'

He led her slowly back to the car and got her settled in. Then he went back into the hospital and came out with two take out coffee cups.

'I hope you like latte' he asked, handing her one of the cups.

'God, you are a full service cop,' she laughed. 'Thank you so very much.'

He took a big sip of his coffee before he started the car.

'Thanks for bringing me here,' she told him. 'Like I said, I never got the chance to do this with my parents and some how it feels so much better.'

'You're welcome,' he said. 'You seem very calm.'

'I am. He looked at peace and so I can be at peace. I'll mourn when his killer is found. Until then, I will be staying on top of you to make sure you're working hard on the case.'

'So, can you tell me about Ben's phone call this morning?'

'I don't think there's much to tell. Is he a suspect?'

'No, we just need to get the whole big picture of everything that happened.'

'Funny, I still think you're not being truthful with me, but what the heck, we have the same goal in mind don't we?' she asked him.

'Yes, Sara, that we do.'

'Well, I was asleep and the phone rang. I usually wake up before Ian does, so I got it. Ben just said there was a patient emergency and he needed to talk to Ian. I woke Ian up and then went back to my room and hung up the phone.'

'You didn't hear any of the conversation?'

'No. Since I was a teenager Ian always told me he had the call and waited until I hung up. I used to try and eavesdrop on his patient phone calls when I was younger.'

'You were a troublemaker were you?'

'I had my moments.'

'So about Ben?'

'Yeah, what about him?'

'You don't sound like a woman in love.'

'I'm a woman who just left the man she'd been with for over five years. I didn't really think I was ready for any sort of a commitment. And I told Ben that. He told me he was happy to wait for me as long as it took.'

'And that's where you left it?'

'That's where I left it.'

'So what do you think; that maybe you two will get together now?' he asked.

'I can only wonder what's going to happen now,' she said,

raising her coffee up to her lips just as the world starting spinning and the wind started whistling through her head. The coffee fell from her hand and she felt sick to her stomach. Her heart was beating hard in her chest, as though trying to break free, and she thought she was going to die. And then it all became clean and she saw him smiling down at her. His face familiar and reassuring, leaning over, kissing her lightly on the lips before he threw back the covers and got out of bed. She watched as he crossed the bedroom to the bathroom and she heard the shower come on. She got out of bed, following him across the room, peeking around the corner, trying to see his face one more time.

'What is it?' he called, seeing her face in the door. 'Are the kids okay?'

'The kids?' she asked.

'You can join me if you want,' he said, holding back the shower curtain.

She crossed the room, reaching up to touch his face, brushing the stubble on his cheek.

'Sara, is everything okay?' he asked, and then she felt dizzy again, and the world was swimming around her, as Detective Grassi looked down at her both from her vision and from the front seat of his car.

'Hang on Sara,' the real detective said. 'I'm taking you back to the hospital.'

And that was the last thing Sara remembered.

Chapter 9

Sara opened her eyes slowly, not sure where she was once again. She was tired of this happening to her and trying to hide it from everyone. She saw the curtains around her bed and heard the beeping from some sort of monitor and guessed she was in the hospital. She craned her head and saw Detective Grassi sprawled in a chair beside the bed, snoring softly.

'I hope you're not supposed to be protecting me,' she mumbled.

He pulled himself up into a more upright position and smiled at her. 'You don't need protection. You need a doctor.'

'Well, then I guess I'm in the right place for that.'

'Do you remember what happened?' he asked.

'Not really. I got dizzy and felt sick and then I think I passed out?'

'That's pretty accurate,' he said. 'But you did say something before you passed out.'

'I did?' she asked. 'What did I say?'

'You were asking if the kids were okay.'

'Kids?' she asked. 'What kids were those?'

'Well, that was my question, actually,' he said.

'I'm sorry. I don't remember any of it.'

'I somehow thought that would be the case.'

'What did the doctors say?' she asked.

'They think you probably had an anxiety attack.'

'Oh, that sounds about right.'

'So how do you feel now?' he asked.

'Like I want to go home and sleep for three or four days in my own bed.'

'Why don't I go and find one of those doctors for you and maybe we can help you reach that goal.'

'Home. Is Ben still there?' she asked.

'Last time I talked to Detective Roberts he was.'

'Does he have to be?' she asked.

'You don't want him there?'

'I really want to be alone,' she said.

'Are you sure that's wise?' he asked. 'Considering all that's happened?'

'How about if I phone a friend and have them come over to stay with me? I don't feel up to any sort of deep philosophical conversation about life or to have him all over me, worrying about everything I'm doing. I swear, if he takes my pulse tonight I might break his wrist.'

Detective Grassi laughed out loud.

'I'm serious,' she insisted.

'I don't doubt that you are. Look, if the doctor says you can go, I'll call Detective Roberts and have her get him out of there. Then I'll get you home myself, okay?'

'Okay.'

And then maybe you'll tell me why you suddenly don't want Ben Douglas around, Matt thought, but he just smiled and pushed through the curtain, searching for a doctor he recognized.

'Dr Stevenson?' he said, almost running into her on the other side of the curtain. 'What are you doing in emergency? It's quite a ways away from the operating rooms isn't it?'

'Detective Grassi,' she recognized him. 'I was called down to intubate a patient. Us anesthesiologists do lots of different things these days.'

'Sorry, I had no idea.'

'What are you doing here?' she asked. 'This is a long way from police headquarters, isn't it?'

'Oh well, us cops do lots of different things these days too. I'm here with a patient. I just want to find her doctor and see if we can get her home.'

'Nothing serious, I hope.'

'I don't think so,' he said. 'Well, nice seeing you again.'

'Detective Roberts, I would just like to repeat that I am not happy about this.'

'Dr. Douglas, I am very much aware of that. I believe you have now told me ten times that you are not happy to be here. Let me assure you that we at the police department realize how inconvenient this is for you but without help from citizens like yourself, we would not be able to solve as many cases as we do,' Detective Roberts informed him, her best fake smile plastered on her face. 'Now, if you'll excuse me, I'm just get some of those mug shot books for you to look through. I'll be right back.'

She let herself out of the interrogation room and nodded to the officer standing on the other side of the door. She walked a few feet down the hallway, pulled out her cell phone and pushed the speed dial.

'Grassi, it's Roberts, can you talk?' she asked.

'Yeah.'

'Okay, I got Dr. Douglas down here, kicking and screaming all the way, but he's here.'

'Good work, Roberts.'

'So what do you want me to do with him?'

'Piss him off.'

'And why is that? Is this part of your theory about pretty girls being innocent?'

'No, I'm pretty sure that they both know something that they're not telling us. I don't think we have a chance at getting anything out of them as long as they're together, but if we can separate them, we might get something.'

'So why do I have to piss him off. Why can't I be the good cop for once?'

'Roberts, you can't play against type.'

'Now don't get mean,' she said.

'No, I think this guy is arrogant and thinks he's quite a bit more clever than the rest of us. I don't think we're going to get anything out of him unless we can knock him a little off balance.'

'Well, I hate to admit it but I was thinking pretty much the same thing,' she said. 'And what are you going to do about the girl? Going to become her best friend?'

'She's a psychologist, she's too clever for that. I'm going to have to actually gain her trust and see if she'll confide in me.'

'Wow, the truth for a change. How do you think that's going to work for you?'

'Well, I've never used it before so I'll have to see what happens.'

'So I'll check in every hour or so?' she asked.

'Yeah, oh I gotta go, the doctor's here.'

Roberts disconnected the phone just in time to see five police officers coming down the hallway, all carrying armfuls of criminal identification books. She smiled to herself, knowing how much this was going to piss Dr. Douglas off.

'Okay boys, lets see how long it's going to take to break this guy,' and then she put on her smile and pushed open the door. 'Dr. Douglas, those books I was telling you about are here.'

And she watched his face fall as he saw the line of officers coming into the room.

Grassi hung up his phone and let himself into the curtained cubicle where the doctor sat on a stool, giving a final listen to Sara's heart.

'Well,' he asked. 'Is the patient going to live?'

'The patient seems just fine,' the doctor said, putting the stethoscope around his neck and jotting something in a chart.

'Can the patient go home?' Sara asked.

'Not alone,' the doctor said. I want somebody with you for

the next twenty four hours otherwise I'm admitting you for observation.'

'I won't be alone,' Sara promised.

'That's what they all say,' the doctor laughed. 'What I usually do at this point is ask you who I should call and then I call them and make sure they stay with you.'

'I'll take care of it,' Detective Grassi said. 'I'll stay with her until someone gets there and I'll make sure she is not alone for at least twenty four hours. I promise.'

'Well, I think I can take your word for it,' the doctor laughed. 'One sec. I'm just going to write you a script for some Ativan just in case you start feeling anxious again. You know about Ativan right?'

'I know all about it,' she said. 'I won't be abusing it, I promise.'

'Good, well I'm only going to give you a couple because you're going to be seeing your family doctor in the next day or so, right?'

'Absolutely,' she promised, not sure if she was going to keep that promise or not.

'Detective?' the doctor asked.

'I'm pretty sure I can take care of that one, too,' he said.

'Good. Then Sara why don't you get dressed and I'll send the nurse in with your prescription and some papers for you to sign.'

'Thanks doctor,' she said, stretching her legs over the side of the bed and standing up. 'Uh, Detective?'

He looked around and then blushed.

'Sorry,' he said, stepping to the other side of the curtain so she could get dressed.

She signed all the forms, picked up her pills and soon they were back in his car and heading for Ian's house. Or maybe it was her house now.

Detective Grassi pulled into the driveway and climbed out of the car. He came around to her side and opened the door, walking to the house with her.

'Can I have your keys?' he asked.

She pulled them out of her backpack and handed them to him.

'Such a gentleman.'

'Actually, I'm being a cop right now,' he smiled, but this time it was his serious smile, not his charming one. 'So, we'll go inside but I want to check out the house first. I need you to stand right by the door and don't move until I've finished looking around, okay?'

'You're serious about this?' she asked.

'Very.'

'Okay, I promise, I'll stay right by the front door.'

And she did while she listened to him go in and out of all the rooms in the house, including closets. Finally he came back into the living room and locked the door behind her.

'It's safe,' he said.

'I could have told you so.'

'Do you have some coffee or tea?' he asked.

'Sorry, Detective, would you like a coffee or tea?'

'Coffee would be great,' he said.

She dropped her pack and went into the kitchen, followed closely by the Detective. It was getting dark out and he closed all the blinds while she got the coffee pot brewing. He pulled out a chair and made himself comfortable at the table, watching her get the cream and sugar. She filled a mug and set it in front of him.

'So are you here for the night?' she asked. 'I really just wanted to be alone; I wasn't kidding about that part.'

'Well, I've been doing some thinking,' he said, sipping his coffee. 'The way I see it you lost a whole bunch of people really close to you in a really short period of time. You've lost your best friend and your brother and your boyfriend is missing and at this point he's presumed to be the victim of foul play. So one of two things can happen now.'

'And what are those two things?' she asked, joining him at the table.

'Well, number one would be that I prove you're some sort of homicidal maniac killing off all those close to you and then I arrest you and throw you in jail for life.'

'Well that sucks,' she said. 'Then I guess I'd like to hear number two.

'Number two is that someone is killing off all those close to you for some undisclosed reason. And you're next.'

'Oh.'

'Yeah.'

'Do we have a third choice?' she asked, trying to make light of the situation.

'Nope.'

'Well, I'll be more than happy to make up a bed for you tonight.'

'Good. Me and Roberts will take turns keeping a close eye on you for the next couple of days. If someone is coming after you, they should be making a move in the next two or three days if they keep following this pattern.'

'I'm just an insignificant little student. Why on earth would anyone be after me and my family?'

'Look, Sara, I'm going to do something I don't usually do here.'

'What's that?'

'I'm going to tell you the truth.'

She laughed out loud.

'No, I'm serious. I don't really want to be honest with you, because frankly I'm not a hundred percent sure that you're not involved in all this somehow.'

'I swear…'

'No, don't go swearing because I know there's something you're not telling me. And even though I'm about to be honest with you, it doesn't mean I'm totally on your side. I'm still going to find out what it is you're holding back from me.'

'You wouldn't believe me if I told you.'

'Try me, Sara. There's not much I haven't seen or heard. And the more I know the more I can try to help you out.'

'Honestly, Matt, I think I'm just going insane. And I don't think you can help me with that.'

'Well, when you're ready to tell me about it, I'll be here to listen.'

'So, what's the big truth you're talking about?' she asked.

'There is only one thing I can find that links all of you together.'

'What's that?'

'Your brother and Ben Douglas were working on a research project together. That is the only link. Your friend Michelle would probably have had some access to it, and that would link you, which would also link your former boyfriend.'

'That's a pretty weak link.'

'Yes it is, but we've solved cases where we've had less to go on than that.'

'So it's a place to start?'

'It's the only place to start right now. I'm going to go through everything I know, and I want you to tell me if you know anything about anybody I've been able to track down.'

'I don't know anything about it, that I do swear to.'

'Maybe you think you don't know anything. But let's go through it just in case and see if anything rings a bell. Okay?'

'Okay.'

'And you're feeling up to it?'

'I'm feeling up to anything that will find Ian's killer.'

'Okay,' he said, pulling his notebook out of his pocket. 'So here's what I got.'

And then went through it all, several times, until she was so exhausted she couldn't even see straight. She finally bid her goodnights and headed to her bedroom.

Sara was upstairs taking a bath, trying to get some of that alone time she had craved, where she could just let go and cry or scream or anything else that would make her feel better. She had hoped to be alone, but since that wasn't going to happen, she had the faucets on the bathtub wide open and she sobbed while the hot water ran into the tub, hoping Grassi wouldn't hear here, but mostly not caring. She had been the strong and vengeful sister all day long and just couldn't manage the façade for one more second.

Downstairs, Grassi was just finishing up some notes and then picked up his cell phone.

'Roberts,' she answered, flipping over her cell phone. She was standing in the hallway and watching Dr. Douglas through the one-way glass.

'Hi, it's me,' Grassi said, sitting in the kitchen and talking softly on the phone.

'How's it going?' she asked. 'You got a new best friend yet?'

'Oh we're bonding nicely. She's not sharing yet but we're getting there. How about you? Is Dr. Douglas still having a good time?'

'Oh, Dr. Douglas is not having a good time. He's been through seven books so far. He was complaining bitterly about missing dinner and being hungry so I sent someone out for take out for him. I guess it's been a while since he's eaten a greasy take out burger. We had to find him some antacid.'

'But he's still there?'

'He's still here. Funny, huh? All that big talk and yet he hasn't left, hasn't asked for a lawyer. Do you think he is maybe a good citizen under all bluster?'

'I doubt it. I think he's probably really worried that if he leaves we'll take a closer look at him and find whatever it is he doesn't want us to find,' Grassi said. 'You are looking, aren't' you?'

'Yeah, I've got two guys running his background with a fine tooth comb. We may not find anything but I'm guessing it will at least make him nervous when he gets home and finds out we've checked out his friends and family.'

'And nervous men…'

'Make big mistakes,' Roberts finished.

'I'm glad you listen to me sometimes,' Grassi said. 'I can be very wise.'

'Whatever. Look, I gotta go. He's causing a fuss again.'

'Are you ready to let him go?'

'No, I've set a personal goal. I'm going to try to keep him here at least another 90 minutes. I want to see how far I can push this guy.'

'Well, call me if you get anything,' Grassi said.

'I will. Are you staying there tonight?'

'No, I've got a cruiser coming by around ten. I'll let them do the night shift and I'll connect with her again sometime tomorrow. I'd like her to miss me and she can't do that if I'm sleeping on her couch.'

'Okay, well you go Grassi.'

'Night, Roberts.'

Chapter 10

Sara sat in the tub for a very long time. The water was running cold by the time her tears had run dry. Shivering, she got out of the tub and dried herself off quickly, then wrapped herself in a flannel robe and crawled under the comforter. She put the radio on softly, hoping the noise would distract her racing mind, because though her body was exhausted from the overwhelming emotions of the day, her brain would not turn itself off. She lay in bed, Kleenex in hand, covers pulled up around her chin, and wished her mother was still alive.

There was a soft knock at the door. She dabbed at her eyes and wondered what he would do if she didn't answer him.

'Yes?'

'Sara,' he said, opening the door a crack.

'Uh-huh?'

'I'm just leaving now. There's a police cruiser out front. I can have the officers come inside and stay with you if you'd like or they can stay in the car.'

'I'll be fine.'

'It would make us all feel better if you weren't alone,' he insisted. 'And because you refuse to let me call any of your friends…'

'Fine, they can stay in the house. I just want to sleep.'

'You sleep. I'll get them settled and then head out for the night.'

'Thanks.'

'We'll talk tomorrow, okay?'

'Good night,' she said. Suddenly feeling safe and cared for, her tired eyes finally grew too heavy to hold open any longer, and she fell asleep.

Sara hadn't heard anything past that moment, the police officers coming in, Detective Grassi leaving, not a thing until her alarm rang at 6:30 that morning. She turned it off and picked up the phone, dialing the number of her faculty advisor. She would probably be waking him up too, but she had to make sure someone could cover her classes today.

'Hello?' a grumbly voice said.

'Professor Harris?'

'Who is this?'

'It's Sara Hunter, professor. I'm sorry to bother you at this time of the morning.'

'Sara, dear, don't you worry about it. The police were around and told us about your brother. I am so very sorry, my dear.'

'Thank you.'

'Is everything else all right?'

'I just wanted to make sure you knew. I didn't want to leave my classes unattended.'

'Sara, don't you worry about that. I've got this week all taken care of. We can meet after that and talk about how much time you're going to need. You need to concentrate on taking care of yourself right now.'

'Thank you, professor.'

'And please make sure someone lets us know about the funeral,' he said. 'There are a lot of people that want to be there for you.'

Funeral? That thought sent shivers up and down her spine.

'Thank you,' she mumbled before hanging up.

Funeral. Oh, God, how do you arrange a funeral?

mind games

When her parents had died, Ian had taken care of everything. She wasn't even going to go to that funeral but her brother had had a long talk with her about closure and healing and said he would hog tie her and carry her there if he had to. She didn't have a clue what to do. And then she realized that it would be alright. Ben would know what to do. She would sleep for a few more hours then call Ben.

Ben had known what to do. Unfortunately, it involved her getting dressed and sitting in his Lexus as he drove to a funeral home. She put on black jeans and a black turtleneck sweater, after having tried on several other outfits and not understanding why what she wore was so important to her. Then she realized that according to her psychology textbooks, she was probably avoiding her real feelings. It was easier to worry about the clothes she was wearing than the feelings she wasn't really dealing with. So she sat in the passenger seat in the Lexus, her jacket wrapped tightly around her, a handful of Kleenex in her hand ready for the inevitable tears.

'How are you doing?' Ben asked, as he turned into the parking lot.

'Fine.'

'Do you mean it?'

'Of course I don't mean it. I'd give you a million dollars right now to take care of all this while I run away and join the French Foreign Legion or something.'

'A million dollars?' He asked her. 'Can I write you a cheque?'

'Yeah, well for cash I might consider it.'

He parked the car and turned it off, but he didn't get out. Instead, her turned to her and took her hand in his.

'Sara, you've had an incredible amount of loss in the last little while. I'm really worried about you.'

'I know Ben, and I appreciate all you've done.'

'Sara, I'd like you to come home with me after we've finished up here.'

'Sorry?'

'I don't want you staying at that house alone. You know how I feel about you, Sara. I'd love for you to come home and be with me. But I don't want you to think that's what this is about. I just don't want you to be alone. I'll make up the spare room and you can stay there until it seems right to maybe take it further.'

'Ben, I just don't know.'

'Sara, I know this isn't a good time for you to make these kinds of decisions. But please don't think I'm trying to force you into anything. I just want to be there for you. I'll just be down the hall if you need anything. Like today. You won't have to phone me, I'll just be there. And I can keep an eye on you.'

'Ben, stop!' she cried.

'I'm sorry.'

'No, I'm sorry. Look, we're sitting in the parking lot of a funeral home. I just can't have this conversation with you right now. Please.'

He dropped her hand and turned away. Sara picked up his hand in hers and squeezed it.

'Ben, please…'

'No, it's my fault,' he said. 'Don't apologize. I have horrible timing. I'm just so worried about you that I don't really know what to do. And that's a position that I'm not really used to being in, you know?'

'I know.'

'Why don't we just go in and pretend that I didn't blurt any of this out?'

'Oh, don't feel bad,' she said.

'I don't,' he promised her. 'I'll just stick around in the background and be here when you need me.'

He came around and opened the door for her.

'Ben, if you were a woman I would say you're pouting now.'

'Maybe I am,' he joked. 'Okay, got your serious face on now?'

'I'm ready.'

He led her inside where a lovely receptionist dressed in a

classic dark suit looked up at them and smiled.

'Hello. May I help you?' she asked.

'It's my brother,' Sara begin, and then out of no where her eyes were full of tears and her throat constricted so tightly she couldn't talk.

The woman stood up quickly and came around her desk, taking Sara's arm and leading her to a private reception room.

'I'm so sorry for your loss,' she crooned, in a practiced voice.

Sara sat in the chair she was offered and started dabbing at her eyes with a Kleenex. Soon she had a fresh box of Kleenex and a steaming cup of tea in front of her and a whole roomful of people that did know how to plan a funeral.

When all was done, Ben shepherded her into the car and took her home. He had really hoped that he would be pulling into his driveway with Sara and her things at this point, but, unfortunately, that wasn't going to happen right now. Ben was becoming concerned because he hadn't had much of an opportunity to monitor her condition in the last while and he was worried about losing track of what was happening to her. But the most interesting thing he discovered was that he actually cared less about her medical condition and more about her. He missed her, missed the time they had been spending together. He realized he had actually grown very fond of her, not just the dream of them working together with her new abilities, but of her. Ben had originally thought that his feelings were inextricably linked with her success as a test subject, but he missed her humour, her smile, even her coffee made with paper towel filters.

'Well, as instructed I will drop you off and not pressure you about anything,' he teased. 'But seriously, Sara, promise you'll call me if you need anything.'

'Ben, why don't you come in and let me make dinner for you,' she offered.

'You sure?'

'Well, not really. After you taste my cooking I'm sure I'll

never see you again.'

'We can do take out?' he offered.

'No, I'm sure I can rustle up a pot of spaghetti or something. Come on in. And you can keep me company until my police escorts arrive for the evening.'

'It sounds like a good plan.'

They had talked and laughed most of the evening and Sara appreciated the distraction. At about nine o'clock a couple of police officers knocked on the front door. Ben said his goodbyes, knowing that even though he wouldn't be there, she would be safe for the night.

After she saw Ben off and settled the police officers in the kitchen, she went upstairs and got ready for bed. As she stood in the bathroom, washing her face, she felt her emotions well up and start to overwhelm her.

'Stop it,' she told herself in the mirror, blinking back the tears. 'You can cry all you want later. Not yet.'

She climbed into bed and tossed and turned for a couple of hours and then gave up sleeping and wandered into Ian's room. She grabbed his robe off the bathroom door and held it close to her. It still smelled like him. Sara curled up on his bed and wrapped the robe around a pillow. She held it close to her and turned on the television. She settled on the local news, pulled her brother's comforter around her and hoped sleep would come soon.

A handsome anchorman with a rugged jaw broke in with a look of concern on his face. 'Local authorities are investigating the scene of a car crash in the southwest just a few hours ago. A '92 Pontiac drove into the side of the local bank, but no driver was found. The owners of the car were home in bed when the officers came to investigate and they didn't even know the car had been stolen. We go now to our reporter in the field. Padma, can you tell us what's happening out there?'

The angle switched to a young brunette standing in a parking lot. 'Thanks, Bruce. Well, like everyone else involved, I'm wondering exactly what happened here last night…'

Sara had a moment of total clarity. One of those moments in life where the wind rustles through the trees and you can almost believe that God is telling you the secrets of the universe and you understand all of them. *I wonder what happened.* As soon as she heard those words leave the reporter's mouth, she realized that was what cued her visions. She even saw a shadowy figure sitting over her chanting I wonder what happened. But that moment of clarity was followed by a sense of panic, as she heard those words and realized what was going to happen next.

'I don't care what happened,' she screamed in her mind. But it was too late. The sound had already started in her head. The wind was blowing stronger than ever, howling like a hurricane between her ears. The room started spinning, slowly at first, and then so quickly that she felt like she was going to be thrown off the bed. Her stomach started to heave and she heard herself retching, as if from miles away. And just when she thought she couldn't stand it, that it was going to kill her this time, it stopped, and she was standing where the reporter had stood moments before. Only there were no cameramen or reporters, just a car coming straight at her. She knew it was aiming for the front window of the bank, and suddenly realized that she was right in between the speeding vehicle and it's intended target. Sara tried to make her muscles respond, she tried to command herself to move out of the way, but it was like she was moving in slow motion, and the car was coming at her in fast forward. Sara screamed, thinking she was going to die and there was nothing she could do.

A screaming sound tore through her head, pulling her from the accident scene. She sat upright, her heart racing and her head pounding. She was trying to catch her breath and trying to find the phone, which wasn't beside the bed where it should be. Then she realized that she was in Ian's room and the phone was on the other side of the bed. She reached over and grabbed it.

'Hello,' she said, still gasping for breath.

'Sara?'

'Yes.'

'Are you okay?'

'Who is this,' she asked, still having a bit of a problem adjusting her view on her two realities.

'It's Detective Grassi. Are you okay?'

'I, uh, I just had a bad dream,' she explained. 'What time is it?'

'It's nine o'clock.'

'At night?'

'In the morning. Sara, are you sure you're okay?'

'Yeah, I'm okay. The phone just woke me up. Sorry.'

'Okay.'

'Detective Grassi…'

'Matt,' he reminded her.

'Matt, why are you calling me other than to let me know that I've overslept?'

'We found Paul Whyte.'

'Oh my God, you did? Where?'

'Sara, I'm sorry. We found his body. It was in a ditch about a hundred miles from here.'

'Oh my God.'

'I need to talk to you about it.'

'Okay, when are you going to be here?' she asked.

'I need you to come here, Sara.'

'Am I a suspect again?' she asked.

'Well, I do need to talk to you in an official capacity to ascertain your whereabouts and all that. But I'm working solo today too.'

'Where's Detective Roberts gone?'

'Her dad had a stroke last night. She had to fly home in the middle of the night. I don't know how long she'll be gone.'

'Detective Grassi, if you have any family you're close to, you need to assign another detective to my case. Preferably an orphan.'

'That's not funny, Sara.'

'I know. It wasn't meant to be.'

Grassi decided to step out for a couple of minutes before Sara got there. He needed fresh air and a trip to the coffee shop at the end of the block was as good an excuse as any. He was just heading back towards the station when he felt a hand on his shoulder. It wasn't a friendly tap on the shoulder, but a firm grab. And Matt reacted like a cop, spinning around, dropping his coffee and grabbing the hand from his shoulder.

'Detective Grassi.'

'Dr. Douglas,' Matt said, releasing the hand now that he had identified the threat.

'You're a little jumpy. Have you seen a doctor about that?'

'Well, I'm a cop. We don't like to have people grab us from behind. It's an occupational hazard. And now I'm a pissed off cop because you made me drop my coffee.'

'Well, I'm a pissed off doctor, so I guess we're even.'

'And why are you a pissed off doctor?' Matt asked, interested that Dr. Douglas didn't seem to feel at all threatened by the detective.

'Because you're bothering my friend.'

'Your friend?'

'Sara Hunter. Detective, I don't know if I can make you understand just what Sara means to me.'

'I understand you're an old family friend.'

'She means so much more than that. And I would be very upset if you caused her any unnecessary pain or suffering.'

'Well, that's not my goal.'

'She's had a lot of loss in her life, Detective. You might think that what you're doing is okay, but it isn't. She needs to rest and have time to recuperate right now.'

'Is she your patient, doctor?' Matt asked.

'She's my friend.'

'Well, then since she's not your patient, I guess I'm not going to take your advice and I'll just continue my investigation.'

'Detective, I'm sure you're used to being in charge and to having people cower before you. But I want you to know I have some friends in very high places. And if I feel that you are causing her any problems, I will have them contact you. And Detective, these are the kind of friends that can have you walking a beat again.'

'Are you threatening me?' Matt asked.

'Just making a promise.'

'Well, I promise you that I'm going to investigate this case to the best of my ability, just like I do with every other case I work on. And as to walking a beat again? Well, there are advantages to that. Less stress and more exercise. That's not such a bad combination, is it?' he asked.

Ben stared at him and then finally turned away, storming off across the street. For a minute, Matt thought it might be fun to give him a ticket for jaywalking, but then he decided his time would be better spent getting another coffee.

2000

Ben Douglas was an upright and reliable young man. He had worked hard all his life, trying to prove he was more than the product of a rich heritage; that that he could actually stand on his own two feet. He had maintained a good grade point average, completed college with honours and got into medical school on his first try. But in medical school, he was no longer the best of the rest, but just one of the best. He was surrounded by the cream of the crop from across the country and his confidence, and then his marks, suffered. In his fourth year he made the only serious error in judgment he had made in his life. He cheated on his final exam. And then Ben Douglas became Dr. Ben Douglas.

Surprised by the guilt he felt, Ben worked three times as hard as all the other residents. He also talked his family into setting up a scholarship for underprivileged students and started doing volunteer time at the local distress centre. As time passed, he eventually came to believe he deserved to be a doctor and his guilt lessened.

And now he sat here, waiting for the legendary head of Beckman pharmaceuticals to join him for lunch. He had applied for a research grant, studying children's surgical experiences, and he was pretty sure he wouldn't have been called to a lunch meeting to be turned down. He sipped his water, and looked towards the door every time it opened, hoping this was about to become his big shining moment.

He recognized Beckman the minute he walked through the door. It wasn't the fact that he was in his mid-sixties, a distinguished and educated looking man. It was the money. Money showed. The Armani suit, the Italian loafers, and it wasn't just the pieces, but how they were all put together. The quiet confidence. Ben recognized it because he had grown up around it. He rose as the maitre d' led his host to the table.

'Dr. Beckman,' Ben smiled, holding out his hand.

Beckman took his hand in a surprisingly firm grip and shook it. 'Dr. Douglas.'

'Pleasure to meet you, sir,' Ben said, as he settled back into his chair.

'You're not going to think so in a few minutes, boy,' Beckman chuckled, as he sat down and opened up the wine list.

'Sir?'

'Oh don't get your knickers in a knot,' Beckman said. 'You've got the grant.'

'Thank you, sir.'

'But there are other things we have to talk about.'

'May I suggest a wine, Dr. Beckman,' Ben offered, trying to smooth out what had become a rough start.

'Why not? Let's see what kind of taste you have.'

'Do you prefer a white or a red?' Ben asked.

'Surprise me.'

'We'll have the Chateau Neuf 1978,' Ben said.

'Good choice. Your parents obviously raised you right.'

'They tried,' Ben laughed.

'Okay, boy, here's the way this is going to work. I'm going to call you Ben, but I'm old fashioned, so you are going to show me the respect due to your elders and call me Dr. Beckman.'

'Yes sir.'

'And no matter what, you've got the grant.'

'Well, thank you sir. I'd like to say…'

'Save the speeches, Ben. There are a whole bunch of strings attached and I'm guessing you're not going to like them much. So I think we should get started.'

The waiter came back and uncorked the wine, serving them.

'We'd like to order now,' Beckman told him. 'I'll take the New York steak, medium rare, with roasted vegetables. Ben?'

'I'll have the same.'

'Good choice,' Beckman said. 'And then we would like to not be disturbed until our lunch is ready. We can pour our own wine.'

'Yes, sir,' the waiter said, closing his order pad and turning away.

'So, Dr. Beckman, what kind of strings are you going to attach to your grant that is going to be so repulsive to me?'

'Well, you can go ahead and do your study. But we're going to double your test subjects.'

'I don't know that I have the resources to handle that.'

'Which is why we've doubled your grant.'

'Sir?'

'Half the subjects are going to be for your own study and the other half are going to be for a study I am running.'

'Well, I'd be more than happy to work on a study with you, Dr. Beckman.'

'It's phase one drug testing on human subjects.'

'What kind of drug.'

'The kind that the FDA doesn't know about.'

'Sir?'

'And neither does the hospital ethics committee. Or for that matter, the patients.'

'Dr. Beckman, I'm afraid that this meeting is over now,' Ben said, pushing away from the table.

'Sit down,' Beckman said harshly. 'And tell me why it is you decided to cheat on your medical school finals.'

'Excuse me?' Ben said, but he didn't leave.

'Your deep dark secret. Have you ever thought about what

would happen if that became public.'

'Yes I have.'

'I'm sure you have. And I'm prepared to let that secret out. Are you prepared to give up your medical career Dr. Douglas?'

'No,' he whispered.

'I didn't think so. I think you're a lot like me actually, and that you'll do what you have to do to prove that what you believe is true.'

Ben took a big sip of his wine, not knowing what to say.

'So, was I right Ben? You don't like the strings I have attached to my grant, do you?'

'No sir.'

'But you're going to go ahead and take it, aren't you?'

There was a long silence. Ben struggled for a way out of this situation, but couldn't find one.

'Yes sir, I'm going to take it.'

'Good,' Beckman said, holding up his glass in a toast. Reluctantly Ben raised his as well. 'I think this is the start of a beautiful friendship.'

'Dr. Beckman, this might be the start of us working together, but this is never going to be the start of a friendship.'

'I like that, you've still got some fight in you,' Beckman laughed, and then drank his wine.

Ben struggled for weeks with his predicament and he realized he was not as good a person as he had thought he was. He couldn't figure any sort of a way out, so his mind had started to figure out a way to live with it. Survival instinct. And that was what led him to start flipping through his address book, and was when he came across the name of his long lost college buddy, Ian Hunter. Ben was sure Ian had finished his PhD and gone into private practice. He had read something about him in the alumni magazine he received. Maybe Ian would be interested in working on a study with him. A legitimate study. The rest would come later. So Ben picked up the phone and dialed the number.

'Hello?'

'Ian?'

'Yes, who's this?'

'Ian, you probably don't remember me. But you got me through second year biology.'

'Ben?' Ian asked, wonder in his voice. 'Ben Douglas?'

'That's me,' Ben laughed. 'How the heck are you?'

'I'm great,' Ian said. 'How about you? Did you manage to get through medical school without copying my notes?'

'Yeah, somehow. I'm a psychiatrist now.'

'Wow, I thought for sure you'd go into surgery.'

'Well, that was the plan. But doing all those rotations in the different specialties really opened up my eyes to what kind of medicine I really wanted to practice.'

'Congratulations.'

'How about you?' Ben asked.

'Got my PhD, did a residency and now people actually put their problems into my hands on a daily basis.'

'I am impressed.'

'Yep, I work mostly with children.'

'That's great,' Ben said.

'And do you remember my little sister? Sara?' Ian asked.

'Sure, she was a cute little tomboy.'

'Well, I think she's actually going to follow in my footsteps. She just applying to university and is interested in a psych major.'

'That's great,' Ben said. 'Look, Ian, I've received this great study grant and I was wondering if you'd be interested in getting together with me and discussing it. I think it might be right up your alley.'

'Well, Ben I have a pretty full plate right now. Our parents died a couple of years ago and I'm kind of raising Sara on top of everything else.'

'Oh, I'm sorry to hear that Ian. But maybe you could spare me a couple of hours anyway. Just in case.'

'Only if you're buying the beer.'

'And it will give us a chance to get caught up, too,' Ben said.

'You're right. Nothing to lose.'

'Well, not much anyway,' Ben laughed.

And from that point on it became easier with each passing day to rationalize what he was doing and start to believe that he was doing good. Because if what Dr. Beckman thought this drug could do was proved, it would be good. Good for the country, good for medicine and very good for him.

Chapter 11

Sara looked decidedly out of place. She had a visitor's pass clipped to her jacket, but she was scared, afraid to touch anything, scared to make eye contact with anyone, as an officer led her through the squad room and over to Detective Grassi's desk.

'Have a seat,' Matt said, pulling out a chair for her.

She looked at him warily, not really wanting to be here long enough to take a seat, but thinking it was best to go along with the nice police officer so he would let her go home, she sat down.

'So, again, I'm really sorry for the loss of your friend,' he told her, not really sure how he should refer to Paul.

'Thank you.'

'It seems you've lost a lot of people very close to you in the last several months.'

'So it seems,' she said, not wanting to offer any information that he didn't ask for and risk having to explain things she wasn't ready to explain.

'Your high school friend and her husband,' he began. 'Your fiancé.'

'Boyfriend. If you recall we broke up before he disappeared.'

'Does that make you happy?'

'That he's dead? Frankly, I really don't care either way. I'm just happy I don't have to deal with him any more.'

'Was he abusive?'

'What?'

'Did he ever hit you?'

'Detective, are you interrogating me? I thought you said that you believed I wasn't involved in this,' she tried.

'Did he ever hit you?' he repeated.

'Detective, you watch too much TV. Sometimes people just don't get along. They fight and then they break up. I thought he was an uncaring asshole and I was pretty sure he was doing his secretary. I'm sure he has some unkind things to say about me too.'

The police officer chuckled under his breath. 'Point taken. What about your friend Michelle?'

'Am I sorry she's dead?' Sara asked, not sure why the detective was bringing her up now.

'No, no I'm sure you are. Can you tell me a little about the circumstances of her death?'

'Well there was a car accident. Don't you have all this in a file somewhere?'

'Sara, I reviewed the entire file this morning. The police officers that went to notify your brother said that you turned up before anyone had a chance to notify you. They suggested that it seemed that you might have known about the deaths before you arrived at your brother's office. Why did you go to your brother's office that morning?'

'I'm always at my brother's office. We're going to be working together and he's been helping me with my research.'

'You had a class that morning, I believe, according to your schedule?'

'I did. But I decided to skip it.'

'The officers on scene said you came in crying and ran to your brother. Did you know that Michelle had been killed?'

She bit her lip and stared at the police detective.

'Is it true?' he prompted her. 'Did you know she had been involved in an accident?'

'I just had a bad feeling all morning,' she whispered. 'When I got there and saw the police, I knew it was her. Don't you ever get feelings about people you're close to?'

'I like to stick to facts in my line of work.'

'It was the strangest thing,' Sara said, probably the most truthful she'd been since she walked in here today.

'Sara, you know that I'm worried about you, don't you?'

'What?'

'Your friend, and your brother, your boyfriend…everyone close to you is turning up dead or missing. I can't help thinking that maybe something is going on here that you might know about and that might be putting you in danger. And we don't have the budget to give you police protection every night until you feel like sharing what you know with me.'

'I'm just a little insignificant psychology student. What would I know?'

'Was your brother just a clinical psychologist? How involved was he in this research project?'

'I don't know anything about that research project. I swear I'm telling you the truth about that, Detective. I was not involved in that at all.'

'And Ben Douglas. How closely did they work together? How involved was he in all this?'

'Ben's been close to my family for a long time. But I don't know about their work.'

'Sara, like I said, there are a lot of deaths in a very small circle here. I need to figure out what's going on and I would really like to make sure no one else dies.'

'I just don't think I can help you,' she told him. 'I don't know anything. I didn't know anything about my brother's patients or his research. I don't know how closely he and Ben worked together. I told you, I'm just the kid sister.'

He stared at her for a long time, and she used every ounce of control she had to maintain her composure and not give him the sign he was looking for.

'I'm having a real problem believing you Sara,' he said, shaking his head as if he was disappointed in her.

'I'm sorry.'

He liked that response and continued on this tact. 'I don't know what I can do to make you trust me. To make you believe that I'm on your side.'

'There's nothing to tell,' she insisted. 'I don't know anything about anything. I don't know what to say to you to make you believe that.'

'You can tell me whatever it is you're holding back. And then I'll believe you. Sara, who are you protecting?'

'Nothing. No one.'

'I wonder if you would tell me if you did know something. I wonder what you think would happen….'

'No!' she screamed, grasping for his arm and trying to stop him before the words came out of his mouth. But it was too late. The room was swirling and she dug her fingers into the detective's wrist, trying to hold on to reality, but those words echoed in her head as the vortex opened and pulled her deep into the void, where she was no longer in control.

She stood there, gun drawn, trying to hold her hand steady as her pulse raced. There was a man not many feet away from her, also with a gun drawn, pointing it directly at her chest. It was a big gun and he was too close to her. She looked down at her Kevlar vest, wondering if it really would stop the bullet. She didn't have long to wonder either, as he took advantage of her moment of uncertainty and pulled the trigger. She felt the thunder against her chest just as she pulled her own trigger. She pulled it five times before he fell down and dropped his gun. And then she looked down at her chest and saw the blood seeping through the holes in the vest.

'Somebody call an ambulance,' a voice yelled in the distance. 'He's going down.'

And she felt gentle hands help her as she sank to the floor. Her breathing was ragged and she knew there was blood in her chest, stopping her lungs from expanding fully. She felt her blood pressure raise as her heart worked harder to try and get oxygenated blood circulating to her vital organs. And then it dawned on her, how surreal this all was. She was watching her body die and it didn't hurt. This must be the shock they always talked about.

'Sara,' a voice called. 'Sara, can you hear me?'

Her eyelids fluttered open, trying to focus on the scene swirling around her. Detective Grassi's face was above hers, his worried eyes trying to find some recognition in hers.

'You're going to hyperventilate,' he said. 'Try and breathe slowly.'

But she couldn't. It was getting worse every time, she was more and more out of control of the reactions to the visions.

'It didn't hurt,' she gasped.

'What didn't hurt?'

More police officers were gathering around, staring down at her.

'When you got shot. Three bullets through a Kevlar vest and a collapsed lung and it didn't hurt, did it?'

He stared down at her, shocked at what she was saying. And then he saw her pupils start to dance again and he focused back on the moment.

'Sara, stay with me. Try and breathe slowly…'

She opened her eyes slowly, afraid she might be overcome by the dizziness again, the room swirling around her, but all was calm. Her hands came to her chest, which still felt bruised where the bullets had struck her, or him, or maybe both of them. She didn't understand it, she just knew it was getting worse and she was afraid it was going to kill her.

'You're awake?' a voice said, pulling her focus from her bruised chest to the corner of the room, where a nurse was scribbling notes in a chart.

'Uh-huh,' she said, her voice feeling gravelly. She pushed herself up into a sitting position, feeling a little shaky but managing to keep herself from falling off the bed.

'Where am I?' she asked.

'You're at the Holy Cross Emergency Room,' the nurse said, coming over and taking her pulse. 'You had a bit of an incident at the police station.'

'Oh, yeah.'

'It's understandable. Detective Grassi told us you just lost your brother. Things like that can cause anxiety attacks.'

'Can I go?' she asked, swinging her legs over the edge of the bed.

'Slow down,' the nurse said, lifting her legs back onto the bed. 'Let me go and get the doctor first, okay?'

'Fine.'

Sara waited for about five minutes, just wanting to be home, and growing more impatient with each passing minute until finally the door opened again.

'Sara?' the doctor entered the room, a lovely looking lady in her mid fifties. She sat on the wheeled stool and pulled herself over to the bed. 'The nurse told me you were back with us. How are you feeling?'

'Embarrassed.'

'Don't be embarrassed. You just had a panic attack and probably hyperventilated. It happens to the best of us in adverse circumstances.'

'Well, I feel a fine now.'

'I just want to make sure that this isn't going to happen again when you get back home. Do you have anyone to stay with you tonight?'

'No,' she said. She knew from her last hospital visit how this was going to go. No point lying to the doctor.

'Do you want me to check you in for the night?'

'No, no I just want to be home. I'll call a friend over.'

'You know, this is the part where we have to figure out if you're telling the truth or just trying to get out of here.'

'I know, the last doctor explained that to me.'

'The last doctor? Have you had an episode like this before?' the doctor asked.

'The day my brother died. After I saw his body in the morgue.'

'So then Sara, what else can we help you with?'

'What do you mean, doctor?'

'Well, I'm not going to ask you how you're doing with your loss, because that is a stupid question you've obviously answered already. But I'd like to give you some brochures about our grief counseling and psychological support services.'

'Oh, really, I'm okay.'

The doctor held out her package of brochures and finally Sara reluctantly took them.

'You don't have to call anyone right away, or even ever. But this way you've got them if you need them, okay?' the doctor asked, her hand resting on Sara's knee, her eyes studying her closely.

'Okay.'

'And were you telling the truth when you said you'd call a friend?'

'Well, no. But I will. My brother's friend will come over, I'm sure.'

'Good girl. I'll just send the nurse back in with some forms you have to sign and then you can be on your way.'

'Thank you very much, doctor.'

After about fifteen minutes she was signed out and heading out the front doors and onto the street. Sara was surprised that Detective Grassi wasn't in the waiting room, but was relieved that she didn't have to face him. She was pretty sure she could find a cab and be home safe and sound in no time. As she pushed through the front door, a horn honked and a car pulled up in front of her. She leaned into the open passenger side window and saw the Detective behind the wheel.

'Good evening, Matt.'

'Sara.'

'Look, I'm really tired. Can we finish this tomorrow maybe?'

'How did you know?' he asked.

'I'm sorry?' she said. 'Know about what?'

'How did you know, Sara? How did you know about my getting shot?'

'I don't really know what you're talking about,' she tried.

'You said three bullets through the vest and I didn't feel any pain. How did you know?'

'I don't know,' she whispered, and then caught herself. 'I don't know what you're talking about.'

He reached over and popped open the passenger door. 'Get in.'

She did as she was told, fastened her seatbelt and tried to blink away the tears that were forming.

'What do you mean you don't know?' he asked.

'I meant I didn't know what you were talking about. I kind of have hallucinations when I have these anxiety attacks and maybe I said something…'

'That was no anxiety attack,' he said. 'You might have fooled me with the first one. But not now.'

'I kind of have an amnesia thing too. I don't really remember when I wake up again.'

'You're lying to me.'

'No.'

'Yes you are,' he said. 'Tell me how you knew!'

'I didn't know. I didn't know anything,' she cried.

'Tell me Sara.'

'Leave me alone,' she said, trying to get the car door open, but he had used the automatic locks and she couldn't get out.

'Tell me right now or I'll put you in jail for the night.'

'Okay,' she screamed and then tried to get herself under control. 'Okay. I'm losing my mind or dying or maybe it's a brain tumor. But this is happening to me, these attacks or episodes or visions or whatever and they're worse and worse all the time and I'm so scared it's going to kill me.'

Chapter 12

Sara stared at the Detective for a moment, terrified of what was going to happen now that she had said this out loud, and then she fell forward, her hands covering her face, and started sobbing uncontrollably. The detective looked over at her and then pulled out into traffic and drove to Sara's house. He grabbed her purse from the floor of the car, fished her keys out and then came around to open the door and help her out of the car. He helped her silently up the walk, opened the door and led her into her house. He sat her on the sofa and then disappeared into the kitchen, coming back with a big glass of amber liquid.

'Here,' he said, handing it to her. 'I was looking for brandy but I guess scotch will have to do.'

She took it from him but just stared at the glass.

'I hate scotch. I can't drink it unless I'm drunk already.'

'Drink it,' he ordered.

She took a sip and tried not to choke on it, as the liquid burned its way down her throat. He pulled the ottoman up and sat down in front of her, his knees almost touching hers.

'Tell me,' he said.

'Detective…'

'Call me Matt, Sara. Please call me Matt.'

'Detective…'

'Tell me.'

'I can't.'

'People are dying, Sara.'

'I don't know. I don't know what's going on; I don't know who's doing it, why it's happening. I don't know anything.'

'Start at the beginning.'

'I don't know when that was.'

'Michelle. The morning your friend died.'

'I don't know what happened. We were driving along, Paul and I, going to work. And I saw the hole in the fence where the accident happened and I just began to think about what had happened and everything started spinning and the next thing I knew it was like I was there. I was reliving the accident from her perspective. And I was screaming and my boyfriend thought I was insane but I made him take me to Ian's office and the police were there already.'

'Did you tell your brother any of this?'

'No. He'd think I was crazy. But it kept happening. I saw my boyfriend with his secretary. I saw horrible things. And then one day I was in Ian's office and it happened and I saw one of his patients, a little boy. I saw this defenseless little boy's father abusing him. And I felt everything and I heard everything and I couldn't make it stop. And when Ian finally pulled me out of it and I told him, he went and talked to his patient. It all turned out to be true.'

'So Ian believed you?'

'Ian believed me.'

'Was he running some tests, or having you see anyone?'

'No. We hadn't talked about anything like that.'

'So, you're having visions, your brother proves that they're real, and yet he doesn't run any medical tests or refer you to anyone or do anything to figure out what was happening to you?'

'That's right.'

'And now he's dead?' Matt said.

'What do you mean?'

'Don't you think he might have known something about what was happening to you? Weren't you suspicious? Why wouldn't he run tests? Do a CAT scan? See what was going on in your brain?'

'I don't know, I'm not a doctor.'

'It's because he knew what was happening to you Sara. He knew about these visions and what caused them.'

'No way, Ian was not involved in this'

'Sara, he knew what caused them. That's why he didn't do any tests. He already knew what caused them.'

'Ian would never do anything to hurt me.'

'I'm sure you're right. He wouldn't do anything to hurt you, but maybe he was trying to find out who had hurt you?'

'No, I refuse to believe it.'

'Sara.'

'No, Detective. No way. My brother had nothing to do with this.'

He took a deep breath and a big gulp from his glass of scotch before continuing.

'Okay, let's leave that for a minute. Do you know why it happens?' he asked. 'What causes it?'

'There's some words, a phrase. When I hear them it brings on one of these visions or attacks.'

'What are the words?'

'I'm not telling you that. These attacks are getting dangerous. They're going to kill me. I can't control anything about them.'

'Sara, don't you see, you could find out what's going on. You could have a vision focused on why this is happening.'

'No, I'm going to do everything in my power not to have another vision.'

'What are the words, Sara?'

'No.'

'I won't let anything happen to you.'

'No, I can't do it.'

He took her hand. 'Sara, I will not let anything happen to you. I swear. That's why I'm trying to do this, to save your life.'

'No.'

'And other people's lives.'

'It's too late, everyone's already gone.'

'No, they're not. What about Detective Roberts?'

'I don't know what you mean.'

'Don't you think it's interesting that she spends the day with Dr. Douglas and then her father is mysteriously taken ill?'

'You said he had a stroke or something.'

'The doctors aren't sure. And he was perfectly healthy.'

'It happens.'

'Yes, it happens. But it doesn't usually happen to everyone you know, does it?'

'It's not my fault.'

'You're right,' Matt said. 'It isn't your fault. But if you can stop it, you have to try. Otherwise, it *will* be your fault if anyone else dies.'

'Don't say that.'

'Sara, please help me.'

She looked in his eyes, trying to decide if she should trust him or not. His hand stayed in the air, reaching out to her, not wavering.

'I'm so scared, Matt.'

'I know you are. I would be too. Please let me help you.'

Slowly, her hand came up and reached out to his. As soon as it was within his reach, he grasped it tightly and held on.

'Please let me help you.'

She looked into his eyes, her fear almost palpable. But she took a deep breath and tried to steady herself.

'I wonder what happened to me,' she whispered.

And immediately it started. The vortex opened, the very air around her seemed to come alive, moving, swirling, thickening so she couldn't pull it into her lungs. She felt sick to her stomach as she was whisked through time and space and then suddenly she was lying on her bed in her room. She couldn't move but she saw someone out of the corner of her eye. A man. Then he turned and he had a syringe in his hand. He sat on the edge of the bed and Sara saw Ben's face come into focus. He smiled at Sara, brushed some hair off her forehead and then injected the drug into her hip. Inside she was screaming but she couldn't do anything to stop him. And then he leaned to her and said the words, the words that had changed her life.

'I wonder what happened,' he whispered.. 'Say it for me Sara.'

And then the vortex opened again and pulled her in, more violently than the first time, like a tornado. Her breath was sucked out of her lungs, as it spun her through the universe, around and around again, until it finally dropped her on the sofa and she opened her eyes and looked up and saw Ben sitting over her again, another syringe in his hand, and she watched as he injected it into her hip and then leaned over and whispered to her again.

'I wonder what happened?' he asked. 'Sara, I wonder what happened. Say it for me.'

She felt her lips trying to move, trying to say the words and as he repeated it a third time the vortex opened again and ripped her from the couch and threw her violently into her brother's office. Ben and Ian both stood there, glaring at each other, anger filling the air.

'Don't do it,' Ben said.

'It's too late, I've already called the reporter. Ben, we can't let this go on. I can't be responsible for any more deaths.'

'We can't stop this, Ian. We're not in control.'

'We are in control. This is our research and our project.'

'Ian, quit being so idealistic. Do you know who's funding us? Do you know how many people are involved in this project? These guys are serious and they are not going to let us just stop. They have given us hundreds of thousands of dollars and they want this project to work. They will not let us walk away.'

'That's why I called the reporter.'

'Ian, they'll kill you.'

'Better they kill me than I let you kill Sara.'

'I'm not going to kill Sara.'

'You've been giving her the injections. What do you think is going to happen?'

'Ian, she can handle it. That's the beauty of it. We were wrong to think we had to use kids. They weren't strong enough to handle it. But Sara is. She's doing beautifully.'

'She thinks she's going insane. She's hyperventilating, her blood pressure's through the roof. Tell me how that is handling it beautifully?'

'She's adapting.'

'You're killing my sister and I'm going to make you stop before it's too late,' Ian said quietly, in that voice that always sent chills up Sara's spine.

'Well, I'm sorry I can't convince you,' Ben said.

'Ben, stay with me. We can talk to the reporter together. I have some evidence.'

'The reporter isn't coming,' Ben said.

'What?'

'His house burned down about an hour ago. It was tragic. No one survived.'

'What are you talking about?'

'Ian, these people are watching us. They know what we're doing. Did you think they would just let you waltz out and talk to the press?'

'They killed him and his entire family?'

Ben reached into his jacket and pulled a gun out, pointing it at Ian.

'Yes, and now it's my turn. I'm not going to let you ruin this for me either.'

'Ben, put that away,' Ian said.

'I'm sorry, Ian. I want to know about the evidence you said you have.'

'No way.'

Ben pointed the gun and pulled the trigger, shooting a hole in Ian's leg. Ian fell to the ground, a scream leaving his mouth as blood spurted from his leg.

'Two arms and two legs,' Ben said. 'We can do this for a while. Why not just tell me now and I'll put you out of your misery.'

'Fuck you,' Ian spat out at him.

Sara watched in horror as the blood pumped out of the wound on his leg and pooled beneath him. It matched the beating of his heart and she knew the bullet had hit an artery. Ian saw it too, she could tell. He knew he was going to bleed to death before Ben would have much of a chance to do anything. Ben was the only one who didn't seem to notice.

'Tell me,' he seethed.

'You'll never find anything,' Ian smiled, a sense of peace spreading through his face. He turned and smiled in the direction where Sara stood watching this replay. 'The only one who will ever know where I put it is Sara. She'll know. Sara will be able to put the pieces together and stop this.'

And then Ian's head fell back. She didn't know if he was unconscious or dead but she felt the tears stinging her eyes.

'Shit,' Ben said, running over and feeling for a pulse but soon he gave up. 'Well, don't you worry Ian, I'll go see Sara and she'll wonder what happened…'

There was a screaming sound in Sara's ears, as the vortex opened and the wind pulled her in. Her arms and legs felt like they were being ripped off. She couldn't breathe, couldn't see, and couldn't move.

'Sara!'

Was that Ian screaming for her? She wanted to feel that peace he had felt at the end. She wanted to let go and let it just end.

'Sara!' the voice screamed barely heard above the storm in her head, and then she felt a sharp pain on her face. And another.

Her eyes fluttered open and she tried to focus but couldn't.

The wind was too strong and it was pulling her in. Her body started to shake and in a moment she realized that someone was shaking her. Her eyes fluttered and finally opened and she saw her living room slowly coming into focus.

'Sara,' the detective screamed at her. 'Pull yourself back.'

He shook her violently again, trying to get her attention; to bring her back from whatever world she had been visiting, but it wasn't working. He shook her again and then pulled back and slapped her face as hard as he could. Her eyes popped wide open and finally, she took a deep breath and felt the oxygen filling her burning lungs.

'I can't breathe,' she gasped.

'You're hyperventilating again,' he said, putting a bag over her mouth. 'Just breathe slowly for another minute, you'll be okay.'

She breathed into the bag, trying to make sense of the images that still danced through her mind.

'Who did it?' Matt asked.

She shook her head, holding the bag tightly over her mouth.

'Tell me what you saw?' he begged her.

'It was too much,' she said. 'There were images on top of images on top of images. I couldn't make sense of any of it.'

'Sara, you have to tell me. It's the only way I can protect you.'

'You can't protect me,' she said, and then despite the paper bag and the racing heart, the trauma in her head was too much for her to digest and she felt the edge of the world starting to grow black.

'Stay with me Sara,' he ordered her, when he saw her pupils start to constrict.

'I can't.'

And then she was out.

Chapter 13

When she awoke again, it was pitch black in the room. She knew she was still on the couch, but there was a blanket tucked tightly around her. She heard a soft noise in the kitchen then felt something cool on her forehead. She looked up and saw the outline of a man leaning over the back of her sofa. As he laid a cool damp cloth over her forehead he noticed she was awake.

'How are you feeling?' he asked.

'You're still here?'

'Of course I'm still here.'

She pushed herself up into a sitting position, pleased she didn't feel faint this time.

'But it's late.'

'Sara, I told you I would protect you, I wouldn't let anything happen to you. I meant it.'

'Thank you.'

'So how are you feeling?'

'Tired,' she admitted. 'I think my brain hurts.'

'That doesn't surprise me. It's been through a lot.'

'Yeah. I have a headache but I'm kind of afraid to take anything.'

'Do you have any idea what happened?' he asked.

'I saw needles. Someone injected me with something and

that's what started all this.'

'What it is, do you know?'

'I don't have a clue. I'm a psych major. I don't know anything about pharmacology. That was more Ian's area.'

'Did Ian have something to do with this?' the detective asked.

She was glad it was dark so he couldn't read the expression on her face. She hoped her voice held steady.

'I was telling you the truth. I couldn't really make anything out; there were just too many images all at once. That's what's scaring me; these things are getting out of control. It's not just the hyperventilating or the blood pressure that's in the stroke range, but my brain is being overwhelmed too. I feel like the synapses are going to explode and I'll just be a burned out mess with my brains seeping out of my ears.'

'We're not going to let that happen,' he said. 'As a matter of fact, we're not going to let any of this happen again. I don't think it's a good idea for you to risk another vision.'

'I think you're right, but how exactly are we going to accomplish that?'

'I don't know. But if I have to take you into the mountains and keep you in a tent away from every other person in the world who speaks English I'll do it. At least until we can find out who is responsible for this.'

'I don't know if I really want to know that or not,' she whispered. 'Maybe I could just live in that tent forever?'

'I know it sounds peaceful right now, Sara, but I don't think it's a good long term solution.'

'Well, it might be worth a try,' she laughed weakly.

'Shh.'

'What?'

'There's a car coming.'

And then they saw the headlights, as the car turned into the driveway. Matt's hand went to the gun in his holster, but despite his warning Sara was at the window, peaking through the curtains.

mind games

'Get back,' he said, pulling the curtain closed.

'Ben!'

'What?'

'Sorry, it's just Ben, Ian's friend.'

'What's he doing here at this time of night?'

'He's a family friend,' she said. 'He drops by all the time. He's probably just here on his way home from the hospital to make sure I'm okay.'

'Sara?' Matt asked, unconvinced by the tone of her voice.

'Really, it's okay,' she said. 'He can stay with me for the rest of the night.'

'If you're sure,' he said, still uncertain.

'Please,' she insisted. 'And can you go out the back? That way I don't have to explain to him why you're here and what happened tonight.'

'Sure.'

'Thank you.'

'Sara, you have to promise me one thing.'

'What,' she asked, walking him to the back door.

'You have to call me in the morning. I swear I'll send the SWAT team over here if I don't hear from you by nine o'clock.'

'I promise.'

He hesitated at the door for a minute, still not totally convinced that leaving was the right thing for him to do.

'Goodnight,' he finally said, closing the door softly behind him, just as the front doorbell rang.

Sara made sure the back door was locked and then took a deep breath and hurried to the front. She peaked through the curtain, making sure it was Ben standing there, and then unlocked the door and let him in. He leaned over and kissed her on the cheek and then closed the door behind him.

'What are you doing here at this time of night?' she asked.

'I just had a feeling that I should check up on you,' he said. 'Is everything okay?'

'Everything's fine.'

'Then why are you still dressed and awake?'

'Oh, I've just been napping on the couch.'

He pulled her into his arms and held her tightly.

'Sara, why didn't you call me?' he asked. 'I could have come over hours ago.'

'There's nothing you could have done.'

'I could have been here for you if nothing else. You don't have to be alone.'

'I just hate to be too much trouble,' she said.

He loosened his grip and held her so he could look into her eyes.

'You are never too much trouble, Sara. I would do anything for you. I love you.'

'I know, you've said that before,' she said, feeling uncomfortable.

'You don't have to say it back,' he laughed. 'Plus, I promised your brother I was going to look after you.'

'I know, I know.'

'Look, you get comfortable on the couch and I'm going to make you something that will help you sleep.'

'I don't want any drugs,' she said, suddenly scared.

'No, I was thinking a hot toddy or something like that,' he laughed. 'If that's okay?'

'That's fine,' she said.

He sat her on the sofa and disappeared into the kitchen. Soon he was back in the living room and sat down on the couch beside her. He handed her a mug of warm liquid. She held it up and took a sniff, her nose crinkling at the acrid aroma of the alcohol. And then she set it down on the table.

'It's better warm,' he said.

'I'm sure it is.'

'You need to drink it, you'll feel better.'

'I'm sure I will.'

'I'm just going to go to the bathroom,' he said. 'I want to see that all gone when I get back.'

'I'll try,' she said.

As soon as she heard the door close, she took some of the

hot liquid in her mouth and swirled it around, then spit it back out into the mug. She took the mug over to one of the plants and emptied it into the soil. Then she raced into the kitchen and rifled through the junk drawer. She found what she was looking for and hurried back to the sofa. She tucked it in under the cushions and then settled herself, too. Ben came back into the room, his jacket and tie off, and his shirt untucked. He joined her on the couch, wrapping his arm around her shoulder and pulling her close to him. He leaned over and kissed her and she let him. He pulled away and smiled at her, pleased she wasn't fighting him any longer. Then he kissed her again, bolder this time, his tongue exploring her mouth.

'You taste like scotch,' he teased.

'Is that what that was?' she asked, stifling a yawn.

'That was part of it. Are you tired?'

'I'm exhausted,' she admitted, truthfully.

'Lie down,' he said, sliding over so her head was cradled in his lap and she could stretch out on the couch. He ran his fingers through her hair and caressed her cheek.

'You're not going to be very comfortable there,' she said, not fighting him though.

'I'll be fine,' he assured her, his voice soft and soothing.

She felt her eyelids growing heavy and eventually they closed and her breathing settled into a regular and even rhythm. He waited, making sure she really was settled. Then he slowly disengaged himself from her, setting her head down on a pillow and listening to her breathing, making sure she really was out. Considering what he had put in the cocktail he gave her, he was pretty sure an earthquake wouldn't disturb her right now. He crossed the room to get his jacket and pulled a case out of the breast pocket. Inside was a syringe and a vial of clear fluid. He filled the syringe and tapped the air out of it, then capped it and set it on the coffee table. He perched on the edge of the couch and pulled the blanket down, exposing her hip. He slid her pants down, so he could inject the drug. When he was happy with the site, he rubbed an alcohol swab over it, grabbed the needle from the coffee table and pulled the cap off with his teeth. He moved the syringe toward her hip, choosing the site he wanted to make contact, when suddenly her hand came up and caught his wrist in hers.

'What are you doing?' she asked.

'Sara?' he asked, shocked.

'What are you doing to me?' she demanded.

She pulled the needle from his grip and tossed it across the room. He was so shocked that she was conscious he didn't have time to react.

'Tell me what you're doing to me,' she demanded, pulling herself into a sitting position. 'I thought you said you loved me.'

'I do love you.'

'Then why are you killing me?'

'I'm not killing you.'

'I'm dying, Ben. Every time it happens I get a little closer.'

'I'm not killing you Sara, I'm enhancing you.'

'Enhancing me?' You're insane.'

'No, Sara, it's exciting. It's a new frontier.'

'It's my brain, my mind, my body. And you've violated it.'

'No, I know you don't understand. I can explain it all to you.'

'I don't want to hear it. I just want you to get out of here.'

'I can't do that.'

'I'll call the police. I swear I will.'

'You'll die, Sara. If I don't give you this last injection, you will die.'

'What do you mean?'

'It's a long story. Can't you just trust me on this one?'

She looked at him, eyebrows raised in shock.

'I guess you can't,' he admitted.

'Maybe you should start at the beginning,' she said, pushing herself into the far corner of the sofa and pulling the blanket tightly around her.

'All right, I guess I owe you that much. Sara, if you can understand how important this is, I know you'll be happy to be a part of it. Do you realize the leaps and bounds you are making for medical research?'

'Ben,' she said quietly. 'Save the rhetoric.'

'It started about two years ago. Ian and I got a grant and we were studying patients who underwent surgery and then reported that they knew what happened, that they had seen the surgery. We were trying to determine whether it was an implanted memory, perhaps something they had overheard a recovery room nurse say, or if the drugs used for the anesthesia were only acting as paralytics and not pushing the patient into unconsciousness, as we had believed.'

'Okay, I'm with you so far.'

'Well, we found that with the patient group from the ages of about twelve years old to sixteen seemed to be having real recollections of events, even though we could prove that they were totally unconscious during the surgery,' he explained, giving her the sanitized and sanctioned version of his story. 'For some reason, we seemed to trigger some sort of vision of the past. We started working with an anesthesiologist, the man who started this project. And then it happened, Sara. It was like a miracle. We finally found the right combination of drugs and we were able to reproduce the results. We were able to take kids, give them the combination of drugs and then induce visions of events from the past.'

'I'm sensing a but here.'

'Well, there were two big buts unfortunately. The first issue was that we could only get them to experience events from the past that were related directly to them in some fashion.'

'Forgetting that this is all horribly unethical, why is that bad?'

'Because it has no commercial value. If we were to use this ability, we needed to be able to prove the benefits of usage. Imagine a police department that could view the crime. Or the CIA being able to inject an agent and he could see what happened in Iraq yesterday. In order to get the grants and study and develop this properly, we had to be able to prove its worth.'

'And the kids?'

'That was the other big problem,' he admitted. 'The kids kept dying.'

'What?'

'We found that after two doses the visions started to get out of control. We had 12 year olds stroking out on us.'

'My God.'

'The third dose seemed to stabilize the visions, but then something happened to their hormones and things got out of control physically. We had to sedate them and put them in a long-term care facility. That is if we got to them soon enough. We've brought in others, doctors, researchers, psychologists, to try and figure out what's happening. But they're still dying. We can't get them stabilized.'

'And this is what you injected me with?' she asked, disbelievingly.

'We believed the problem was because of their age, they were pubescent and the drugs were stimulating something in their systems. We postulated that if we could find the ideal candidate, someone older whose hormone levels had stabilized, who was perhaps between twenty and twenty five years old, we could avoid that problem.'

'What did your animal testing show you?' she asked.

'We haven't done any animal testing, nothing in the labs,' he admitted. 'We're testing this in the real world in real time.'

'What?'

'It's about the money, Sara. We can't afford to wait twenty years for the testing to all be approved.'

'And you did this to me?' she asked again.

'You were the perfect candidate,' he said. 'You fit all the criteria.'

'So I'm going to die?'

'I don't think so. You have to let me give you the third shot, to stabilize your condition. And then we have to go to the clinic so I can run some tests, but there seem to be no signs of any other problems with you.'

'Did my brother know about this?' she asked.

'Not when I started,' Ben admitted. 'We talked about using you, but he absolutely forbade it.'

'And you did it anyway?'

'Sara, you were the perfect candidate. And I fell in love with you. How perfect would that be? My research and you as our prize subject. We could do this together.'

'You're insane.'

'I'm not, you're just in shock,' he said. 'You just need to think about this for a while. Let it settle in.'

'Tell me what happens if I don't let you give me that next shot,' she demanded.

'You already know, Sara. It gets out of control. You start having visions repeatedly. Your respiration goes crazy, your blood pressure and heart rate go crazy, and the vision won't end. Each one will get worse and worse. And then you'll get stuck in one you can't get out of. Then you'll either shoot your blood pressure up so high that you'll stroke out, or you heart will beat so fast it will almost explode, or neurons will start misfiring in your brain and you'll wind up on life support in some long term rehab hospital in a permanent vegetative state. Sara, I don't want to lose you for the research, but mostly I really don't want to lose you. And I don't think you want to end up that way either, do you?'

'No.'

'Then please let me do this. Sara, I swear I wouldn't do anything to hurt you. I would have never given you the first injection if I didn't think it was safe. I just wanted big things for you. For us. Please let me help you.'

'How can you expect me to make a decision like that right now?'

'You know, Sara, I could have just said the words and sent you off into another vision, and then when you were helpless I could have injected you. But I didn't. And I still won't. It's totally your decision.'

'You killed Ian.'

'What are you talking about?'

'I saw it. You killed Ian. You shot him in the leg and he fell down . You were going to torture him.'

'You went back and saw that?' he asked. 'You had a vision about that?'

'I had to. I had to know what happened.'

'You didn't see everything.'

'What did I miss that would make me think you were doing the right thing? My God, you shot my brother.'

'He hid our research. He was going to go to the press and tell them everything.'

'He was doing what he thought was right and you shot him.'

'I was doing what I thought was right. I was protecting you.'

'And yourself?' she asked. 'You can't tell me you weren't trying to save yourself.'

'You're right, they would have killed me. And if they killed me, you would have died too. No one knew I had started the series of injections on you. If I died, Sara, you died.'

She just started at him, not knowing what to believe.

'Please,' he said, reaching over and putting a hand on her knee.

Sara shivered and withdrew from him, pulling herself back further into the corner of the sofa. 'You're a monster.'

'Did you see where Ian hid the research when you had your vision?' Ben asked her.

'He was dying.'

'You're right, he was dying. And just before he did, he turned and he looked into the corner of the room and he smiled. Oh my God, Sara, did he see you? Was it more than a vision? Have we created something greater here?'

'I don't know what you're talking about.'

'Were you in that room with us?'

'It's your research, asshole, you figure it out.'

'Sara, I'm sorry, but I have to do this. It's for your own

safety. I wonder…'

She reached down into the cushions on the sofa and pulled up a gun pointed directly at his head.

'I'll have two bullets in your brain before you get that last word out,' she interrupted.

'A gun?'

'You didn't know Ian had this, did you?'

'Put it down, Sara.'

'He must have been worried about what was going on for a long time. He got this gun six or eight months ago.'

'Give me the gun, Sara.'

'So if Ian believed in this project so much, why did he feel the need to buy himself a gun? Who was he protecting himself from?'

'Oh, Sara, please don't do this.'

'Now that's just funny coming from you after what you've done to me.'

'When did you do it?' he asked. 'When did you have your vision and find out it was me?'

'A while ago.'

'Tell me what you saw? I don't think you saw everything and I want to fill in the missing pieces for you. Sara, I need you to know everything about this so you can trust me again.'

'No, I don't think so. I think you should talk to the police. You can tell them everything.'

'If you call the police you will die,' he was getting frustrated and it was beginning to show. 'They'll never let me treat you.'

'No, but they can take me to a hospital and the doctors can help me.'

'Sara, you have to understand something. They won't let you live. The people I am working for, they are very dangerous people. I knew I was taking a big chance when I decided to accept the offer from them, but it was the only way I could carry on my research. But if you go to the police or to a hospital, they will not hesitate to kill you before anyone can find out what is going on. They will do anything to protect this research. Sara, your only hope is letting me help you. And then come with me, let me do some studies, play along with me and when I've got the money, we can disappear.'

'I thought you said they were dangerous and powerful. Won't they just find us?' she asked.

'Sara, I will have twenty five million dollars if this research is successful, maybe more. It is a lot easier to hide with that kind of money. But it has to be your decision. I've told you everything I can.'

She stared at him for a few moments, wishing her brother were here. He would know what to do. She didn't. She just knew she didn't want to die. Not here and not now. Not yet. She slowly reached over to the coffee table and set the gun down. There were tears streaming down her cheeks when she looked back at Ben.

'Okay,' she whispered, meekly, not really believing she was saying it.

'Thank you,' he gushed, but she couldn't help wondering if it was because she was going to be saved or if it was his research he was happiest about.

'Does it hurt?' she asked.

'A little burning. Just like a local anesthetic. It only lasts about ten seconds and then you'll just get sleepy and when you go to sleep, I'll instigate a vision. Only this time, you'll feel in control, you'll be able to direct where it goes and when it ends. Your vital signs will stay within normal limits and when you wake up you won't feel like you've just run a marathon.'

'Where do you need to inject it?'

'Glutes,' he said.

She turned around on the couch and offered him her exposed hip. Her heart was racing and her brain was screaming at her to run, but she just sat there, trying to control her breathing, as he retrieved the syringe she had thrown across the room and checked the dose.

'Are you ready?' he asked.

She nodded her head, unable to speak, knowing her life

was never going to be the same from this moment onwards.

He brought the needle close to her hip and paused, looking up to smile reassuringly at her. She thought she saw some love in his eyes, but she turned away. And as she did, the room exploded around her. Sara dove to the floor, not sure what had happened but feeling safer on the floor than on the couch. There was another massive explosion and Ben fell on top of her. She opened her eyes, wanting to ask him what had happened, but screamed when she saw a black mark on the side of his head, a hole, that was slowly dripping blood and brain matter onto the carpet beside her.

She screamed again when Ben seemed to move, rolling off of her so she was free. She felt someone reach for her arm and pull her up. It was Detective Grassi, his gun drawn, arm reaching down to her.

'What the fuck was that?' he asked.

'You shot him?'

'He was trying to kill you and you were just going to sit there and let him?'

'He was trying to save me,' she said. 'He said he had to give me that last injection or I was going to die.'

Sara started frantically looking for the missing hypodermic again, terrified it had broken this time.

'You lied to me.' Grassi said.

'Yes, I did.'

'You saw this in your vision. You knew it was him and you didn't tell me.'

'You're right. I didn't tell you because I was afraid you'd do something stupid like shoot him. And oh look, I was right.'

'Okay, I'm just going to call this in and then we need to get you to the hospital.'

'I can't believe you shot him,' she said.

'Sara, you're in shock and you're not making sense. Why don't you just go get a glass of water or something while I call this in. Please.'

She slapped his face, shocked by the red outline of her

hand that appeared on his cheek. She hadn't meant to hit him that hard.

'I am not in shock. Couldn't you have just wounded him or something? Now we have no chance of finding out what is going on or who is behind this. Or what kind of poison they have been injecting into my body.'

'That's why we're taking you to the hospital.'

'Right, so I can have one more vision, blow a few synapses and wind up a vegetable? Does that sound like a good plan to you?'

'It sounds like the only plan we have.'

'Well, I actually had a plan where I was going to go with Ben and find out who was behind all this and maybe get my hands on his lab books so when I did finally get to a hospital, someone could make sense of all this and help me.'

'You should have shared your plan with me then, before I thought I was saving your life.'

'What were you doing out there anyway, spying on me?'

'Yes. I am a cop you know, it's what we do. Especially when we think someone is lying to us and we're trying to get to the bottom of a series of deaths.'

'Fuck.'

'Come on, let's get to the hospital. Or do you want an ambulance?'

'I don't want to die.'

'I won't let you die.'

'Look, you've seen my last two visions or attacks or whatever these are. Don't you think they're getting a little more violent, a little harder to break out of each time?'

'Yes, but I think the only chance we have of helping you with that is at a hospital.'

'Well, that's not exactly true,' a voice said, from the direction of the kitchen door.

They both turned, shocked. Matt's gun came up, pointing at the shadow that loomed in the corner of the doorway.

'Who are you?' Matt demanded, in his deep, no nonsense

cop voice.

'Don't tell me you didn't lock the back door behind you?' she said.

'Identify yourself.' Matt ordered again, ignoring Sara.

Slowly, the shadow moved forward into the half light of the living room and an elderly man appeared, holding a gun of his own.

'I can help her,' he said, not letting the gun drop. Sara couldn't help but notice it was pointed at her head.

'Put the gun down,' Matt instructed, his aim not wavering.

'All right, if it makes you feel better, I will put the gun down,' he complied, setting it gently on the floor. 'But please don't shoot me. Because if you do, she'll wonder what happened next.'

Sara didn't realize the words had even come out of his mouth and then suddenly the vortex was upon her. She crashed to the floor, hitting some piece of furniture on the way down but registering nothing other than a dull pain. The winds pulled her through the past; flashing so many images at her she couldn't keep track of them, let alone make sense of them.

'Help me,' she whispered, before she totally lost consciousness.

'What have you done?' Matt yelled, cocking the trigger of the gun.

'Dear boy, it would be very unwise of you to shoot me,' he said and turned his attention to Sara. 'She needs me.'

'You're trying to kill her.'

'No, I very much do not want her to die. What I am trying to do is make a point here. No matter what you think you believe about what is going on here, she needs that third injection to live. That is the truth.'

'And why am I supposed to believe that?'

'Look at her,' he said sadly. 'The arms are twitching, see that is a sign that her neurons are starting to fire out of control. She is having trouble getting enough oxygen; hear her gasp for breath? See the faint blue outline around her lips. Cyanosis.

Soon her body will try to hyperventilate and then if we don't help her, she will start to suffer from oxygen starvation and her brain will start to die, cell by cell. That is if her heart lasts that long. But she is young and healthy. I'm guessing her heart will be able to withstand this even if her brain can't.'

'You bastard!'

'We have to give her the injection. Please dear boy, let me do that for her. Then you can shoot me later.'

Matt stood there, helpless, watching as she gasped for breath and her limbs twitched out of control. He could almost see her heart beating in her chest.

'All right,' he screamed. 'All right, do it. But then back away from her.'

'Can I check her blood pressure?'

'You will back away. I'll call the paramedics and they can look after her.'

'Fine, fine.'

The old man pulled a small container out of his breast pocket, pulled a syringe out of that and prepared it for his patient. He gently swabbed a patch of her skin and injected the drug into her muscle. He stepped backwards, a few paces, and watched her for signs of recovery. And slowly, her breathing came back to within normal limits and her limbs quieted. Matt looked relieved as he slowly sidled over to her, trying to focus his attention on his prisoner while double checking on Sara. He slowly kneeled to the ground, his gun still pointed at the elderly doctor, and he put a hand gently on her neck, turning for a split second to feel her pulse and make sure she was really okay. And that split second was all it took. He felt a stabbing pain in the arm that held his gun and looked down, to see an empty syringe still sticking out of his bicep and a satisfied elderly gentleman smiling down at him.

'One of the biggest mistakes you young people make is assuming that because we're old that we're slow. It's not always true, you know.'

Matt felt his head spinning and tried to speak, but his lips wouldn't form the words. The gun dropped from his hand, which was quite useless now, as the rest of his body slowly began to tingle as well.

'You must have known she is far too valuable to us to just let her go.'

Matt fell over on his side, struggling to keep his eyes open, desperately wanting to see what happened to Sara.

'I'll take good care of her, I promise,' the man said, bending over and closing Matt's eyes. 'She's very valuable to us. We'll take very good care of her.'

And that was the last thing Matt heard. The man pulled out his cell phone and pushed a speed dial button.

'Dr. Beckman here. I'm ready for the ambulance at the home address please.'

Chapter 14

Matt opened his eyes, blinking rapidly, a sense of panic overtaking him. He tried to sit up but found he couldn't move his hands and feet. He tried to shout out, but his voice was hoarse, his throat dry and only a faint croak escaped.

'It's okay Detective Grassi, you're in the hospital,' said a voice from the corner of the room.

He watched as the nurse turned on a small bedside light and held a glass of water with a bendable straw up to his mouth. He began to sip greedily but she gently pulled the straw from his mouth.

'Slowly, slowly, you don't want to make yourself sick.'

'How long?' he croaked.

'You've been here three days,' she said, putting the straw back to his mouth.

'My legs?' he croaked.

'We had to put you in restraints. You had some interesting drugs in your system and you were having some violent moments. It was for your own safety.'

'Oh.'

'I think we can get rid of these now, if you've had enough water for a moment.'

'Fine,' he whispered, feeling a little more certain of his

voice.

She set the water on the bedside table and undid his restraints, giving his wrists and ankles a little rub.

'Thank you,' he said.

'I should go get the doctor,' she said. 'Will you promise to lie still and be good for a couple of minutes until I get back?'

'Yes.' Not that he had much choice, as he barely had the strength to nod his head.

'All right, I'll be right back then.'

Matt watched her walk out of the room and tried to get his mind to focus on what the hell had happened to him. He wasn't sure why Roberts wasn't here. He knew they were working on a case together and remembered that he had been attacked, but that was all he could remember. He needed to see the doctor and then he needed to find out what was going on and find out who had put him here.

Sara's eyes opened. She tried to look around and see where she was, a sense of panic overtaking her. Her muscles weren't reacting properly to the orders her brain was giving them and she was having a hard time seeing around the room. She tried to talk but her throat was parched and her lips cracked. She couldn't get a sound out.

'Are you awake?' she heard a voice from the corner ask.

She tried to move her arms and legs, but found them restrained tightly to the bed. A nurse walked from the corner of the room and turned on a bedside light. He picked up a glass of water with a bendable straw and held it to her lips.

'Sip slowly. We've had to keep you sedated for a couple of days. I don't want you making yourself sick.'

Sara fought the urge to greedily suck the water down, and sipped slowly as she was instructed. The nurse took the water away and set it on the bedside table, then felt her pulse.

'How are you feeling?' he asked.

'Okay,' she croaked. 'Where am I?'

'At our research facility. That's all you need to know for now.'

'My arms?' she asked.

'We had to restrain you for obvious reasons. We don't want you to hurt yourself or any of us.'

'I won't,' she promised.

'You must think I haven't done this before,' he laughed. 'We'll just keep them on you for now and see how it goes.

'Please,' she cried. 'What happened to Detective Grassi?'

'I'm afraid Dr. Beckman took care of him.'

'What do you mean?' she asked.

'Well, Dr. Beckman rarely gets his drugs mixed up, so I'm pretty sure that your Detective went to sleep and never woke up again. But don't worry; it's a very peaceful way to go.'

'No,' she whispered.

'I'm just going to get your doctor. I'm sure he'll want to look you over and make sure everything's okay. I'll be right back.'

She watched him go, knowing she probably had just this one moment alone.

'I wondered what happened?' she said out loud, bracing herself for the vortex that would momentarily overtake her.

The doctor deflated the blood pressure cuff, removed it from Matt's arm and smiled at him.

'Everything seems in good working order. You should be out of here in a couple of days.'

'Doctor, I'm afraid I don't remember why I'm here.'

'Really?'

'Really,' Matt said.

'What do you remember?'

'I was investigating a case. A psychologist and his secretary had died and we were trying to determine if it was coincidental or if the deaths were related. I think I had been interviewing the man's sister. There was something going on there but after interviewing the girl, I don't really remember anything.'

'Well, there must have been some sort of an amnesiac in that interesting cocktail of drugs we found in you. You're a very lucky man, Detective Grassi, because with that mixture of medications they gave you, someone really wanted you dead. But I guess the amnesiacs were their back up plan, so if for some reason you didn't die, you wouldn't remember anything.'

'So what happened?' Matt asked. 'Who tried to kill me?'

'Well, your coworkers will have to fill in the details for you, but I believe they found you at the girl's house, unconscious. There was a dead man with bullets from your gun in his head and the girl was missing. The neighbours called the police because an ambulance had come to the house, picked someone up and left, but all the doors were open. When the police got there, they found you on the floor. Luckily they brought you here and I was on call. I'm pretty good at drug overdoses after all these years in the ER, and I was able to counteract almost everything they had in your system.'

'Almost everything?'

'Almost. For the ones I couldn't, we supported you. We had you on a respirator for a day, and I thought we were going to have to put you on dialysis. But you are a nice young healthy, stubborn man and your body fought like I have never seen a body fight before.'

'So it paid to quit smoking?'

The doctor laughed. 'Yes it did, and what we need to do now is try you on a soft diet, get some strength back into you and notify your captain that you're back in the land of the living. I think he was most anxious to talk to you.'

'That sounds good. I need a few holes filled in this memory of mine right now.'

The vortex had been gentler this time, soft and soothing and had taken her to a safe and calm vision, a place where she didn't feel panic and fear. So she couldn't understand why suddenly she was feeling pain and shaking, as if the vision had changed. But then as it faded and she began to focus back on the room around her, she understood. A doctor stood above her, slapping her face and shaking her shoulders, forcing her from her vision. She blinked hard, as he slapped her again.

'Stop,' she cried. 'Please stop.'

The doctor smiled down at her, letting her fall back onto the bed.

'You're a very clever girl,' he smiled at her. 'I didn't think you'd have your wits about you so soon.'

'I'm getting used to working under pressure.'

'Did you have a vision? Did you see your escape?' he asked.

'How did you know?'

'What else would you want to see?' he asked, and then his expression softened. 'Unless it was that detective?'

'I saw you kill him in real life,' she said. 'I didn't need to have a vision and relive it.'

'Give me the device,' he ordered the nurse, who handed him a small electronic unit. 'This is going to keep you from having visions until I want you to have one.'

'What, it blocks my brainwaves or something?' she asked.

'Oh, nothing that refined, I'm afraid. It's programmed for your key words. If the sensor hears them, it delivers a severe electrical shock, which breaks you out of the vision.'

'Oh.'

'I do mean a severe shock, my dear. Please don't think you can withstand it.'

'I won't.'

He chuckled at her as he wrapped the device around her arm and taped it firmly in place.

'Sorry, this is a little archaic, in a couple of days we'll implant a permanent one just under the skin on your chest. I will have a remote control that will turn it off when I need you to work. But for now, we have to use this. As I said, I wasn't expecting you to think so rationally quite so quickly.'

'I hear you're used to dealing with prepubescent children. I'm guessing at this point they were quaking with fear and begging for their parents.'

'Actually you're right about that,' he said. 'Nurse, I'll need the batteries checked on this every two hours. I don't trust that she won't be testing it out as often as she can stand it.'

'Yes, Doctor.'

'But you know I could save you a lot of trouble right now and just tell you it is going to hurt like hell if you try it.'

'I'm sure it will,' Sara agreed.

'But sometimes a demonstration is always for the better, isn't it?' he asked, turning to leave the room.

'No need,' she said. 'I'll behave.'

'But then you'll always wonder what happened,' the doctor laughed, letting himself out the door while the device recognized the magic words and crackled to life. An electrical current surged through Sara's arm just as the vortex was opening around her and she began screaming while her consciousness was ripped back to the present.

He closed the door behind him and joined the other man at the nursing station, where they could watch the room on closed circuit television.

'It worked, didn't it?' he smiled.

'It worked, Andrew, she's perfect.'

'Fournier, I'm trusting you to be careful with her. She is the first subject that has made it this far. No matter what, we cannot lose her.'

'I'll do what I have to do,' Fournier said. 'I may not be as good as you, the great Beckman, but I do have some skills, Andrew.'

The two men smiled and continue to stare at the television monitor, proud of their creation.

Matt Grassi sat on the hospital bed. He was in his jeans and shirt, happy to be out of those stupid hospital pajamas. The doctor was supposed to be around in another couple of hours to discharge him. He was looking forward to that; a week in the hospital was almost more than he could take. He had papers strewn all over the bed, trying to review the cases he had been working on and see what he could remember about the mysterious Sara Hunter and why he had been at her house interviewing. He poured over the case files of her brother's murder, her best friend's car accident, the disappearance and subsequent murder of her boyfriend and now her brother's research partner, Ben Douglas. It all seemed to centre around Sara. Everyone else was dead and she was alive. There had to be something she knew, something that he might have suspected and that's why he was over at her house that night. He just couldn't seem to put the links together.

The doctor finally showed up and cleared him for discharge. Matt packed everything into his overnight bag slung it over his shoulder, ignored the orderly waiting with a wheelchair, and started down the hallway.

'Detective Grassi?'

He turned and saw a woman in her mid fifties, grey hair, running towards him, lab coat flapping in the breeze she was creating.

'I'm sorry?'

'Detective Grassi, I'm Dr. Stephenson. We've spoken before.'

'I'm sorry Doctor,' Matt apologized, putting on his charming smile. 'My memory is a little fuzzy right now.'

'I'm sure it is. I've been going over your chart and I'd say you're lucky to be alive, let alone have any memory left.'

'Were you one of my doctors?' he asked.

'I'm an anesthesiologist here at the hospital.'

'I remember,' he said. 'You were doing some research?'

'You were hoping I could give you some information on a doctor you were looking for.'

'Did you?' he asked, remembering she hadn't, but curious as to how she would answer the question.

'I didn't help you out at all,' she admitted. 'But I also wasn't totally truthful with you.'

'And why was that?' he asked.

'Detective Grassi, we have to talk.'

'I'm sure we do.'

'But I don't feel really comfortable talking about it at the hospital. I'm not sure if anyone else here is involved with this project, so I'd rather go somewhere else, where no one knows me.'

'Well, if it hasn't been towed, I'm told they left my car in the parkade.'

'No, I'll meet you. Do you know the restaurant across from the Sheraton downtown?'

'Sure.'

'I'll meet you there in thirty minutes. Get a booth.'

Matt sat inside the restaurant. It was packed with a lunch hour crowd, and noisy, which he was sure were the reasons Dr. Stephenson had chosen it. She walked through the door and saw him right away, hanging her coat on the rack and sliding into the booth across from him. She ran her hands through her spiky hair, and slid the menu over to the side of the table just as their waitress appeared.

'Are you ready?' she asked.

'I'll have the bacon cheeseburger, fries and gravy,' she said. 'With a large Coke.'

'I'll have the soup and salad,' Matt said, handing the menu to the waitress. He watched as she walked away and turned back to his lunch partner. 'Isn't that kind of food supposed to be bad for your heart?'

'Detective Grassi, I think that with what I've gotten myself involved in, cholesterol is the least of my worries.'

He laughed. 'So, are you going to share with me what you're involved in?'

'Well, a million years ago, when I was in medical school, my lab partner the first year was a man named Andrew Beckman.'

'Of Beckman Pharmaceuticals?' Grassi asked.

'Yes. Now, Andrew was an okay student and an average intern but he was driven. We both went into anesthesiology and through the luck of the draw, did our residency in the same hospital. Andrew was convinced that patient's could see things while they were unconscious. He kept a notebook and wrote down the things they said, or questioned them when they woke up. He was reprimanded a couple of times regarding his inappropriate behavior. Then, he got a job at a hospital in another city and that was the last I heard of him for several years.'

'I'm guessing that's not the end of the story.'

'The next thing I heard was that he got fired. I never heard why, but you rarely do, although eventually gossip starts filtering through the grapevine. And the grapevine was saying that he had been experimenting with some drug cocktails on some unsuspecting patients.'

'To what end?'

'No one knew for sure. He wasn't exactly forthcoming with his experiments, so he lost his license. But while he was doing this illegal research, he stumbled upon a new local anesthetic and the bastard patented it and made a million dollars. And that's how Beckman Pharmaceuticals was formed.'

'So have you heard from him since?'

'Not directly,' she said, pausing while the waitress put her plate down in front of her and she proceeded to drown her French fries in ketchup. 'But one day a Dr. Smith came to see me.'

'Smith?'

'Yeah, I'd never heard of him, and I figured out later it was probably not his real name. Apparently he was a hotshot professor of anesthesiology from somewhere. And he was working with Beckman on a research project. He told me Beckman couldn't stop talking about me and what a brilliant doctor I was, and how he needed me working on this research project with him.'

'Did this surprise you?' Grassi asked, through a mouthful of salad. 'To have these people clambering after you after all those years?'

'It should have. But I'm human, Detective. They were flattering me and I was enjoying it. And so I signed on.'

'And what was the research project about?'

'Well, there's the rub. It was about finding a combination of anesthetic and the right patient who would remember what they had seen in the OR while they were supposedly asleep.'

'Just what was Beckman doing before he got fired.'

'Pretty much. We always joke that there's three levels of anesthesia: asleep, awake and dead. Beckman honestly believes there is another level in there. A level where they can have a vision of something that's going on that they're not really present for.'

'So why didn't you back out?'

'Because I tried it on a patient.'

'You what?' he asked.

'I tried it on a patient. I was led to believe that we had the official okay for human testing and that the ethics department at my hospital had approved the study also. And then once I'd done it, they admitted it was all forged and fake.'

'So why didn't you go and tell someone?'

'Because I had no evidence. I didn't have copies of any of the documents. All I had were chart notes on the patient I had tested. I would have lost my license too. I was scared, Detective Grassi. I didn't know how to get out of it.'

'So then why are you telling me this now?'

'Because it's time. Because I want to sleep at night. I suspected that patients had been dying, but when he attacked you that was the first time I had proof he was actually killing people. I guess it was the straw that broke the camel's back.'

'I should probably advise you at this point that I'm going to have to arrest you.'

'You can arrest me if you want, Detective. But I think you need me right now. So let me help you. I swear I won't leave the country or disappear.'

The two parted company after lunch. Matt had some things to think over; he wanted to check out Dr. Stephenson's past and see if he could trust what she was saying. But first, he needed to go back to the scene of the crime. He drove over to Sara Hunter's house and parked in the driveway. The house was still circled with yellow crime scene tape and an officer stood guard outside the front door. Matt parked, sat in his car and stared for a few minutes, trying to force his brain to remember something. He finally got out, flashed his badge to the officer standing out front and then circled the outside of the house. He stopped near the back door, putting his hand on the door frame, hoping the house might share a memory with him. There was nothing. He opened the door and let himself in, as he had apparently done a week ago. He stood inside the door, listening for a whisper, a hint, a gust of wind that might spark a memory. He took a few steps in to the living room and stood above the bloodstain on the carpet, his brain hurting from the strain.

'I wonder what happened here?' he whispered to no one. And then he froze, as he heard her voice whisper back *I wonder what happened?* He turned to the couch and saw her lying there, fighting for breath, limbs twitching, eyes moving like she was caught in a horrendous nightmare.

'Sara?' he called to her.

'Help me,' she whispered to him, tears on her cheeks, her voice cracking, as she was fading away from him.

And he had wanted to help her, tried to help her and why couldn't he?

'Was it me, dear boy?' he heard the voice and spun around, expecting to see a benign looking elderly man crossing the room. But the room was empty. At least his memory wasn't quite so empty any longer. He knew where to start looking.

Matt raced out to his car and put it into gear, speeding towards the university medical school. He had to find a doctor. And when he found that doctor, he was pretty sure that Sara would be close by.

Chapter 15

'What is she trying to do?' the doctor asked, racing into the room in response to his emergency page. He surveyed his patient quickly, trying to ascertain her status.

'I don't know,' the nurse told him. 'She just keeps saying it. She goes into the vision and then the electrical current cuts in. As soon as it stops and she does it again.'

'She's going to kill herself.'

'Possibly.'

'Or at least she's going to cause some permanent damage,' the doctor said.

'I am aware of that, Dr. Fournier, that's why I called you.'

'Sara,' he said, shaking her roughly by the shoulders. 'Sara do you hear me? You're going to damage yourself. You need to stop doing this.'

'I can't,' Sara said, before another electrical shock took her breath away.

'What are you trying to see, what are you trying to discover?' he asked. 'Maybe I can tell you what you need to know.'

'You would never tell me the truth,' she gasped. 'I can't trust anything you would say.'

'Try me. Please, dear girl, you can't just keep doing this to yourself.'

'You can't stop me,' she cried. 'I wonder what happened.'

She screamed as more electrical current burned into her arm. The doctor dropped her back onto the bed.

'Sedate her,' he ordered.

'Are you sure?' the nurse asked. 'We don't know how it will interact with everything else we've put in her system over the last couple of days.'

'Do it,' he repeated. 'Keep her sedated until I can figure out how to get her under control.'

'Yes sir,' the nurse acquiesced. He filled a syringe and walked over to the bed, injecting it into the IV that was set up now in Sara's arm. 'You don't know what you're doing to yourself, girl.'

The two men stood and watched her. She fought the drugs, trying to stay conscious and in control.

'Just relax,' Fournier told her.

'No,' she mumbled. 'No, just let me go.'

'Just relax and don't fight it,' he soothed her. 'You can't win, dear, you can't win.'

Finally her eyes closed and her body relaxed. Fournier quickly checked her vital signs and then wrote some notes in the chart at the foot of her bed.

'I don't want her awake again until we're ready,' he instructed the nurse. 'Do you understand?'

'Yes doctor.'

And then he stormed out of the room. The nurse took a cloth and gently wiped the sweat off Sara's forehead before settling down at her bedside with his novel. Outside her door, Dr. Fournier pulled out his cell phone and dialed a number.

'Beckman Pharmaceuticals,' a pleasant voice said.

'Dr. Beckman please. Dr. Yves Fournier returning his call.'

'One moment doctor and I'll connect you.'

After a couple of minutes of seventies pop music blasting in his ear, the call was finally answered.

'Well,' the gruff voice barked at him.

'It worked, Andrew.'

'It did?'

'She's the most amazing subject I've seen. She can have visions at the drop of the hat and her vitals are rock steady. It's amazing to see after witnessing all the others.'

'We really did it?' Beckman asked. 'She's really stable?'

'She's brilliant, Andrew. Ben Douglas was right all along about the ages of the subjects,' he said. 'But we do have a couple of problems to work out still.'

'What kind of problems?' Beckman asked. 'Tell me you're not going to lose her?'

'No, she's perfectly stable. She's just not quite as obedient as the younger subjects.'

'Well, figure it out, Yves. Do whatever you have to do, but we have to have a success right now. I need to be able to tell the others that we have a success.'

'I understand. I'll figure out a way to tame her.'

'Without losing her.'

'Well, that does make it more difficult, doesn't it?' he laughed, but already the hint of an idea was forming in the corner of his mind.

Detective Matt Grassi walked up to the counter, his best smile on his face and a map of the university in his hand. He looked lost and harried. He wasn't, but he knew that looking slightly out of control would get him a lot more sympathetic help that storming in here waving a search warrant. He fumbled in his pocket for his wallet and pulled his detective badge out to show the lovely young woman standing at the counter waiting to greet him.

'Good afternoon,' he smiled at the young receptionist. 'I'm Detective Matt Grassi and I wonder if you could help me out?'

'Well, I can certainly try Detective,' she smiled back at him. 'What are you looking for?'

'I need to find a doctor.'

'For yourself?' she joked. 'You look very healthy to me.'

'Not for me,' he laughed with her. 'It's for a case. Now, I

know what this doctor looks like, but I don't know anything else about him.'

'What school he went to?' she tried.

'No.'

'Age, year he graduated?'

'Sorry.'

'Specialty?' she tried one last time.

He smiled slowly at her persistence, because he guessed it had just paid off. 'Anesthesiology.'

'Can you guess his approximate age, Detective?' she asked.

'Call me Matt.'

'I'm Linda.'

'Well, Linda, he looked older but he moved fast.'

'Detective?'

'Sorry, I'm guessing he's about thirty years older than me.'

'Mid fifties?' she asked.

'You're too kind. Let's try early to mid sixties instead.'

'All right, well that gives us some place to start,' she giggled. 'I can get some residency yearbooks and provide you a table to work at, but I'm afraid you're on your own after that.'

'That's okay because that's miles ahead of where I was an hour ago,' he smiled, and then made himself comfortable at the table she had led him to.

Sara opened her eyes slowly. Her brain was foggy and her mind was working very slowly. She wanted to try to gather her wits about her before she let them know she was awake. But she felt like she was swimming through molasses.

'Wakey, wakey,' she heard the doctor's voice call to her and then a nasty smell under her nose shocked her and her eyes blinked open.

'That's better,' he smiled at her.

'Good morning,' she tried a weak joke.

'Yes, well it's no longer morning.'

'Have you decided to trust me?' she asked.

'Have you decided to cooperate? He asked her.

'Of course, I'll cooperate fully and do whatever you want

me to,' she said, as sincerely as she could muster. 'Just don't hurt me anymore.'

'Yes, just as I thought. Nothing's changed.'

'No, really,' she insisted. 'I mean it.'

'Well, I'm glad you're serious about it, because I've come up with a way to help you stick to that resolution.'

She looked down at her arm where the appliance had been, only to notice there was just a dressing there, covering her burns.

'No, I've removed it,' he explained. 'I realize that you would just fight it until you died and that wouldn't accomplish anything.'

'So you do trust me?'

'No, dear, I don't trust you. But I think I've figured out a way that I can at least control you now.'

He nodded to the nurse, who went out into the corridor and came back with a small boy. The child was about ten years old, but looked underfed and under rested, with deep dark circles under his eyes. He had the appliance strapped to his arm.

'What are you doing?' she asked the doctor, trying to control her fear.

'I am teaching you that if you don't obey me somebody will suffer. And since you don't seem to care if it's you, I thought I would test a theory and see if you cared if it happened to someone else.'

'I'll do what you say,' she promised, and this time she was sincere.

'I'm sure you will. But I feel it important that you know I'm serious about this.'

'After everything else you've done, I'm pretty sure you're serious about this.'

'Yes, well I always like a little demonstration just to prove the point. So, you were so anxious to have a vision, why don't you say the magic words?'

'No, I'm fine,' she said. 'I won't do anything unless you want me to. I swear.'

'I want you to do this.'

'No.'

'But you said you'd do what I wanted.'

'I meant with research, with experimenting with me. Not this.'

'But Sara, this is what I want. I want you to say your cue phrase.'

'No,' she whispered, tears in her eyes. 'Please don't make me do this.'

'All right then, I won't make you do it,' he smiled, patting her hand and turning to leave.

'Thank you,' she whispered.

'I wonder what happened?' he hissed, as he opened the door and left the room.

She felt the gentle breeze start to sweep over her as the child sitting in the chair across from her started to scream as the electricity jolted through his tiny little arm.

Matt sat at the table and flipped through the seventeenth yearbook, photos swimming before his eyes. He flipped page after page, and the receptionist brought him yet another coffee, a service he was quite grateful for. And then he flipped over final page and he saw the face. That face smiling, as it had smiled at him while he lay dying on the floor. A face Matt would never forget again. He read the biographical information below the photo and then asked the receptionist to photocopy the page for him. He used her computer and did a google search, finding what he needed on the first try and printing it off. Now he had somewhere to start.

He took the papers and raced out to his car, driving across the campus and parking in a handicapped spot in front of the hospital. He threw his police ID on the dashboard so he wouldn't be towed and then raced inside. The line up for the elevator was long, so he pushed through the door and raced up the stairs. He ran past the receptionist on the floor, despite the fact that she was calling after him, and pushed his way into Dr. Stephenson's office.

'Detective Grassi?' she asked, looking up from her Dictaphone, shocked to see him standing there trying to catch his breath.

'This is the doctor that tried to kill me,' he told her, tossing the picture on her desk.

'Detective Grassi, have a seat and try and catch your breath. You've just been released from the hospital and you don't look very good right now. Do you want me to page your doctor for you?'

Matt did sit down but pushed the photo across her desk. 'Do you know this man?'

Dr. Stephenson looked down at the photocopy and studied it for a minute.

'Yes,' she said. 'That's Andrew Beckman.'

'Good. Now, please look at these,' he slid the other papers in front of her.'

'What's this?'

'This is the research team employed by Beckman Pharmaceuticals. I'd like to know if your Dr. Smith is one of these people?'

'This one,' she said, pointing to a photograph.

'Dr. Yves Fournier. Do you know anything about him?'

'Other than that one visit to my office, I have never heard of him before.'

'Okay, Dr. Stephenson, here's the way this is going to play out. You're going to have to deal with your licensing committees and you are probably going to go to jail. There is not a lot I can do to help you. But if you help me, I will make sure that whatever court is judging you knows that you cooperated.'

She stared down at her desk, not really knowing what to say.

'You said that people were dying,' Matt continued the pressure.

'Yes I did.'

'Doesn't that go against everything you were taught as a

doctor?'

'Yes, it does.'

'You have to help me Dr. Stephenson. At least three people that I know of have died so far. I almost died. And Sara Hunter is missing.'

'There's more than that,' she whispered. 'Somewhere out there is a research facility with some children that he has been experimenting on.'

'You were involved in this?' he asked.

'No. After that first patient my part only involved lab work But I'm not a stupid woman and I was able to figure some of it out. The rest of it came from a letter I received today.'

'A letter?' Matt asked. 'From who?'

'A Dr. Ian Hunter. He is a psychologist…'

'Was a psychologist…'

'He's dead?' she asked. 'I guess I knew that. He wouldn't have sent out a letter like this if he was alive and safe.'

'Do you have the letter?'

'I burned it. I read it and I was terrified. I didn't know what to do or how to get out of this. I threw it in the fireplace and then started packing my bags. I was going to try to get out of the country before anyone could find me.'

'But you're still here.'

'Don't kid yourself. I was leaving. I got as far as the city limits before I had calmed down a bit. Detective, I realized that I was partly responsible for what had happened. I had to try and do something to make it right. I couldn't do that if I was hiding out in Panama, could I?'

'You realize you're putting yourself in danger?' he asked.

'I am fully aware of that. But I'll help you out. Please just tell me what you need me to do.'

'Well, I think we should get you some place safe first,' Matt suggested.

'No. If I disappear they'll know something is up. This way, we've got some time before anyone catches on.'

'I can't protect you if you're out in the open like this.'

'I don't want your protection. I want to do something. Please tell me what you want me to do.'

'Well, the first thing I need may just be a personal favour. Is there any way you can call a doctor in another city and get some information on a patient?'

'Probably, if I can convince him that I've got some sort of relationship to the patient. Who is it?'

'Here's the name of the doctor and his number,' Matt said, pulling a paper from his wallet. 'The patient's name is Samuel Roberts.'

'Can you tell me a little bit about him? Just so I don't sound like I'm lying to this doctor when I'm lying to him?'

'It's my partner's father. He had a stroke a few days into this investigation and my partner had to fly home. I'm just wondering though if it really was a stroke or if something else might have happened to him.'

'Okay. I'll see what I can find out. Do you want to wait and see if I get through to the doctor right now?' she asked.

'No, I have some other things to do. Call me on my cell phone when you know something.'

'I will,' she said, pulling his business card out of her rolodex. 'Detective Grassi, this missing girl...do you know if she was having any medical treatments? Getting any sort of injections?'

'They were injecting her,' Matt confirmed.

'Then I'm afraid I have to tell you that she is probably already dead,' she said softly.

'No, she's not,' he said. 'I'm still a little fuzzy on the details, but they figured out how to stabilize her. She was having these visions and her heart was going crazy and she thought she was going to die.'

'They get more out of control as time goes on. The patient usually doesn't survive beyond two weeks unless they're put into a chemically induced coma.'

'The night she disappeared, the night I was attacked, Andrew Beckman was there. He gave her a third injection and said she'd be fine.'

'And was she?'

'I think so, I think her heart rate had slowed down but that's right when he attacked me.'

'It's amazing,' she said. 'I can't believe they did it.'

'Doctor?'

'Detective, I'm horrified with their methods but the discovery is amazing. They are uncovering parts of the mind that we have never understood.'

'And how many people have they killed to do it?'

'I know, I know. And we have to find that poor girl, because they might not kill her but I cannot believe her life is going to be easy.'

Chapter 16

'No,' Sara screamed, arching her back as the pain seared through her.

'Why do you fight me on everything I ask?' he said, turning the dial to off. But secretly he would be disappointed if she didn't.

'I don't know,' she admitted, trying to straighten herself up in the chair. 'You ask me to do things that don't sit really well with my conscience.'

'I don't want to hurt you.'

'And I don't want to be hurt.'

'Good. So now I want you to do what I tell you. Please, Sara, let's not do this every day.'

'You're right,' Sara said. 'Let's not. Why don't we go to the zoo or have a picnic instead?'

'Okay, okay. I want you to go to the bank robbery from last week.'

'Look, can't we make a deal?' Sara asked. 'How about if I tell you where the money is and you promise to tell the police who the robbers are after I've seen them?'

'No.'

'But they shot two bank tellers.'

'I know my dear. But how would you have me tell the

police that I knew who the robbers were without arising some suspicion?'

'I'm not sure. But you're a clever man doctor.'

'And I'm a late man, Sara. We've been arguing for almost the entire day in here and you've given me one vision and it was not what I wanted. So we're going to call it quits for today. Tomorrow, there will be a child in here. And every time you say no to me, they will feel the pain. I'd like you to think very carefully about that tonight and then tomorrow, maybe we can take some journeys through your visions,' he turned to the nurse standing by her side. 'Take her back to her room and lock her up for the night.'

'You know, I can't control where I go in my visions.'

'How do you know if you're not even going to try?'

The nurse undid her restraints and took her arm firmly in his grasp. She let herself be led past the doctor and towards the door.

'Why don't you just kill me?' she asked him as she was pulled through the door. 'You've killed everyone else I cared about.'

'Sara, you are far too valuable. You and I have a lot of research to do before our relationship is over. But years from now, you can rest assured that you will have made a major contribution to medical science. What you have done here will touch thousands of lives. Far more than if you had just earned your degree and become a psychologist.'

Sara turned from him in disgust and hurried down the hall with the nurse.

'Do you have a name other than nurse?' Sara asked.

'Of course,' he said.

'Well?'

'We're not allowed to share our names. The doctor believes that if the patients are allowed to call us by name, we might get more attached to them.'

'And what's so wrong with that?'

'Well, it's hard to stand there and watch him zap a patient

you've bonded with. Sort of goes against my training.'

'Don't you think I'd be more cooperative if we developed a bond of some sort.'

'It's possible, but Sara, I'm afraid if I were in your position I would fight with everything I had to get as far from this place as I could. No matter who got in my way.'

'Is that your advice to me?' she asked.

'God, no. They're willing to kill to make you have a vision. You should know that by now. My advice as your nurse is to quit worrying about your conscience and start worrying about your survival. You may not have an outstanding quality of life here, Sara, but at least you have a life. And where there's life, there's hope.'

'There may be hope, but there's no point. Everyone's gone.'

'Yes. Everyone's gone. And your life is changed forever. But as long as you're alive, you will have these visions. So that's the starting point. Now you have to decide where to go from there.'

He opened the door to her room.

'Easy for you to say, asshole,' she responded, walking through the open door.

'Hey. shouldn't you be a little nicer to the man who is going to go and get your dinner for you?' he joked.

'You can't starve me, they won't let you.'

'You're right about that,' he said. 'I'll be back in about twenty minutes.'

And then he closed and locked her door.

She sat down on the bed. She had already searched the room for anything she could use as a weapon. And there was nothing. No point searching again. And she was sure there were video cameras everywhere, so that even if she did find something they would be in here in seconds to take it from her. But that didn't matter. She knew where she was going from here. Somehow, she was going to kill that bastard doctor. And then with her brother's death avenged, nothing else mattered.

The door opened and Sara looked up, expecting her nurse

with the dinner tray. But it wasn't. It was Dr. Fournier.

'What's wrong? What's happened?' she asked, concerned about the change in her routine. He must want something from her.

'Come with me, dear, I want to take a little walk. I think you need to see our clinic.'

She stood up uncertainly. He nodded and the nurse came in after him, taking Sara's arm and pulling her out the door and along the corridor.

'What did you want me to see?' she asked.

'Well, you've seen this floor; you've seen our rooms here and our little laboratory. But I thought I would like you to see upstairs. It's where we keep some of the really ill children.'

'And why do you want me to see the children?'

'Because, Sara, I've been told that we aren't moving along fast enough. We're not going to play our little games any longer, we have to get serious. I want you to see these poor little children and know that you are the only one that can save them.'

'Me?' she asked, following him into the elevator.

'There is something inside you that allowed this drug to work. If we can find that, we can save these children. But conversely, Sara, you can kill them too. Every time you don't cooperate with us, we will kill one of these children. Plain and simple. So I want you to see them, so that when you make your choice in the laboratory tomorrow, you are making an informed choice.'

She didn't know what to say, so rode the rest of the way in silence. When the elevator doors opened, she really was speechless. They walked into an elevated room that looked almost like mission control, looking out over a huge circle of intensive care beds. There were several nurses manning the monitors. She took a step forward and looked through the glass. All the beds were full of children of various ages. But the one thing they had in common was that they were all unconscious. Some were hooked up to respirators, some were breathing on their own. Sara looked back at the monitors, trying to understand the brain wave read outs showing on the EEGs.

'Are they in comas?' Sara asked.

'Yes. Some are medically induced and some were created by Mother Nature to save them from what was happening to their brains.'

She put her hands on the glass, as if she could reach out and heal them. 'How many?'

'That isn't important.'

'It isn't important?' she gasped.

'We are still studying them, Sara. They are hooked up to an incredible array of monitors and we have specialists in here, interpreting the read outs and other tests, trying to figure out a pathway to reach into their brains. This is one of the best equipped ICUs you'll find in the country, my dear. The things we are uncovering with our research is amazing.'

'They're children.'

'They are patients. And we are learning so much from each of them. Hopefully what we learn from them will prevent the next generation of subjects from dying.

She turned and started at him, trying to decide if there was anything human left inside him. And then, before she realized what she was doing, she slapped his face. Hard. There was a red hand print already forming on his cheek. But he didn't flinch. He didn't even blink hard. He just stared at her and smiled slowly.

'I think I've accomplished what I need to here,' he told the nurse. 'Take her back to her room.'

Sara picked at her dinner and, after her plate was taken away, she turned in. There was nothing else to do. No television, no magazines or newspapers. There was a deck of playing cards but she was tired of solitaire. She lay in bed and started at the ceiling. The nights were interminable. Nothing to do but think and nothing to distract her. And tonight, the images that were dancing across her closed eyelids were especially horrifying. No matter where she tried to make her mind go, she kept coming back to those beds and those poor children, sick and helpless, slowly dying while the doctors picked at their last shreds of dignity, trying to find out where their experiments had gone wrong. And all Sara could do was to lie in bed and pray for the relief sleep would finally bring her.

Matt Grassi lay on his couch, having given up on his bed. He hadn't been sleeping well at all since he got out of the hospital. He didn't like losing someone he was supposed to protect and the fact that he had no leads on Sara was not helping matters. And he sure as hell didn't like that fact that someone had almost killed him. It seems he was stuck with this investigation that was going nowhere. His cell phone started vibrating, bouncing its way across the coffee table. He turned and grabbed it, flipping it open.

'Grassi,' he said.

'Detective Grassi, I'm so sorry to wake you.'

'Who is this?'

'It's Dr. Stephenson.'

'What is it?' he asked, sitting up and paying attention now.

'I've just had some rather unsettling results about your partner's father. It seems it wasn't so much a stroke as they first thought. After I suggested a careful drug screening and what to screen for, they found traces in his system.'

'Oh my God.'

'Well, I guess they wanted your partner out of the way and that was the quickest way to make it happen, short of actually killing her.'

'I guess they weren't ready to kill a police officer.'

'Yet. They've since tried, if you recall.'

'I've got to call her…' Matt started.

'I've already spoken to her and the doctors have arranged for police protection. I came up with quite a good story about loan sharks and mob money. And with the drugs in his system, the doctors and the police all found it quite believable.'

'Thank you,' Grassi said.

'There's more Detective,' she said, before he could hang up. 'I had an idea about how we could find the girl.'

'How's that?'

'Well, you had mentioned that Dr. Ben Douglas was seeing some patients at a private clinic?'

'That's what Sara told me. When I found out he was linked to this research group, I figured this private clinic was too much of a coincidence and probably had something to do with his research, but we haven't been able to locate it yet.'

'Well, I've managed to track down the clinic through a couple of internal referrals Dr. Douglas made for some surgical patients. I can't imagine he'd be affiliated with more than one private clinic so this must be what you're looking for.'

'I think I'm impressed with your detective work.'

'The other thing I discovered was that Dr. Yves Fournier has privileges at that same clinic. And I'm sure if you could get into the records you will probably find that Beckman Pharmaceuticals has something to do with it, too.'

'Okay, that's good. Do you think anyone is suspicious of you checking this out?'

'No, I kept it very quiet. And just to cover my tracks, I asked a bunch of questions about several other doctors too. If anyone questions it, I'll just tell them I have a friend with a sick son and I was trying to find a facility for them.'

'Doctor, you appear to be a born liar. Now give me the address of this place.'

'I thought I'd come pick you up and we could go together,' she said.

'No, doctor, it's too dangerous. Just give me the address.'

'Detective, if you go in there with your gun and badge they're just going to send you away until you have a warrant. If I go in as a doctor, I stand a much better chance of getting somewhere.'

'It's too dangerous.'

'So is getting out of bed.'

'Doctor.'

'I don't have to tell you where it is at all,' she said. 'And unless you start listening to me I won't.'

'Okay.'

'Really?' she asked, not believing her threat had actually worked.

'Yes. But I'll drive. When can you be ready?'

'How about for eight thirty tomorrow morning?'

'How about twenty minutes?' he asked.

'Again, detective, if we have a chance of getting in there, we need to show up during regular daylight hours, not in the middle of the night.'

'Okay, okay. I'll be at your office at eight o'clock.'

'They're not going to kill her, Detective. They need her alive,' the doctor tried to reassure him.

'It's what they're doing to her to get her to cooperate that I'm worried about.'

'It's nighttime. I'm guessing she's sleeping, like we should be. They'll want her well rested for the days ahead. That's what I would want, anyway.'

'I hope you're right, doctor.'

'So do I.'

Sara lay in bed, thinking carefully. It was probably three o'clock in the morning. The guards were bored with watching her sleep and she didn't think she'd draw any attention to herself. Sara was working on her visions. Each night she would lie here quietly and force herself to have as many as she could. She didn't have to say her cue line out loud anymore, she could just think about it and off she went. She didn't know if Fournier was right about being able to control where her visions took her or not, but she was going to try everything in her power to make it happen. It would be the one way she could get free of these people. But mostly she wanted to know how she was going to kill Dr. Fournier. That was something that preoccupied her thoughts during the dark lonely nights. And she prayed that the first vision she could control would show her how she was going to kill Fournier. It sounded cold and harsh when she stopped to think about it, so she didn't think about it for long. Besides, all she really had to do was think about him with those children, about the pain and suffering he caused them, anything to get results from his experiments.

'I wonder what happened,' she whispered quietly, so softly there was barely a breath passing over her lips.

And what used to be a harsh gale force wind but was now a gentle tropical breeze blew through her mind and swept her away. But as always, it didn't sweep her to where she wanted. She was in a living room, watching a boy watch TV. It was Saturday morning cartoons and he was giggling away. He laughed and giggled some more as the program came to an end, and then stood up and walked to the television, changing to channel.

'Yves Lawrence Fournier, you are not going to watch TV all morning. You need to go out and play; it's a beautiful sunny day out there.'

'Yes, mother, just one more show please.'

He didn't wait for her answer and was singing along with the theme song of the next show as he sat back down on the couch. But in that moment when he had reached up to change the channel she had seen a small flash of gold, and she thought she might know how she could get out of this hell hole.

When the breeze was gone, she laid in bed, quietly listening to see if anyone had caught on, if they were coming to try and stop her. But the corridors were quiet. The guard had probably been watching TV and hadn't noticed a thing. Sara tried to figure out the missing pieces of the puzzle and how she could use this little piece of knowledge to her advantage.

Detective Grassi disconnected the phone and set it on the table. It was too early in the morning to call his partner, and he had nothing new to add, since everything was already taken care of as far as protection for her and her family. He reached for the remote and turned off the television, determined to get some sleep so he'd be on his best game tomorrow. He rolled off the couch and made himself return to his bed. But he wasn't any better off than he had been a couple of hours ago, his eyes refused to close, his brain refused to turn off and he started at the ceiling. He couldn't stop thinking of Sara, of where she was and how she was being treated, or if she was even still alive. But mostly he was worried about whether she was scared. It was his fault she was there and he could picture her all alone in her bed at night, terrified of what was going to happen to her tomorrow.

Chapter 17

Matt drove the car down the country road, away from the clinic. It had ended up taking them two days to get past the front gates of the private clinic. They had finally been granted an appointment with the director, but when they arrived, he had unfortunately been called off on a medical emergency. The appointment was rescheduled for two days later and the pair was escorted off the property by a very serious looking security guard. Matt was pissed off but trying not to let it show. There was total silence in the car. Christine Stephenson sat still as a stone beside him, the anger that was emanating from her equaling the frustration that was oozing from his pores. She wasn't used to being denied access to a patient and he wasn't used to being denied access to anything. But if he could get a search warrant today, it would be an entirely different story tomorrow morning. He was just running through a list of sympathetic judges in his mind when Dr. Stevenson grabbed the dashboard.

'Watch out!' she screamed, bracing herself.

Matt saw it at the exact same instant the doctor had screamed. A girl, with bare feet, in a torn t-shirt and jeans, was, running out onto the road waving them down. He slammed on the brakes and veered out of the way. He threw the car into park and jumped out on the road before it was fully stopped.

'Are you fucking crazy?' he yelled, letting his anger spill into his voice.

'Matt?' she asked, thinking her eyes were deceiving her.

'Sara?' he asked, as much disbelief in his voice as there was in hers.

'You're dead,' she said, starting to cry. 'Oh my God, this is just a vision.

'I'm here Sara,' he told her.

'It's not fair,' she screamed. 'It's not fair. I didn't ask for any of this to happen to me.'

'Sara, it's okay.' He heard the car door open and turned to see Dr. Stephenson get out of the car.

She took a few steps towards him. 'Detective Grassi?'

'It's okay,' Matt said. 'It's okay.'

'I didn't make it out,' she cried. 'I'm still a prisoner. Why is this happening to me?'

Matt hurried over to where she stood and reached out to take her hand. She stopped crying when she felt his skin on hers, and looked down at his hand.

'You feel so real,' she said. 'Maybe I'm dying. Maybe that third injection didn't work.'

'I'm real, Sara,' he said. 'I'm real and you're safe.'

'You're not real. You died.'

'I didn't die. The neighbours called the police and they got me to the hospital in time. I'm real and you're safe.'

'I'm really out?' she asked. 'I really made it out of there?'

'You're really safe and you really made it out of there,' he confirmed.

She almost fell into his arms, tears flowing freely now.

'Thank God,' she cried.

'Come on, we need to get out of here,' he said, leading her back to the car. 'Dr. Stephenson, can you drive?'

'Who's she?' Sara asked, the tears stopping as fear begin to overtake her again.

'She's a friend,' Matt explained. 'She's on our side.'

'She's a doctor. What kind of doctor is she?'

'Sara, she knows all about it. She was part of the project. Now she wants to help.'

'And you trust her?' Sara asked, pulling away from him, as he was trying to get her into the car.

'Yes, I do,' Matt said, simply.

For a moment she hesitated, looking like she was ready to run, and then she changed her mind and climbed into the back seat, followed by Matt.

'Where to?' the doctor asked from the front seat.

'Home?' Sara practically begged.

'It's not safe,' Matt said. 'Nowhere that we usually go would be safe. Let's go to one of those motels on the city limits. We'll check in for the night until we can decide what to do.'

'I don't have any clothes or anything,' Sara said, looking down at her legs and trying to brush away the stains.

Matt looked at her jeans and realized they were covered with blood.

'I'm sorry,' Sara said, trying to cover them up.

'I'm not going to ask you anything,' Matt said. 'Just tell me that you're okay and I don't need to know anything else.'

'I've never hurt anyone before,' she said. She sat up straight in the backseat, pulling away from Matt.

'It's okay Sara. You had to get out of there. Whatever you had to do is okay.'

'Is that where he's keeping the children?' Dr. Stephenson asked from the front seat, trying to change the subject.

'It's where they are,' she confirmed. 'Some of them are very sick. It was horrifying.'

'We should go back,' Matt said, pulling his cell phone out. 'I can have half the police force there in thirty minutes.'

'No,' Sara interrupted, taking the cell phone from his hand. 'We can't just go in and close the place down. Half of those kids will die.'

'We have to do something,' Matt said. 'We can't just let them keep the kids locked up there, experimenting on them.'

'We need to figure out how to help them medically, not just get them out of there.'

'Sara, I think I can try to help them,' Dr. Stephenson tried to reassure her.

'Maybe you can, but if the police go in they won't let you touch them. They'll put them all in ambulances and take them off to the nearest hospital where they will die. We have to come up with a better plan. When I was in there I swore that if I got out I would try and rescue them.'

'What's your plan?' Matt asked.

'I don't really know. I can't think right now,' she said. 'I'm hungry and I'm tired. If we could just get something to eat and have a little nap, I promise I'll tell you everything after that.'

'I think that's a good idea,' Dr. Stephenson said.

'Okay, but room service in the room. I don't want a lot of people seeing us. They are going to be looking for you.'

Matt checked into the motel and got adjoining rooms for them. He settled Dr. Stephenson in one room and then opened the door to the other room for Sara. Now that he had found her there was no way he was letting her out of his sight again. He ordered food for her and by the time he rolled the empty tray outside of the room, she was asleep on the bed. He sat on the bed beside her, pulling his gun out and setting it on his lap. His eyes were heavy from too little sleep and too much stress over the last few weeks. He decided a few hours of sleep wouldn't hurt him either.

Sara turned over and Matt's eyes popped open, his hand gripping the gun.

'You okay?' he asked, eyes scanning the darkened room.

'I'm okay. Actually, I almost feel human again. How long have I slept?'

He turned to look at the clock on the bedside table, 'It's two thirty in the morning.'

'Wow that was a long nap. I'm sorry.'

'You obviously needed it.

'Where's Dr. Stephenson?' Sara asked.

'She's sleeping.' he said, after checking the adjoining room. 'I guess she was worn out too.'

Matt put his gun on the bedside table and sat down. 'Do you want some tea or something?'

'No, I'm just going to get a glass of water and go to the bathroom. Then I'll tell you everything I know, okay?'

'Okay.'

Matt piled some pillows behind him and got comfortable. Sara came back from the bathroom, just in her t-shirt, and climbed under the covers.

'I'm glad you didn't die,' she said. 'But why were you on that road at the same time I was there?'

'It must have been fate helping us out. We had just left the clinic,' Matt said. 'Dr. Stephenson did some investigating and found that Ben Douglas had sent some kids to that clinic. We assumed they were some kids that had been experimented on, so we decided to check it out and see what we could find. I thought if the kids were there, you probably would be too.'

'But you didn't find anything?' she asked.

'We didn't get past the reception desk,' he said. 'We were supposed to have an appointment with the director but he kept putting us off. They were very insistent that we were not coming in without the director's authorization or a search warrant.'

'So it was just coincidence?' she asked.

'I guess it was. How did you end up on that road?'

'Well, after they tried to kill you and kidnapped me, I woke up in the clinic, in a hospital bed, fully restrained. I'd been doped up for I don't know how long and my brain was fuzzy. There was a doctor there, Dr. Fournier, and he explained that we were going to work together and figure out why I hadn't died like all the others. He was there from the moment I woke up and he never left me alone. Have a vision. That was his favourite phrase. Find out what happened here, find out what happened there.'

'And did you?'

'Have you ever been tortured?' Sara asked.

'No.'

'Well, I have been now. They started with electricity, so I would only have a vision when they wanted me to. When that didn't work, they brought in one of the children. Anytime I didn't do what they wanted, they zapped the kid. So then that's when I started doing almost what they wanted.'

'Almost?'

'I was practicing at night,' she explained. 'That third injection did stabilize whatever was happening to me and I learned that I could have a vision without trauma. Fournier thinks I should be able to control the visions, tell them where to take me, what to show me.'

'Can you?'

'No. Once in a while I've seen something that's sort of related to what I want, but it's just coincidental. One thing I learned, though, is that I don't just have visions of things that have happened in the past. Some of the things I've seen haven't happened yet.'

'What?'

'It's rare. Or at least right now it is. Maybe I'll get better at the future stuff. But it's happened a couple of times.'

'How did you do it, Sara? How did you get out of there?'

'Well, I had a vision of Fournier when he was little and I noticed he wore a medic-alert bracelet. The next day, when he was checking my eyes, he held my head steady with that arm and I could see that he was allergic to a whole bunch of antibiotics. So I told them I had a bladder infection and they started me on antibiotics.'

'Don't they do a lab test first?'

'Any woman knows that they put you on antibiotics before the labs come back. And that's what they did. I started palming my pills. I had forty-eight hours before they could culture my urine to prove I was fine. Forty-eight hours to try to get out of there before they caught on to me. I took a syringe from one of the sharps containers. Then I filled it with the antibiotics and carried it in my pocket, waiting for the right moment.'

She took a sip of the water she had brought back from the bathroom with her.

'You don't have to go on,' he said.

'Yes I do. You need to know the whole story,' she took another sip of water and then pulled the covers up around her.

'Are you cold?' he asked. 'I can turn the heat up.'

'It's not my body, it's more like my soul,' she said. 'It's comfort I need, Matt, not heat.'

He moved closer to her, taking her hand.

'So he took me into the lab one day and sent the nurse out for something. We were alone. I pretended to faint. He came over to take my pulse and I jabbed him with the hypodermic needle. In a matter of seconds he was on the ground, clutching his throat, trying to get a breath through his swollen throat. I sat there and watched him die, Matt.'

'You did what you had to do.'

'And then the nurse came back into the room.'

'And she let you go?'

'He was named Vince and he was six feet tall. I thought I was going to die. He pulled a scalpel out of the drawer and walked over to me. I couldn't talk. I knew I should be begging and pleading for my life, but I couldn't open my mouth. And to be honest, I was happy it was going to be over soon. But then he handed me the scalpel.'

'What?'

'He said that the only way my escape would be believable was if I hurt him. Then he could still look after the children.'

'So what did you do?' Matt asked gently.

'I cut him. He made me promise I would bring help back for the kids. Then he told me to knock him over the head. I did and gave him a good bruise I imagine, and he pretended he was knocked out.'

'And you?'

'He told me where the fire escape was and I got my butt out of there before anyone else could notice I was gone.'

He squeezed her hand and smiled down at her. 'You are amazing.'

'I'm not amazing. But I'm changing my Master's thesis subject. I'm going to write about the survival instinct because I've learned what a person will do to survive.'

'And what about the kids?'

'Tell me, is that doctor next door really going to help us?' she asked.

'She says she is ready to go to jail if she has to, and I believe her'

'Well, then lets talk about the kids in the morning over breakfast. She needs to hear everything if she is really going to help. But Matt, if she can do anything, you have to keep her out of jail.'

'I don't know if I can do that.'

'You don't understand, you have to promise me that you will. If you don't Matt, I'll disappear and I'll take her with me.'

'All I can promise you is that I'll do everything in my power to help.'

'That's a start but it's still not enough,' she said. 'You'll understand tomorrow.'

She settled in under the covers.

'Are you going back to sleep?' he asked.

'The other thing I'm learning is to sleep and eat whenever you can, because you never know when you'll get a chance to do it again,' she said. 'That goes for you too. Come on, get under the covers and get some solid sleep.'

'No, I'm on guard duty. I'll watch out for you.'

'Matt, if anything happens we can take care of it together. For now, I need to sleep and I need to feel you next to me, so I feel safe.'

She noted his hesitation and looked up at him.

'Please,' she said softly.

He pulled off his t-shirt and climbed under the covers beside her. She wrapped her arms around him, holding him tightly. He held her, trying to make her feel safe. And soon her breathing slowed and she was asleep, though her grip on him never loosened.

In the morning, they sat around the table, their breakfast dishes empty, and the waitress faithfully refilling their coffee cups. They had filled Dr. Stephenson in on everything that had happened during Sara's escape and then she told them about the children and what she wanted to do.

'So, that's the vision I had. I know where we end up and I know the kids are there so I guess we saved at least some of them but I still don't know how.' Sara said. 'Do you think we can do it?'

'Sara, do you always see the truth?' Dr. Stephenson asked. 'Or maybe I should ask if the future can change? What if this vision you had was just a dream? I mean a dream that anyone could have. What if you were just hoping that's where we might end up? In a nice peaceful country ranch?'

'I don't know. I don't know enough about any of this yet. I know I don't always see what I want to see, sometimes I just can't get a vision or I go somewhere strange, like opening day at Disneyland or something. But this one came through loud and strong. I saw the hospital we built and I saw some of the kids actually outside playing. I don't know if it's true or not but I think we have to try, Dr. Stephenson.'

'Well, if we're going to work together, you should probably call me Chris.'

'Well, Chris, you and I are in this no matter what. Matt, you're a different story. You have a career and you don't have to be here. As a matter of fact, if you were smart you would go right back to the police precinct and pretend none of this had happened.'

'You didn't see me in the vision, did you?' he asked.

'No I didn't. But Matt, what I see is limited, like a little vignette of the day, a slice of what might be. You could have been there with us, just doing something else.'

'You can't really believe that I could just walk away from all this.'

'Matt, it's different for you,' she said, laying her hand gently on his. 'I had no choice about getting involved in this thanks to Ben. Chris can't get out either because of the choices she made. But you, you have a career and a life. You were just investigating this as part of your job. You've done nothing wrong. Matt you could go back to work right after breakfast and nothing in your life would change. I totally understand you not wanting to give up your life to pursue some crazy woman who is having insane visions and a megalomaniacal doctor…sorry Chris.'

'No offence taken,' Chris laughed.

'And I have to be honest, Matt, if I had the choice to turn around and walk out of here, I might just do it.'

'You wouldn't.'

'I would be very tempted.'

'You're trying to make it simple for me to walk away,' he said. 'But this is not an easy decision. I don't believe your vision, Sara. I don't think I would leave you to our own devices and just walk away from you. I also find it hard to believe I can just walk away from my job, the law, and become some sort of vigilante. It would be so much easier if you could have lied to me and just told me you saw me there with you.'

'I couldn't do that to you.'

'So you're not going to make this easy, huh?'

'I guess not.'

'Well, Sara, Chris, I don't think I can just go back to work and forget about those kids. I need to help.'

'I didn't think you could Matt.'

'Well, we know where we're going to wind up,' Sara said. 'I just wish I knew how we were going to get there.'

Chapter 18

Sara was scared. She hadn't been out in public since her escape. And she was alone. Matt was parked in the underground parkade, waiting for her. She thought that the two of them together might draw a little too much attention. But if she was alone, especially with her new hair colour, she might not be noticed walking down the busy hospital corridor. Every time she passed someone wearing a lab coat, a shiver went up and down her spine. Sara worked hard to keep her panic under control as she wound her way through the corridors to neurology, where she checked in and waited for her appointment.

After breakfast at the hotel, Sara had gone back to her room claiming she needed to rest. She lay down and pretended to nap, while Matt and Chris hung out in the other room. But instead of sleeping, she had forced herself to have visions. She lay on the bed all afternoon, forcing herself to try and see more; to figure out what they were going to do and how they were going to do it. The minute she recovered from one vision, she would write down everything she could remember, every little detail, in case it was something important, something that would make a difference to their fate. Then she put the pen down and whispered to herself *I wonder what happened* and she would be back into another vision. By early evening, when Matt and Chris came in to check on her, she was so exhausted she could barely talk. Chris checked her vital signs and Matt fussed over her, both worried she was pushing herself too far. But her vital signs were stable and they were able to get her to eat a bit of a supper. Finally, they left her alone and she slept for almost eighteen hours.

Matt woke her up for a room service breakfast the next morning. Sara stretched and pulled the covers tightly around her.

'Come on,' Matt said, pulling the covers away.

'I don't want to get up,' she protested.

'How are you feeling?'

'Better,' she said, stretching again and then sitting up. 'Can I have some coffee?'

Matt poured two cups, keeping one for himself.

'You scared me yesterday,' Matt told her, sipping his coffee.

'I had to try and find out what was going to happen.'

'It won't help us if you put yourself in a coma or worse.'

'I know. But I think I can control it.'

'You just slept for eighteen hours, Sara. You drained yourself yesterday.'

'But I'm fine today.'

'Sure, today, right now. But how long do you think your body can take this.'

'We can't have this fight every time I try and have a vision.'

'It's not a fight, it's a discussion.'

'We need to find a middle ground somewhere,' she said. 'You need to figure out that I can't give this up.'

'And you need to figure out that I'm not willing to let you die.'

'That's a goal I can live with,' she laughed.

Somehow he was looking at her differently, today. She wasn't quite sure what it meant, but it was different.

'Did any of these visions help us though?' he asked. 'Did we learn anything we didn't know already?'

'No.'

'But…'

'But what if they had?'

'And what if I lost you?'

'I think I need to go see a doctor,' she said.

'Are you okay?'

'The visions may not have helped. But there was a name I heard a couple of times when I was at the clinic. Dr. Peter Schmidt.'

'Do you know him?' Matt asked. 'What kind of a doctor is he?'

'I don't know anything about him. But if the visions aren't going to be helpful, then maybe we should try it your way.'

'I'll get you an appointment right after breakfast.'

'I'm sorry I scared you,' she said.

Dr. Peter Schmidt had turned out to be a neurologist and it was actually Chris who was able to get an emergency appointment within a couple of days for a fictitious patient. And that was how Sara came to be in his waiting room, trying to be inconspicuous while she waited for the nurse to call her name.

Eventually, a nurse came out, showed her to an exam room and left her with a history form to fill out. She didn't bother, since she had no intention of becoming a real patient of this doctor.

'Ms. Jones?' he asked, coming in and perching on a stool.

'Yes.'

'Dr. Schmidt,' he introduced himself, shaking her hand. 'Now, did the nurse leave you a questionnaire to fill out?' he asked.

'Uh, yes she did. But one of the problems I'm having right now is seeing things clearly.'

'Okay, well we'll get someone to help you out with that after we're finished here. In the meantime, are you on any medications?'

'No.'

'Parents alive and healthy?'

'They died in a fire. But they were healthy before that. There are no diseases or anything that I know of in our family.'

'And you're having some problems with your eyes?'

'I am definitely having a problem seeing things,' she admitted.

He pulled a penlight out of his pocket and turned it on. He put one hand on her forehead and then held the light up to her eyes.

'Just follow the light please,' he instructed her. 'Any other problems?'

'Well I've been having some dizzy spells.'

'Tell me about those.'

'I get this swimming feeling in my head, I feel like there is a strong wind blowing in my brain and sometimes I feel nauseous.'

'How often does this happen?' he asked.

'Well, it's hard to say time-wise, but it always happens right before I have a vision.'

Despite the shock he must have felt, you had to give him credit, the penlight never stopped moving and his voice never wavered.

'Visions?' he said, finally turning the light off and then holding his hands up to her. 'Squeeze my fingers please.'

She took his fingers in her hands and squeezed as hard as she could. 'Yes, visions. Have you heard of Beckman Pharmaceuticals?'

He pulled his hands away from hers and wheeled his chair backwards. 'I think I'll get a nurse to help you fill out that form before we go on.'

'Dr. Schmidt, you need to hear me out. I was injected.'

'I'm afraid I don't know what you're talking about.'

'I was injected three times. And guess what? It worked. My brain didn't turn to gelatin and ooze out my ears. I now have controlled visions.'

'No!' he gasped. 'It's not possible.'

'It's true.'

'How did you know about me?' he asked.

'I had a vision, Dr. Schmidt and you were in it,' she lied.

'But I've never done any of the injections; I've only worked with the patients afterwards. The ones that didn't stabilize.'

'I know. That's what I saw. And you didn't do it for the research or the money. You did it to try and help the kids. I saw that too.' She was watching his face carefully for a reaction, but she was getting everything right, she could tell.

'I don't even know what to say,' he told her. 'I had no idea there had been any successes.'

'Well apparently I'm the one. And I wasn't exactly a volunteer.'

'Beckman doesn't believe in volunteers. He believes in taking what he needs when he needs it. But why haven't they told us about you?'

'I guess I'm a secret. They've been keeping me in Dr. Fournier's lab for the last little while. I think they wanted to find out what made me tick before they told anyone. But I saw the kids, Dr. Schmidt. How can you let them do that? It's like a horror movie.'

'I'm only one man and there was nothing I could do to stop them. I thought I might be able to help one or two of those children afterwards and that's why I've stayed at the clinic.'

'Well, we think we can help them out in greater numbers than that. And we think that maybe you can help us do it.'

'Me? How?'

'Well, there's the puzzle. My visions don't always tell me exactly what I need to know. So I know where we're going to end up but I don't know exactly how we're going to get there.'

'And where do you end up?'

'We build a hospital and we rescue the kids. We're in the country and it's beautiful and peaceful. There are horses to ride and pathways to walk and a river to swim in. But the best part is I saw some of the kids waking up. There's hope, Dr. Schmidt.'

'And who is this we?' he asked.

'I don't think I can give you anyone's names right now. But they do know yours. Nothing personal but we're all in a great deal of danger.'

'I understand. I have to think about all this,' he said. 'It's a lot to consider. I mean, if we're in hiding in the country somewhere that would mean I've given up my career here.'

'Yes, it would. But when the police make the connection between you and those children at the private clinic, you'll be lucky if all you lose is your career.'

'Are you threatening me?' he asked.

'No, it's not a threat. It's a promise. I'm telling you what is going to happen to you. By associating with these people, regardless of what your intent was, you ended your career. The police are already investigating and they're getting closer to the truth every day.'

'So, what is it that I am supposed do for you?' he asked. 'Did you see that part?'

'You help us, Dr. Schmidt. You come along and you help us.'

'I see.'

'It's a leap of faith, Dr. Schmidt. If you want to try and help those kids badly enough, you'll take it.'

Sara hurried down the hospital corridor, afraid of being followed. She had a business card with Dr. Schmidt's private number on it and was to phone him in a couple of days. She pushed through the front door and found Matt parked in a no parking zone, his police ID sitting on the dashboard. She took a last peek over her shoulder, making sure she was alone, and then hurried towards the car and let herself in.

'Well?' Matt asked, as she buckled her seatbelt.

'It was fine,' she said. 'We're supposed to call him in a couple of days.'

'Are you okay, Sara? Did anyone see you?'

'Actually, Matt, it was strangely exhilarating. I think I know why you like being a cop now.'

'Don't you go getting all cocky. That was only one person and you managed to get out safely. It doesn't always happen that way.'

'I know, I know. Now get me out of here before my adrenaline rush ends and I realize how dangerous it was to go back into that place!'

'Are you going to be able to do the next one?' he asked.

'Oh yeah,' she smiled. 'I'm ready to face these people. Make them own up to what they've done to those kids.'

'And to you, Sara,' he said, reaching over and taking her hand.

'And to me.'

On her next foray into the hospital she wore a business suit and carried a brief case. She was a pharmacy rep, off to see one of the hospital administrators. Her cover wasn't going to last more than two minutes after she was through the door, but she was getting better at this, learning how to play the part and how to manipulate people. She was shown through the door by the receptionist, given a cup of coffee then left alone with Sylvia Jorgenson.

'Ms. Jones, I don't believe we've met.'

'No, we haven't. I'm actually really new to this territory and I thought I would stop by and we could get to know one another.'

'Well, you know it's generally the medical staff the deal with the pharmaceutical reps,' she explained.

'I am aware of that. Except for the rep from Beckman Pharmaceuticals. I understand that you seem to deal specifically with them.'

'I don't really think that my relationship with the Beckman rep has anything to do with you, Ms. Jones.'

'Well, funnily enough it does.'

'I'm sorry?'

'Well, I know the reason that you meet with the rep has nothing to do with ordering drugs or discussing budgets or research grants. It has to do with giving them confidential patient records and in turn, they give you a lot of money.'

'They donate to the hospital, but that's public record.'

'They also donate to you, Ms. Jorgenson. I believe you put most of the money into an account in the Cayman Islands. Because, of course, if you get caught turning over medical records, you'll be forced into and early and dishonorable retirement.'

'Well, that's true, if I were doing such things. But I am in a position of responsibility here and I would never allow anyone access to our patient records unless they were legally entitled.'

'Well, I'm afraid you're lying to me now. As a matter of fact, I have a list of records here that you gave out last week.'

Sara pulled a list of names out of her purse and pushed it across the desk so the woman could read it. Thank God Matt was good with computers and Chris still had access to the hospital systems.

'How did you get this? How could you even know about it?' she asked, horror crossing her face.

'Because I saw it.'

'How could you see it?' she asked. 'I took every precaution.'

'Because I'm one of the people that Beckman has been experimenting on. Because I've been having visions for months. And because I think it's time to put a stop to this and I think you might feel that way too.'

'What?'

'You know what I'm talking about. You may not be injecting patients but you are funneling them to these people. You are responsible, Sylvia, as much as the man who injected me and as much as Beckman himself.'

'No,' she whimpered, tears streaming down her face.

'Yes. And your career is over. One way or the other. But I'm offering you a way out that might help you sleep nights.'

'What do you mean?'

'We're going to save those children. Those children who were leading perfectly normal lives until you gave their records to a representative of Beckman Pharmaceuticals.'

'You can't save them. Beckman is too powerful. And I'm only one person.'

'But soon we'll be more than one person. We'll be strong and powerful and we'll have one thing they don't have.'

'What's that?'

'We'll have visions and we'll know when they're coming,' Sara said, much more confidently than she felt.

'But what can I possibly do? I'm a business person, a hospital administrator.'

'Sylvia, you are going to be invaluable to us. You are going to help us acquire equipment and funding and help us set up the hospital that I've seen in my visions. And eventually, you will even turn over the money from your offshore account. You hold a great deal of power, Sylvia, more than maybe you even realize. You can be an integral part of helping to save these children. And perhaps you can heal your soul at the same time.'

'I need to think,' Sylvia said. 'This is all happening too fast.'

'I know you need some time. I'll call you in a couple of days and see what you've decided to do. But I have to warn you, that if you do anything stupid in the meantime, like telling your friends at Beckman Pharmaceuticals about my visit, I'll know about it. And we probably won't be so forgiving the second time around.'

'You would kill me?'

'No. Worse than that, we would turn you over to the police.'

Sara made her way out of the hospital, fighting the urge to constantly look over her shoulder to see if she was being followed or had been recognized. She breathed a sigh of relief when she pushed through the front doors and Matt pulled the car up to meet her.

'How'd it go?' he asked, as she climbed in and fastened her seatbelt.

'Good, I think.'

'You think?'

'Well, she started crying and got all emotional.'

'I warned you that might happen.'

'I know. But it always worries me when people get desperate. What if she gets crazy and calls Beckman.'

'But you saw her helping us in your vision.'

'I did see her in my vision.'

'Helping us, right?'

'I might have kind of stretched the truth a bit.'

'Fuck.'

'Just drive, Matt.'

He pulled out into traffic.

'You lied to me about your vision.'

'Would you have let me come and see her if I had told you the truth?' Sara asked.

'Probably not. At least not until we had more proof.'

'But we found the proof. You found her bank accounts and you found that list of patients.'

'Sara, that list could have been anything. And some honest people have Cayman bank accounts. That didn't really prove anything.'

'Except that I was right in the end. She is involved.'

'I thought you and I were going to meet on some middle ground where we stopped lying to each other and worked on these plans together?' Matt asked.

'I thought we were.'

'Sara, it's only compromise when both people give something up.'

'Remember, Matt, it's me that will wind up back in the lab if we get caught.'

'And me that will end up getting shot and killed trying to keep them from taking you.'

'You'll be the lucky one.'

'I'm serious.'

'So am I.'

'Sara, that's not funny.'

'I'm tired; take me back to the hotel.'

'You look tired. Do you feel okay? Do you think we should

have a doctor examine you?'

'Uh, I don't think I'm ready to see another doctor yet,' she said. 'I think a nice steak, a couple of hours in bed and I'll be good as new.'

'Are you pushing yourself too hard with the visions again?'

'I might be,' Sara admitted. 'But there's no other choice. And besides, I see me in all these visions I keep having. So I'm guessing that somehow I get through it all right.'

They drove the rest of the way in silence. Sara had closed her eyes and Matt let her be, hoping she would get some rest. He drove in silence to the new hotel, the third one they had checked into. He liked to change locations every couple of weeks to make sure they weren't leaving a trail. Matt had returned to his job, his life and his apartment, as had Dr. Stevenson. When he came to the hotel in the evening, they would discuss their plans and then he would go home for a few hours sleep.

Matt pulled into the lot and put the car in park.

'We're here,' Matt whispered softly to Sara.

'I'm awake,' she said, forcing her eyes open. 'Thanks for the ride.'

'Okay, well you try and rest, okay? No more visions for a few days.'

'I won't argue,' she agreed and then leaned over and kissed him on the cheek. 'I'll see you later.'

Sara walked quickly through the lobby and took the elevator to her floor. She let herself into the room and did a quick look around, satisfied that everything was the way she had left it. She changed into a pair of jeans and a sweater and hung her suit up, smoothing out the creases with her fingers. She had another meeting in a few days and had to look like a young business professional again. She had memorized the room service menu so picked up the phone and ordered a cheese omelet with toast. Sara was sick of restaurant food but had no choice. She sat down on the bed and turned on the television, flipping through the channels to see if anything would catch her interest for a couple of hours, but nothing did. She finally settled on the news. A few minutes later there was a knock at her door.

'Room service,' the voice called out.

Sara jumped off the bed and hurried across the room to let them in. She was supposed to check through the peephole and make sure it was room service, but she only did that when Matt was around. She was less cautious when he wasn't there to lecture. The minute she opened the door, she realized Matt had been right to worry. It wasn't anyone from room service. It was a man in a dark suit, smiling at her.

'Sara?' he asked.

'Yes.'

'Dr. Beckman sent me to get you.'

'Dr. Beckman?' she asked. 'I think you must have me mixed up with someone else. I don't know a Dr. Beckman.'

'Well, he certainly knows you.'

Sara's stomach danced as the adrenalin surged through her system. Fight or flight, it screamed but she had no idea what to do. In a moment of panic she lunged for the door and tried to slam it, hoping she could get the night lock on and have a minute to call for help. The man was big and strong and fast and he flung himself at the door the moment he saw her trying to close it. Then he was in the room and she was backing up, trying to find a safe corner but knowing that soon there would be nothing but a wall behind her.

'Sara, we can do this the easy way or the hard way. But I am not leaving this room without you.'

'What's the easy way?' she asked.

'You grab your coat and we walk down to my car.'

'And the hard way?'

'Well, it involves handcuffs and pain and maybe even a little blood. But either way, you'll end up in my car and headed back towards the clinic.'

'Well, I never like to take a car trip unless I can stop at Starbucks first,' she joked, trying to buy some time. 'What

mind games

about if I agree to go with you if we can stop at Starbucks on the way there?'

'Yeah, well I'm not such a big coffee fan myself,' he laughed. 'So what's it going to be?'

He was almost on top of her now and there was no where else for her to go. Her back was up against the bureau. She was reaching frantically behind her, trying to find something to grab. She found a bottle of hair spray and she brought it around and sprayed him in the eyes. He screamed, but he managed to grab her with one hand while he rubbed his eyes with the other. She struggled against his grasp and when she couldn't get free, she sank her teeth into this arm. Then she kicked with all her might and managed to make contact with his groin, which knocked him to the floor. Sara grabbed her briefcase off the floor and swung it as hard as she could, but he saw it coming and ducked out of the way, and she just barely grazed his forehead.

'You little bitch,' he shouted, grabbing at her leg and pulling her down.

Sara hit the corner of the bed on the way down and the wind was knocked out of her. She lay there, trying to catch her breath before he got up. He was leaning on the dresser, trying to pull himself up. She rolled over and crawled to the bathroom, so she could get a get the door closed and slow him down for a minute. She had her hand on the sink and was just pulling herself up when she felt his hand on her ankle. He heaved and pulled her across the room. Sara felt something metal on the countertop and she wrapped her fingers around it, trying to pull it with her. She lay on the floor, looking up to his angry face, still trying to catch her breath. The man leaned down to pull her up and just as his fingers curled around her collar, she threw herself at him, her hand curled around the object she had pulled from the bathroom counter. The next thing she saw was the scissors making contact with his left eye. There was a moment of resistance and then they went all the way in, the force of her blow crunching bone . She felt her stomach begin to heave as he fell backwards, the scissors buried to the hilt in his eye. She braced herself, expecting him to come after her again, angrier than ever. But he hit the ground and didn't move again.

Sara stood up, breathing heavily, trying not to throw up. She turned away from the body and hurried to the window. She knew there would be others out there and needed to know how many. There was a man leaning against a black town car that was parked in front of the hotel doors. Sara looked at the phone and thought about calling Matt, but she realized the other man would probably come looking for her long before Matt could get here. She grabbed her coat and hurried out into the corridor, wishing she had time to try and have a vision. Maybe just this once it would show her what to do. But instead of a vision something else caught her eye and she reached out and pulled the fire alarm. It was only moments before panicked faces started to appear out of rooms up and down the corridor, wondering what to do. Panic was good, she thought, no one would notice her and she would have time to get lost in the crowd.

'Ladies and gentlemen,' the public address system crackled to life above Sara's head. 'Please leave your rooms immediately. Please us the stairs. You will be informed when it is safe to return to the hotel.'

Sara joined the crowd that was forming and hurried down the stairs. Outside, they gathered at the far corner of the parking lot and she buried herself in the middle of the mass of people watching as fire trucks pulled up. The man in the black town car had been asked to move his car out of the way, but now he was standing at the front of the crowd, scanning the exits, trying to find Sara and his partner. Firefighters were everywhere and the buzzing of the alarm was finally shut off. Sara was beginning to worry, certain they would be allowed back to their rooms shortly, and then she would be in plain view. She was looking around, trying to figure out which way she should go next when she saw Matt's car pull up. He parked and got out of the car, racing to the fire captain and flashing his badge. Sara slowly made her way across the back of the crowd and let herself into the back seat of his car, where she stayed down low on the floor. In a couple of minutes, Matt returned to his car and pulled his cell phone out.

'Matt, I'm here,' she whispered.

'What?' he asked, turning around and trying to look over the seat.

'Turn around and act normal.'

'Sara, what's going on?' he asked.

'Get me out of here, Matt. Drive normally, don't draw attention to yourself but get me out of here.'

Matt fought back the questions he had and put the car in drive. He did as instructed and drove into traffic, twisting and turning down the busy city streets, checking the rearview mirror to ensure they weren't being followed. When he was satisfied they were safe enough and far enough from the hotel, he pulled into a parking lot and turned the car off. Matt got out and opened the back door, helping Sara out.

'What the hell happened back there?' he asked.

'I can't do this anymore,' she said, and then burst into tears. 'They found me. They were going to take me back to the clinic. Oh, God, Matt, I think I may have killed someone.'

He took her in his arms and rubbed her back.

'It's going to be okay.'

'No, it isn't going to be okay. No matter what I do they find me. I can't do this any more.'

He held her tightly. 'I know you can't. We've asked so much of you, but now it's our turn. I've got some good news for you Sara.'

'What do you mean?' she asked, wiping at her eyes with her sleeve.

'Get back into the car. I want to take you for a ride.'

Sara got into the front seat and Matt pulled out into the street. He got onto the highway and drove out of the city. He left the highway and they wound through side roads, eventually finishing their trip on a very old unused gravel road, before Matt finally pulled off into a long driveway. There were several out buildings and what looked like some sort of main communal building. Matt pulled up in front of it and turned the car off.

'What is it?' she asked.

'It's an old hotel. You know, the kind where you went when you wanted to escape from the world? No TV, no phones, no electricity.'

'You're kidding.'

'And one of our new partners bought it a couple of weeks ago. We've been trying to get it ready for you.'

She got out of the car and looked around. 'This isn't the place. It's not the place I saw in my vision'

'No, you're right, this isn't the place. It's too close to the city to be safe. They'd find us too quickly. But it's safe for now and it's where you're going to stay for a while.'

'I can't. There are still people I have to see. We're not finished Matt.'

'Yes you can Sara. We've been worried about you. You're just exhausting yourself with these visions, you have dark circles under your eyes, you sleep eighteen hours a day if I let you and you hardly smile any more. You need to rest. I can finish things up. I can find the last people we need to talk to. We have enough information now that Chris and I can take care of things. And what happened today just proves that we can't keep you in the city.'

'You mean it's over?' she asked. 'It's finally over?'

'For a little while. You can be at peace for a little while,' he said. 'I'll finish the planning and clean up the last of the stuff in the city. We'll use this as a staging area before we leave.'

'Please tell me there are flush toilets?' she asked.

He laughed and wrapped his arms around her. 'Let me show you around.'

Chapter 19

It was cold out here. Summer was ending and fall was around the corner. When the sun went down in the evening, you could feel the chill in the air. She had been at the abandoned hotel since the day Matt first brought her here. The site had originally been built as a retreat. A safe place in the woods with no phones, no power, no television or radio, where all the burned out city dwellers could come to recharge their batteries. But it had gone bankrupt and closed, sitting empty for several years before Dr. Peter Schmidt had bought it at auction. Though he was a neurologist by day, he had a dream of leaving the city and breeding horses. At least that's what he had told the real estate agent who sold it to him.

In reality he could care less about horses. Matt had found the place; Christine had approached him and instructed him to purchase the property. Slowly, their group brought out supplies. They came from different directions at different times and on different days, to ensure that the increased activity would not draw attention to either themselves or the location. Before long the pantries were full, the rooms clean and the beds made up and ready for visitors. There was a generator, a big tank of gas and the well had been serviced. Matt came out on his days off and cut firewood for Sara. They wanted to avoid using the generator as much as possible, so she needed the firewood.

The first week had been a relief. Sara felt safe, she felt rested and stopped worrying about everything. But after the first week she started to feel isolated and alone. There was way too much time to think. She thought about Ian and her friend Michelle and even her parents and felt herself falling into an abyss. Sara knew all about depression. She had studied it in school, worked with a patient who had it, and learned all about the medications and ways to treat it from her brother. She though she could fight it, but it settled on her like a fog, making everything dull and gray. She didn't want to get out of bed most mornings and was terrified that she would lose her focus and not be ready when they needed her. And then one day when Matt was up, he took her for a run through the woods. It had started as a walk, but then he dared her to a race and the next thing she knew she was at the finish line, smiling, and she actually felt a little better. She started exercising regularly, running through the forest for an hour a day, and she did sit ups, chin ups and anything else she could think of. Not only did it make her feel better, it also made the days pass more quickly.

She spent her days outside, while the weather was still warm, walking under the canopy of trees, reading or just thinking. She had started to get more visitors too, with different members of their group coming out to meet her, ask questions about the clinic or the treatments. They all wanted to see the circus act of course, and she never let them down. She would have a vision and tell them whatever secrets she had seen, and they became believers. During this settling time, Matt was still working as a police detective, running the investigation of her disappearance. It was strange to think that he was trying to find her when he knew exactly where she was.

Sara had also come up with a plan on how they were going to try and save the children. What she had in mind was dangerous but there was nothing else she had been able to come up with that had any chance of working. The biggest problem was going to be to convincing Matt and Chris that her plan would work. Especially when she didn't have a vision to back it up.

Sara was peeling potatoes for a pot of soup that bubbled on top of the stove. Her cooking skills had improved considerably over the last several weeks. Cooking was one of the things she had been doing to help pass the time. She heard a car approaching. She dropped the potato and pulled the gun out of the holster that she now wore all the time, and dropped behind the counter. She peered over the edge of the counter, not relaxing until she actually saw the car and recognized the driver as Matt. She holstered the gun and picked up her potato again. He would see the smoke coming from the cookhouse and find her. She watched as he carried his duffel bag to the room he had made his own, and then crossed to the wood shed and had a look inside. Satisfied, he walked over to the cookhouse and let himself in. Sara poured him a cup of coffee and set it on the table where he had made himself comfortable.

'How's it going?' he asked.

'Okay,' she said. 'It's been kind of quiet.'

'I know, I'm sorry I couldn't get up here sooner.'

'No, it's okay, I know you've been busy on that case of the missing psychology student. How's that going, did you find her yet?' she laughed.

'Yeah, it's proving a little harder than I thought,' he laughed back. 'Seems she doesn't want to be found.'

'Well, I know how that goes. Just as long as you don't find her too quickly.'

'Trust me; I think she's pretty well hidden. It smells good in here.'

'Thanks. I've got some beef barley soup on the stove for supper. You're staying, right?'

'I'm staying.'

'Good. And then there's some fresh made biscuits…'

'You made fresh biscuits?' he asked.

'It's okay; they're not quite like hockey pucks any more. I think I figured out what I was doing wrong.'

'So they're as good as my grandma's?'

'Well, I wouldn't get your hopes too high. But at least you won't break a tooth on them.'

'All this time alone is doing you some good then?'

'I wouldn't go that far either,' she laughed. 'But I do have an apple crisp for dessert.'

'I am impressed.'

'Well, I think I'll go do some chores if you don't need any help in here. Although the wood shed still looks pretty full.'

'I've been chopping some wood,' Sara admitted.

'I told you I didn't want you doing that.'

'Matt, I'm going crazy here. You and Chris are out there, putting together our team, gathering supplies, living your lives, and I'm stuck here. I can't bake biscuits all day long.'

'But what if you hurt yourself and none of us got out here for a couple of days to find you?'

'I'll be fine.'

'Sara, do you know how important you are to saving these children?'

'Yes, I know, my blood holds the key to whatever they did to me. Well, I promise that if I am bleeding to death, I'll do it over a bucket so the doctors can still run all their experiments on me.'

'Don't be like that. Please.'

She could only look at him for a minute, until she felt the tears well up in her eyes and she turned back to the sink to peel the potatoes. Matt knew she was lonely and emotional, but he also knew there was nothing he could do about it. He wanted to wrap her in his arms and make this all go away. But he couldn't. And he didn't want to cross that line with her. Frustrated, he pushed away from the table and she heard the door close behind him. In a couple of minutes she heard the sound of the axe cutting into the wood as he dealt with his feelings the only way he knew how.

Sara cried and then dried her tears, finished making supper, and set the table as the sun started to hang low in the sky. She watched out the window as Matt started to clean up his mess. She pulled on her jacket and joined him in the yard, silently helping to stack the wood.

'You don't have to help,' he said.

'I know, but it'll be getting cold out here soon. You know Matt, I'm really sorry…'

'You don't have to apologize. Sara, you're out here all alone, you have no one to share any of this with. And then there's all the loss…'

'Don't.'

'I know. I know it hurts. But I don't know what to do for you. We have to keep you out of sight. They can't find you.'

'I know, I know. But then every time you come and visit me I dump on you.'

'It's okay,' he smiled. 'I really don't mind.'

'Well, dinner's almost ready,' she said, stacking the last of the kindling.

'I'll just wash up real quick and be right in,' he said, smiling sadly at her.

Sara turned back into the cookhouse and pulled the soup pot off the hot stove and set it on the table. She opened the oven and peeked at the apple crisp, happy that is was just beginning to brown around the edges. It would have been nice if she'd had a freezer and she could have served it with ice cream, the way her mom always had but this would have to do. Maybe a little canned milk over top would taste just as good.

Matt joined her in the kitchen, looking neat in a clean shirt and freshly washed face. The hair at the base of his neck was still damp and she could smell the slightly musky smell of his afternoon's work. She pulled her focus back to the kitchen, trying to shake off how she was feeling about him, and ladled out some soup.

'Can you pass me one of those hockey pucks?' he laughed, holding his hand out for a biscuit.

'You're lucky it's not a hockey puck or I'd be beating you over the head with it right now.'

'Assault on a police officer is a very serious charge.'

'I'm missing, remember? First they'd have to find me.'

'Yeah, well I'm misdirecting this investigation as best as I can, but don't get too cocky.'

'I won't. How's the soup.'

'The soup's wonderful. You really are getting better at this cooking thing.'

'Even the biscuits?' she asked.

'Even the biscuits,' he agreed, taking a big bite.

'Good.'

They ate in silence for a few moments before she was brave enough to broach the subject.

'So, how's it going out there?' she asked.

'Good.'

'Are we almost ready?'

'We're getting there.'

'Did you find a place for us to go?'

'Sara, we agreed that we weren't going to tell you about what we were doing, just in case they found you.'

'I know, I know. But I think I've figured out a way for us to get to the kids out of the clinic.'

'Really?' he asked. 'Have you had some sort of vision or something?'

'No. You know I haven't been able to see anything about how we did it, no matter how hard I've tried. I just can't do it.'

'So what have you figured out then?' he asked.

'I have to go back there.'

'Nope.'

'What do you mean nope?'

'It's too dangerous. We'll find them and then we'll rescue them.'

'When?'

'When the investigation is over.'

'Matt, when? Five months? Five years? How many kids will die before then? How many more people will they do this to? We have to do something now. So as soon as you guys have everything ready, I need to go back to the clinic.'

'I'm never going to let that happen.'

'Can't we just discuss this?' she asked.

'No. We can discuss books or movies or politics but we will never discuss you going back there.'

'Now you're just being pig headed.'

'Maybe.'

'It's the only way, Matt.'

'I don't care.'

'Matt, what is wrong with you? We have to talk about this. I mean, I don't want to go back there either, but I don't know what else to do? Do you have any other ideas?'

'We're not going to talk about it. Christine and I and the others will work out some way to get those kids out.'

'You'll never do it without somebody on the inside,' she said.

'We'll see.'

'If I have to walk to the highway and hitchhike back to the city, I will do it.'

'Not if I handcuff you to the stove.'

'Matt,' she yelled at him. 'Stop this. It's is hard enough for me to even think about going back to that place. I can't stand you being angry with me right now.'

'And you don't think it's hard for me?' he asked. 'Thinking about you being back there? The things they might do to you? I can't do anything to protect you once you're inside.'

'I know it's hard, but it should be my decision. I'm the one who'll be in danger.'

'And it's me who would have to live with it. Sara, I can't let you do it.'

'You don't have a choice as to what I do or don't do.'

'Sara, I love you, I can't let you do this!'

'What?'

'I love you,' he said, and then pushed away from the table and raced outside.

Sara watched him go, her heart swelling with joy at his

words. Then she realized that it didn't matter. She had a job to do and if he was going to stand in her way, she had to steel herself and forget her feelings. There would be a time for a personal life some other day. She tidied up the kitchen, and prepared what she could for the morning.

In her room she lit a candle and changed into her pajamas. Someone had brought her some thick flannel nightgowns from the city, and she was very happy to have them. She crawled into bed and opened the book she had been reading. But everything distracted her, a crackle of a log in the fire, the sound of an owl in a tree outside her door. She put her book down and crossed to the window. Sara noticed a candle lit in his room and watched to see if he would go to bed or sit up for a while. But the candle didn't move and she couldn't see anything else through the thick shadows. She went back to bed and picked up her book again, turning pages, reading the same words over and over until nothing made any sense. She finally put the book down and blew out the candle, pulling the covers tightly around her neck and willing sleep to overtake her troubled mind. But that didn't work either. Finally, after tossing and turning until her bed sheets were totally twisted around her, she gave up. She pushed the blankets back and got up, taking an afghan off the end of the bed and pulling it tightly around her shoulders. She opened the door quietly and walked across the parking lot to the room Matt was staying in. She opened the door a crack, peeking in to see if he was awake. He sat bolt upright, sensing her presence.

'Sara? What's wrong?'

'I love you, too.' she sobbed through the open door.

Matt held back the covers and Sara ran to the bed, crawling in beside him and burying her head in his shoulder. He wrapped the covers tightly around both of them and held her while she cried.

'Aren't we a pair?' he asked.

When it was dark and quiet and she had finished crying, she lay in his arms, holding him tightly, afraid he would be taken away from her too.

'How long are you staying out here this time?' she asked.

'Two days.'

'You know, no matter what happens between us, no matter how we feel, we still have to do this thing,' she said.

'I know we do,' he said.

'So I think we should keep this between us.'

'It's probably a good idea,' he agreed, his hands running through her hair. 'But you know there's not really anything to keep secret.'

'But there's going to be,' she said.

'You don't think we should just leave it like this?' he asked. 'It would be the smart thing to do, just be friends and not get emotionally involved.'

'I know,' she said, her hands finding his face in the dark and pulling it close to hers. And she kissed him. And no matter what he thought might be best, he didn't fight it. And as she kissed him again, he realized how long he had been fighting his feelings, forcing them deep inside himself. And now, they were free, and he found himself tearing at her clothes, suddenly hungry for the feel of her skin against his. He felt her hands tearing at his clothes too, fueling the fire that was burning inside him. And then suddenly her night gown was over her head and his hands were on her skin, exploring her body, trying to memorize her shape, her curves. Her legs were open to him and a soft moan escaped her lips as his hand caressed her. She was warm and wet and was pushing his hand away, pulling herself onto him. Suddenly they were together, he was inside her and he couldn't tell where she began and he ended. A white heat overtook him as they began to move together, their rhythm slow and almost painful at first, then quickening, until he almost couldn't catch his breath. He felt a moan building up deep within her and then suddenly a sound to match hers rose up from him. He was out of control and they were lost in each other. She fell on top of him and he wrapped her arms around him, too exhausted to speak. After a few minutes she slowly rolled off him and pulled the blankets up around them, as the chilly air slowly penetrated their haze.

'Matt?' she whispered, not sure if he was still awake.

'Yeah?'

'I lied to you.'

'You're not really a woman?' he teased.

'Uh, I'm a woman.'

'You're not really having visions?'

'Sorry, that's not it either.'

'What did you lie to me about then?' he asked. 'And don't be afraid to tell me. It's going to have to be pretty serious for me to get pissed off at you right now.'

'When we were at my house and I had that first vision with you there, I did see who did it. I saw Ben inject me.'

'Yeah, I was pretty sure you knew.'

'And you never said anything?' she asked.

'He was dead, you were safe. I figured you'd tell me when you were ready to.'

She kissed his hand. 'There's something else.'

'What?'

'I saw Ben shoot Ian. But that's not all, I think Ian knew I would see that in a vision, or at least he hoped I would. He told Ben he had evidence and that I would know where to find it.'

Matt lifted his head slightly. 'Evidence?'

'Yeah, that's all he said. I think he was trying to make sure I knew about it without giving too much away to Ben.'

'So, did he tell you where it was?'

'He just said I would know where it was.'

'And do you? Can you have a vision about it or something?'

'I don't have to. He had a hiding spot in the backyard when we were kids. I think that's where he put it, whatever it is. Because he knew I would be able to find it.'

'But you can't go home, Sara.'

'I know,' she said. 'But I can draw you a map and you can go there, when it's safe. And once again, Detective Matthew Grassi will save the day.'

'Well, at least we'll have something other than these crazy stories. We'll have some concrete evidence.'

'You hope,' she said.

He didn't answer. Instead, he just wrapped his arms around her as she pulled the blankets tightly around them, and they drifted off to sleep.

He woke at dawn, the light peaking through a crack in the curtain. He wanted to close it, so this moment together would last longer, but he knew the minute he moved, she would wake up. And then she moved, twisting a bit.

'Are you awake?' he whispered.

'Shh.' She instructed him. 'Don't say anything. Don't ruin this moment.'

Her hands were warm as they explored his body. The need was suddenly there again, but he held himself in check, while she slowly traced his body with her fingers. Her warm mouth covered his and he was lost to her again. His hands began to move as well, exploring the curves of her hips, her buttocks and her breasts. Her breath quickened as he found a nipple and her back arched as a moment of pleasure surprised her. She had her hand around him, slowly caressing him, increasing the pressure and stroking faster until his breath was coming in short gasps. He rolled on top of her, and she opened herself to him. He raised himself up on his elbows, watching her face as she slowly guided him inside her. He thrust himself inside her and her eyes closed lost in a moment between pain and pleasure, then she relaxed and wrapped her legs around his, pulling herself up to meet him.

He watched her face, while he slowly moved into her and then pulled away, teasing her, teasing himself. He felt her trying to draw him deeper inside her and he resisted the urge to let go, trying to stay in control. He didn't want this to be another groping in the dark session like last night; he wanted to memorize her face, her body, the feel of her. And then she pulled him down, wrapping her arms around his neck and kissing him, while their hips came together with explosive electricity. At that moment he did lose himself again, pushing deeper and deeper within her, kissing her lips, her breasts, her ears, just wanting every part of them to connect. She moaned and thrust up to meet him, losing control as her body gave itself up to him. He felt her body begin to twitch in pleasure and he began to shudder in concert with her. When it was over, he couldn't move, exhausted from the overwhelming emotions that were running through him.

'We were meant to be together,' she said. 'Remember that, no matter what happens next.'

'What do you mean?' he asked.

'Matt, I don't think we're going to have the opportunity to be alone like this again for a long time. But you have to remember that fate doesn't bring two people together like this unless they are meant to stay together. We have to have faith.'

'Have you had a vision?' he asked.

'It doesn't matter. Just promise me you'll believe in us.'

'I'll believe in us,' he said.

'Okay, now promise me you'll put some wood on the fire and then come back to bed?' she giggled.

'I promise,' he said, hurrying across the cold floor and doing as he was told. After the fire was stoked and he was back in bed, lying beside her with one of his arms draped across her waist, she took his hand in hers and twined her fingers through them.

'I wonder what happened?' she asked softly.

The breeze started blowing gently, reminding her of a warm Caribbean beach, and she swam the current of warm air to where her vision was taking her. The wind deposited her on a wooden porch, where she sat sipping a glass of lemonade and enjoying the warm sun on her face. She watched the road, waiting for a car to appear, the one she knew was coming. And eventually, she heard an engine off in the distance, and the tires crunching the gravel road, as a car slowly approached. She was content. She knew that once it got here, they would be together. The car pulled up, stopping almost in front of her. The engine was turned off and the door opened. She watched as a foot slowly extended from the car and crunched as it hit the gravel road. And then her eyes opened and she was back in the abandoned hotel, the fire crackling and the warmth of his body against hers. She smiled and tears welled up in her eyes. She knew that he would be waiting for her when this was all over.

A week later Christine Stevenson turned up at the hotel. She sat at the table with Sara, drinking freshly brewed coffee and trying one of Sara's oatmeal cookies.

'This is good,' Chris told her.

'Forget the cookies. You have something to tell me. I can see it on your face.'

'We're ready,' Chris said. 'We're ready to go.'

'You've found the place.'

'We found the place a month ago and it's almost set up and ready. We can start moving the kids in as soon as we can get them out of the clinic.'

Sara felt tears stinging her eyes. 'I can't believe it.'

'Believe it,' Chris said, taking her hand and giving it a squeeze. 'We've already got a skeleton staff out there. The others will start coming here over the next few days. They'll be needed to escort the kids to the new facility.'

'Is Matt coming out?' Sara asked.

'He couldn't get away from work.'

'What?'

'I'm sorry, I'm lying to you. He couldn't do it, Sara. He couldn't deliver you back to those people. I told him I would take you and make sure you were safe.'

'I understand,' she said sadly. 'When do we leave?'

'Whenever you're ready. It's totally up to you.'

'All right then, first thing in the morning. We'll have a hearty breakfast and then get if over with.'

'Are you really sure want to go through with this?' Chris asked. 'We could come up with some other plan.'

'I don't want to do it but there is no other way, is there?'

Chapter 20

She stood there, in the driveway of Ian's house – her house, all alone. Chris had dropped her off at the end of the block, and was parked out of sight, watching to make sure everything went as planned. It had been months since Sara had escaped the clinic. Months of trying to plan and scheme and figure out how they could beat an organization that had unlimited funds and resources. It had been both frustrating and enlightening. But it was over and now she was back in the city, back where Beckman could find her. If anything serious happened to her, the others were ready; they would carry on without her. So she came home, back to the place of her childhood, where first her parents and then her brother had raised and cared for her. Sara needed some closure. She needed to say goodbye to Ian. It was fitting that what started here so long ago would now end here. At least it had sounded good when she had rehearsed it in her head, but standing here in the driveway, she was scared.

Sara took a deep breath and pulled the keys out of her pocket. She let herself into the house and stood in the doorway, listening for a noise, any clue that someone might be in there waiting for her. There was nothing. The house was dark and cool and quiet and appeared to be pretty much in the state she had left it. The air smelled stale. Sara closed the door behind her and locked it tightly. Then she hurried into the kitchen and checked the back door. It was locked. The windows were shut and she pulled the curtains tightly closed as well. She hurried to her bedroom and grabbed a suitcase from the closet, tossing in a few weeks worth of clothes. When she was satisfied with what she had packed, she walked down to Ian's bedroom.

Sara sat on the bed and put his pillow to her face. It didn't smell like him any more. Nothing in here smelled like him or even felt like him anymore. There was a thin layer of dust covering everything and even the air smelled dusty. The room didn't look like anyone lived here and it made her sad. She realized there was nothing here that meant anything to her any longer. Ian was in her heart but he wasn't in this house. She hurried back to her room and closed her suitcase, then stopped in the living room and grabbed one of the photo albums from the bookshelf. She opened it up and took out a picture of her parents and a picture of Ian and her together. That was all she needed. She tucked them in the pocket of her suitcase, took a deep breath, picked up the suitcase and put her hand on the front door.

'I love you, Ian' she said, before she turned the handle. 'I'm going to find the person who did this to you.'

She opened the door and there were two men standing there. For a moment she thought about running or putting up a fight, but there was no way she would even make it halfway across the living room.

'Hi there,' she smiled. 'Would one of you mind taking my bag for me?' she asked, holding up the suitcase.

One of them did take the bag and then the other took her arm and they led her off to the dark sedan waiting on the street.

'Mom,' Matt said. 'Mom, please calm down.'

'I'm worried about you.'

'Mom, it's not serious,' he said. 'I have to help someone who's going into witness protection and I will be out of touch for a while. I just wanted to let you know so that you wouldn't worry.'

'But how can I not worry about you when I'm not going to be hearing from you.'

'Mom, you have to trust that if you don't hear from me I'm okay. If anything happens you'll hear.'

'I never wanted you to be a police officer. I always thought you should be a doctor.'

'Mom, that's not much safer either these days,' he laughed.

'I love you, Matthew. You call me if you can, okay?'

'I love you too mom.'

He hung up the phone and sat there for a moment. His paperwork was signed and he was basically out of here. Personal leave. He had convinced his captain that when Sara disappeared from his custody the second time, he began to doubt his ability as a police officer. He told them he couldn't face another case, losing another witness, his gut just wasn't in it any longer and that he needed time to think. He thought the witness protection thing sounded good enough to keep his mom from worrying about him too much. He had a small box of his belongings sitting on his desk, smaller than he had expected. It looked as though he hadn't made much of a mark on this place. Matt took one last look around and picked up the box. He was done here. He needed to get out.

Fournier may have been gone, but there were other doctors happy to have Sara back, including the great Beckman himself. She was settled into the same room she had occupied before. She was assigned around the clock nursing, all strapping young men well over six feet tall, including her old nurse. The first day he was in and taking her vital signs he leaned close to her and whispered in her ear.

'Vince.'

'What?' she asked.

'My name is Vince. I thought you should know that.'

'Thanks.'

'Are you back to help the kids?' he asked. 'Or did they really just get lucky and capture you.'

She stared in his eyes for a long time and wondered how to answer him. 'I wish I knew for sure if I could trust you or not.'

'I let you attack me with a scalpel.'

'But you've been here a very long time,' she said.

'Here, take my hand. Can you have a vision about me? Maybe it will tell you that I'm on your side.'

If he was willing to take that chance, he must be telling the truth, she thought. And then told him, 'We're going to try and help those kids.'

He smiled as he wrapped the blood pressure cuff around her arm.

Sara's days were interminable and unchanging. She got up, showered and dressed, had breakfast and then was taken to the lab. Some days they wanted her to have visions. Some days they just wanted to measure her reactions, sample her tissues, take pictures of her brain. It didn't matter to her. She knew they wouldn't find out anything that would help them in the short time she was going to be there.

'Sara!'

'What?' she said, shaking herself out of her fugue.

'Were you having a vision?' the doctor asking, sitting safely behind the console, monitoring all the beeps and pings that were being emitted from the electrodes and sensors taped to her body.

'No.'

'Are you sure?' he asked.

'I was daydreaming.'

'About what?'

'About nothing...'

She saw his hand move over toward the button for the electrical current. It was how they checked her honesty.

'About how nice my life used to be. About how I enjoyed getting up, going to school, studying, dating.'

'Thank you.'

'About how I was never going to be able to do those things again. Do you realize I will never have a date again?'

'Thank you.'

'I'll never have a man love me, hold me, touch my hair. I'll never have children. I'll probably never even have a dog. Do you realize that?'

'Thank you Sara. Please just relax for a few minutes while I take some further readings.'

'Sorry doctor, I didn't mean to interrupt your research.'

Christine Stephenson was very nervous. She was always nervous these days. She was afraid that she was being watched or being followed or maybe both. Since Sara had disappeared and Detective Grassi was now Mr. Grassi, she felt alone and unprotected. At least she wasn't in jail, but she didn't know if it was a good thing that she was free. Maybe jail would actually be safer.

She carried on with her regular routine, seeing patients, working in the operating room, joking and carrying on as though everything was normal. At night, though, she sat in her tightly locked house and worked in the darkened basement. She was copying all of her lab notes, putting together a package that would hopefully protect her. She was going to mail it to her lawyer with instructions for him to turn it over to the police if she suddenly turned up dead. It wasn't something Matt had agreed to when they had last met, but it was something she just felt safer doing; having some insurance, or vengeance if they got to her.

But with every noise, ever creak and groan of the foundation, every car that drove by, she froze. She stopped working, expecting someone breaking through her front door, and then when it didn't happen she got back to work until the next noise disturbed her.

Matt stood in front of the punching bag, sweat rolling off his forehead. He had been working out a lot. He was frustrated. He was never good with inactivity and all he was doing was waiting. Waiting for something to happen. And he didn't like it. He hit the bag again, and then when he was exhausted, he showered, changed and headed to the bar next door. He was there every day at 3:00, just like he was supposed to be. And every day at 3:00 he ordered his beer, drank it and then went home, because nothing happened. No one was ever there.

He crossed the street and pushed the door open. He stopped at the bar to order a beer and then settled at his favourite table, tossing his gym bag down by his feet. He sipped the beer and watched the baseball game on the old TV set. He was actually getting interested in it when he heard the chair beside him scrape the floor as someone pulled it out.

'Christine?' he said, standing up and helping her with the chair.

'Matt,' she said, slipping into the chair and settling at the table. 'How are you?'

'I'm fine,' he said. 'Can I get you a drink?'

'A glass of white wine would be nice,' she said.

Matt hurried to the bar and came back with a glass of wine for her.

'How did you know how to find me?' he asked, looking around to see if anyone was watching them. They had this conversation carefully mapped out, just in case anyone was following them.

'I asked around,' she said. 'People tell doctors everything.'

'Well, you're looking good,' he said, lifting his glass to her.

'You too.'

'What brings you here?'

'Well, Detective…'

'It's just Matt now.'

'I've bought some land. I found a lovely parcel of land in the mountains and I think I'm ready to retire. I thought I might raise some horses, maybe get a couple of dogs to keep me company and just disappear.'

'That sounds nice.'

'I know I won't be able to run away from what I've done, but it will give me a quiet place where I can try and sort things out.'

'When do you take possession?' Matt asked.

'I got a quick possession date. I'm hoping to be up there next week. Tuesday is my last day at the hospital.' Right now I've had some contractors checking things out, getting the buildings into shape, that sort of thing.

'Well, that sounds nice.'

'And you Matt?' she asked, putting her hand over his. 'Are you okay?'

'I'm okay. I can't stop thinking about her.'

'I know, neither can I.'

'Aren't you going to reassure me that she's okay? You always used to.'

'I don't know if she is okay,' Chris said. 'I used to think I knew everything. Now, I'm not so sure. Just think positive thoughts Matt. Send a message out into the universe for her.'

'I will Chris,' he said, standing up and hugging the woman as she prepared to leave. 'Thanks for coming by.'

Sara lay in bed, staring up at the ceiling and trying to figure out what time it was. It was hard sometimes, especially if she dozed off. But it seemed dark and it was very quiet so she pulled the covers up around her neck, tucking herself in tightly, and whispered.

'I wonder what happened.'

Tonight it was working and the breeze blew her gently across the night skies and into Matt's apartment. It was winter and the curtains were closed. Matt was asleep on the couch, a hockey game playing on the television. There were a couple of empty beer bottles on the table. He looked young, younger than when she had known him. She tried to turn, looking for a calendar, and she found one by the kitchen door. It was opened to April 1999.

'Damn,' she cried. 'Why can't I make myself go where I need to go?'

'He shoots, he scores. This game is going to go down in history, tied at twelve twelve, we're going to be playing until midnight if this keeps up.'

The TV was blasting away and she wished she was

corporeal and could turn it down so she could concentrate. She had to think. There had to be something in the apartment, some sort of clue, something she was missing. The universe had to have brought her here for some reason. But she didn't see anything. She wished she could turn the TV off, cover him up with a blanket, and brush the hair off his face. But she was nothing but a ghost looking back at this piece of time. She turned back to the calendar, and noticed the date he had circled, Tuesday April 20th, 1999.

'I'm sorry, Matt,' she called to him, as she felt the vision fading around her.

Matt woke up the next morning stiff from spending the night sprawled across his desk, where he had fallen asleep. He stretched out the kinks and went into the kitchen to make a pot of coffee. Then he came back and turned the news on. He felt so much more light hearted this morning, knowing there was a date; that something going to happen at last. He wasn't good at sitting and waiting. The coffee pot beeped and he went to the kitchen and poured a cup for himself. Then he went back to the desk and ripped the top sheet off the yellow legal pad that was sitting there. He read it and smiled. *Tuesday night*, it said, in big bold black print. He fed it through the shredder and then decided it was time to start packing. There were only a few days to get everything sorted and ready to go. He just hoped Sara had somehow managed to see it.

Chapter 21

'You know, you're doing this all wrong,' Sara said, lying on the exam table, with still more electrodes attached to her body. She had a new confidence this morning, even if she hadn't been able to get a message from Matt, she had seen him and she knew the end was in sight.

'Sara, just lay quietly please.'

'I mean it. I have a really good idea and I think you should listen to me.'

'If I listen to you will you promise to lie quietly for a while?' he asked her.

'Yes.'

'I knew this was going to happen.'

'What?'

'That you would get bored. You need stimulation to keep you satisfied.'

'Well, I learned that in first year psych and it took you this long to figure it out, doctor?'

'I suggested they just keep you sedated, as it would be infinitely easier.'

'You were going to listen to me, I believe?' she asked.

'What's your idea, Sara?'

'You need me to work with the children.'

'The children are fine.'

'The children aren't fine,' Sara said, sitting up. 'The children are dying or turning psychotic or having breakdowns and you have over half of them in chemically induced comas in intensive care. I wouldn't say that was fine.'

'How do you know this?'

'I saw some of it when I was here the last time. I also learned a lot of things when I escaped.'

'Well, I can neither confirm nor deny...'

'You don't have to. I know it's true. I can work with them.'

'Lay down Sara.'

'I'm the only one who can work with them. I'm the only one who knows what they're going through. I'm the only one who can explain to them what's happening and try and help them.'

'It's an idea we've already discussed.'

'And?'

'It was tossed around but we didn't think we'd be able to carry it out.'

'It's a great idea.'

'But we can't trust you.'

'You're right, you couldn't trust me before. But I'm a changed woman.'

'Of course you are.'

'I'm serious. I'm stuck here, I'm never getting out and even if I did, I wouldn't stop having visions. At least here I could work with the kids. It's the kind of work I've been trained for; it would make my time here worthwhile.'

'Lay down Sara.'

'No. I want to do this.'

'Sara, you know I have to get these readings. Please don't make me sedate you.'

'One kid. Give me just one kid and I'll show you what I can do.'

'Okay, I'll bring it up at the next meeting.'

'Promise?'

'Yes, I promise.'

'When's your next meeting?'

'Tomorrow morning.'

She lay back down on the bed. 'Okay, get your readings.'

'Thank you Sara.'

'No, thank you, doctor.'

They gave her a room with two very comfortable arm chairs. The walls were covered with bookshelves filled with books for every age. There were toy chests in the corner, filled with toys for every age group. She couldn't see the cameras, but knew without a doubt that they were being filmed and recorded. There was nothing she could do about that.

She sat across from a young girl, who looked to be about ten or eleven years old. The girl had dark circles under her eyes. She looked malnourished and exhausted. Her hair was dull and falling out, and her skin sallow. She wasn't very talkative and she wouldn't make eye contact. Sara sat there and tried to get her thoughts in order. She had never seen a patient on her own before. There had always been a supervisor, taking her through a pre-session conference, reviewing charts, discussing what would be the best tact to take during the interview. Helping her to plan the therapy and treatment, helping her to decide what questions to ask, and then sitting through the session with her, quietly directing her from the sidelines, steering her back on track if need be. Here she was on her own, with a very scared and unhealthy child sitting across from her. And for a moment, she was overwhelmed. She thought she might hyperventilate. She had sixty minutes with this young girl. Just one hour to try and get through to her and let her know she was going to be all right.

'My name is Sara,' she started.

'Hi,' was the timid response, though there was still no eye contact. These kids had learned they had to respond or there would be some sort of punishment.

'Can you tell me your name?'

'Jessica.'

mind games

'Jessica, do you know why you're here?'

'So they can test me.'

'That's right. You have some special powers now and they want to try to help you use them.'

'Are you going to test me too?'

'No Jessica, I'm going to help you learn to control these powers, so that they're not so scary for you.'

'I'm not scared.'

'I know, you're a big brave girl. The doctors told me that you try and help the other kids when they have the scary dreams. But I think I can help you not be scared by them ever again. Would you let me try that?'

'I guess.'

Sara still didn't believe the response. This little girl didn't trust anyone here, but she had learned to lie and to tell them what they wanted to hear, just as Sara had learned to do.

'Jessica, can I hold your hand for a minute?' Sara asked, holding out her own hand.

Slowly, Jessica stretched her hand out to Sara and Sara took it in hers, surprised at how light it felt, how dry the skin was to the touch. Sara held on tightly and closed her eyes.

'I wonder what happened?' she whispered, praying her vision might show her something that could help this girl.

And then the most amazing thing happened. The breeze began to blow and she let herself drift on its current to the spot she was meant to be. When the wind dropped her and she looked up and saw Jessica staring at her. But this wasn't the Jessica that was sitting in the room with her. This Jessica was a strong and healthy young girl, in jeans and a t-shirt, swinging on the monkey bars in a playground.

'Jessica?' Sara asked.

'I'm Jessie. That's what everyone used to call me.'

'Where are we?'

'What are you doing here?' Jessie asked, dropping from the monkey bars to the ground. You can't come in here.'

'Where are we?'

'You're in my mind and I want you to get out. This is the only place I can be alone and play.'

'We're in your mind?'

'So how did you get in here?' Jessie asked.

'I don't know for sure. I have the same special powers you do. I have scary dreams and visions. I was trying to see if I could figure out what happened to get you here. But it brought me here instead.'

'Why did you let them give you the scary dreams?'

'I didn't let them,' Sara said. 'They did it without my permission. Just like they did to you.'

'Do you have the scary dreams all the time?'

'No, now my dreams are nice. I want to help you learn how to make yours nice too.'

'So how'd you get in my mind?'

'Jessie, how do you know we're in your mind? Has this happened before?'

'Some of us kids can do it, go into each others minds. It's how we play.'

'You do this all the time?' Sara asked.

'Uh-huh.'

'Do the doctors know?'

'No. If they knew they'd just want to do more tests on us. This is our secret,' she said. 'But Sara?'

'Yes.'

'There are some other kids. I've gone into their mind before and they're really sick and they can't play. Can you help them too?'

'We're going to try.'

'Are you going to tell the doctors about this?' she asked.

'No, I'm going to keep this a secret too. Now can you keep a secret for me?' Sara asked.

'Sure.'

'We're going to try and rescue you. To get you out of this clinic.'

'Really?'

'Really. And I need you to tell the other kids, in their minds if you can. But you have to be very careful to keep it a secret.'

'I will.'

'Because when my friends come, you have to be ready to do exactly what they say so we can get out of here quickly.'

'Okay.'

'I'm glad you showed me this, Jessie,' Sara said. 'You're a very brave little girl.'

Then the breeze began to blow again and Sara opened her eyes. She was in the arm chair, but she was laying back, her head lolling over to one side, the young girl gently shaking her shoulder.

'Jessie?'

'Jessica,' the girl said.

'Did I fall asleep?' Sara asked, confused.

'I think so.'

'But I thought we were talking.'

'You talked to me, then you said something and closed your eyes. I had to wake you up because I need to go to the bathroom.'

'I had the strangest dream.'

'Please, I really have to go to the bathroom,' Jessica said.

Sara shook her head, trying to clear the cobwebs, and then got up and pushed the intercom button, to get them to open the doors.

'I'll see you on Tuesday,' Jessica said, as she followed the nurse back to her room.

'Tuesday?' Sara asked.

'Yeah, that's when you said you'd see me again.'

And then Sara remembered the vision she had had, the calendar in Matt's place, with the Tuesday circled. And she wondered if maybe she had got a message from Matt after all.

Christine had a smile on her face as she strolled up the sidewalk to Sylvia Jorgenson's house. She and the hospital administrator were becoming friends and Christine was picking her up to take her out to the hotel. There was a sold sign on the woman's front lawn, as there was on Christine's house too. Christine knocked on the front door, smiling to herself, glad that this waiting was over and they would soon be on the move. She had lost several nights sleep afraid that she had been discovered but now, finally, she felt she might be safe. She knocked on the door again, wondering what was taking Sylvia so long. She was supposed to be ready and waiting. Chris knocked a third time and then twisted the door handle, surprised to find that it was unlocked and it swung open for her. She moved slowly into the house.

'Sylvia?' she called out. 'Sylvia, it's Christine. Are you ready to go?'

There was no response. Christine heard a noise behind her and jumped, only to find it was Matt at the door.

'What's taking so long?' he asked.

'I don't know, she didn't answer the door and she doesn't seem to be home.'

Matt pulled his gun out of the holster. 'Get behind me.'

She obeyed his order, as the tone of his voice left no room for argument. Matt slowly made his way through the main floor of the house, room by room. When nothing turned up, they climbed the stairs to check out the bedrooms. The door to the master bedroom was closed. He opened it slowly and Christine screamed as she saw what was behind it. Sylvia lay on the floor, a bottle of pills and an envelope with Christine's name on it beside her.

'Oh my God,' Christine said, racing over and checking her pulse. But the woman's arm was cold and stiff and she knew it was too late to do anything.

'Is she dead?' Matt asked.

'Yes.'

'Shit!'

'I know, such a waste. Such a shame.'

'I'm sorry, but the only thing I care about right now is that she might just have totally screwed up our plan and given us away.'

mind games

'What do you mean?'

'Well, if the new owners of this house had stumbled across her body tomorrow when they take possession, what do you think would happen?'

'They would call the police.'

'That's right. They would call the police and there would be an investigation. They would check out her bank accounts trace what she had been doing for the past few months. And Chris, if we could find out all that stuff about her, you can be sure they will find it too. One thing will lead to another and that other thing can lead straight to us.'

'I never thought about that.'

'We have to do something,' Matt said. 'We can't let them find her like this.'

'What are we going to do?'

'Stay here. Gather up the pill bottles and that letter and I'll be right back.'

Christine did as she was told, putting everything in her purse. Matt returned with a gas can and took the cap off it, pouring gasoline all over the room.

'Matt, we can't do this.'

'We have to. We can't let them find her.'

'But they'll still find her, they'll still investigate.'

'Yes, but they'll be investigating the wiring, to find out why there was a short in the garage below the master bedroom, which in turn set this can of gasoline on fire. It will buy us some time.'

'Oh, poor Sylvia. No matter what she did she deserves to die with a little more dignity than this.'

'She can die with dignity or we can live a few more days, Christine. You make the choice.'

'You're right,' she sighed. 'There's too much at stake. I'll wait for you in the car.'

Matt took the gas can back to the garage and soaked some old rags. Then he found a hammer and a nail, and pounded the nail through an electrical cord. He dropped a match onto the pile of rags and left the garage, locking the door behind him. He went back to the car and got in, waiting to make sure that the fire was burning .

'Did you read the letter?' he asked Christine.

'Yes.'

'And what did she have to say?'

'She was very upset. She said that nothing she could do would ever make up for what she had done, she still couldn't live with herself. She couldn't bear to meet the children . She left me the numbers for all her Cayman bank accounts and just wanted to die in peace.'

'I can't say I'm totally surprised,' he said.

'There was something else in there,' Christine said, opening another piece of paper that was on her lap.

'What is it?'

'It's some financial information. Sylvia was helping us get everything set up, but what we didn't know was that she was funneling money into an off shore account.'

'She was stealing for herself too?'

'No, Matt, she was stealing for us. It looks as though she's transferred money from all the bank accounts of all the people Beckman Pharmaceuticals had involved in this project. She's managed to transfer almost all the money that Beckman paid out for this project to us.'

'She's been hacking into people's accounts?' he asked. 'What if someone goes to the police?'

'And what would they say? That the money they were paid under the table for their participation in an illegal research project resulting in the death and severe injury of several children was stolen from their bank accounts?'

'I guess you're right.'

'She was brilliant. There's millions of dollars in this account.'

'Millions?' he whistled. 'That should keep us going for quite a while.'

'Yes it should. It's too bad she didn't stay around and work with us. She could have done so much good. We need someone like her if we're going to fight against a company like Beckman Pharmaceuticals.'

'It's such a waste. Enough people have died already.'

'Maybe she will be the last one.'

Chapter 22

It was Tuesday. Sara was sure of that because Vince had told her. He never told her what day it was unless she asked, but this morning he had come in with a smile on his face, singing.

'Tuesday, Tuesday,' he sang, throwing back the curtains.

'Don't you mean Monday, Monday?' she asked.

'That was yesterday.'

'Oh!'

'Just wanted to make sure you knew what day it was.'

'Thanks.'

'When?' he whispered, while he took her pulse.

'I don't know. It didn't she me anything specifically, but I have a feeling.'

He wrapped the blood pressure cuff around her arm. 'I would trust your feelings more than most.'

'Then I think it's midnight. Twelve o'clock midnight.'

It was hard to keep track of the days and time when you didn't have a calendar, television or radio. And then she smiled, almost certain she would see Matt later today.

Sara thought that time would fly, since she knew she would soon be free. Instead, it turned in to one of the longest days in her life. She was ready. She didn't know what the plan was but she was ready for whatever was going to happen. She had visited Matt's apartment two more times in her visions, trying to get some confirmation, but all she did was get more useless information from his past. She had told Vince that something was going to happen soon but that was all she knew. Regardless, he was ready to help out.

She had gone through her normal routine during the day, but now it was night. She was alone in her room and the clock was moving very slowly. She did have a watch, Vince had tucked it under her pillow at bedtime, so she would know what time it was. She lay on her bed, and watched the hands move slowly, until they finally reached eleven o'clock. The day was almost over and nothing had happened yet. Then the door to her room opened and Vince poked his head in.

'You awake, Sara?' he asked.

'What do you want?'

'One of the doctors wants to see you,' he said, acting for the cameras.

'At this time of night.'

'Yeah, they're curious about your REM sleep. Come on, let's go.'

Sara got out of bed and put on her slippers and sweater. She trudged over to where Vince stood; he took her arm as per usual and led her down the hallway.

'What's going on?' she asked.

'I'm not sure. But I saw some cars passing by on the road outside. I thought you better be ready if it's them. How are you feeling?'

'I'm nervous,' she whispered. 'I'm glad nobody wants to check my blood pressure right now.'

'Me too.'

They walked further down the hall and he opened a door. It wasn't the lab, but some sort of electrical room.

'You sure they didn't see us come in here?' Sara asked.

'I put enough sedatives in the night guard's coffee to keep him out until Christmas. We're good to go.'

'And are you sure if we cut the power here that none of the

kids in the ICU will die?'

'All the hospital systems are on a backup generator. It will come on thirty seconds after the main power goes out. But it won't power any secondary systems, like computers or phones.'

'Okay. So now we wait for the troops to arrive.'

Matt was parked about a mile from the clinic. He had driven by a couple of times, checking for an unusual activity on the roads, but it seemed like business at usual. He was in an ambulance, wearing a paramedic uniform, with Christine Stevenson and a nurse both out of sight in the back. He stared at his watch, watching the hands move slowly, minute by minute, creeping towards the time they put their plan into action.

'How are you doing, Matt?' Christine asked from the back.

'Okay.'

'There's still some coffee in the thermos if you want some.'

'I think I've had enough caffeine for the night,' he said. 'I'm already pretty jumpy.'

'Yeah, me too.'

'How's our patient doing?'

Christine knocked on the hard plastic head of the resuscitation dummy that was strapped to the gurney.

'He's hanging in there. But do you think we're really going to fool anyone?'

'I'm hoping that we'll just get a cursory glance with a flashlight through the back window. The dummy will fool them.'

'And if they come in?'

'Then things may get a lot more violent than we had planned on.'

'Do you mind if I say a quick prayer for that to not happen?'

'I wish you would,' he said. And then with one last glance at his watch, he reached down for the key and turned on the ignition.

Sara, still in the electrical room, stood up and tried to

stretch her legs. They were cramped from sitting in one position for such a long time. Vince was rubbing his thighs, but being much more stoic about his discomfort than she was.

'You okay?' he asked.

'Yeah, just edgy I guess. Sometimes my legs get jumpy when I'm nervous, enclosed in a confined space and trying to avoid capture.'

He laughed. 'Why don't you talk to me? Keep your mind from wandering.'

'What do you want to talk about?'

'I don't know. Tell me what you're going to do tomorrow when you're free.'

'The first thing I'm going to do is have a coffee. I've been dreaming about coffee. I can't believe that these guys won't let me have any.'

'They're afraid of the caffeine affecting the test results.'

'Yeah, but they'd have a happier test subject. Then after I've had two or three cups of coffee, I'm going to have the longest hottest shower you can imagine. And best of all, no one will be knocking on the door telling me it's time to get out and get to the lab.'

'Those are good goals.'

'What about you, Vince? What are you going to do tomorrow?'

'I don't know. It's been a long time since I was unemployed.'

'Well, technically you'll have a pretty important job. You'll be training all the other nurses.'

'What, you're not going to give me a single day off?' he asked. 'Man, you're tougher than old Beckman is.'

She laughed. 'What time is it now?'

'Ten more minutes if it's them,' he said.

'What if it's not them?' she asked.

'It has to be them,' he said. 'What about television? Do you miss TV? Or magazines?'

'I even miss the commercials,' she laughed.

Matt slowed the ambulance as he approached the gate. The guard came out of the shack and shone his flashlight into the driver's side, illuminating Matt's face.

'Evening,' the guard said. 'Can I help you?'

'Yes, I've got a patient here. Transfer from Dr. Christine Stevenson to Dr. Andrew Beckman.'

'I wasn't told about any new patients arriving tonight.'

'I've got a copy of the orders right here,' Matt said.

'I'll need to see those.'

Matt leaned over and reached beside his seat. He came up with his gun pointed at the guard's face.

'Hey, mister, take it easy,' the guard said, slowly backing up to the guardhouse.

'Stop right there,' Matt ordered, opening the door to the ambulance and getting out. 'Up against the front of the ambulance.'

The guard leaned against the vehicle and Matt cuffed his hands securely behind him. He led him back into the guardhouse with Christine following closely behind. She pulled a syringe out of her pocket and uncapped it. She ripped the guard's shirt sleeve open and held the needle to his arm.

'Any allergies, sir?' she asked.

'Christine!' Matt chastised her.

'I'm sorry, I can't help myself.' She finished her injection and the guard slowly sank to the floor.

'How long will he be out?'

'Oh, he's good until late morning at least,' she said.

Matt ripped out the telephone line and then pushed the button to open the gate. Two seconds later, all the lights went out and the clinic was totally dark.

'One minute until midnight,' Vince said.

Sara took a deep breath and held the wire cutters to the main cable leading to the circuit box.

'You want me to do that?' Vince asked.

'No, I'd really like to,' she said. 'As long as you're sure I won't get electrocuted.'

'No, those are safe, they're made for electricians.'

'How long?'

'Thirty seconds.'

They sat there in silence, Sara with the wire cutters ready, Vince with this watch.

'And five, four, three, two, one.'

Sara pushed the cutters with all her strength and the wire snapped in half. Then they stood in the dark.

'It worked,' she said nervously.

'Yep, now we better start getting the kids together.'

Sara opened the door a crack and peered out. She couldn't see anyone down the hall and pushed the door open the rest of the way. She made her way out and turned to tell Vince that the coast was clear when she hit a brick wall. At least it felt like a brick wall. She was looking up at another one of her nurses, a big angry man who had just blindsided her and looked perfectly happy to have a reason to throw another punch.

'What are you doing out of your room, Sara?' he asked.

Sara tried to form words, but her head was swimming.

'I think you've been causing some trouble. We better get you back to your room until Dr. Beckman can talk to you.'

'I'm not going back,' she said.

'Oh yes you are, one way or the other.'

Just as he leaned over to pick her up, the electrical room door opened again, but quickly and violently, and made contact with his head. Vince followed through with a tackle that would have made his high school football team proud. But the men were evenly matched and Sara watched as the other nurse seemed to be besting Vince. She went back into the closet and felt around, looking for something she could use as a weapon. And then she found something, groaning at the weight as she picked it up. It was the longest wrench she had ever seen, and heavy. She came out of the closet and blinked her eyes, trying to adjust to the emergency lights and make sure that she was aiming for the right man. Then she swung it like a baseball bat and made contact with the nurse's head. He stopped fighting and slumped on top of Vince.

'You okay?' Sara asked.

'Yeah, thanks,' he said, pushing the unconscious man off him as he got up. He wiped his bloody nose on his shirt sleeve and steadied himself against the wall.

'You okay to keep going?' she asked.

'I'm fine,' he said. 'Just a little dizzy for a second. I must have gotten up too fast.'

'Or been hit in the head by a six foot three, two hundred and fifty pound goon.'

'Yeah, or that. Okay, let's get going.'

Vince led her down the hall and into the first room.

'Jessica?' Sara asked, surprised to see the girl sitting up on her bed waiting for them.

'I told you I'd see you Tuesday,' Jessie said quietly.

One by one, they woke the kids up and got them to the nursing station, which was currently empty as one of the nurses on duty was unconscious and the other was aiding and abetting the escape. Jessie kept the kids remarkably calm throughout all of this. She was talking softly to them while Vince was quickly emptying the pharmacy shelves behind the nursing station into a duffel bag.

Matt pulled through the front gates, his headlights the only ones visible for miles, until suddenly a whole line of headlights turned on behind him. A caravan of vehicles followed him into the clinic grounds as they pulled up in front of the main doors. Matt was buzzed in by the night nurse, who was ensconced behind a glass panel, making her feel more courageous about letting strangers in at night.

'Yes?'

'We've got a patient to admit. Dr. Beckman is expecting us.'

'I have no paperwork on this admission,' she said, scanning her sheets. 'I'll have to call Dr. Beckman.'

'Please don't do that,' Matt said, bringing his gun up so she could see it.

'This is bullet proof glass,' she explained while she picked up the phone. 'There will be a security guard here in under thirty seconds.'

Matt pointed the gun over her left shoulder and pulled the trigger. The glass shattered around her. The nurse screamed and ducked, her hands covering her head as thousands of shards of glass rained down over her.

'Was it Dr. Beckman who told you this was bullet proof glass?' he asked, as he jumped over the counter, ripping her phone cord out of the wall and picking her up off the floor. 'Now, I wonder if you could buzz these nice people in and take us to the nursing station on the first floor.'

There was terror on her face but she pushed the buzzer and everyone who had gathered behind him followed as she led him down the hall. Through the dimly lit corridor, he saw a group of people crowded around the nursing station, at the far end of the hallway. His pace quickened and his heart raced as strained to see if Sara was there. They saw his group coming and Sara slowly stood up, trying to pick Matt's face out of the crowd.

'Sara?' he yelled down the hallway.

'Matt!' she called, racing to meet him and throwing herself into his arms.

'You're okay?' he asked.

'I'm fine. I'm okay.' And then she kissed him.

'I guess our secret is out,' he laughed, looking into her eyes, making sure she really was okay.

She let go of him. 'I'm sorry, I couldn't help myself.'

'Me either,' he said. 'Now we've got to get these kids out of here. Is this all of them from this floor?'

'Yes.'

Matt turned back to the people behind him. 'Okay, team one, these are yours. Two kids to one adult. And remember to take your assigned routes back. We don't want a huge caravan heading down the highway.'

Sara turned to the kids. 'All right, guys, these are the people that Jessie told you about. They've got cars outside and they're going to take you to the safe place we talked about. It's very important that you go very quickly and quietly and do exactly as they say. Any questions?'

'Shouldn't we go to the bathroom before we go for a car trip?' one of the little girls asked.

'Only if you have to go right now. We're kind of in a hurry.'

As the team starting taking the kids out, Matt stood beside her and took her hand in his.

'Where are the rest of them?' he asked.

'Upstairs.'

Vince handed the duffel bag full of medications to another nurse then joined Matt and Sara. 'Are we ready to go upstairs?'

'Matt, this is the nurse I told you about. Vince, this is Matt.'

'And I'm Christine Stevenson,' she said, joining them. 'I'm the designated doctor on this mission.'

Vince nodded at them and led the way down the hallway to the stairwell. The stairwell was empty and when they reached the ICU, Matt had the two duty nurses handcuffed and in a closet before an alarm could sounded.

'Oh my God,' Matt said, when he looked at the children laying in the ICU.

Christine stared for a moment too, and then turned to Vince.

'Okay, what have we got?' she asked.

'There are four who can be moved,' Vince said. 'The other two are on full life support. I don't think they could survive a move.'

'We can't leave any of the kids behind,' Sara said.

'We have to Sara. They'll die if we try to move them.'

'Vince?' she asked, hoping for back up

'They have a chance if we leave them here, even though it's a small one,' he confirmed.

'Chris, I thought we weren't going to leave anyone?' Sara tried again.

'Matt, I think you should take her down to the ambulance,' Chris instructed. 'We can handle this.'

'No,' Sara said. 'I'm not going anywhere. We agreed we weren't going to leave anyone behind.'

Chris took Sara's hand in hers and squeezed it gently. 'Sara, the ones who are being kept alive by machines are already gone. There's nothing we can do for them. But I'm not willing to be the one to pulls the plug. We need to leave them here. Maybe one day if we will learn how to reverse what's been done to them we can come back.'

'No,' she said.

'You know it's for the best,' Chris said.

Matt put his arm around her shoulder. 'Why don't we let the medical people do what they have to do and get out of their way.'

'Matt?'

'Come on,' he said, as he gently led her back down the stairs and to the main floor. 'Let's go wait in the car. They don't need our help any more.'

Sara let him lead her down the stairs and through the main hallway. All the staff was handcuffed and anesthetized. Phones and surveillance equipment had been ripped out of the walls. It might have been overkill but Matt knew it would take quite a bit of time to load the kids up, and he wanted to make sure if someone woke up sooner than expected, that they wouldn't be able to call for help.

When he was satisfied, he led Sara out the front entrance and opened the door of the ambulance for her. She climbed in and he got in the driver's side and closed the door.

'Are you warm enough?' he asked.

'I'm fine.'

'Do you want anything to eat or drink?'

'I'm fine,' she said sharply.

'You don't sound fine.'

'I never thought we'd have to leave any of them behind,' she said. 'I thought I could save them all.'

Matt had no answer, so he just held her hand while they watched the patients being loaded into a line of vans and slowly driven off.

It was hours later and the sun was just beginning to break the horizon when the back of the ambulance was opened and a small child put on the stretcher. Chris and Vince climbed in the back.

'Is that it?' Matt asked.

'That's all of them,' Chris said. 'Let's get out of here.'

'I'll second that,' Sara said. 'I'll be happy to never see this place again.'

'Matt?' Chris asked when he still hadn't started the engine.

'I just don't feel good about this,' he said. 'It seems as though it was all too easy.'

'Or, it went exactly as planned,' Sara said. 'Now let's get out of here and we can talk about it later. Day shift will start arriving in the next hour or so. All we need is one person to decide to come in early and we're done for.'

Matt still didn't feel totally at ease, but he knew getting away from here was a good idea. He started the engine and turned the ambulance for the main road.

'It's not too late, we can stop them.'

'No.'

'But Dr. Beckman, they've got all the test subjects. We can't lose all that valuable data.'

'We're not going to lose it you fool, we're going to gain more data than you could ever imagine.'

'I don't understand.'

'Look, Dr.. Clark, do you think that Sara was open and forthcoming with you about her visions when you had her in the lab?'

'Not totally, that's why I wanted to use stronger techniques on her.'

'Well, I've found that she doesn't react well to pressure. But if she thinks she's free, she'll be very open and honest. She'll think she's saving all those children.'

'But she is free, Dr. Beckman.'

'She thinks she is free, Dr. Clark, and that is an entirely

different story.'

'I don't know what you mean?'

'We have some people with her. Some people that she will learn to trust implicitly. But those people will be reporting to us. They are also equipped with homing beacons, which they will plant on some of the cars. We will be able to trace them no matter where they go.'

'That's brilliant,' Dr. Clark said.

'Yes it is,' Beckman smiled. 'And I think we'll make much faster progress than we have been doing thus far.'

The sun was almost up and the sky losing the last of its morning pinks and golds, as it slowly turned a solid blue. Chris was unloading the ambulance and Vince had already disappeared into the bunkhouse that was serving as their temporary hospital. The place looked different now that Sara wasn't alone. There was smoke coming out of all the chimneys, cars were parked safely under the blanket of trees and there were people everywhere. She leaned against the ambulance, still in her pajamas with her sweater wrapped tightly around her against the morning chill, and watched as everyone hurried to their tasks. It appeared they all had a purpose right now, except for her. She slowly made her way across the grounds to her old room, closed the curtains tightly and crawled into bed.

For a while her mind wandered, going over the plans, wondering if they had forgotten or overlooked something. The children were set up in their temporary quarters and the medical personnel briefed and given their schedules. Everyone was on duty until they were in the permanent location. You ate, slept and worked until it was time for your team to leave. And starting tomorrow, a few people a day would leave, taking different routes, but all headed for the same destination. The Promised Land, as they had started to call it. And finally, after concentrating on the thought of them all being there safely, she drifted off to sleep.

Matt patrolled the road while everyone was getting settled, making sure they hadn't been followed. After a few hours he was finally satisfied and made his way back to the main grounds. The grounds were almost deserted by now, as everyone was finally settled, so with nothing left to do he made his way back to Sara's room. He opened the door quietly trying not to disturb her, knowing she had gone to bed hours ago. He pulled off his jeans and shirt, put another log on the fire then climbed into bed beside her. She felt cold as she snuggled up against him, and he tucked the covers tightly around them.

'Are we safe?' she asked. 'No bad guys out there following us or snooping around?'

'No bad guys.'

'So we're safe?'

'I don't know,' he said. 'I've got a bad feeling Sara. It was just too easy. We waltzed in there and took those kids.'

'Well, you might have waltzed in there but I'm pretty sure I'm going to have a black eye in the morning.'

'I'm serious. I don't know why they would have let us get away without a fight.'

'Unless they really weren't prepared. Maybe they didn't think we would actually do it.'

'Or they may have planted someone in our group,' he said.

'You are such a cop,' she teased. 'You have an overly suspicious mind.'

'My overly suspicious mind is what has kept you alive so far.'

'Okay, supposing you're right,' she said. 'There's an easy answer.'

'What's that?' he asked her.

'I meet with everyone before we send them out. I can have a vision; do a reading so to speak.'

'You can't direct your visions.'

'I know that and you know that but they don't know that.'

'You can't have that many visions in one day.'

'I won't do everyone at once. I'll just do the ones that are leaving that day. I should be okay with three or four a day. Even if they're fake visions.'

'I don't know.'

'We can do this, Matt, we can fake them out.'

'Oh, you're getting devious too,' he laughed.

'I've been hanging around you too long. But can we deal with it tomorrow? I'm exhausted.'

'It is tomorrow.'

'Okay, the day after tomorrow then?'

'The day after tomorrow. That's when the first group is scheduled to leave. We can deal with it then.'

But she was already snoring softly, so he wrapped his arms around her, closed his eyes and was asleep almost as quickly.

Chapter 23

She room was cold, chilled from the damp night air. She sat in an armchair and pulled a blanket tightly around her shoulders. Sara had moved the armchair in front of the window to watch the sunrise, but missed the warm bed she had just climbed out of. She heard Matt stirring behind her, but knew he wasn't really awake. She curled her legs under her as she watched the skies grow pink. She was tired, tired to her very soul, not just because she hadn't been getting enough sleep or because she was stressed. She'd been having visions at a breakneck pace, and was starting to feel as though her brain was going to melt. She had started doing some work with the kids, but mainly she and Matt had been interviewing everyone before they left, trying to see if they had a traitor in their midst. Sara was trusting her life to this group of people she didn't really know. A group of people who had originally been willing to be a part of Beckman's experiments, through their own personal choice or blackmail, and she was terrified.

Every night, she and Matt would sit in front of the fire, and he would show her pictures of the people who were leaving the next day. Then they would make their plans, decide what they were going to do and what kind of vision she should tell them she had. Sometimes, when Matt would fix the fire or go for more wood, she would try to have a vision. But try as she might to concentrate on the photograph, she would end up seeing them grocery shopping in the local supermarket or swimming in a summer pond. Everything except what she really wanted to see. Trying to direct her brain to show her the things she wanted to see was turning out to be a very frustrating experience.

Sara would sit in the hospital for hours, watching Christine and Vince sit with one of the patients, calming the child when they woke up from a nightmare or vision. It was hard to tell the difference sometimes. They would hold the child in their arms for hours until they went back to sleep, at peace with the world again. But a part of her couldn't help wondering if this was all an act. She wondered, as she watched Peter Schmidt pouring over EEG readings and enter the data into his laptop computer, or as she watched any number of people go about their day to day business, if they really were all on the same side.

They left in small groups, twos and threes, children and adults, and they all drove in different directions. But they would all wind up in the same place. The Promised Land, that magical place where everything would be right with the world. Soon it would just be Matt and Sara left.

Sara pulled herself out of her reverie and turned back to the window. The sun was just peeking above the horizon, sending a faint light shooting out into the darkened night sky, and there were the first signs of life outside her window. Someone was packing up a station wagon and a van, the next two vehicles to hit the road. She could see smoke coming out of the kitchen chimney, as someone prepared an early breakfast for the travelers. Her stomach growled but she didn't want to leave her little cocoon just yet.

'What are you doing up?' she heard from just over her shoulder, and then Matt's scruffy face gave her neck a quick nuzzle.

'I woke up early and I wanted to watch the sunrise.'

'It's freezing in here,' he said, hurrying over to the fire

place. He stirred up the embers and piled some wood on top of them. Then he came back to the armchair and slid in beside Sara. She reluctantly gave up some of her blanket to him. 'You should be trying to get as much sleep as you can, Sara.'

'I know, but it's hard. There's so many things running through my brain that it's hard to shut it off.'

'I know, but you have to make sure you don't burn yourself out. We need you Sara. We need you well and healthy. I need you.'

'I know, sleep well, eat well, live long and prosper.'

'Something like that.'

'So, is this the second to last group to go this morning?' she asked.

'This is it. We'll pack your team up after lunch and then we're out of here.'

'Matt, I had a vision. I know what…'

'Don't Sara, not yet. Let's just enjoy the sunrise, okay?'

Sara cuddled up closer to him, trying to memorize the feel of his body, but she didn't say a word. Together, they stared out the window and watched the group of people outside load up one of the cars and then drive off down the road to the Promised Land.

Sara took the dish that Christine offered her, warm from the wash water with soap suds dripping off it. She dried it off and put it in the cupboard.

'That's it,' Christine said.

Sara just stared at her, as if willing more dirty dishes to appear. And when they didn't, she turned and hung the towel on the rack and headed back to her room. She pulled her suitcase out from under the bed and opened it. Sara opened the dresser and started transferring her clothes from the drawer into the suitcase. She pulled out one of Matt's sweaters that was mixed up with hers. Sara sat on the bed and held the sweater close to her, her heart already hurting at the thought of him leaving her later today. She looked down at the sweater and made her decision.

mind games

'I wonder what happened,' she whispered to herself.

The gentle breeze blew, growing stronger than she had felt it for a long time. It dropped her off in the middle of the forest in the pitch black night. She looked around, trying to get her bearings, and saw a sliver of light as one of the hotel room doors opened then closed quickly. She walked over and saw a set of keys laying on the step outside the door. She bent down, picked up the keys and then crossed over to the vehicles that were still left in the parking lot. She used the key to open the door, and then reached under the seat and stuck some sort of device to it.

'Sara…'

She looked around, wondering who had caught her.

'Sara…'

And then her eyes blinked open as Matt was shaking her and calling out her name.

'Matt?'

'Sara, what are you doing?' he asked.

'I had a vision.'

'You were twitching, like you were having a convulsion or something.'

'I must just be tired.'

'Do you need help? Should I get a doctor' he asked.

'No,' she said. 'Matt, I had a vision.'

'What was it about?'

'I saw someone leaving their car keys out on the stoop late last night. Then someone else took them and put something in one of the cars.'

'Are you sure?'

'Yes,' she said, her breath coming more quickly, matching her racing heart. 'Matt, I think someone planted a bug in one of the cars. There's a spy here with us. I saw us driving into the Promised Land and we were being followed by a line of dark sedans, filled with armed men. They wanted to take us all back to the lab.'

'Sara, are you sure?'

'I'm sure. I was so scared.'

'It's okay.'

'What are we going to do?'

'We're going to search the cars, see if we can find anything.'

'We can't lead Beckman to the ranch,' she said. 'I can't go back there again.'

'You won't have to,' Matt said, pulling her into his arms and holding her tightly. 'Sara, can you remember if it was a man or a woman?'

'I think it was a man.'

'For sure Sara?'

'Yes, I'm pretty sure.'

'I have an idea,' he said. 'Do you think you can lie to someone. Look them straight in the face and tell them a lie?'

'I used to be terrible at lying, but I'm getting much better at it lately.'

'Okay, well we're going to give something a try.'

Later, Matt pulled out his duffel bag and started packing too. When they were done, he did a quick sweep of the room, making sure there was nothing forgotten, nothing that would leave a clue as to who had been there. He leaned over to pick up Sara's suitcase, but she pushed him away and picked it up herself, went out the door and put it in the back seat of the van. Then she turned and headed back toward Christine's room. Matt silently followed closely behind her. Sara knocked on the door and Christine opened it and stepped aside to let them in.

'Well, I think everything's ready,' Matt said.

'The kids are all ready to go,' Christine added. 'Sara?'

'No.'

'Sorry?' Christine asked.

'I'm not going.'

'Excuse me,' Christine said, looking first at Sara and then at Matt. Finally, she got up and turned for the door. 'I'll leave you two alone for a minute.'

'What do you mean you're not going?' Matt asked.

'I don't want to go,' she cried. 'Matt I know what you're

planning and I want to stay with you.'

'You had a vision?' he asked. 'And never told me?'

'I didn't have to have a vision to know what you're planning. You're going to sacrifice yourself for the group.'

'Not for the group.'

'For what then? What is this big martyr complex you have going on? Why do you have to go out there and throw yourself to those Beckman dogs? Why?' she screamed, tears streaming down her face.

'For you.'

'What?'

'I'm doing it for you, Sara. To keep you safe. I want to make sure they'll never find you.'

'But Matt, I can't live knowing you're out there in danger.'

'Sara, you know this is the only way,' Matt said softly, knowing how hard this was for her because it was twice as hard for him.

'Matt, I love you,' she cried, throwing those words out into the cold cruel world. Hoping that they would be returned again.

'I love you too,' he said. 'But if you stay with me, then we're both dead. You have to stay with the team. I'll try and keep them off your trail.'

'No, someone else can take the kids,' Sara said, tears flowing freely, her voice breaking with desperation. 'Christine will be fine with them.'

'Sara, you know you're the only one who can work with them. You're the only one who can teach them what it's like to live with visions and how to deal with it.'

'It's not fair,' she cried. 'I never wanted this to be my life. I just wanted to be a psychologist, work with my brother, maybe have a family some day. I didn't ask for any of this.'

'I know you didn't Sara. Neither did I. I didn't wake up one day and say, I know, I'm going to be a renegade cop and spend the rest of my life being hunted. But this is the shit we've wound up with and we have to do the best we can with it. If we give up, if we don't stick to the plan, it's not just our lives that will be affected but the lives of all these children.'

'I don't care.'

'Yes you do. You wouldn't be able to sleep another night if you let them die.'

'Fuck you, fuck them, fuck it all!'

'Are you almost ready?' a voice asked from the hallway.

'Come on in,' Sara called, wiping her eyes. 'We're not ever going to be finished with this argument.'

'Are we ready to leave then?' Christine asked.

'So, are you ready to do this?' Matt asked Sara, sitting her down on the couch.

'I'm ready.' Sara whispered.

'Christine,' Matt said, turning to the doctor and taking her hand. 'We want Sara to try and do a reading of you. She's had an unsettling vision and we want to see if we can clarify what's going on.'

'I didn't know you could control your visions,' Christine said. 'When did this happen?'

'I don't know for sure if I can,' Sara admitted. 'But what I saw was so strong I need to try.'

'It must have been quite a vision,' Christine said.

'It was.'

'Are we okay?' Matt said.

Sara reached up to Christine. 'Christine, can I try?'

'Go ahead,' Christine said.

'Give me your hand.'

Christine complied and Matt put his hand on his gun, as he watched Christine carefully.

'Do you really have to do that?' Christine asked.

'Just a safety precaution in case Sara sees anything that might make you want to hurt us.'

'I told you I'm on your side.'

'A lot of people have told us a lot of things, Christine. We just have to make sure. And you said she could try this,' he reminded her.

'I know, I know,' she said. 'I'm just in a hurry to get out of here. The car is packed, the kids are ready to go and I'm not going to relax until we're safe at the Promised Land.'

'And I'm not going to feel safe until Sara says we're safe.'

'Ready?' Sara asked, looking up at her, still holding her hand.

'Fine, go ahead,' she gave in.

'I wonder what happened,' Sara said, and then stared intently into Christine's eyes as the gentle breeze blew inside her head.

The hotel room disappeared and for a minute she thought she might actually see Christine's life. But instead she was walking down a country road, seeing a group of cabin's at the end. She was happy, the sun was beating down upon her shoulders and she was happy. It felt so good to be relaxed. She looked down at the road and saw the little puffs of dust her feet kicked up with every step. She felt so relaxed and so happy, she never wanted to leave this place. Then she felt the breeze begin to blow again, and slowly it lifted her out of her reverie. Slowly the room was coming back into focus and she released the doctor's hand.

'Well?' Matt asked, hoping she had had time to gather her wits about her.

'She's fine,' Sara said. 'Let her go and pack up the van.'

'I'll send Alex in,' Christine said. 'He's the last one. That is if you want to play this little game with him too?'

'Yes, please send him in,' Matt instructed her, his hand on Sara's shoulder.

Alex came into the room and stood in the doorway. 'Christine said you wanted to see me?'

'Have a seat,' Matt said. 'Sara had a bad vision last night and we just want her to do a quick reading on you and make sure everything is okay.'

'Is this something new you're doing?' Alex asked.

'Yes, she's getting better with her visions and we think she can control them now. Maybe we can figure out what the vision she had last night means. Is that okay with you?'

'That's fine,' the man said uncertainly. 'What do I do?'

'Have a seat,' Sara said. 'And give me your hand.'

He held out his hand and Sara took it. Matt had his hand back on his gun and Sara whispered the words to herself. The room swirled and she felt slightly nauseous, probably from doing this so many times during the last few days. This time she was in a university lecture hall. There were hundreds of students, all diligently working over their papers. And there was Ian, filling in blanks with his pencil, three other identically sharpened pencils were lined up on his desk, just in case. Ian had always been so anal about things like that when he was younger. She focused on the exam booklet, Psychology 101. This was his first year psychology final, Sara realized. The subject that changed his future. He had wanted to be an engineer originally, but Psych 101 had changed the course of his life and brought them to where they were now. Then Sara felt herself pulled out of that vision and the hotel room came back into focus. She looked up at Matt.

'There's something we need to discuss,' Sara said, her pulse racing, but sticking to their prearranged script.

'Sara?'

'Right now, Matt, I think I know…'

'Everything's okay, Sara,' Matt said. 'Thanks, Alex, we'll meet you out by the van in a couple of minutes.'

Alex smiled and left the room quickly..

Sara turned to Matt, worry on her face. 'Why did you do that? Why did you interrupt me?'

'I'm sorry,' he said.

'There's a tracking device on one of those cars. I thought we were going to try and get some information out of Alex. Make him think we knew what he was up to. But you just let him go.'

'I know that was the plan, Sara, but when I saw the look on his face we didn't have to say anything else. He was scared. He already suspects that you know something.'

'Then why'd you let him go?' she asked.

'Because I'm a detective and I'm going to detect.'

'We can't let him get away.'

'We're not going to let him get away. But I'm hoping I can get a little more information out of him first.' Matt sat down beside her. 'I'm going out there and let them know I've changed the teams. Then he will be pretty sure something is going on. You guys are going to take my car and I'll take the van and try and lead Beckman in the opposite direction.'

'How do you know it's the van that's bugged?'

'Because I already found the bugs.' He said. 'I just didn't know who put them there.'

'You left them there?' Sara asked. 'Are you crazy?'

'Sara, I'll keep Alex with me for a few days and let him report in, so they'll think everything is okay.'

'And then what?' she asked.

'I'll deal with him,' Matt said.

'You can't do that, Matt.'

'It's a good break, Sara. They'll follow me for a while and I can lead them in the opposite direction, just like I planned.'

'So what's so good about that?' she asked. 'You were going to do that already.'

'I was going to do that by exposing myself. This way, they'll just be following the tracking devices; they won't be a car length behind me. And Alex will be reporting to them that everything is going as planned.'

'So you expect me to be happy about this?'

'It's safer.'

'Nothing's safe,' she said.

'Sara, it's the way it has to be.'

'No. We'll need you as our second driver now,' she told him. 'We're going to be one man short.'

'You'll be okay. You can drive the car.'

'Why can't you stay with us?' she asked. 'We really need you to stay with us.'

'Sara, we can't argue about this all day. We already agreed that you were going to go with the kids and I was going to go in the other direction.'

'We didn't really agree. We just stopped discussing that whole subject. And besides, back then my heart wasn't breaking at the thought of maybe never seeing you again.'

A horn honked.

'Sara, we have to go,' Matt said.

'No, not yet.'

Matt crossed to the door and opened it, calling outside. 'Christine, change of plans. You guys are going to take the car. Can you get Sara's stuff loaded into it too?'

'Matt?' Sara asked, tears streaming down her face again.

'Sara, please, you have to go.'

She ran across the room and wrapped her arms around Matt, planting kisses all over his face, trying to make this moment last forever..

'I love you,' she said, finally pulling herself away from him. 'And if you don't come back to me I am going to hunt you down and kill you myself.'

'I love you too, Sara. I'll swear I'll be back.'

Her hand went up to his cheek and she just held it there, smiling up at him, blinking back her tears.

'Tell Phil about the tracking devices when you're on the road,' Matt told Sara. 'They should know why we did the big switch and what we're up against.'

'I will.'

'And send Alex in to see me.'

She finally let him go and turned away, walking slowly to the door where Christine was waiting for her. The older woman took her bag and led her outside, draping an arm over her shoulder as she broke into tears.

As she left the room, Matt fought the urge to run after her. Instead, he watched through the window, as she wiped her eyes dry and helped Christine load the two kids into the back seat of the car and get them buckled in. Phil was unloading the van and transferring everything into the trunk of Matt's car. Then Sara went over and spoke to Alex, pointing up to the room where

Matt waited for him. Alex started towards the room as Phil closed the trunk and waved to Matt. He waved back, feeling his heart breaking as the car slowly pulled out of the parking lot and headed for the highway. He pulled out his gun, checked the cartridge and then put it back in the holster. He waited for Alex to get to the room and smiled broadly when the man finally came in.

'You wanted to see me?' Alex said.

'Yeah, we have a little change of plans and I need your help,' Matt said.

'Sure, whatever I can do.'

After he had explained his plan to Alex, they loaded up their suitcases and got into the van. Matt pulled out onto the highway but turned in the opposite direction that Sara had taken. He felt his heart sink as he thought of her driving away from him, but then he turned his mind to the task at hand. He had to lead Dr. Beckman on a merry chase across the country.

Chapter 24

They were taking the back roads. Their group had some of the healthier kids and there was no great urgency to get to their destination. It's the journey, Sara joked, not the destination. The first night they pulled into a cheap motel in a town Sara had never heard of before and piled the kids into the room with them. Christine stayed in the room watching cartoons with them, while she and Phil crossed the street to get some take out from the local restaurant.

'What do kids like to eat?' Sara asked, reading over the menu.

'Well, at the clinic we ensured they got five vegetables and four fruits servings a day, combined with whole grains, lean protein and less than thirty percent fats in their diets. They weren't allowed any simple carbohydrates, anything refined and definitely no soda pop.'

'Have you decided?' the waitress asked.

'Yes,' Sara said. 'We'll have five double cheeseburgers, five large fries and five large cokes please.'

'Sure. Anything for desert?'

'Yeah, is your chocolate cake good?'

'Three layers of Dutch chocolate covered with the richest homemade icing you've ever tasted.'

'Okay, five pieces of chocolate cake with ice cream.'

'To stay or to go?'

'To go please.'

'All right. That'll be about ten minutes. 'Forty three dollars and eighty cents total.'

Sara pulled out her wallet and counted the cash, throwing in a couple of dollars for the waitress.

'You folks new to town?' the waitress asked, while she put the money in the till.

'Just passing through,' Sara said. 'We're taking the kids to visit the grandparents.'

'Well you have a safe trip,' she smiled and then hurried off to another customer.

They carried the bags back to the hotel room and listened to the joyful shrieks of the kids as they unpacked the juicy burgers and French fries. Sara's mother's voice echoed in her head; these kids should be eating at the table, not sitting on the bed and making a mess. But as she watched the smiles on their faces when she passed around the soda pop, she decided messy sheets for a night or two would be okay. She opened up her foil wrapped burger and bit into it, juice dripping down her chin. She grabbed a package of ketchup and tried to open it with her greasy fingers. When her hands slipped a blob of ketchup flew across the room and landed on Chris's cheek. For a moment there was silence, until Chris reached into her pop, pulled out an ice cube and threw it back at Sara. Giggles erupted throughout the room and Sara was momentarily surprised to find that she, too, was laughing.

Matt sat in the restaurant. Half a patty melt lay congealing on the plate in front of him. He played with the French fries for a few minutes but this was not the most appetizing food he had ever eaten.

'You finished there, dear?' the waitress asked.

'Yeah, thanks,' he said, sliding his plate to the edge of the table.

'I'm sorry dear, I don't cook them, just serve them. If

you're still hungry, I would suggest you try some apple pie and ice cream. That's about the best thing we got here.'

'Yes, please,' Matt smiled, grateful for the advice. 'And I'll take some more coffee too, please.'

'I'll be right back.'

She finished clearing the table and then headed for the kitchen.

'Did you order more coffee?' Alex asked, sliding into the table across from Matt.

'Yep.'

'Well, I filled the van and checked the oil and the radiator. Everything looks good.'

'Thanks.'

'So, are we planning on putting on this many miles tomorrow?' Alex asked.

'Probably.'

'Do you think we're being followed?' Alex asked.

'I'm sure of it. I haven't spotted them yet, but this has been far too easy, don't you think?'

'Well, I guess.'

'Think about it, Alex. We're up against Beckman Pharmaceuticals. We've stolen their prize research subjects and they are now at huge risk of having their experiments discovered. Don't you think they'd be trying to do something to stop us?'

'I guess. You don't think we just got lucky, had a good plan and good timing and got away with it?'

'This is real life, Alex, not television. There aren't any happy endings. Things don't all get wrapped up in sixty minutes or less.'

'I guess I'm just not used to this cloak and dagger stuff,' Alex said as the waitress came back to fill their coffees and deliver Matt's pie.'

'Well, better safe than sorry,' Matt said. 'We are going to be on the road for three or four more days and then we'll ditch the van, get a new car and head for the Promised Land.'

'So why do you call it the Promised Land? What is it, a ranch or something?'

'We call it the promised land because it's where the kids can find their salvation,' Matt said. 'Or at least we hope we can salvage their brains, minds and bodies.'

'Why won't you tell me where it is? I mean Sara did that reading on me and everything was okay, wasn't it?'

'Yes, yes, everything was fine. It's just the way we're operating. Only one person on each team knows and then if anyone gets caught, it lessens the chances of us being found out.'

'I understand. It's kind of frustrating though.'

'I know. But just a few more days,' Matt assured him.

'So, are we going to find a hotel soon?'

'No, we've got a van. I figured we could take turns driving and sleeping. It's harder to hit a moving target, right?'

'Right,' Alex said. 'Do I have time for a piece of pie?'

'Go ahead,' Matt said. 'We've got plenty of time.'

'Sara, they haven't eaten a vegetable for two days,' Phil said. 'Let's at least get some carrot sticks or something like that.'

'They had strawberries on their pancakes this morning,' she argued. 'Besides, did you see how happy they were last night?'

'Yes I did. But as a nurse I still have their welfare in mind.'

'Oh, a couple more days and we'll be at the Promised Land and then you and the dieticians can make sure they get all those yummy whole grains and raw vegetables and whatever else it is you think they need. Tonight, I'm going to make sure they get chicken fingers with barbeque sauce and French fries.'

'How about a glass of milk instead of the coke?'

'How about orange soda?' she asked. 'There's got to be some orange in it somewhere doesn't there?'

'I'm pretty sure it's just food colouring.'

'Okay, we'll get pickles on the side. Pickles are good for you.'

'Okay pickles.'

'And apple pie. There's fruit in that.'

'Okay, you win. I won't argue for the next two days I promise.'

She kissed him on the cheek. 'Thanks.'

'So, this is what I really want to know. Are you doing this for the kids or are you really doing to for yourself?'

'Why, Phil, you have a very suspicious mind.'

'That's because I'm used to dealing with patients like you,' he laughed. 'But seriously, Sara, how are you doing?'

'I'm okay.'

'You look a little tired.'

'I'm feeling better. I had a hard time just before we left, having all those visions about everyone. But I'm starting to feel better.'

'You know, you of all people should be watching what you eat and taking some vitamins. Your body needs good food and rest to strengthen and heal.'

'And sleep more and drink less coffee, I know, I know.'

'I am serious about this. We have no idea what these visions do to you.'

'I know what they do to me,' she said. 'And I will take better care of myself. But not until we get to the Promised Land. For now, we have a couple more days where all that matters is getting these kids there safe and sound.'

'You know how much we need you there too?'

'I know you have to experiment on me and see what makes me different from them.'

'No, Sara, because you're the only one that has ever successfully got through to these kids. I've seen you with Jessie. I don't know what you're doing, but somehow you are getting through to her. She smiles more, has put on some weight, and makes eye contact when she talks to you.'

'It's because I found her.'

'What?'

'That first day, when I had a vision to see what had happened to her and figure out how to deal with her trauma, I found the real Jessie. She was hiding deep inside her mind. The part of her that was outside was only the part that she needed to stay alive while she was at the clinic. But the real Jessie had created this beautiful park and was playing on the monkey bars in her mind.'

'And you went into her mind?' he asked.

'I don't know how it happened. I thought it might be a dream. But it was as though we shared a vision or a dream or something. But I found her and convinced her it was safe to come back out again.'

'Can the other kids do it too?'

'I don't know. She told me that they play together at night. But I don't know if she goes into their minds or if the others can do it too. Or maybe it's all just a weird dream. Whatever it is, we won't be able to figure it out until we get to the Promised Land and can spend some quality time working with them.'

'So if we can fix their bodies, you can get into their minds and try and fix them?'

'I hope so. There's a lot of trauma to overcome, but if I can get Jessie to trust me and teach me what she does, we might be able to help them come out of the places they are hiding in.'

He grabbed the take out bag the waitress gave them and they crossed the street to the motel.

'Then, starting tomorrow, you're taking your vitamins and sticking to two cups of coffee a day and not a drop more.'

'Oh, yet more torture forced upon me by Beckman Pharmaceuticals,' she laughed.

'Matt, I need a bed and a shower,' Alex said, as they were pulling into a gas station to fill up the van.

'Yeah, I'm tired of sleeping on that foam mattress in the back too.'

'And we're both starting to smell a little ripe,' Alex joked. 'You can only wash up so well in a gas station bathroom.'

'I know. Let's stay on the road until dark and then we'll find a motel this evening.'

'That sounds like the best thing you've ever suggested.'

'Okay, you fill it up; I'm going to buy us some breakfast.

What do you feel like?'

'I'll take a large coffee and one of those chocolate donuts, you know with the powdered sugar on them.'

'You want some potato chips for later?' Matt asked.

'Yeah, but not those salt and vinegar ones, they make me too thirsty. Get the barbeque ones this time.'

'Man, we need a woman,' Matt said. 'Maybe I should have taken Sara up on her offer to come with us.'

Matt crossed the parking lot and made his way into the convenience store. He went up and down the aisles, picking out potato chips, soda pop, chocolate bars, and throwing in a couple of apples and bananas for good measure. He really didn't want all this junk food. As a matter of fact he was feeling pretty crappy from eating in cheap diners and munching on too much junk after being on the road for several days. What he did want to do was give Alex some time alone to make his phone call. He knew the man had a cell phone secreted away and arranged to give him three or four opportunities a day to use it. And he always made sure that he could watch. So he stood by the magazine rack and pretended to leaf through a car magazines while he watched Alex out of the corner of his eye. When Alex had finally hung up and tucked the phone back into his pocket, Matt made his way to the counter to pay for his purchases and the gas.

'Everything okay?' Alex asked, as Matt came back to the van.

'Yeah, just day dreaming over new models coming out,' Matt said, holding up the car magazine. 'Some day, when I win the lottery, I'm hoping to be able to afford something old and Italian and spend my days restoring it.'

'Every man's dream,' Alex said. 'An old car, a fridge full of beer and a woman who leaves him alone with them.'

'Yeah, well maybe I'll have some time when we're at the Promised Land. After all, I doubt they're going to let me treat patients, so I'll have to put myself to some use. I guess keeping the cars in running order will be of some help.'

'I guess there won't be much need for security if we do a good job of this.'

'I hope you're right,' Matt said, which was the first time he hadn't lied to Alex since they'd hit the road. 'I really hope you're right.'

'Sara,' a hand gently touched her shoulder. 'Sara, we're there.'

She opened her eyes, trying to get her bearings. She looked out the window and saw the forest rising up around her, and several cars and vans parked among the trees. Slowly, her exhausted brain started to function again and she realized where she was.

'We're here?'

'The Promised Land.'

'Hallelujah,' she laughed. 'I'm sorry I fell asleep.'

'It's okay. Our passengers slept most of the way too. I would have woke you up if I needed you.'

'Thanks Christine.'

Sara undid her seatbelt and got out of the car, closing the door quietly, trying not to disturb the kids in the back seat. Some cabin doors were opened and curious faces looked out. A few people started coming over to greet them. She took a deep breath and enjoyed the joy of knowing the she didn't have to run and hide any more. She felt the sun on her face and inhaled the sweetness of the air and realized she could be happy here, for as long as the project took.

'It's beautiful isn't it?' Chris said.

'The air smells wonderful. It smells of freedom.'

'You made it,' a friendly voice greeted them, attached to a face that Sara didn't recognize at first.

'We did,' Chris said.

'You're the last ones. We were starting to get worried about you.'

'Everything's fine. We just had some rain, so it slowed us down a bit. But we're all here now.'

'Welcome home. We've got your rooms ready. We're

keeping all the kids in the hospital for their first night, just to make sure they're stable.'

'That's a good idea,' Chris agreed.

'I should be there too,' Sara said.

'Are you all right?' they both asked simultaneously.

'I'm fine,' Sara said. 'I've been stable since the third injection. I just thought I should be there for the kids.'

'I don't think we've met,' the man said, finally, extending his hand in greeting. 'Dan Jackson. I'm a psychiatrist. I worked in the same office as your brother's friend Ben. I believe we met briefly once when you were at the office.'

'I remember,' she said, taking his hand. 'And I'm the freak with the visions, Sara Hunter.'

He laughed again. 'Well, patient is oriented to person, place and time with sense of humour intact.'

'It's a fine line between sanity and the alternative,' Chris joked.

'All joking aside, Sara, it wouldn't hurt to have a quick look at you, too.'

'I know, you guys are all curious about me. I guess the testing might as well begin today instead of tomorrow.'

He put a hand on her shoulder and looked directly into her eyes.

'This isn't Beckman's Clinic, Sara, you're in charge here,' Peter said. 'You don't have to do anything you don't want to.'

'I know, but the only way we're going to help the kids is to find out what the difference is between us. And while you're doing that, I'm going to see if I can teach the kids to control the visions on their own. One way or the other, we're going to get through to them.'

'Well, advancing medical science and all can wait,' Chris said. 'I think a better treatment right now would be a hot shower and change of clothes. Why don't you show us where we'll be staying, then you can show us around the place.'

'It's okay,' she said.

'Sara, we're going to be here for a while. Let's get settled and have a cup of tea, like civilized people.'

Sara smiled. 'A cup of tea would be nice.'

A couple of nurses were taking the kids from the van. More people appeared to help unload the car.

'Okay, I'll get the kids settled. You can follow the guys with the suitcases to your cabins and then I'll meet you in the mess hall in an hour?' Dan said.

Sara was overwhelmed and wrapped her arms around Chris as they started towards their cabins. 'Thank you so much for getting me here.'

'I didn't have any choice,' she said. 'These kids need us.'

Matt sat on a fallen log, in front of the campfire he had started when he got up that morning. It was late in the season to be camping, but he had bought a small tent and convinced Alex it was safer than staying in hotels all the time. They had been on the road for almost two weeks and he was tired of driving twenty four hours a day, and tired of keeping up the pretense with Alex. He woke up early, fixed the fire and put the coffee on. His stomach was growling but he let it growl. He would stop for breakfast later, if he had any appetite left. Finally, when he was on his second cup of coffee, he heard some rumblings from inside the tent. After a few minutes the zipper opened and Alex came out, pulling his coat on.

'Wow, it's a chilly morning,' he said. 'I don't think we're going to be camping too much longer.'

'You're probably right.'

'Hey, you've got the coffee on and everything. Why didn't you get me up, I could have helped you with the fire, gathered some wood.'

'Naw, you were sleeping,. No use both of us being up.'

'I guess you miss Sara a lot, huh?'

Alex sat on the log on the other side of the fire, and filled his coffee cup. 'Yes, that I do. More than I thought I would.'

'Love's rough.'

'It is.'

'So, when do you think we're going to head for the

Promised Land? Get you back together with your lady?'

'Oh, not for a long time,' Matt said. 'There's lots of sins to repent before one gets to the Promised Land.'

Alex laughed. 'That's very funny.'

'One of the first things I have to do, Alex, is ask you what it's like.'

'What do you mean?'

'What's it like to be a traitor?'

'I'm sorry, I don't follow you,' Alex said.

Matt pulled out his gun. He had had it on his lap, tucked under his coat so Alex couldn't see it.

'Whoa, man, you don't need that. We're friends here.'

'I'm not friends with people who work for Beckman Pharmaceuticals.'

'I don't work for Beckman,' Alex protested. 'I left them to come with you guys. At the risk of probably never working anywhere professionally again.'

'If you quit Beckman Pharmaceuticals, then why have you been calling them on your cell phone two or three times a day?'

'I don't have a cell phone.'

'Not true. You're not supposed to have a cell phone. You were supposed to turn in all cell phones and pagers or any other devices that could be traced or tracked. But you've been hiding one and making a lot of calls. Every time we stopped somewhere and my back was turned, you were on the phone.'

'Matt…'

'Don't bother Alex,' he said, his voice suddenly sounding like the cop he used to be. 'Give me the cell phone or I'll shoot you right now.'

Alex hesitated but only for a moment. He finally reached into the inside pocket of his jacket and pulled out the cell phone. He tossed it across to Matt who caught it in his free hand. He turned the phone on and checked the memory.

'All these calls are to the same number.'

'Look, my mom has been sick. I just wanted to stay in touch.'

'Should we call mom and see how she's doing today then?' Matt said, pushing the redial button.

'Well sure, but it won't be my mom that answers of course...'

'How convenient. Who will it be, her next door neighbour, who just happens to work for Beckman Pharmaceuticals? Maybe a friendly doctor who said he'd check in on her.'

'I didn't have a choice,' Alex said, his head falling in defeat.

'And why is that?'

'I'd rather not say. Look, just keep the phone, we can head out and I'll be free of them.'

'Just like that, you'd quit and come with us?'

'I don't want to die,' Alex said.

'Then tell me why you had no choice.'

'They caught me with one of the kids.'

'What?'

'It was one of the brain dead ones. So it's not like I was hurting anyone.'

'Oh my God,' Matt said. 'You sick fuck.'

'I'd been at that stupid clinic for so long, no social life, no friends. What do you think was going to happen?'

'Well, most people would go jogging or play cards or even see someone about it. Only someone as disgusting as you would molest a brain dead child.'

'Well it was a girl and she was a teenager. It's not like I'm queer or anything.'

'No, you're worse,' Matt said. 'Stand up.'

'What?'

'Stand up; we're going for a walk.'

'You can't kill me.'

'Walk.'

'If I stop phoning in, they'll know something is up. They'll stop following you and start looking for Sara again. You need to keep me alive.'

'You know, I probably would have until now. Walk!'

Alex looked around for a way out, as Matt led him down

overran over grown hiking path. He hadn't been here since he was a child, but he knew it led to a steep ravine where several hikers had slipped and fallen to their deaths over the years. They walked in silence until there was no where left to go.

'What now?' Alex asked, turning around to look at Matt.

'You keep walking.'

'I can't get down there.'

'That's the point,' Matt confirmed.

'I won't do it,' Alex said, getting suddenly braver. 'You'll have to shoot me and then when they find me, they'll trace the bullet back to you.'

'I'm not going to shoot you,' Matt said.

'Then we're at a stalemate.'

'No we're not,' Matt said, lunging for Alex.

The man took a step backwards, trying to avoid the blow, but he overstepped and found himself hanging in mid air, with nothing to grab onto. After a moment of defying gravity, his body plummeted backwards, plunging over the cliff. Matt took a couple of cautious steps forward and looked over the edge. Alex's body was laying at an awkward angle on the rocks below. He holstered his gun and slowly headed back to the van. He put out the fire, but left everything else in place, to make it look like Alex had been out camping, gone for an early morning walk and had a horrible accident. Three days later he threw the cell phone into the Atlantic Ocean. He then got back into the van and continued to drive further away from the one place on earth he really wanted to be.

Chapter 25

Sara sat on the floor wearing jeans and a sweatshirt, surrounded by pillows. It was cold outside; but she had tossed her jacket on the floor just inside the door when she entered the warm cabin.

'How are you doing today?' she asked the girl sitting on the floor, waiting for her.

'Good.'

Sara barely recognized Jessie. There was almost nothing left of the unhealthy waif that had been in the clinic, dying in little bits and pieces. Now, she was a vivacious young tomboy, climbing trees and riding horses, racing around and exhausting the people she talked into playing with her. She was even starting to make plans and set goals for her future. She still had terrible nightmares that sent her heart racing and the medical team into a panic, but slowly Sara was teaching her how to control her attacks and overcome the terror. Jessie had even decided she was going to be a psychologist when she grew up, just like Sara.

'You're thinking too hard,' Jessie said.

Sara opened her eyes and stared at the girl sitting cross-legged on the floor across from her.

'I can't help it.'

'Well, you have to help it if you ever want this to work,' Jessie said. 'I told you it's like dreaming. You just have to get really relaxed and then almost go to sleep. Not get all stressed out.'

'Jessie, you're not the adult here.'

'Yeah, but I'm the one who knows how to have those dreams. And if you want me to teach you, you have to listen to me.'

'I'm listening,' Sara said.

'Then relax. You can't try so hard or it won't happen.'

Sara closed her eyes again and took a deep breath. 'Okay, I'm ready.'

'All right. Just drift. Just say your keys words and picture the playground where you saw me. Let the wind blow you there. Ride it like you're surfing.'

'Okay.'

Sara closed her eyes and tried to remember what she knew about meditation, removing all thoughts from her mind. *I wonder what happened*, she thought in her head, and as the breeze started blowing inside her brain, she pictured herself playing on the monkey bars that Jessie loved so much and willed the breeze to blow her there. Then suddenly, she was hanging upside down from the monkey bars, right next to Jessie.

'I did it!' Sara yelled.

'Well sort of,' Jessie said.

'What do you mean sort of?'

'You were sort of drifting. You almost made it and then you started drifting away. So I pulled you in.'

'Jessie, I told you not to do that.'

'I know, but you looked so sad when you didn't make it in the last five times. And I kind of wanted to play.'

'It is a nice playground,' Sara admitted.

'Thanks. I made it myself. Want to go on the swings?'

'How about this, we'll swing for a couple of minutes and then we have to try again, okay?'

'Okay,' Jessie said. 'Last one there is a rotten egg.'

mind games

Jessie jumped down off the monkey bars and raced over to the swings. Sara climbed down a little more gingerly. She knew that she couldn't get hurt in here, but she couldn't help herself. Then she raced off after Jessie, her longer legs allowing her to catch up. They climbed on the swings at almost the same time and pushed themselves higher and higher.

'This is fun,' Jessie squealed.

'I haven't been on a swing for years,' Sara said. 'I forgot how much I loved them.'

'Okay, on the count of three, we jump off.'

'No, it's too high for me, Jessie.'

'Sara, you can't get hurt, remember?'

'I know that's true, I know we're not really swinging, but I just can't make myself do this.'

'No, this is really cool,' Jessie said. 'We jump off when the swing is at its highest and then we fly across the park.'

'We fly?'

'Sure. Sara, it's your mind. You can do anything you want to if you just believe it.'

'Okay, we fly,' Sara said. 'What do I do?'

'Jump off then picture yourself flying after me, all the way back to the monkey bars. I just pretend I'm on an air current like a glider plane.'

'Okay, on the count of three,' Sara agreed. 'One, two…three….'

And she let go of the swing and felt herself flying through the air until she hit a brick wall and everything went black.

'Oh my God,' Sara said, hitting the ground. She wanted to lie down, and try to catch her breath.

But Sara was already lying down on the pillows in the cabin. For a minute she was confused, had she fallen asleep again? Was this just a dream? She opened her eyes to see if Jessie was okay, but Jessie's eyes were still closed and her eyeballs were moving rapidly back and forth, like she was in REM sleep. Her arms and legs were twitching and whimpering sounds were coming from her tightly clenched mouth.

'Jessie?' Sara asked, trying to regain her bearings and push herself up off the floor. 'Jessie, where are you?'

Sara finally caught her breath and pushed herself up off the floor. She put her hands on the girl's shoulder and shook her gently, but got no reaction. She took her wrist and felt her pulse, which was racing.

'Jessie, come back to me,' Sara said, her voice a little firmer. She tried pinching her arm and got no reaction to the pain. 'Jessie!'

There was still no reaction. Sara knew she should push the panic button they had installed in the cabin, which would bring a medical response team running. But she had another idea and held Jessie's hand tightly.

'I wonder what happened?'

The breeze blew and she did what she was best at; she followed it to where it took her, hoping that would be where Jessie was too. She was by the river, strolling down the path on a sunny summer day.

'Jessie?' she called. 'Jessie where are you?'

'You traitored us,' she heard someone scream. 'Why did you do that?'

'Jessie, is that you? Where are you?' Sara called, racing down the path.

'You have a phone,' the voice continued yelling. It was definitely one of the children. 'You told on us.'

And then Sara heard a noise that seemed to split the forest in two. After that, there was total silence. Sara ran harder, to where she thought she had heard Jessie's voice.

She stopped suddenly when she saw a gun lying on the pathway. And then she felt a pain in her chest and she looked down and saw blood staining the front of her shirt.

'Help me?' she called out, dropping to her knees.

But there was no one around, as she slowly collapsed to the ground, just the wind blowing past her ears.

Sara opened her eyes, free from her vision but still feeling like she'd been kicked in the chest where the bullet had gone.

She dropped Jessie's arm and then slapped her face as hard as she could.

'Wake up Jessie,' she said. 'Wake up and come back to me right now.'

She raced over to the panic button, pushed it, and then hurried back to the girl, whose eyelids were starting to flutter open.

'That's a girl,' Sara said, digging her knuckles into Jessie's breastbone, trying to cause a pain response. 'Wake up and come back to me.'

Jessie's eyes popped open and she focused on Sara's face.

'I had a bad dream,' she said, and then fell over in a faint.

The door to the cabin opened and a medical team came racing in.

'She got caught in a bad vision,' Sara said, as someone wrapped a blood pressure cuff around Jessie's arm. 'I think she's just fainted.'

And then Sara felt the world start spinning and did the same thing.

It was late at night and the compound was dark, except for the lights burning in the mess hall. The leadership group sat around the table, a pot of coffee in the middle of them.

'Well, I'll start,' Peter said. 'I've spent all afternoon with Jessie and she seems okay. I think Sara was right and she just fainted after having a scary vision.'

'What was her vision of?' Chris asked.

'She won't say,' Sara said. 'But I'm pretty sure it had something to do with Beckman.'

'And your vision?' Chris asked.

'Well, I have no idea what I was really seeing. Someone was accusing someone of being a traitor and then someone got shot. I didn't see any faces. I don't know if I managed to tap into Jessie's vision or if it was just random.'

'You think she got trapped in a vision?' Vince asked.

'I don't know. I've been trying to get inside Jessie's visions, or dreams as she calls them, for weeks. All I can manage is to see a playground and then I'm so exhausted I just fall asleep.'

'So we don't know what she's seeing?' Peter asked.

'I have no idea. But I don't think she got trapped in it. I think she made herself stay inside it to see the ending. She was fighting me when I was trying to bring her out of it.'

'Do we need to sedate her for a while?' Phil asked. 'Or put her on a portable monitor or something?'

'No,' Peter said. 'Physiologically I think she's okay. But Sara had a vision while this was happening and she passed out too. I think what we should focus on is what you are trying to do. Sara, you haven't been physiologically stressed by your visions in a long time.'

'I'm not trying to do anything,' Sara said. 'Except to help Jessie.'

'By doing what?' Chris asked.

'I told you, I was just trying to see if I could get into one of her visions.'

'Well, we're going to have to get Jessie to tell us what she saw.'

'I think this has brought up several problems we need to address,' Sara said. 'Like how does somebody living here get their hands on a gun?'

'So you think this vision is real, that it will come true?' Peter asked.

'I don't think we can take a chance that it isn't real, doctor, do you?' she asked sarcastically.

'Well, you know we have guns here,' Phil said, trying to avoid a fight. 'We all agreed we needed them. But they're kept in a locked cupboard.'

'What kind of lock?' Sara asked.

'It's a heavy duty combination lock,' Phil said. 'I bought it myself.'

'And none of us realized that any number of these kids can have a vision at any time and see the combination.'

'Good point,' Vince said. 'So I guess we should switch to locks with keys?'

'I think so,' Sara said. 'And don't try to hide the keys. Whoever gets them needs to wear them around their neck at all times. If you try and hide them, someone will have a vision and see where they're hidden eventually.'

'What else?' Chris asked. 'What other problems do you think we have?'

'I think it's possible that we might have a traitor here. Someone with a cell phone who is reporting on us.'

'How are we going to find them?' Vince asked. 'Obviously they've been able to keep it secret so far.'

'A cabin search?' Phil suggested.

'If we don't pick the right cabin first, it will just give them time to get rid of the phone. I want to find this person. I don't want them hiding out here. It puts us all at risk.'

'It may be too late already,' Vince said.

'I know,' Sara said. 'But let's operate on the assumption that we're not too late. And after we catch them and find out what's going on, we can make our plans.'

'So how do we catch them?' Phil asked.

'We have to have someone watching Jessie. I think she may know more than she's willing to tell us. But we have to be subtle. We can't let her think we're suspicious of her or she'll really start hiding thing,' Vince said. 'Remember, underneath it all she is a scared little girl.'

'Do we need to watch her twenty four hours a day?' Phil asked.

'No, it was definitely daylight when I heard the gunshot. I think we can just keep our eye on her from breakfast to dinner.'

'For how long?'

'For as long as it takes.'

When Sara woke up several days later, she felt funny. Not sick or tired, just funny. It was as though there was something tickling her brain. She had a shower and went to the mess hall for breakfast but all she was in the mood for was coffee. And then she looked outside. She didn't know if it was the angle of the sun or the crispness in the air, but something in her mind just clicked and she knew today was the day. She tried to get through the morning, but her mind was wandering, so she cancelled the rest of her appointments and went to find Phil.

'I need a gun,' she said, when he opened the cabin door.

'Good morning to you too,' he laughed. 'Who are you planning on shooting?'

'The traitor. I'm pretty sure today's the day,' she said.

'Did you have a vision?' he asked.

'I just have a feeling.'

'Well, I supposed that is better than anything else we've got right now,' he said. 'We need to keep a close eye on Jessie today then.'

'Yes we do. And Phil, I don't want her anywhere near that path.'

'But the vision?'

'Look, Phil, I don't know if it was her that shot someone in my vision or not. But I'm not letting Jessie try to kill anyone. She's a little girl and we have to protect her. Now, obviously, someone has lost their key to the gun cabinet and doesn't know it yet. So if it's Jessie that comes here to get a gun, I want you to stop her. Don't let her leave.'

'But what about our traitor?'

'I'll take care of whoever it is.'

'Sara?'

'Phil, I've already done a lot of things that I never thought I would. I can do this.'

'Your vision showed someone getting shot.'

'Yes, my vision showed someone getting shot. But we don't know who and we don't know if it was even a real vision or some crazy dream,' she said. 'Don't you think that now would be as good a time as any to figure that out?'

'I think you're crazy,' he said.

'But you'll do what I'm asking?'

'I'll do it, but I'm going to tell the others. I won't keep this a secret.'

'You will also tell them not to stop me.'

'I don't think anyone would try,' he laughed, handing her a weapon. 'You know how to use this?'

'Yes.'

'Okay, be careful, Sara, these bullets are real, not like the ones in your visions.'

The day dragged by slowly. Sara sat on her porch holding a paperback. She was trying to read but couldn't concentrate and found herself reading the same paragraph over and over again. She finally closed the book and took a sip of tea. The air was warm with the sweet smell of early crocus and daffodils in the air. The worst of the winter was behind them. But there was still a chill that sent the occasional shiver through her body. Or maybe it was nerves.

'Sara,' Vince said, jogging across the grounds and waving to her. 'We just caught Jessie breaking into the gun cabinet.'

'So it's started?' Sara asked. 'The vision was real?'

'I think so.'

Sara stood up and went into the cabin. She came back out with the gun, checking the safety and the cartridge.

'I wish you would let me go with you,' Vince said.

'You weren't in the vision,' she told him.

'You keep saying you don't know if the visions are infallible or not. I could have been a couple of feet behind you.'

'I know, but I don't want to take a chance and let this person get away. Okay?'

'Not okay, but you better get going,' he said, stepping aside so she could come down the steps. 'Before you make yourself crazy.'

'Thanks.'

'Good luck,' he called after her, as she started down the path that led to the river.

Sara hurried down the pathway as quickly as she could, trying to stick to the soft snow and avoiding crunching through anything that would warn someone she was coming. She got to the bend in the path she had seen in the vision, and stopped dead in her tracks when she saw someone several yards in front of her, talking on a cell phone. Sara moved off the pathway and into the forest, trying to get close enough to listen in on the conversation without giving herself away. She hid behind a tree, praying the woman wouldn't turn around and see her.

'Yes, Dr. Beckman please,' she said into the phone.

'Beckman.'

'It's me.'

'I haven't heard from you in a while. I was worried.'

'You should be worried. You have no idea what it's like here.'

'Now, now, don't get yourself all worked up. Tell me what's happening.'

'You're not here, Beckman, surrounded by these freaks. Every morning when I get up I wonder if one of them has had a vision about me. I'm not safe here.'

'You have to do this. You are our only link to the group.'

'No, it's too dangerous. I'm throwing this phone away as soon as I hang up. I'll keep in touch, but I'll do it when it's safe for me. If I stay here it's on my terms, not yours.'

'That's not the deal we had agreed upon.'

'No it isn't. But you're not here and I am.'

'Do you know what I can do for you? I can make you rich.'

'But you can't hide me from these people. I wouldn't be safe anywhere in the world. Wherever I went, one of them will just have a vision and they would find me. It's my way or no way.'

'Fine, fine. So when can I expect to hear from you?'

'When it's safe. I won't promise any times or dates. Maybe when we go into town for supplies.'

'Well, tell me where you are at least, the homing devices we planted have just led to dead ends.'

'No, I can't tell you. If I do, they'll know I told. I can't do anything that will leave too strong an emotional trail for them to follow.'

'I don't like this one bit,' he said.

'I didn't think you would,' she said, and then hung up the

phone. She took a few steps closer to the river and tossed the phone as far as she could, watching it sink to the bottom. She turned towards the pathway. She would have to walk until her mind was at peace. If she didn't it would act like a beacon to one of these people and she was sure she would be found out. As she stepped onto the pathway, Sara came out from her hiding place, gun drawn.

'Sara, what are you doing out here?'

'Hello Christine.'

'It's such a beautiful day, isn't it? I just had to come out for a walk and get some fresh air.'

'Lots of fresh air back at the compound.'

'You know what I mean.'

'How is the cell phone reception out here?'

'I'm sorry?'

'Or do you have one of those satellite phones? I imagine Beckman would spare no expense, would he?'

'I don't know what you're talking about. Look, I have to get back; I have to see one of the kids in the hospital.'

'How could you do it?' Sara sobbed.

'Sara, if I've done anything to upset you…'

'I know you were worried about someone having a vision about your phone calls,' Sara tried to regain her composure. 'Well, it's too late. Someone did have a vision, a couple of weeks ago.'

'What? Look, I did have a cell phone. I know it's not allowed but my mother is quite ill. She's in a nursing home and I was just talking to her nurse to see how she's doing.'

'Don't bother lying to me,' Sara cried. 'I trusted you. How could you do this to me? To all of us?'

For a moment Christine looked around desperately, frantically searching for a story that would cover her, that would make Sara put her gun down. But nothing came to mind. She was going to try and run, when there was a noise behind her. And then Vince stepped out from where he had hidden himself off the pathway. Christine turned to her right and Phil, too, joined them on the pathway, taking hold of Christine's arm.

'What are you doing here?' Sara asked.

'We're here to help you,' Vince said.

'What's going to happen to me?' Christine asked.

'Well, in Sara's vision, someone was shot and died out here. I'd like to take you back though, avoid the bloodshed,' Phil said.

'And do what to me there?'

'You need to tell us what you've told them,' Sara said. 'Then maybe we can try and throw Beckman off our trail.'

'And then you'll kill me?'

'We're not Beckman, Christine,' Vince said. 'We don't kill people as our first line of defense.'

'But I'll be under house arrest.'

'That's pretty much a given for now.'

'And you won't let me treat the children?'

'I don't think you're going to have anything to do with the children for a while,' Sara said.

Christine sighed deeply, wondering what it felt like to get shot, wondering if it would be a quick death and finally this would be all over with. But she slowly put her hands up in the air, in a show of surrender.

'Let's try plan B.'

Phil pulled her down the pathway, back towards the ranch. Vince came over to Sara and took the gun from her, wrapping his arm around her shoulder.

'You're not alone, Sara,' he said. 'You don't ever have to go through anything alone again.'

'We better get back,' she said, blinking back the tears that welled in her eyes.

It was dark and Sara brought two mugs of hot chocolate to bed. She handed one to Jessie, who was snuggled in under the covers already, and she set hers on the nightstand and crawled under the covers herself.

'I'm so glad you're safe,' Jessie said, sipping her drink.

'I know. But Jessie, we have to talk about this. You can't keep secrets from me. We can't help you if you don't tell us about your visions or your dreams.'

'I was afraid that you would get hurt. I saw you hiding behind a tree and you had a gun, and then I heard the gunshots but I couldn't see who got shot and who was okay.' The words spilled from Jessie now.

'I know sweetie,' Sara said, wrapping her arms around Jessie's shoulders. 'But this isn't like the clinic. We're all working together now. We're all on the same side.'

'It's hard though. When I see these things they scare me. And I feel like I'm the only one who can fix them.'

'I know. I do too. But we have to work really hard to try and learn how to ask each other for help, okay?'

'Or no more sleepovers?' Jessie asked.

'Oh, Jessie, you can always come and sleep over. Honey, we all make mistakes and I would never punish you for making a mistake. We'll always be friends no matter what, okay?'

'Okay.' Jessie said, and they clinked their mugs in agreement.

When Jessie was asleep, Sara wrapped herself in a coat and sat out on the front stoop of the cottage. She had poured herself another hot chocolate from the thermos and sipped it in the icy night air.

'What are you doing out here?' Vince asked, joining her on the stoop.

'Thinking.'

'You couldn't do that inside?'

'I was afraid I would wake Jessie. What are you doing out here?'

'I was coming to see how you were doing.'

'Did you talk to Christine?' she asked.

'We did.'

'And what did she say?'

'She said that Beckman had her mother. Apparently her mother really was in a nursing home. And when Beckman got wind that she was taking early retirement, he suspected something was up. So her mother was mysteriously transferred to another nursing home and Beckman's been blackmailing her since.'

'Do you believe her?'

'I don't know. We'll have to see what we can find out.'

'It's such a blow,' Sara said. 'I thought we were safe here.'

'We still might be,' Vince said. 'She swears she didn't tell him where we were. And if he knew, don't you think he'd be here already?'

'I suppose.'

'All we can do is wait and see.'

'Well, if I could manage to figure out how to control my visions, maybe I could see something.'

'Don't stress out about it, Sara.'

'What good are they anyway?' Sara asked. 'I can't control where I go or what I see. Is this the big success Beckman was looking for? I can't teach the kids how to control theirs. What good is any of this?'

'We have had successes, even if they're small. We haven't lost a single child.'

'We sedate most of them at night, Vince, is that a victory?'

'Sara...'

'And the woman I thought I could trust most in the world betrayed us,' she cried, bitter tears filling her eyes. 'I'm sorry. I just can't seem to stop doing this.'

Vince put his arm around Sara and pulled her close to him.

Chapter 26

Vince sat across from Sara and laid down a playing card on the table.

'And thirty-one for five,' he said triumphantly, moving his pegs in the cribbage board.

'Remind me never to play this game with you again,' she said, pulling up the crib and counting the cards. 'Nothing.'

'Oh, tough luck,' Vince joked.

'Tell me again why we didn't leave you with Beckman?' Sara asked.

'Because you would have missed my wry humour and card playing skills.'

'Whatever,' she said, rolling her eyes.

Peter put a thermos of coffee on the table and sat down..

'I made a fresh pot,' he said. 'Anyone want a refill?'

'Please,' Vince said, sliding his cup across the table.

'Not me,' Sara said. 'I'd like to sleep tonight.'

'You are way too young to be having trouble with caffeine,' Peter said. 'When I was in my twenties I would drink five pots a night while I was studying.'

'Well, you were a medical student. Wasn't it a prerequisite to be able to drink lots of coffee and be able to go without sleep for five years?'

'Yeah, I think that was on the entrance exam,' Peter laughed. 'So, can a lonely doctor who can't sleep get dealt in on this hand?'

'Sure,' Sara said. 'It'll look much better for me if Vince beats us both. Then I won't look like a total loser.'

'No worries there,' Peter laughed. 'I may be a good doctor but I'm not the world's greatest card player.'

'Good.'

'Sara!' a voice yelled from the entrance to the mess hall.

Sara turned, and Vince was already halfway out of his chair.

'Jessie?' he asked, racing across the room. He grabbed her wrist and found her pulse. 'What's wrong, honey?'

'Sara, quick, you have to come to my room.'

'What is it?' Sara asked, joining Vince, her hand on the girl's head trying to calm her down.

'Please, it's an emergency. I had a nightmare and you have to come to my room.'

'Jessie, what's going on?' Sara asked.

'Sara, I'm scared. You have to come back to my room and help me sleep right now!'

'Okay,' Sara said, taking Jessie's hand. 'Peter?'

'I'll get my bag and be there in a minute.'

'Just you!' Jessie said firmly, pulling Sara out the door. 'No doctors.'

'I'm coming, sweetie. You just need to calm down for a minute.'

'No doctors.'

'I'll go with her,' Sara said to the two men. 'I'll push the panic button if I need you.'

'It was a very scary dream,' Jessie continued.

'What did you dream about?' Sara asked.

'Monsters,' Jessie said. 'Really bad monsters. And they were chasing a policeman.'

Sara's heart skipped a beat when she heard that. Without another moment's hesitation, she followed Jessie across the compound.

mind games

'Let's go to my cabin,' Sara said.

'No, we need to go to mine,' Jessie said, trying to pull her faster.

'We'll wake up the other kids,' Sara tried to explain.

'They'll be okay,' Jessie said. She pulled Sara up the stairs to her cabin and threw open the door. They hurried inside and Jessie climbed up on the bed, trying to pull Sara down beside her.

'Lie down on the bed,' Jessie told her.

'Why, Jessie? What's going on?'

'I have to go back to sleep. It's very late.'

Sara was confused, but she lay down beside Jessie. The girl cuddled up beside her and whispered in Sara's ear.

'Go to sleep,' she whispered. 'Make your mind empty and go to sleep. Think about swinging on the playground.'

Sara felt her eyes grow heavy and tried to blink them open.

'It's okay to go to sleep,' Jessie said.

Sara tried to force her eyes open but she couldn't do it, and her breathing slowed as she fell into a deep sleep.

'Okay, everyone ready?' Jessie whispered, as she lay down beside Sara and closed her eyes too.

Sara was dreaming. She was running through a wheat field, chasing the little puppy she had when she was nine, and then the wheat field ended and there was a playground. Jessie hung upside down on the monkey bars, like she always did. But there were other kids there as well. Some were on the swings, some on the seesaw and some just sitting on the ground watching her.

'Okay, Jessie, what is it?' Sara asked. 'Why did you want me to come into your dream?'

'Come on up here, we have to fly to a place.'

'Not until you tell me what's going on.'

'It's important,' Jessie said.

Sara clambered up the monkey bars, balancing on the top beside Jessie. She looked over at Jessie who nodded, and then they both jumped off the monkey bars and caught a current, like seagulls at the shore. The pure joy of being free of gravity and soaring through the air made Sara forget for a moment why she was here. And then she noticed Jessie veering off to the left and she followed.

'Where are we going Jessie?' Sara asked again.

'To the place.'

'What place?'

'The place where Matt is right now.'

'Matt?' she asked. 'Where is he?'

'I didn't recognize it,' Jessie explained, turning and checking behind her.

Sara looked too, and she saw a bunch of kids flying behind them, gliding through the air just as they were.

'What is going on?' Sara asked.

'It's not much further,' Jessie said, as the crested a hill.

And then Sara realized where they were, she knew where they were going. And she felt tears fill her eyes. She and Jessie set down on the sidewalk in front of the house, and the other kids remained in the air, soaring on the currents.

'Do you know this place?' Jessie asked.

'It's the house I grew up in,' Sara said. 'My brother Ian and I used to live here after my parents died.'

'Well, this is where Matt is,' Jessie said. 'He's in the backyard.'

'I need to see him.'

'He can't see you.'

'I know. Why did you bring me here, Jessie? What's wrong?'

'That,' Jessie said, pointing across the street at a dark blue town car parked in front of the fire hydrant. 'There are two men in the front seat and Dr. Beckman is in the backseat.'

'Are you sure?' Sara asked. 'How do you know Dr. Beckman?'

'He was at the clinic when they transferred me from the hospital,' Jessie said. 'He told me his name and that he would be looking after me from now on. And then he put that electrical thing on my arm. I'll never forget him, Sara.'

'Okay, we've got to get out of here. I've got to call the police and get some help for Matt.'

'No, it's okay,' Jessie said. 'That's why the other kids came with us.'

'What are you talking about?'

'Let's go see what he's doing,' Jessie said, taking Sara's hand and leading her around to the back yard.

And there he was. Her heart skipped a beat. It had been so long since she'd seen him. She walked across the lawn and laid her hand on his shoulder, hoping he could feel her presence. But he didn't stop chopping at the hedge along the fence.

'What's he doing?' Jessie asked.

'He's trying to find our burial ground,' Sara said. 'My brother and I had a secret box that we buried in the ground, where we hid things that we didn't want mom and dad to see. We put a cross on the spot and pretended it was where we buried our goldfish.'

'That's silly,' Jessie laughed. 'But why does he want to dig that up?'

'Because before my brother died, he hid a secret book in there; a book that might have some answers that will help the really sick kids.'

'He better dig faster,' Jessie said, pointing to the side fence, where the two henchmen were watching Matt.

'Jessie, we have to get out of here,' Sara said again. 'I can call the police and they can come here and help Matt.'

'Sara, don't be mad at me,' Jessie said.

Matt finished cutting the hedge and now had a clear field to dig in. He pulled out the worn wooden cross and sunk the shovel into the ground.

'Why would I be mad at you?' Sara asked.

'I've kept another secret from you,' Jessie said. 'Sara, I'm really sorry, but the other kids wouldn't let me tell you. They were afraid you would start experimenting on them.'

Sara knelt down and put her hands on Jessie's shoulders.

'Jessie, I need you to calm down. Just take a deep breath for me, okay?'

Jessie took a deep breath in and the let it out noisily.

'I'm not going to get mad at you, I promise. But we have to do something to help Matt. Those men are going to kill him once he finds that book. You have to tell me what we can do right now or we have to go back so I can call the police, okay?'

Jessie nodded and looked up at the other kids, still soaring overhead. One by one they touched down beside her, joined hands and closed their eyes. Sara released her grip on Jessie and took a step back, unsure of what was happening. And then, in front of her, the air began to shimmer. And slowly the shimmering formed a shape and started to solidify until finally a man stood in front of her.

'This is Dr. Beckman,' Jessie said.

'He can see us?' Sara asked, noting the look of surprise on his face.

'We brought him in with us to play,' Jessie explained.

'Dr. Beckman?' Sara asked. 'You're not what I expected.'

'What did you do to me?' he asked. 'I was sitting in the car…'

'You're on my turf now,' Sara said, trying to sound more sure of herself than she felt.

'You're a foolish girl,' he said. 'Coming back here.'

'Dr. Beckman, I don't know if you realize the gravity of your situation,' Sara said. 'Actually, I don't know if I do either.'

'You're the one that should be scared,' he said. 'I have two armed men standing behind that fence. Hardly a fair fight for you and a few kids.'

'Call them,' Jessie said. 'I dare you.'

'Impertinent child.'

'No, please, call them,' Sara said. 'Let's get this over with.'

'Boyd! Harding!' he yelled across the yard, yielding no results at all.

'I guess they can't hear you.'

'Over here,' he yelled much more loudly.

'Sorry Dr. Beckman, but they really can't hear you. Like I

said, I don't think you realize the gravity of your situation.'

'What are you talking about?'

Sara turned and checked out Matt's progress. As best as she could estimate, he was digging about two feet to the left of where the box was, so she knew they had another few minutes.

'Come with me,' she said, grabbing the old man by the arm and pulling him roughly back to the front of the house and across the street. She stopped in front of his car and motioned for him to look inside the back window. 'Anyone you know?'

Beckman leaned over and peered in the window. His face grew gray and he stumbled backwards as he recognized himself, in the backseat, head angled precariously over his shoulder.

'Am I dead?' he asked.

'Not yet.'

'What is this?'

'You're asking me? This is the result of your little experiments. I'm sure it will take years for us to figure out exactly how it works.'

'Put me back.'

'No,' Sara said. 'Not until you agree to call off your men and leave.'

'And why should I do that. I intend to recover that book and get rid of Detective Grassi once and for all.'

'Jessie,' Sara called. 'I need some rope, maybe a skipping rope please. Do you think you can find one somewhere?'

One materialized in Sara's hand and amazed, she unraveled it.

'What are you going to do?' he asked. 'Make me jump rope until I have a heart attack?'

Sara whipped the rope around his neck and grabbed the other end. She tightened the rope until Beckman was bent over backwards and making gurgling sounds, his arthritic fingers trying to loosen the rope from his neck.

'If you don't call them off and get out of here, I'll kill you,' she said.

'You won't do it,' he gasped.

'Don't test me, Dr. Beckman. You've killed everyone else I care about. I'm not letting you kill Matt.'

'Your psychological tests say you're incapable of violence.'

'Well, those were done long before you started rewiring my brain. You have no idea what I'm capable of right now.'

'Let me go,' he ordered, obviously used to that tone of voice working for him.

'Not until you agree to get out of here and leave us alone,' she repeated. 'My arms are getting tired, Beckman, decide right now or it's over.'

She tightened the rope just a bit, trying to convince him that she was capable of killing him. She pulled once more, and the rope cut deeply into his skin. For a moment she actually believed she could do this.

'Okay,' he said.

'What?'

'Okay, you win.'

She loosened the rope. 'Tell me.'

'I'll call off my men and we'll drive out of here. We won't follow Detective Grassi.'

'Just remember, Beckman, we're going to be standing here watching you. And if you don't do exactly what you promised, we will yank you back here and I will kill you.'

'I understand,' he said, still bent over trying to get his breath back.

'Jessie,' Sara called again. 'Dr. Beckman is ready to go back now.'

Jessie looked around at the other kids and they all closed their eyes again, in deep concentration. And then Beckman started to shimmer and faded out before her eyes. She saw him sit up in the back seat, rubbing his neck where he still felt the pressure from the rope. For a minute, she was worried that he wasn't going to do it, but then he pulled out his cell phone and dialed a number.

'Come back to the car right now,' he said gruffly into the phone.

And then he snapped it shut and watched the two men run across the street and back to the car.

'What's wrong?' the first one asked, opening the door and slipping in behind the wheel.

'Something's come up,' Beckman said. 'We have to get back to the office right now.'

'But Grassi's still back there.'

'It doesn't matter,' Beckman roared. 'This is more important. Now get us out of here.'

The car started up and sped off down the street without another word being spoken. Sara watched it disappear into the distance and then crossed the street to where Jessie and the other kids waited for her.

'You guys okay?' she asked the kids.

'I'm just tired,' Jessie explained. 'That's all.'

'Can we stay until Matt gets out of here safely?' Sara asked.

'Sure,' Jessie said.

And they watched as Matt finally found the shoebox hidden in the ground. He pulled it up and dusted it off, before he opened it. Inside was a notebook safely tucked away inside a zippered plastic bag. Matt tucked it into his jacket and then hurried out front to his car. They all watched as he drove off, in the opposite direction as Beckman.

'Okay?' Jessie asked, 'Can we go now?'

Sara nodded and closed her eyes. 'Yes, we can.'

Sara sat up in bed, gasping for breath, her heart racing so fast she was afraid it was going to explode. Jessie sat up beside her, her hand on Sara's forehead, concern in her eyes. The kids were all circled around the bed, watching Sara gasping for breath.

'We did good, didn't we?' one of them asked.

'We did very good,' Jessie said.

'What's wrong with her?' another one asked.

'I think it's because she's grown up,' Jessie said. 'Now go to bed. I'll look after her.'

Sara was still breathing heavily, but she felt her heart begin to return to a more normal rhythm.

'Jessie, what was that?' Sara asked. 'Where did we just go?'

'You had a bad dream,' Jessie said. 'Don't you remember?'

'We were outside my brother's house…'

'You woke all the other children up,' Jessie continued. 'It must have been very scary.'

'Jessie,' Sara lay back in bed, feeling more confused. 'Are you trying to trick me?'

'Just go back to sleep,' Jessie said. 'Just go back to sleep and you won't even remember your dream in the morning. That's what you always tell me.'

'You're right,' Sara said, feeling suddenly exhausted. 'Goodnight Jessie.'

There was a knock on the door and Jessie pulled the covers up around Sara and then hurried over to the door and opened it.

'Did you have the door locked?' Phil asked. 'Jessie, you know the rules about that.'

'I'm sorry, it must have locked accidentally.'

'Are you feeling better now?' he asked.

'Yes, Sara calmed me down. She's sleeping now.'

Phil looked around Jessie and saw Sara's form sleeping peacefully on her bed.

'Well, you need to get back into bed too,' Phil said, opening the door and coming into the room. 'Come on, back into bed and I'll tuck you in.'

Jessie obeyed, climbing into bed beside Sara. Phil leaned over and tucked the covers tightly around her and kissed her on the forehead.

'Sweet dreams,' he said, before he turned and left.

'I'll have sweet dreams now,' she smiled, and closed her eyes.

The Promised Land

The ranch was beautiful. So beautiful, in fact, that everyone had stopped calling it that many months ago. They all called it the Promised Land now and some of them even started calling it home. It had originally been a dude ranch, and that's what they still called it in the telephone book. But there were never any vacancies if anyone called for a reservation.

As the kids felt better and were released from the hospital, they were assigned to bunk houses, each with a nurse in charge of them, and they were settling in and becoming little families. Everyone else had staked a claim in the main house or the various cabins. Sara had taken a small cabin with a fieldstone fireplace and a nice porch on the front. She had settled in quickly, unpacking and getting rid of her suitcases, but she left half the closet and half the dresser drawers empty for Matt's arrival. She refused to let anyone suggest there might be any other outcome.

As well as the cabins and the main house there were two barns, the first housing a huge stable of horses that the kids soon were in love with. The second barn had been converted into a state of the art hospital.

This wasn't the way it would stay forever. They had dreams of building more cabins so everyone could have more privacy, but those plans were well in the future. The immediate task at hand was treating these kids. Christine was allowed back in the lab, under supervision, and she worked hours a day, trying to unravel the chemical formula that Beckman had developed. Sara worked even harder, dealing with the children's mental well being, as well as her own.

Recovery was taking a lot longer than Sara had hoped it would, but at least they were safe for the moment. Everything else would come with time. Including Matt. She hadn't had a single vision about his since she arrived here, but her heart told her he was coming back to her, even if her mystical brain wasn't ready to.

Sara had been enjoying the warm spring day. She spent the morning in the barns with some of the kids, brushing horses and mucking stalls. Then she cleaned up and found some freshly made lemonade in the kitchen. She poured herself a glass and sat on the top stair of her porch, waiting. It was too early, she knew that. Early every morning, for the last week or so, since the weather had changed and she had hung up her winter jacket, she had sat on the step. It had been over six months since she had seen Matt. And there was something about the temperature, the smell of the air, the angle of the sun, that convinced her he was on his way back to her, just like that vision she had so many months ago. So though it was too early in the day, because he had come back closer to evening in her vision, but she couldn't help herself. She missed him a lot and she had waited a long, long time for his return and her patience was wearing thin as the days passed by. So she sat on the porch, with a big glass of lemonade, and waited for the sun to travel across the sky and bring him home. People walked by her all day long, but everyone left her alone. They all knew what she was doing and they left her alone with her thoughts. The sun began to sink, and everyone was gathering at the picnic tables by the barns, for the first picnic of the season. Sara sat on the porch and waved as they walked by, not ready to give up her vigil for the day just yet.

Finally, she heard car tires crunching the gravel on the road, and she looked up to see an old, beat up Mustang driving up the road, heading towards her. This was the car he came in, she had seen it in her vision. And when the car stopped, the door would open, and a brown loafer, followed by a leg swathed in well-worn denim, would emerge. She stopped her mind right there, wanting to live this one moment in the present, not lost in the memory of a vision.

The car did stop and the door did open. A foot in a brown loafer stepped out, pulling the rest of him out after it. His jeans were well worn and loose, his green Yale sweatshirt bringing out the green in his eyes. His face broke out into a slow smile when he saw her waiting for him.

'You saw me coming?' he asked, closing the car door and sauntering over to her.

'I did. A few months ago.'

'You still having trouble with that?' he asked, approaching her slowly, tentatively.

'It's getting better every day'

She too was timid. It had been a long time since they had touched each other. But finally she set her lemonade down and stood up slowly. He crossed to where she stood, leaning against the railings, his hand on the banister just inches from her waist.

'So is it okay?' she asked. 'Do they know about this place or are we safe?'

'I think it's okay, I think we're safe,' he said. 'I've done everything I could. We'll just have to keep our eyes open and be careful. Can't you tell, Sara'

'I've stopped asking' she admitted. 'I can't control the answers I get and I don't always like them. Besides, good or bad I don't think we were meant to know our own futures. I think we were meant to live them.'

'I think that's good thinking,' he agreed.

'So, it took you a long time to get here,' she said.

'I know. But I had to make sure. There was a lot to do. I went to Ian's house.'

'You did?'

'And you were right.'

'You found something? You found what he left for us?'

'Yes,' he reached into his jacket and pulled out a spiral bound notebook.

'It's a lab book,' she said.

'Is that good?'

Sara was flipping the pages, trying to interpret the notes.

'I think it's good,' she said. 'I don't understand all of this but I think it will give the doctors a good place to start.'

'Good,' Matt said. 'Then it was all worth it. So that's one of the reasons it took so long.'

'I understand. You know, Matt, I'm really sorry you got dragged into all of this. It's the thing I've felt the worst about since I've got here and had time to think,' she laughed uncomfortably.

'No,' he stopped her. 'If I hadn't gotten involved with this, I would never have met you.'

'And your life would have been normal and you wouldn't have had to spend a year on the run. Or become a rogue cop,' she teased.

'But doesn't that make me sexier?' he asked. 'I thought you girls liked bad boys.'

Sara laughed out loud. 'I guess I never thought of it that way.'

'It would have been a waste of a life. Maybe this isn't the way I planned meeting the woman I loved, but it doesn't matter, it was all worth it. I wouldn't change anything if it meant giving you up. I know it's been a long time since I've seen you, but I love you Sara. It's what's gotten me through every day. I just pray you still feel the same way about me?'

She looked at him and smiled, tears in her eyes, and all she could do was nod. But he understood and he took her hand in his and stared down into her eyes, drinking in the sight of her after being apart for so long.

She stared back at him for a minute. 'I wonder…'

'No!' he yelled, pulling away from her. 'Don't!'

'I was just going to say I wonder if there's more lemonade in the kitchen. But if you're not interested, that's fine.'

He laughed. 'Lemonade would be great.'

She held out her hand and he took it.

'Come with me Detective. I'll get you some lemonade and I'll introduce you to some of the kids we've been working with. I think you'll be proud of what we've done here.'

And just like the vision she'd had, they walked off into the sunset.

About the Author

Deborah Nicholson, a medical transcriptionist by day, has always loved the arts and fed that love by working and volunteering at the Calgary Centre for Performing arts, with the Calgary Philharmonic Orchestra, The Calgary International Children's Festival, Alberta Theatre Projects and as House Manager for Theatre Calgary. After leaving the Centre she found she missed the theatre, which led to the creation of the Kate Carpenter Mystery Series.

Since being published, Deborah has done several workshops and readings to encourage people who dream of writing to stop dreaming and start writing. She has made numerous appearances on television including: The Breakfast Show, Shaw Television and was a featured guest star in 'The Letters'.

Deborah is a great supporter of charity and volunteerism and donates 10% of all profits of her novels to charity.

Deborah has an extensive backlist, and a couple of new novels, appearing in EBook format coming soon. Stay connected at www.deborahnicholson.com.

Photo © Deborah Nicholson

7258425R00178

Printed in Great Britain
by Amazon.co.uk, Ltd.,
Marston Gate.